Raven Rebellion

ALSO BY K HANSON

Fantasy:
Storm Raven

Thriller:
The Azrael Initiative
Morgan is Missing

Raven Rebellion

K Hanson

DEDICATION

I dedicate this book to my wonderful wife, Bobbi. I'm so thankful to have found the perfect co-captain for navigating the seas of life.

ACKNOWLEDGMENTS

I want to thank Bobbi, my family, and my friends for all of their encouragement as I've worked on this book. I especially want to thank the people who have read it and provided the hard feedback that I needed.

Thank you to my editor, Rachel Libke, for challenging me and helping me find, craft, and refine the words to bring this story to life.

Thank you to Kale Lawrence for another fantastic cover.

Finally, thank you, reader, for reading my book. I hope you enjoy your journey with Nereyda.

The World of

Storm Raven

Shattered Sea

Freyport

Ascaya

Cambisian Empire

Antalia

Trabizan   Gorenix

Mining
Complex

Kleifar

Glamol
Forest

Manisa

Stalsta Federation

Bosarazi Desert

To Mariana

To Takondwa

CHAPTER ONE

Nereyda would be damned if she'd let a tiny bridge get in her and her crew's way. Weeks of hiking across the continent had left their legs aching, their throats parched, and their stomachs empty. The days they had lost as they trudged through the thick forest hadn't done them any favors either, but at least they had evaded any Imperial patrols. Now, a guarded bridge interrupted their journey back to Lord Devrim's estate in Ascaya, where Nereyda hoped to reunite with the one person who might be their ally. Normally, they'd be able to handle such a problem with ease. However, her crew and the Islanders who were with them displayed heavy steps, slumped shoulders, and unfocused eyes that showed the toll that their enslavement in the mines and the long journey had taken. On any other day, any single member of her crew could kill the two guards standing just on this side of the bridge, especially if they were surprised, but the guardhouse across the river worried Nereyda. It looked like it could house up to twenty guards at a time, and a small stable with three horses stood next to it. Nereyda didn't want to face a barracks full of well-armed and rested guards, and she definitely didn't want any of them running off to get reinforcements.

"What do you think, Captain?" said Elvar, the old quartermaster, as he ran his hands through his graying beard.

"The crew isn't ready for a fight. Keep them here and I'll go see if I can talk to those guards."

"What are you going to say?"

"I don't know." Nereyda shrugged and gave him a smile. "I'll just use my irresistible charm."

"That's what I'm afraid of."

Nereyda gave Elvar a wink and a pat on the shoulder, then swaggered down the road toward the bridge.

The guards wore forest-green tunics, with gleaming bits of chain mail showing at the collars. Swords hung from their belts. They leaned against the posts on either side of the bridge and focused more on their conversation with each other than the road.

As Nereyda approached the guards, they tensed up and reached for their swords. One of them, who had a clean-shaven face under his shiny helmet, asked, "Who are you? Why do you need to cross?"

Nereyda pushed her black hair out of her eyes and fixed him with her purple gaze. "We're some tired travelers hoping to make it to the village ahead. You wouldn't want to get in the way of loyal citizens of the Empire, would you?"

The guard narrowed his eyes at Nereyda and took a moment to glance over her shoulder at the group a way up the road behind her. "After the attack at the mines, we aren't taking any chances. Nobody crosses without a permit. I also don't like the look of you and your friends."

"I agree, we could all use a bath." She wrinkled her nose. "We've been on the road for weeks, so what do you expect?"

The guard shook his head. "No, not that. You all have weapons, and none of you is wearing an Imperial uniform. We have reports of escaped slaves from the mines. We can't take the risk that you might be some of them."

"I suppose it's not good enough to promise that we'll behave ourselves?"

"Unfortunately not."

"If you let us through, I'll buy both you and your friend a drink at the tavern in town. I can be pretty good company, or so people tell me."

"I don't doubt that. But my orders are clear."

"If the promise of my company isn't enough, maybe you're looking for a bit more of a spark." Nereyda reached down to the storm she knew was in her stomach. Through her exhaustion, it proved difficult to find. A flutter in her stomach told her she had almost found it. She focused on that feeling, honing in on it. When she latched on to it, electricity jolted through her body. As it coursed through her arm to her fingertips, she sent tendrils of lightning over the ground next to her. She smiled at the talkative guard and winked at the other, forcing herself to ignore the intense tingling sensation that coursed through her nerves. "Is that enough for you?"

The guards' faces turned white.

Before he could respond, a woman's voice shouted from the bridge. "Stop! What's going on here?"

Nereyda glanced over the guard's shoulder to see a woman in an officer's uniform rushing over the bridge. She held her helmet in her right hand, revealing dark skin and a tight braid of black hair pulled back behind her head. Her sharp cheekbones and slightly hooked nose combined with her rigid posture to give off a commanding presence.

She stopped between the guards and fixed Nereyda with piercing emerald eyes. "I'm Guard Captain Limbani and I'm in charge of this outpost. Who are you? What was that trick you were just using?"

"I'm nobody special. We're finishing a very long journey. We fought for the Empire in the battle at the mines and are returning home."

"You fought for the Empire? You're not in uniform." Limbani's eyes widened. "It's you. It must be."

"Yes, it is me. Who do you think I am?"

"You're that pirate."

Nereyda set a hand on her hip, resting it near the grip of her cutlass. "If I'm a pirate, I'm not a very good one since I don't have a ship."

Limbani held her hands up and shook her head. "No need to reach for your sword. I'm not going to arrest you. I mean you're the pirate that Lord Devrim mentioned. He gave us instructions to watch for you."

Nereyda arched an eyebrow. "Really? Why would he care about me?"

"I couldn't say. At any rate, I was instructed to lend you a horse as soon as you arrived, so that you could make for Lord Devrim's estate with all haste."

"What about my crew? They've walked a long way with me. Can they come with us?"

The guard captain shook her head. "No, not at this time. We don't have enough horses for them. They can stay here at our barracks for the time being, or at least until they're rested enough to make the journey."

"You're inviting a bunch of pirates into your barracks? I don't think

3

you know what you're asking for, but fine, that will do for now. Show me to the horse you want me to take and I'll be off."

"Very well, come with me." The officer turned to the guards. "See that the others cross safely and are made comfortable in the barracks. They are considered guests of our lord and are to be treated with every courtesy."

Nereyda smirked as she thought of her crew being guests in a guardhouse.

Limbani beckoned to her. "Follow me, Captain . . ."

"Just Nereyda is fine." She walked beside her as they crossed the bridge. "Did you ever think you'd play host to a bunch of pirates?"

"I just follow my lord's orders."

"You can speak frankly with me, soldier. I promise not to rat you out to Devrim," Nereyda said with a devious grin.

Limbani scrunched her face up, then nodded. "Fine. I do think it is rather unorthodox that Lord Devrim has chosen to accommodate . . . people like you."

"You're still being polite. You really want to call us nasty, rotten criminals, don't you?"

Limbani raised an eyebrow at Nereyda. "You're the one who said it."

Nereyda laughed. She enjoyed the chance to tease a soldier who wasn't allowed to retaliate. "It's okay to think we are. After all, I think most of you Imperial soldiers are mindless minions who just follow the orders of people who claim to be better than you. But what makes them better, really?"

Limbani took a deep breath. "Lord Devrim's different than the others."

"We'll see, I guess." Nereyda had hoped to get more of a rise out of Limbani, but the officer's composure impressed her. "Are you from around here?"

"No. My family is from Takondwa."

"How did you end up all the way up here?"

"That is a story for friends." Limbani picked up their pace.

Nereyda and the officer rode in silence under the clear afternoon sky. They followed the road as it wound between rolling green hills. Eventually, they arrived at a familiar town. The two halves of Ascaya sat on either side of a river, with a bridge connecting them. They crossed the bridge and turned at the crossroads in the center of town. This path took them uphill through a forest before it opened to a clearing with a sprawling mansion.

"Wait here while I let Lord Devrim know that you have arrived," Limbani said.

"I can't come with you? Wouldn't that save everybody some time?"

"It wouldn't be proper. As a guest, your arrival must be announced."

Nereyda rolled her eyes. "I don't know if you've noticed, but propriety isn't exactly a priority for me."

The officer declined to respond and instead dismounted and unlocked the gate ahead of them, then pulled her horse through behind her.

As Nereyda waited, she looked around the grounds. A hedge almost as tall as Nereyda wrapped around the perimeter of the estate. From atop her horse, Nereyda looked over the hedge at the large house. The building featured a terraced structure. It had three stories, with each level being smaller than the one beneath it. The second and third floor each had a balcony on top of the floor below. Aside from the mansion, the estate grounds had gardens and a stable in the corner.

Officer Limbani strode back to her. "Lord Devrim will see you now. Just head in through the front door." She pointed toward a large double door in the center of the house, directly in front of the gate. "I will take your horse. Wagons will bring your crew into town, so you will be able to meet them at the tavern not long after you're done here."

Nereyda dismounted and passed the reins to Limbani. "Thanks for the escort. I hope you enjoyed hanging out with a nasty criminal like me."

She allowed herself a small smile. "It has been an educational, but pleasant, experience."

"Good. Maybe I'll see you around, Limbani."

"Perhaps. Good day, Captain Nereyda."

She rode back down the hill, with the other horse in tow.

Nereyda turned to the house and sauntered up the front path. As she arrived at the doors and reached up to use a brass knocker, she reflected that going in through the front entrance felt strange. The last time she had been at this house, she had snuck in by climbing to the third-floor balcony and finding an unlocked door. Her intent had been to rob the place, but she had instead stumbled into the beginnings of a rebellion. In exchange for her silence, Devrim had given her some supplies to help Nereyda free her crew from the mines. Now, it was time to see why he wanted to see her and if he'd be willing to help her and her crew yet again.

She knocked on the door three times and waited. A few seconds passed before the door opened.

"Ah, you must be Captain Nereyda," said a well-dressed man. "I am Karim and I serve as head of house for Lord Devrim."

"You're in charge of a lot of house, then."

"Indeed. My lord has done well and I am lucky to be in his service."

"Where can I find Devrim?"

"Lord Devrim is in his study upstairs." Karim gestured up the stairway that ascended from the foyer. "Allow me to show you to him."

"No, I know where it is. Thanks, though." She started up the stairs as the butler sputtered his objections.

She made her way up to the third floor and found the room where she had first surprised Devrim and his friend. Nereyda pushed through the door without knocking, and spotted Devrim sitting at his desk across the room. He ignored the creak of the door and focused on writing on a document on his desk.

"You want me to wait while you finish that?" asked Nereyda.

Devrim looked up and gave her a smile, framed by stubble. "Ah, Nereyda, I was just finishing a letter. I expected Karim to show you up."

"He offered, but I told him I knew the way. He's very particular about being proper."

"Yes, he is. It's the reason I hired him, actually. As someone who is new to being nobility, I needed someone who could help me keep all of our protocols straight."

"Limbani said you wanted to talk to me, which is convenient because I was coming here to talk to you anyway. But why the rush? Why go to the trouble of lending me a horse to get here?"

"Why don't you sit down? Then we can get to business."

Nereyda pulled a chair up to the rich mahogany desk and waited as the warm glow of a lamp flickered. Devrim lacked the gaudy jewelry so common among nobles, though she took a moment to appreciate the fine dark green tailored shirt that fit well on his athletic build. Nereyda made herself look back up at his face.

"Now that we're comfortable," said Devrim, "you said you were on your way to talk to me? What did you want to talk about?"

"After the battle at the mines, my crew and I needed somewhere to go. Without any real friends anywhere, the only person I thought might help us was you. You asked for a distraction and a bloody nose for the Empire. I think freeing every slave in the mines is quite a bit more than what you asked for. Since I more than held up my end of our bargain, I came to ask for something."

Devrim studied her face for a moment, his eyes narrowed. "And what is it that you want from me?"

"I want a ship large enough for my crew and the Islanders who are with us."

"A ship? If I had one to give, you could have her right now. But, sadly, Ascaya doesn't have much of a port."

"I thought that you were rich and that the Emperor personally made you a noble. All of that wealth and power, and you can't even do a small favor for me? What's the point, then?"

Devrim grunted. "My wealth and power can get me quite a bit, but not that, I'm afraid. Buying a fully armed ship large enough would raise more suspicion than I would like." He frowned as he glanced at the trees swaying outside the window. "And it was the previous Emperor who promoted me to nobility. I believe that the current occupant of the palace regrets his father's decision."

"So what can you do to get a ship for us? I'd say we've more than earned your help."

He returned his attention to her. "You have, but there is only so much I can do. Why is this so important to you?"

Nereyda rose and paced in front of the desk. "You really have to ask? The sea has been my home for as long as I can remember. And it's been home for most of my crew." She waved in the direction of the village. "How would you feel if your own home was taken from you? Wouldn't you do everything you could to get back there?"

"In that case, maybe there is something we can do, but it will not be easy. And that takes us to why I wanted to bring you here."

Nereyda crossed her arms and raised her eyebrows at him. "I'm listening."

"As you know, we're working on bringing change to the Empire and reforming it to better serve its people."

"I remember that. You said you were going to try to work within the system and with the other nobles to make it happen."

"Yes, that would be my preference, but I don't believe that approach will get the job done by itself. I think the time has come for a real rebellion."

Nereyda leaned back against a bookcase, staring down at Devrim with suspicion. "I see where this is going."

Devrim rose and strode over to Nereyda. "I need people who know how to fight. I've recruited some from my own lands and from other sympathetic nobles, but it is not enough. With your crew, though, I think we could get a real start on assembling our army."

Nereyda shook her head. "We're pirates, not soldiers. We already got mixed up in a battle and I think we've had enough. Besides, fifty of us isn't really much of an army."

"Then don't be soldiers. Be pirates," he said with eagerness lighting up his eyes. "We're not going to win against the Empire in open battle anyway. We need to fight dirty. And who better for that than a bunch of pirates?"

"Well, I do like it dirty." Nereyda gave him a grin.

She caught a hint of a smile on his face before he cleared his throat and moved on. "Then you'll be perfect for what we need to do."

Nereyda was almost tempted, but then remembered Brynja's betrayal at the mines and a cold feeling came over her as she recalled the sting of her first mate's actions. "So, if we help you with this whole war, I'm supposed to trust that you'll give us a ship? Hardly seems like a good bet."

"It's the best I can do right now. But you have my word that you'll have your ship."

Nereyda sighed. "I need to think about what's best for my crew, and the Islander friends we have with us. You're asking us to do all of the work before we see any reward. That's not the kind of deal I can trust. And we barely made it out of the battle at the mines. We're not up for an entire war." She backed toward the door. "We'll just have to find our own way."

He moved to block her path and glared down at her. "And how exactly do you plan to do that?" he asked in a heated tone.

"We'll go get our own ship." Nereyda's eyes flashed with defiance.

"Alone? You think you can do this without my help?"

"Of course. We know how to steal things and I don't need you holding my hand to do it. There's a port just north of here, right?" She brushed past him.

"There is. But this isn't a good idea, Nereyda." He caught her arm. "And we need you in this fight."

"This fight isn't ours." Nereyda shook out of his grasp and strode out of the room, ignoring Devrim's yells for her to come back.

CHAPTER TWO

As she rode back down the hill to the guard station, Limbani shook her head. She didn't know how her lord could ally himself with someone as unreliable as a pirate. Nereyda was amusing enough to chat with during their ride up to the estate, but someone without any respect for authority could become a liability rather than an asset. The pirate's purple eyes and perky button nose had worked together to mock Limbani with every smirk. Still, Limbani had faith that Lord Devrim knew what he was doing. He had not let her down before and always seemed to pick the right people for the job at hand, even if they were unorthodox. The guard captain herself was not the most conventional choice for her position. She would keep an eye on the pirate captain, though. If Nereyda turned against her lord, Limbani wouldn't hesitate to kill her, though she hoped it wouldn't come to that.

She brought her horse to a trot. The bridge where she was stationed stood at the edge of Lord Devrim's land. Normally, lords would not militarize their borders, but Devrim hadn't wanted to take any chances after the disaster at the mines had thrown the western reaches of the Cambisian Empire into chaos. They were on the lookout for any stray Stalstan troops, escaped prisoners, or even Imperial troops who had deserted. Limbani suspected though that the biggest reason Devrim stationed them at the bridge was to watch for Captain Nereyda and her crew. Limbani didn't know how he knew to expect them, but he apparently had.

The stable stood outside the abandoned tavern that they had

converted into a barracks. As she dismounted and handed the reins to the stable master, he said, "You'd better get inside. The pirates aren't exactly the most reasonable of guests."

"I never would have guessed. Nobody's died yet, I hope?"

"Not that I know of, but I wouldn't wait."

Limbani walked at a quick pace toward the tavern door. Even as she approached it, she could hear yelling and singing inside.

She opened the door and found a chaotic scene of pirates with drinking mugs in their hands shouting and singing a rather unflattering song about the Empire. Several pirates flung insults at the guards, and some even threw food at them. To their credit, her own soldiers did not retaliate, and merely brandished their weapons while her lieutenant tried to order their guests to settle down. The pirates were either oblivious or intentionally ignoring any efforts to settle them down. Meanwhile, the Islanders who had accompanied the pirates, recognizable by the strand of beads they each had in their hair, sat at some tables in the corner, keeping themselves as far away as possible and casting nervous glances at the two groups.

As she shoved her way into the fray, Limbani whistled above the noise. Her troops came to attention, but the pirates kept up their frivolity. Adnan, her lieutenant, hurried over to her.

"What's going on here?" Limbani asked. "How did things get so out of hand?"

"Captain, as soon as we showed our . . . guests into the barracks, they immediately broke into the old tavern storage area in the basement and found an old stash of liquor. Ever since, they've been drinking and getting increasingly loud and belligerent."

"Have they threatened or attacked you at all?"

"No, Captain, that's why we haven't made any effort to remove them. They haven't done anything to provoke violence. They've just been singing and yelling at us. I ordered the men to be ready in case anything wild happened."

"And what of these other people? The Islanders in the corner?"

"They've been sitting quietly. None of them have bothered to help themselves to any drink. One of them seems to be in charge, though. He keeps telling them to keep out of it, and they listen."

"I'll start with him."

Limbani pushed her way through the crowd, dodging an apple on the way, to the quiet group in the corner, where the Islanders talked among themselves while keeping an eye on the crazy proceedings around them. As she got closer, she saw that their strands of beads had a variety of colors. Most common were red, blue, and yellow, with a smattering of green and white. A couple had black beads.

"Hello there, I'm Captain Limbani. Is any of you in charge here?"

One of the Islanders let out a hearty laugh. "I don't think anybody is in charge here, including you, Captain. But I can speak for my friends."

"Good. What's your name, friend?"

The Islander with wild black hair stood up and strode over to her. One strand of hair featured a set of beads. A few blue, some red, and a single white one at the end. "I'm Jax," he said with a smile across his broad face as he held out his hand and greeted her with friendly dark eyes.

Limbani took his hand. "A pleasure to meet you, Jax. So how did you end up with these pirates?"

"They were with us in the mines. They put Nereyda with us because they thought she'd lead her crew to rebel and escape. Instead, she got us to do it, so their plan didn't work out too well. When the Stalstans attacked, we fought together and kind of stuck with each other afterward. We didn't have anywhere else to go and this lot seemed fine."

"They're making a mess and making my men nervous. We're on the edge of something triggering a fight."

"I don't think the pirates want a fight. Most of them have been locked up for months and they only want the chance to unwind. You can't really blame them for wanting to let loose."

"I suppose not. And what about all of you?"

Jax shrugged. "We're not exactly the rowdy type. And we've just finished a long journey, so we just appreciate the chance to sit down."

"Aside from Nereyda, do you know whom I could talk to to help get them settled down?"

"I don't know most of them, but there is one named Elvar who seems close to Nereyda. He might be the closest thing to a leader without her around."

"Can you point this Elvar out?"

"Of course. You see the older man sitting at a table across the tavern?" Jax pointed.

Limbani followed his gesture and spotted the man, who was sipping his drink and singing along with a smile, though far less boisterously than his crew mates.

"Care to come along and introduce me?"

Jax shrugged. "I suppose. I don't know him very well, but I've got nothing better to do."

Jax and Limbani made their way around the crowd of singing pirates and stood above the older pirate.

"Hey Elvar," said Jax.

"Why hello, did you decide you wanted a drink, Jax? Take a seat right here and I'll get you a drink." Elvar slapped the bench next to him.

"No, I'm good for now, thank you. Our host, Captain Limbani, wanted to speak with you."

Elvar eyed Limbani with suspicion. Lines crinkled across his forehead, his face showing the wear of years at sea. "This Imperial? I've seen enough of you to last a lifetime."

Limbani clenched her teeth, but kept her face passive.

"I can understand that," said Jax. "But they haven't shot you yet. And they've let you drink their alcohol. They can't all be bad, can they?"

"Fine, I'll give this one a chance. Sit down and we'll see if you're different."

Limbani sat next to Elvar, and Jax took a spot on her other side.

"So," said Elvar, still giving Limbani a hard look, though the wrinkles near his eyes carried a slight smile, "what can I do for you?"

Limbani met his gaze and said, "You and your crew are our guests, and we're happy that your crew seems to be getting comfortable, but perhaps they're a bit too comfortable."

"And who are you to tell us that we're too comfortable? That's easy for you to say when you get a bed to sleep in, decent food, and get to see the sun. I bet even you have a drink or two on your days off. Us, though—we've been stuck underground. Pirates are used to doing whatever they want, whenever they want. You try living in a hole without the kiss of fresh air on your face, drink to warm your soul, or even the freedom to take a piss without asking permission, and see if you don't get a bit thirsty when you come out. It was Imperials who put us in that hole to begin with. I don't particularly feel like telling my people to settle down on the word of another Imperial dog, even one who speaks with words rather than the whip."

"Mister Elvar—"

"Elvar is fine."

"Elvar then," Limbani said, maintaining a gentle, respectful tone. "Perhaps my uniform has led you to make some assumptions about me, but I can assure you I am quite different, if my appearance didn't already hint at that."

"What about your appearance?"

"Well, I'm a woman and my skin doesn't exactly blend in."

"That doesn't mean much to me. My captain is a woman and we have people of all colors in the crew."

"It may not mean much to a pirate, but it means something in the Empire."

"Is that right? And what does it mean?"

"It means that I'm not just a trained Imperial dog, as you put it. I know that the Empire isn't perfect. I don't think I could serve anywhere other than in Lord Devrim's guard. I'd never serve in a place like the mines."

"If you're in uniform, I'm not sure you get much of a choice, do you? You have to follow orders, right?"

"Within reason. Some are more willing to follow unsavory orders than others. I'd sooner desert than do some of the things I've heard about."

"So you'd be willing to break the rules if the situation called for it?"

Limbani shrugged. "I suppose."

"In that case," Elvar said as he slid his mug toward her, "finish this."

"I'm on duty."

"I know." Elvar smirked, his eyes full of mischief. "That's the point. I want to see if you're telling the truth."

"I said I'd disobey orders if the situation called for it. How does that relate to this case?"

"If you drink that, I'll get the crew to settle down." He winked at her.

Jax chuckled as he watched from the other side of Limbani.

Limbani stared down at the mug, filled almost to the brim with amber ale. Drinking on duty went against everything she'd learned as a member of a lord's household guard. While it wasn't a major offense, if one broke the rules once, it became easier to do it again. She'd seen it in some of the less successful guard candidates. And as captain, she needed to set an example for her unit. Still, she also needed to do her job, and that meant preventing a riot in the barracks. And if this helped earn the respect of their guests, that might be helpful long-term, as well.

She glanced around the room at her troops. When she felt confident that none of them were watching her, she lifted the mug and drained the liquid in it. She winced as she repressed the urge to burp.

"Wow," said Elvar. He gave her an impressed nod. "I just wanted you to finish it. You didn't need to chug the whole thing."

"I know. I wanted to get it done before I changed my mind."

"Well, I'm proud of you." Elvar clapped her on the back. "Maybe you're not just another hopeless Imperial after all."

"I've done my part. Now it's your turn to hold up your end of the deal."

"Indeed it is, lass." Elvar climbed off the bench onto the table itself, standing above the crowd, then whistled. "Hey, all of you."

At the sound of their quartermaster's voice, the pirates quieted down and looked at him.

"After our wonderful host here," he said as he waved toward Limbani, "had a bit of a drink with me, I've decided that these guards aren't as bad as the other Imperials we've gotten to know."

Lieutenant Adnan looked at Limbani curiously, which she returned by flicking her gaze away and straightening her posture.

"We've had some good fun," continued Elvar, "but I think maybe we should take a rest and let our hosts relax."

"We're still thirsty!" cried someone from the crowd.

"I am too, and we can still drink. Let's just try to keep it down, at least for a while. Besides, we don't want to wear ourselves out before our own captain comes back. You all know that Nereyda would feel left out if we drank ourselves into the ground before she had a chance to join the fun."

The pirates all laughed and nodded their heads.

"Very well, it seems you all agree. Then let's all sit down and play nice until she gets back. After that, I'm sure she'll let us loose again."

The pirates all raised their mugs to that and let out a final cheer before quieting down to merely a dull roar. Elvar climbed back down and smiled at the guard captain. "How was that?"

"I wish you hadn't called me out for drinking on the job in front of my soldiers. And I'm not excited about letting them loose again when

Nereyda gets back. That said, I thank you for buying us some time of peace and quiet."

"I'm afraid that's all I can get for you, even if I was inclined to ask for more from them. If I push too hard, they'll just ignore me."

"How do you keep order with these kinds of people?" She gave an incredulous wave toward the crowd. "How does your captain get anything done?"

"They don't listen to us because we have a certain position. They listen to us because they respect us. Anyone on the crew can leave at any time. We only stay together because we can all pull together around a common cause. The good news for me is that I'm not the one who has to come up with that common cause. Captain Nereyda does a mighty fine job of that, then getting the crew to agree to go along with the method."

"Sounds like your captain has it all figured out."

"Most of the time, yes. And when she makes mistakes, she fixes them."

"I'll have to talk more with her when she gets back from speaking with Lord Devrim."

"That you will. Despite your positions, or maybe because of them, I think you two have more in common than you might think."

"I'd better get back to my job, but now that you've gotten your people to calm down, I can do that with more peace of mind. I thank you again."

"You're most welcome." Elvar nodded at Limbani as she stood up.

Jax eyed her with a last look of amusement before he slid over to Elvar and began a conversation.

Limbani shoved through the throng of people to her lieutenant. "That seems to have settled them, for the time being."

He looked at her with worry etched across his forehead. He leaned in and whispered, "Can I speak to you outside, ma'am?"

She gave Adnan a quizzical look. "Yes, we can slip out for a moment. Lead the way."

After they left the barracks, Adnan paced back and forth for a moment.

"What did you want to speak to me about, Lieutenant?"

He stopped pacing and looked at her with a frown. "You do know I should report you for that drink, right? I don't want to do it, but if I don't, then I'm on the line for an infraction as well. If I were the only one who knew, then maybe I could hide it, but . . ."

"Absolutely report it," she said in a firm voice. "Even if you were the only one who knew, that's the right thing to do. Don't put yourself in trouble on my account. I chose to take that drink. I could have refused and thought of a different way to approach the problem. I'll bear the consequences."

"I'm sorry, Captain." He still gave her a remorseful look, but his face relaxed.

"Don't be sorry. Go, write the report and have it delivered to Lord Devrim. I'll keep an eye on things here."

"Very well. Just don't have a second drink while I'm not here to stop you," he said with a slight smile.

Limbani shot him an amused look. "Don't be impertinent."

He gave a small bow and left. Limbani went back inside and returned her attention to the band of pirates and the group of Islanders. While she wasn't too concerned about what her punishment might be for her infraction, she wondered what else might happen if they had to spend much more time with these people. Soon though, the wagons would take them into Ascaya to stay at the tavern, where they would be someone else's problem.

CHAPTER THREE

Commander Erhan of Boscada sat in a dark corner of the Harbinger Tavern, a run-down tavern in a tiny village on the western coast of the Empire. He glanced back down at the note in his hand. I know you're looking for a certain pirate. Meet me at the Harbinger Tavern. Erhan knew nothing about who had sent it or how they had known where to send the courier. The messenger wouldn't answer any of his questions. Still, Erhan needed any information he could find, so he had to take this opportunity. If it went badly, he trusted in his ability with a blade.

As he waited, he watched the shady patrons around him. The Imperial officer in him wanted to investigate them. The former Imperial officer, perhaps, he reminded himself. Erhan was not sure of his current status in the Cambisian Empire.

After being captured at the battle of the mines, Erhan was likely marked as missing in action. While he could report to any Imperial military outpost to begin the process of being reinstated, that would also mean explaining where he had been. He doubted that his superiors would look kindly upon his agreement to work with Foreign Minister Audo of the Stalsta Federation. Apprehending the pirate and witch Nereyda would be for the greater good of the Empire, even if it meant delivering her to an enemy nation. Still, Erhan didn't think his superiors would agree with that.

However, it would mean defeating the person most responsible for destroying Erhan's life and career. His back ached at the memory of how she had tossed him against a wall with a blast of wind. She had inhuman abilities that nobody should be allowed to possess, and he aimed to stop her before she could cause more damage.

He pulled himself from his thoughts as a cloaked man strode across the tavern and slid into the seat across from Erhan. A hood draped over the man's head, leaving all but his strong jaw veiled in shadow. His broad shoulders carried a powerful confidence.

"You are Commander Erhan," said the man. It was not a question. A damp aroma wafted across the table.

Every instinct yelled to Erhan that he should walk out, but his hunger for information about Nereyda kept him there. "I am. And who are you? Your message implied that you could help me find a certain person that I'm looking for, but didn't give me much else."

The man gave a dismissive wave. "Who I am does not matter. In fact, I prefer if people don't know who I am. I'm not one for public attention."

"Fine, then," said Erhan. "As long as the information you can provide is good, I do not care who you are. Do you know where the pirate known as Nereyda is?"

"I do not, but I do know that she and her crew were seen going north from the mines."

Erhan scoffed. "If you can't give me more than that, you're wasting my time." He rose and took a step toward the door. Before he could take another step, the cloaked man sprang in front of Erhan.

He placed his left hand on Erhan's shoulder. "Sit down, please." A sharp pain in Erhan's side punctuated the request.

Erhan glanced down at the dagger pressed against his torso. He chastised himself for letting the man catch him off guard, then nodded and sat again.

The man returned to his seat. "Thank you. Now, think. What would pirates be looking for?"

The commander rubbed his chin, allowing adrenaline to sharpen his focus. "A ship, of course, but where would they get one? Antalia is too heavily guarded. And the only other port to the north is . . ." His eyes widened. "Of course, I think I know where they're going. There's an Imperial outpost there. The captain is a friend and might be able to help."

"Good. Once our meeting is done though, you'd better move quickly if you want to get ahead of them."

Erhan tried to study the man across from him, but couldn't get a read on him through the shadow of his hood. "Why do you want to help me? What do you get out of this?"

"I don't particularly care about your mission, but I am being paid handsomely by my employer. That is good enough for me. What my employer wants, however, is of much more significance: that you bring this Nereyda to me. And, yes, I do mean that you should bring her to me rather than to your Stalstan friends." The cloaked man let his words hang in the air.

Erhan's heart pounded in his chest. How did this man know about that? "What Stalstan friends do you mean?"

"Don't play innocent with me. We know that you've had a conversation with their foreign minister. If you don't want anyone else to know, I suggest that you cooperate."

Erhan reached under the table for the dagger at his side.

The man didn't flinch. "Do you really want to test me again? Besides, I wouldn't advise killing me. I am just a messenger. If I don't report back, I can't guarantee the safety of your secret."

"How did you know?" Erhan kept his hand on his dagger.

"My employer is well connected. Don't worry too much; I believe we are the only ones in the Empire who know about your meeting. If it helps, once you have brought her to us, we can help you get back to your position within the Imperial Navy without having your time away questioned uncomfortably."

After pondering for a moment, Erhan relaxed and let go of his dagger. "You seem to know exactly what to say to get me to work with you."

"My employer gave me all of the information I need, and I know how to use it well."

"Can I ask who your employer is?"

"You can ask, but I won't tell you. At least not yet. Once you've proven you can be trusted, maybe they will see fit to reveal themselves or allow me to tell you who they are."

"If you can't tell me who you work for, then can you tell me what is their interest in Nereyda?"

"I've only heard rumors about what happened at the mines. Is it true that she can command lightning?"

"Among other things, yes."

"Then you know that she is a threat to the Empire, and every other nation. The gods punished us for meddling with powers like hers. If we allow her to go unchecked, she won't be alone for long. I don't know how we'll be punished this time, but I know that I don't want to find out."

"The foreign minister recommended that I invoke the Rite of Inquisition."

"He's done his research, then. That is a rather obscure piece of history. I do not think anybody has ever called an Inquisition." The cloaked man stroked his chin. "Maybe that's a better approach than what I had in mind, actually. Instead of bringing her to me, take her to Goremia and show the priests what she can do."

"I don't understand why waste time on an Inquisition at all. Nereyda is dangerous. The sooner we catch and deal with her the better. Why not do it ourselves and be done with it?"

"Do you think she's going to be the last person to have these abilities? Do you want to protect your precious Empire from more of her kind?" he asked in an urgent voice. "If she can get these abilities, so can others, and we need to learn as much about them as we can. The priests who will oversee the Inquisition will be prepared to extract information from her. After your journey north, whether you capture her or not, go to Goremia and talk to the priests that reside in the temple there. If you've captured her, they can deal with her. If not, they can tell you what you need to start an Inquisition."

"How do I get them to talk to me? I can't tell them who I really am without drawing attention from the military."

"I'm sure you can figure out a good story to tell them. I have faith in you." The man slid out of the booth. "You have much to do, so I'll leave you to it now."

"How will I contact you if I have questions?"

"You won't. We have eyes all over the Empire, though, so if it seems like we need to meet, I'll find you." The man started to turn away, then stopped. "I almost forgot. Here is something to help start covering your expenses." He pulled a sack of coins out of his cloak and set it on the table. "Good luck," he said with a nod. With that, the cloaked man walked across the tavern with quiet footsteps and left.

Erhan remained, looking down at the table and contemplating the wild turns that had taken him to this path.

CHAPTER FOUR

As she waited for Devrim's wagons to carry her crew into town, Nereyda wandered to the edge of Ascaya and found the trail that would take her to the old man who had helped her when she washed up ashore after her raft had been destroyed in a storm. She figured he'd appreciate knowing that she was still alive, and he had seemed to know more about her powers than he had let on. She followed the path through the forest and along the side of a gently rolling creek. Eventually, the dirt of the path gave way to sand and she emerged from the trees. Nereyda paused at the edge of the beach and gazed out at the sea. Though she had been tired from the long day, the sight of the ocean rejuvenated her.

She slipped her boots off of her feet and set them aside in the sand, then waded out into the water. Nereyda closed her eyes as the cool waves lapped at her ankles and feet. The scent of salt drifted in the air as the sea mist kissed her face. The waves whispered to her as they splashed against the shore.

"Feels like home, doesn't it?" asked a voice from down the beach to Nereyda's left.

She glanced over to see the familiar old man shuffling over the sand toward her with a walking stick in his right hand, his shack in the distance behind him. "Yes. It's really the only home I've ever known. Coming back to it fills me with energy I didn't realize I'd been missing."

The man waded out into the water next to her. Wild silver hair framed his tan and weathered face. "Perhaps your connection with the sea goes deeper than living your life on a ship."

Nereyda narrowed her eyes. "What do you mean?"

"I'm sure you remember when you washed up on my beach. You said a storm destroyed your raft, but the only storm had been on the edge of the horizon. There was no way you should have made it to shore."

Nereyda shrugged, but his words unnerved her. "I guess I was lucky."

"No, not even luck would have helped you survive, and I think you know that."

"I'm not sure I got your name before."

"Forgive me. My name is Manu."

"So, Manu, what do you think happened? The sea decided to push me to shore without drowning me?"

The man chuckled. "You might be closer to the truth than you think. Many years ago, people had abilities that we no longer possess. They could command the elements and do extraordinary things." His eyes sparkled as he spoke.

"You sound like a priest. That's what they say. They also say that the gods punished us for it."

He laughed. "They would say that. If anyone did have those talents, they would be a threat to the established order and priests want things to stay as they are."

"How do you know about all of this?"

"Much of it comes from legends passed down through generations, but there are enough hints that have survived in the histories to make people like me think there is some truth to the stories."

"And you studied these histories?"

He nodded. "I did, when I was back at the University of Varanasi in Hariana. A couple of colleagues and I were working on piecing the clues together. We even thought we had located a place mentioned in the legends. A place of power. My friends left on an expedition to find it, but they were never heard from again. The news that I received is that their ship was wrecked somewhere south of the Shattered Sea."

As he mentioned the location, Nereyda turned and faced him directly.

"After their disappearance," he continued, "I lost the heart for academic pursuits and left the continent. I've had a quiet existence here ever since."

"You said they were shipwrecked just south of the Shattered Sea?"

"Yes. Why?"

"I think I might have something that you'll want to see."

Nereyda held her open hand out over the water and found the cluster of power inside herself. A column of water slowly stretched up to touch her palm. It was a calm, clear tendril reaching up from the ocean. Then she closed her hand and the water splashed back down. She glanced over her shoulder and smiled as Manu's eyes widened.

"I've read about such abilities, and I had a feeling about you." Excitement left his voice breathless. "Even so, it's quite something else to see this for real."

"I think I found the island your friends were searching for. And that place of power exists. I know because I took that power."

"Come with me. We need to talk about this. I need to hear everything." Manu turned and shuffled up the beach back toward his shack, which had graying walls as weathered as himself.

Nereyda grabbed her boots and followed after him.

As they entered his home, he leaned his walking stick against the wall. As they passed through the tiny living room that also served as the entryway, Nereyda saw a bookshelf that sat in the corner, packed with books in several languages. She understood Cambisian and recognized Stalstan, but the others featured characters she had never even seen before.

"I'm going to make some tea, and I want to hear everything. Please sit." Manu pointed to a small table in his kitchen. "Start while I get the tea ready."

Nereyda began by telling him how she got captured by the Empire, then shipwrecked on the island near the Shattered Sea. When he set a cup of tea in front of her, she described the ruins she had found in the middle of the island and how she had absorbed some sort of energy from a fountain.

Manu's mouth hung open. "Amazing," he said. "Simply amazing. That sounds exactly like what we had read about before my friends left on their journey." Manu looked at her with studious eyes, the natural academic returning to the surface. "Did your ability start showing right away?"

"No, I felt something inside me, but didn't know what it meant right away," said Nereyda. "I didn't have much time to think about it because some crazy fire demon chased me through the ruins. I escaped into the forest, but it pursued me. I thought it was going to kill me, but I somehow threw it into a pool of water with a blast of wind."

He tilted his head. "So your new abilities only showed when you were under duress?"

"That's right, at least for a while. During a battle, I managed to start figuring out how to use them on command. It still takes quite a bit of concentration, but I can do it."

"How does it feel when you do it?"

"That depends on what I do."

"Is there anything else you can do?"

"So far, I can throw wind, shoot lightning, create and control water, and freeze things. If there's anything else I can do, I haven't seen it yet."

"That's quite a wide range of talents."

Nereyda shrugged. "I don't know why I have these skills in particular, but they've been useful so far."

"How so?"

Nereyda took a few minutes to tell Manu about everything that had happened at the mines.

"You've certainly been through quite an ordeal," he said. "It's amazing to me that you've acquired so many skills and learned to use them relatively quickly."

"Has it been quick? It's felt like it's taken me forever to get to this point."

"From what I've read, it should take years of study to control one element. To control water, for instance, people would spend hours each day sitting in pools, attuning themselves to the water."

"I've been living on a ship for years. Maybe some of that has rubbed off and helped me."

"Perhaps you're right. You said that you started controlling these abilities during the battle at the mines?"

"That's right."

"So you still hadn't learned that control when you washed up on my beach. Most interesting."

"How so? What does that mean?" Nereyda stood up and paced the room. "What does any of this mean? Why can I do these things and nobody else can? Do I have to figure out all of this on my own?"

"I'm not sure yet what any of it means. But I want to warn you to be careful. Don't let too much of your power come out at once. A person can only take so much of it flowing through them. Push too hard, and something inside you might very well burst."

"Good, another thing to worry about. I'll keep that in mind. Bursting would be inconvenient."

"You do not, however, need to be alone in this. I would very much like to study your abilities. I wish we were back at my home university so I could refer to the materials there."

"I'd like to know more about them, too. I'll make you a deal. You help me learn more about these abilities, and when I get a ship, I'll take you to the eastern continent myself, and we can take a look at these texts to see what else we can learn."

The old man beamed at her. "That's a very generous offer, and I hope we can make that journey together." He gazed out the window over the ocean with energy in his eyes. "Oh, I hope some of my old colleagues are there. They thought we were crazy for pursuing our studies. Now I can prove them wrong and maybe make the loss of my friends mean something." He looked back at her. "You said you need to get a ship first. How do you plan to do that?"

"We'll find one and take it. Lord Devrim wants us to help him with something in exchange for getting a ship afterward, but I'm not willing to pay the cost of his help. We'll just end up doing it on our own."

"If you do end up working with Devrim, be careful with him. I don't know much of him, but what I do know is that he is an ambitious man," he said with a tone of caution.

"You think he wants to take advantage of me? Trust me, I agree with that. He offered a lopsided deal and was quite upset when I turned it down."

"I don't necessarily think he's dangerous, and his ambition by itself doesn't make him untrustworthy. A lot of people like him, and that speaks to his character. But someone who rises from nothing to his position doesn't usually become content. He'll be hungry for more. Make sure that whatever you do for him takes you closer to your goal, and that he's not using you."

"I'll keep my eyes open, but I may not have much choice. I do appreciate the advice though." Nereyda looked out the window at the setting sun. "I should get back to town before it gets dark. My crew should have arrived at the inn by now and I want to spend some time with them before calling it a night."

"Very well. Thank you for coming by. It was good to see you again."

"Thanks for the tea. I'll come back soon and we can see what I can do with this." Nereyda concentrated and produced a spark of lightning at her fingertips.

"I look forward to it," said Manu with a smile.

Nereyda pulled the door shut behind her and hiked back toward town.

Dusk had settled by the time she arrived at the tavern. The sounds of drunken singing came through the walls.

She opened the door and smiled at the jolly scene. Elvar's voice shouted, "Captain!"

The noise died down, and the crew turned to look at her, smiles on their faces.

"Captain, I have a drink for you," said Elvar. Crew members made way for him as he elbowed his way through the crowd. "Where have you been? What did you talk with Devrim about?"

She took the drink Elvar offered. "Never mind that. We're going to go get a ship."

The crew cheered, then quieted as Elvar asked, "How are we going to do that?"

"There's a dock up north. We're going to steal a ship, then get the hell out of this place. We'll keep it nice and quiet, then sail for Freyport to restock. But we'll worry about that tomorrow. Tonight, we celebrate our freedom."

With that, the mood picked back up, and the crew enjoyed their drinks and jokes.

Drink in hand, Nereyda spotted Jax sitting across the tavern in a corner with the rest of the Islanders, where they were quietly drinking their own drinks. It reminded her of how the Islanders had walked a short distance from the pirates as they hiked north from the mines. She swaggered over and took a seat right next to Jax. "Why so glum?" she asked. "We're out of the mines and finally in a place where we can relax."

"It's how we are. If it was just us, it'd be different. But it's tough for us to get used to non-Islanders. It takes time, that's all."

"I hope you do become comfortable with us. I'm surprised that fighting our way out of the mines didn't break the ice enough for you."

Jax shrugged and cracked a broad genuine smile.

Nereyda found it refreshing how Jax and the rest of the Islanders were so quick to wear their emotions. It gave them an authentic honesty that was rare.

"It's hard to shake old habits, I suppose," said Jax. "Looks like we're together for the long haul, so we'll have time to become friends."

"Listen, you helped us in the mines when you didn't need to. You don't have to stay with us. You can go off and find a way home or do whatever you want."

"You helped us at least as much as we helped you. We wouldn't have even started trying to escape without you. We want to stick with you. Just promise me that if you get a ship, you'll take us home to the Shattered Sea."

Nereyda nodded. "I can do that. It's a long way, but I suppose what's one more detour after everything we've gone through?" She paused to take a sip. "So that's your goal, then? Get home?"

"I can't speak for everyone. Some of them may wish to stick with you. I'm thinking of that myself, after seeing all of you in action. But I know some of the others have families in the islands, and they want to go back to them."

"Why join us? Don't you like it quiet?"

"Not all the time, and we're born to love the sea, just as you all do. I could see that kind of life growing on me."

"How did you end up in the mines in the first place? We got captured in a raid gone bad, but I don't see you and your people as the marauder type."

"We're not. We were settlers on one of the islands in the Shattered Sea. We were trying to expand our reach toward the south, but it didn't go unnoticed by the Cambisians. They landed two ships of marines on the island and rounded us up. We—" His voice broke and he averted his gaze.

Nereyda put a reassuring hand on his shoulder. "What happened?"

He tensed at her touch, but didn't pull away. "We were lucky that we could help the children escape in one of our small and fast ships, but there wasn't room for everyone. The rest of us tried to slow the Imperials down." He bit his lip and stared down at the table. "We—we lost some people. Eventually, when we were sure the young ones had gotten away, we surrendered, and then the rest you know. Not much to tell between that and the mines."

"Did you have a child among those that escaped?"

"I have no children, no." His voice caught as a tear slid down his cheek. "But some of my friends who have been killed, either in the battle on the island or in the mines, did. I may adopt one or two of the children if I return home, if they haven't been already. If they arrived at our capital safely, I know they will be well taken care of while we're all gone. Still, I think I owe it to my friends who died."

"That's why you all stood and fought with us at the mines."

Jax nodded.

"Thank you for sharing your story with me, Jax. I know that couldn't have been easy."

"No; but it feels good to open up to someone new."

"I'm glad you chose me. You can always talk to me, if you need someone to listen." She gestured toward the strand of beads in his hair. "Can you tell me about those?"

"Oh, these?" Jax toyed with the beads for a moment. "They're a way of marking our individual achievements." His fingers traced along each bead. "Blue for leading a fishing expedition, red for helping to build a ship, and white for volunteering to colonize another island."

"You've got quite a few of them."

Jax gave her a humble smile. "Not as many as some."

"What about the yellow and green others have?"

"Yellow is for serving aboard a patrol ship and green is for leading a scouting expedition on another island."

"Maybe I should start handing out beads. You all have earned more than a few." She glanced around at the other Islanders and said in a raised voice, "In the meantime, if you're going to be part of our crew, I insist that all of you join us and get to know us tonight. Grab your drinks, stand up, and meet the rest of your crew. And it is your crew, because tonight you join it until we can return you to your home."

The Islanders glanced around at each other, hesitating.

Nereyda grabbed Jax by the elbow and pulled him up. "Up, I said. Come with me. There is booze to drink, and it goes down much better when you're not sulking in a corner."

CHAPTER FIVE

Nereyda and her crew crept through the darkness toward the docks of Fethia. The lights of lanterns sparkled in the single Imperial frigate docked there. A few silhouettes stood or walked around the ship. The waves splashing against the hull and the creak of the ship swaying were the only sounds from that direction. A large number of voices shouted, chattered, and sang from the lone tavern in town. Two sailors stumbled out, leaning against the wall.

Good. That meant that there would only be a token skeleton crew on the ship to deal with.

"Okay, you all stay on shore. I'm going to swim to the ship and deal with any sentries," Nereyda said.

"Are you sure you want to go alone?" Elvar asked from over her left shoulder. "I remember the last time you went onto an enemy ship alone. You got surrounded and almost couldn't fight your way out."

"'Almost' is the key word in that sentence."

"Fine, we'll stay here," agreed Elvar. "But as soon as you are clear or if you're in trouble, let us know and we'll run out to the ship."

"Sounds good. We won't have much time to get the ship up and sailing before that garrison in the tavern figures out something is wrong. While they might be drunk, there will still be more of them than us, and if they board the ship before we can sail, we'll be trapped in a fight."

"We'll have to be fast then."

Nereyda crept to the edge of the water. She took off her black boots and squeezed them under her belt to keep them secure for the swim to the ship. She waded out until it was deep enough to swim. Silently, she slipped through the dark water toward the ship. In her dark clothing, she blended in with the nighttime waves.

One or two soldiers stood nearby on the dock, while a few others roamed the deck, casually glancing out over the water. Their gazes kept returning to the tavern, where their comrades enjoyed the night off. They didn't seem too concerned with the prospect of being attacked at a quiet village, especially when no enemies had made their presence known.

Nereyda and her crew, which now included the newly joined Islanders, would change that very soon.

She reached the side of the ship and slipped around the hull to the side opposite the dock, then climbed up using the ropes and portholes that she could reach. At the top of the hull, she peeked through a gap in the railing supports. A breeze chilled her through her drenched clothing, and she fought to suppress a shiver. The deck creaked as a guard sauntered past her. Nereyda ducked her head down. When his steps began to get quieter, she reached to the top of the railing and pulled herself over, landing lightly on her feet in a crouch.

She padded over the deck and crept up behind the guard. She dared not even breathe as she got within arm's reach.

A board groaned under her foot and the guard started to turn around. Nereyda struck him on the back of the head with the hilt of her cutlass, then supported him as she lowered his unconscious body to the deck.

Now, there was only a guard at the aft of the ship, one at the bow, and the two on the dock. She crouch-walked up the stairway to the aftercastle, where the helm wheel was. The single guard stared out over the ocean and leaned against the railing with his back to Nereyda.

She slowly strode up to him, pulled her cutlass back to ready a thrust, and then he whirled around.

A familiar face. Erhan.

His face had become gaunter and his brown hair had grown a couple of inches longer than his standard military cut, but his strong shoulders and jaw still projected resolve.

"Hello pirate," he said, venom in his voice.

Nereyda took a step back as her mouth hung open and her sword arm faltered for a moment. "What are you doing here?"

"I heard a rumor that some pirates were in the area, looking for a ship. So I guessed and hoped that I'd find you and your crew here."

"Well, my crew isn't here right now. It's just me."

"You're even more talented than I thought if you plan on sailing this ship all by yourself. Then you won't mind if we capture and execute the people hiding in the bushes on the beach."

Nereyda needed to stall as she searched for an escape route. "What do you want, Erhan? We just want to leave, and then you never have to worry about us again."

"Because of you, I lost my commission. You destroyed my life, so it's only fair that I do likewise to you." He gave Nereyda a smug smile.

"Then how the hell are you here? Who are these soldiers and sailors if they're not under your command?"

"An old navy friend owed me a favor, so I called it in. And after I told him about everything you've done, he was eager to help out."

Nereyda heard footsteps behind her and glanced over her shoulder. Another guard crept up behind her, with his sword pointed at her back. The tip dug into her skin, making her wince.

"Now, drop your sword before I have him run you through."

"Fine, fine," she said. She made a show of holding her sword out before letting it fall from her grasp. She held her hands up in surrender. After a moment, she pulled her back away from the sword tip, spun to her right, and dropped her elbow straight into the gut of the man who had captured her. With her other hand, she wrenched his sword from his hand, then knelt and picked hers up. A sword in each hand, she kicked the doubled-over guard onto the deck and faced Erhan.

He reached into his jacket and pulled out a whistle and blew into it, letting out a shrill note.

Nereyda winced at the loud, high-pitched noise, but set her discomfort aside when she heard the sounds of battle from the beach. Forgetting Erhan, she vaulted off the aftercastle and sprinted across the gangway to the dock. The two guards grabbed at her, but she held her swords to either side and cut them down as she ran past. She didn't have time to play with her food right now.

Dashing down the length of the dock, she found her crew facing off against a large number of soldiers. The Imperials used their numbers to their advantage. When the front rank slowed from exertion, an officer blew a whistle and a fresh rank pressed forward and gave their comrades a chance to rest. This constant cycle of fresh troops pushed the pirates and Islanders to the edge of the water.

A group of three Imperials ran over to her and blocked her path. One came forward to face her while the other two watched.

The wet sand squished between Nereyda's bare toes as she lunged with a quick thrust toward his stomach. With a flick of his wrist, he swept her blade to the side. She feinted to her left, and he took the bait. Seizing the opening, she surged forward and drove her elbow into his gut.

He clutched his belly and staggered back, while the next soldier charged, his sword raised overhead. Almost too late, Nereyda blocked the blow. Pain jolted through her arm at the impact. She counterattacked, but struck his unwavering shield.

Between moves, Nereyda reached toward some of her power.

A swing toward her right shoulder. She dodged with a sidestep, and her concentration broke.

She turned her focus inward and tried again.

Her opponent lunged toward her. Nereyda batted his sword away, but lost her focus once again.

The third soldier strode up to take his turn.

With their relentless attack, Nereyda would never have time to channel her power. She needed all of her energy and focus to keep up with the constant rotation of rested opponents.

Rather than wait for an attack from her new challenger, Nereyda unleashed a flurry of strikes against him. He kept his defenses up, but she forced him back several steps toward his two comrades.

Before he could recover his stance, she rolled to the side and thrust her sword into one of the waiting soldiers. While this cut down the number of enemies, the remaining ones fought even harder after seeing their friend fall. They stopped taking turns and instead attacked her at the same time.

In between blocks, Nereyda chanced a glance at the beach. Her pirates and the Islanders had been pressed far enough back to where they were wading in water up to their ankles and could no longer retreat.

Gunshots echoed from the forest at the upper edge of the beach. Nereyda expected some of her people to fall, but only saw Imperials collapse in the sand. Their comrades paused in confusion, and her crew pressed the attack.

As Nereyda's people took advantage of the distraction, more troops in uniform surged out of the forest—except their uniforms featured the green of Devrim's household guard.

Nereyda recognized Limbani leading the way as they charged into the Imperials. With renewed hope and energy, Nereyda finished off her opponents, then helped the others clean up the beach. Once the area was clear, Nereyda slipped her boots back on, then approached Limbani.

"What are you doing here?" Nereyda asked.

The officer looked at Nereyda with a focused, serious face. "Devrim thought you might do something crazy. Guess he was right."

A horn sounded in the distance.

"Come on," said Limbani. "Reinforcements are coming."

Nereyda looked back longingly at the ship. They had come so close to having a way out.

"We need to leave," said Limbani as she tugged on Nereyda's shoulder.

"How long do we have?" asked Nereyda.

"Not sure. Minutes."

"Too long to get that ship ready." Nereyda sighed, then relented. As Nereyda and her people followed Limbani off of the beach, she resigned herself to a much longer fight for a ship.

CHAPTER SIX

Clutching the travel permit that Commander Erhan had given to her, Brynja approached the high, dark walls of Antalia with the Storm Raven crew. Well, her half of the crew. The half that had been released after Brynja turned Nereyda over to Erhan. Bringing Nereyda to Erhan was supposed to have bought freedom for the entire Storm Raven crew, but the commander had changed the deal at the last minute. Brynja hadn't had any choice but to accept, unless she wanted to end up right back in the mines that had broken her.

Not that she truly had her freedom yet. Part of her terms with Erhan was that she and her crew enter the service of the Empire as privateers. Still, serving the rest of their sentence on a ship was far better than being stuck below ground.

A pair of guards kept watch next to the gate. "What's your business in Antalia?" asked the one on the right.

"We're reporting for duty."

The guard studied her, then glanced over her crew. Their time on the road from the mines had left them haggard and dirty, but the Imperials had provided enough supplies and rations to stay healthy.

As the guard looked them over, Brynja fidgeted with a loose braid of straw-blonde hair that rested on her shoulder.

"You're reporting for duty without uniforms?" the guard asked.

"We're supposed to be privateers. Do they have uniforms?"

He sneered at her. "Oh, so you're not real soldiers, just criminals for hire."

Brynja swallowed. "Commander Erhan gave us this pass." She

handed him her travel permit. "He told us that this was part of our sentence."

He scanned her paperwork. "This all seems to be in order. I'll let you in, but it doesn't mean I think you deserve it. The naval station is down at the harbor. You can't miss it. Go there and report to the admiral. He'll decide where to put you." The guard knocked on a smaller door built into the gate. "Oi, open up. These people are cleared."

The door clicked open and swung out from the gate. Brynja stepped into the city and led her crew past the inner guards who glared at them without speaking. She turned her gaze away and focused on getting to the station at the harbor with as little trouble as possible. As they made their way through the once familiar city, they passed by the occasional subdued citizen and through the main square where a platform with three gallows stood in the middle. The nooses hung empty, ready for the next people that the Empire decided needed to be punished.

Once, Antalia had been a loosely governed port of the Cambisian Empire, and a haven for pirates, smugglers, and thieves who did business on or near the continent. Then, the Emperor had decided to crack down on those unsavory professions, and made Antalia an example by purging the criminal elements and their associates and bringing the city directly under military control.

As the vast harbor came into view, a forest of masts rose into the sky. Naval ships of all sizes stood docked, with more floating out in the middle of the water. A massive building with the Cambisian flag fluttering above it stood at the midpoint of the coast. Brynja recognized it as the old city administration building, but the large number of marines moving around, in, and out of it suggested that it had been taken over by the martial authority that had assumed control of Antalia.

They entered the building, and Brynja spotted a uniformed man at a desk. He glanced up at them, with a raised eyebrow at their rugged appearance. "May I help you? Are you lost?"

"No," said Brynja. "We're reporting for duty as privateers." She passed him the paperwork from Commander Erhan that marked them as legitimate recruits.

"I see. You're Brynja, then?" He tapped a line on the paper and glanced up.

She nodded.

The man frowned.

"Admiral Mansur is quite busy at the moment," he said, "but if you wait in that room over there, he'll see you when he's available."

Another marine ushered them into a room with a scattering of empty chairs, enough that about half of her group of sixteen could sit.

After Brynja had been staring out a window at nothing in particular for an hour, a marine marched into the room and addressed the crew. "Is there a Brynja here?"

"Yes, I'm Brynja," she said as she stood.

"Excellent. Admiral Mansur will see you now. Please follow me."

As she followed, she adjusted her shirt. Her time in the mines had left her thin, so her clothing felt a bit too loose.

The marine led her up to the third floor and into a spacious office that overlooked the harbor outside. A man in a uniform that seemed to have more medals than bare fabric sat at a large desk, his attention on a document that lay in front of him. He glanced up as Brynja entered the office with the marine.

"This is Brynja, sir."

"Thank you, Ensign. You may step outside."

The man nodded and left.

"Come forward and stand in front of me."

Brynja obeyed and stood across the desk from him.

Cool gray eyes studied her above a hawkish nose. "So you're the pirate." He pointed at the paper in front of him, apparently given to him by the clerk. "It says here that you were captured. Not a very good pirate, are you?"

She didn't know what to say, so she remained silent.

"I asked you a question, sailor."

Brynja swallowed and averted her gaze. "No."

"What was that, sailor? Are you talking to me or someone out the window? When you address a superior officer, you look him in the eye."

She forced herself to meet his gaze. "No, I'm not a good pirate."

"That's what I thought." He sneered. "If you let yourself get captured, what use are you to me as a privateer?"

"We'll follow your orders, sir. We've learned our lesson in the mines."

He snorted with derision. "You don't have the typical attitude that most privateers have, I'll give you that. It seems that the mines did their job. You seem like the obedient sort. I can't tell if the mines broke you or just taught you the error of your ways, but I think we can find a use for you. Do you know what a privateer does?"

"I'm not sure. It's like a mercenary of some sort, isn't it?"

"Sometimes they're mercenaries, but not in your case. You're still serving a sentence, so you will not be paid beyond what you need for rations and supplies. Privateers serve to augment the Imperial fleet. You will attack enemies of the Cambisian Empire, but you won't fly the official flag of our navy. That way, if you're captured, it makes a diplomatic incident less likely. It means you're expendable. Doubly so for a rotten pirate like you."

Brynja's calloused spirit ignored the insult. "What will be our first assignment, sir?"

"You and your crew, along with whoever else I assign to be with you, will take a frigate and harass the Stalstan Empire. After their stunt at the mines, we need to take the fight to them. 'Brynja' sounds like a Stalstan name. You have the blonde hair and blue eyes of a Stalstan, as well. Will your heritage be a problem for you on this mission?"

"No, I have very little attachment to Stalsta. I barely remember my parents, and I've lived my life on the sea."

The admiral nodded. "Excellent, then I'll leave you assigned to this campaign."

"Who will be in command? Me?"

He gave a dark laugh. "Not entirely. You'll be in command of your crew's operations on the ship, but you will also have a representative of the navy with you. Most of the time, he will be there to observe and make sure that you are doing what you are supposed to be doing. However, if he gives you an instruction, you are to consider it an order that bears my own authority. Also, this representative is our insurance policy that you won't hijack the vessel. You will need to report back at prescribed intervals, and your representative will need to be with you, alive. If you fail to return entirely, you will be considered pirates and enemies of the state. If my representative is dead or unaccounted for, you will lose your status as a privateer and be sent to finish your sentence somewhere far less enjoyable. The mines are gone, but I have other choices that are equally unpleasant. I also do not hesitate to hand out punishment myself. Oh, and because you are pirates and may not mind being on the run from the law, I am also going to keep one of your crew mates here at all times."

"What if your representative dies in battle or because of illness? Will we be held responsible even if it's through no fault of our own?"

"You should not be picking battles that put anyone on your ship at significant risk. I do not want you attacking Stalstan warships on your own. For now, your purpose is to harass their trading operations. If you encounter a war vessel or anything that is an even match or better than your own ship, you are to retreat. If the representative falls ill, you are to return to port. We'll find you a new representative for the duration of the other's absence."

"Understood. When do we start this mission?"

"You will report to the Tavara tomorrow. Ilker will meet you there as my delegate to your ship, and you can begin preparations."

"Do you have quarters for my crew and me until then?"

"Take this." He passed her a sealed envelope. "Bring it to any inn in town that has enough rooms for your crew, and they will need to accommodate you. If you face any resistance, report it and the owner of said establishment will be dealt with."

CHAPTER SEVEN

Despite the morning chill in the air, Limbani's palms were sweaty underneath her riding gloves as she passed the reins of her horse to the stablehand. After helping to rescue the pirates from their ill-fated attempt to steal a ship, Adnan had finally submitted his report about the drink she had while on duty. She had received an order from Lord Devrim to report to his office first thing in the morning. A dewy smell hit her nose, and the rising sun streamed through the trees that surrounded the estate as she strode across the grounds to the servants' entrance.

She followed the familiar route to her lord's office on the third floor. She found the door closed, so she rapped on it with three sharp taps.

"Come in," called the voice of Devrim from within.

As Limbani pushed through the door, Devrim remained in his seat at the desk and watched her cross the room. She stood straight at attention in front of him. "Reporting as instructed, my lord."

"Yes. Good job with helping our pirate friends. Despite their recklessness, I anticipate them being valuable allies. However, I received a disturbing report about your recent behavior."

"I understand, sir. I have no excuses for my actions."

He frowned at her. "Is it true that you drank alcohol on duty, Captain Limbani?"

"It is, sir."

"I'm surprised that you of all people would break a regulation like that. Can you explain why you did it?"

"Our . . . guests were getting out of hand, and the fastest way of getting them to settle down was to accept a drink from their quartermaster. It worked, as he got them to quiet down right after that."

Devrim raised an eyebrow. "Did the pirate captain rub off on you during your ride together yesterday?"

"Excuse me, sir? I'm far from a pirate. It was a lapse in judgment, and it will not happen again. I will accept any punishment that you deem appropriate."

Devrim cracked a smile. "I'm just teasing you, Limbani. I have no desire to punish you. I know that this isn't like you. We're both facing quite a change in circumstances, and we have to figure out how to deal with it."

"So you won't take disciplinary action?"

"Do you think it's necessary? Will it help you avoid a repeat incident?"

"I am already set on avoiding a repeat, sir. However, it will not set a good example for the rest of the unit. Give me an undesirable post or something of the sort."

"If you insist on a punitive assignment, then I have something just for you. Whenever you are on duty, you will remain in the company of our guests. You will see to their needs and even accompany them if the situation calls for them to have a guide. In your off-hours, I also want you to spend time with them. During that time, you may socialize or drink or whatever you wish to do. But I want you to get to know them."

"So my punishment is to be a babysitter?"

"If that's how you choose to view it, I suppose so. But the fact that you look down on such an assignment makes it a good punishment, doesn't it? Besides, if you're going to be leading the rest of our forces alongside them, you will need them to trust and respect you."

That caught Limbani off guard. "What do you mean by leading the rest of our forces?"

"I mean that I am putting you in command of all regular guard and military units that are part of our growing resistance. You're a general now. Captain Nereyda and her people will remain separate from that chain of command. I don't think it would go well to mix a bunch of pirates in with regular soldiers. If someone with your exemplary record can be led astray, even if it was for a mere sip of a drink, I can only imagine how some of our less disciplined people would behave. We don't need their influence spreading, as useful as they may be in the fights to come."

Limbani bowed her head. "Thank you for this honor, sir. I'll do my best to make you proud. Although it seems strange to get a promotion at the same time as getting chastised for my infraction."

"Oh, I had already planned to grant this position to you. However, Adnan's report gave me the perfect opportunity to make you nervous and have a little bit of fun at your expense."

Limbani laughed and relaxed her shoulders. "I hope it was entertaining, sir."

"Of course. You'll forgive me for making you nervous?"

"Certainly."

"And while I appreciate your professionalism, it is quite okay to turn that off at times."

"It's something I need to work on, sir."

"Spend some time with Nereyda, and I'm sure she'll be happy to help you with that."

"Yes, sir."

"Now, I need to speak with Nereyda today. Could you please go and fetch her from the tavern down below as soon as possible? I wish to have breakfast with her and go over her role in the rebellion."

"Of course. I'll go get her at once." Limbani bowed as she backed out of the office, then returned to the stables. Part of her looked forward to waking the pirate up, knowing that she had spent the night drinking with her crew.

Before long, she tied her horse to a post outside the tavern where the pirates and Islanders had taken up residence again. Limbani walked in, took the staircase to the room that the captain had claimed, and raised her hand to the door.

CHAPTER EIGHT

A knock sounded at the door and shattered Nereyda's peaceful sleep.

She rolled over and covered her head with her pillow. Her head hurt from a night of drinking with her crew, and she wanted to sleep it off. Normally she didn't drink so much, but she had needed to drink away her disappointment at failing to secure a ship.

Another knock.

Nereyda pulled the pillow from her face and threw it at the door. Squinting her eyes against the morning light streaming in through her window, she rolled out of bed.

The knock came again, louder and more urgently this time.

"I'm coming, settle down," she said as she staggered to the door. Nereyda reached for the door and pulled it open, revealing Limbani standing in the doorway in a crisp uniform.

"Sorry for waking you, ma'am, but my Lord Devrim has summoned you to his estate for breakfast and a meeting." Despite her courteous tone, the slight smile on Limbani's lips suggested she wasn't sorry at all.

"What time is it? Isn't it a little early for breakfast?" Nereyda asked with a scowl.

"It's nearly eight; two hours since sunrise, ma'am."

"Clearly Devrim has never worked with pirates before. We're rarely up before noon when we're on land." She started to push the door shut. "Come back in another two hours."

The door caught on something. Nereyda looked down to see the woman's boot blocking the way. "Sorry, ma'am, but my lord is insistent that you join him now. I'd think you would be a bit more grateful after he sent us to bail you out."

Nereyda considered grabbing her cutlass and sticking the guard captain in the gut to get some more sleep, but decided that would put a damper on her relationship with Devrim and decrease her chances of getting a ship. "Fine, I'll be out in a minute. Also, don't call me ma'am."

"What should I call you then? Captain?"

Nereyda shook her head, then winced at her headache. "No, my crew calls me Captain. Nereyda is fine."

"I'm not sure I'm comfortable with that. I was raised to treat a fellow officer with respect. Addressing you so casually feels like a breach of etiquette."

"A breach of etiquette, you say? Then you should definitely call me Nereyda, or even Reyda." Despite her hangover, she gave a wink. "Also, isn't it disrespectful to call a person something she doesn't want to be called? I think it'd be politer to call me what I want."

Limbani frowned. "I've never thought about that."

"Most haven't." Nereyda sighed. "If you insist on taking me with you, give me a minute to get dressed."

After Nereyda dressed, she joined the guard captain out in the hallway and headed downstairs. She stopped to chug a mug of water at the bar, then followed Limbani out of the tavern.

Normally, she'd chat with her companion as they walked, but her headache left her in an unsocial mood. Nereyda trudged behind Limbani up the hill to the estate, then her escort led her into the house and showed her to the same dining room where she had shared breakfast with Devrim before. Once again, the table was strewn with a feast.

The lord himself sat at the head of the table with a half-empty plate, reading a letter set next to him on the table. He glanced up and his eyebrows raised as he spotted Nereyda. "Ah, Captain, I see that Limbani roused you. Please, take a seat and help yourself." He waved at the food covering the table.

"Thanks," said Nereyda as she sat down in the chair on Devrim's right hand and began to pile her plate with food.

"You seem quiet and hungry this morning."

"I'm not a morning person when I'm on land, especially after a night with my crew."

Devrim placed a hand on her arm. "I'm sorry your plan to take that ship didn't work."

His gesture surprised Nereyda. After she resisted the urge to push him away, she enjoyed the reassuring strength of his gentle touch. "It's no use dwelling on it. I appreciate the assist on getting out of there alive, though."

"It's not exactly the resounding blow I'd imagined we'd use to start our rebellion, but it was no trouble." He pulled his hand back. "I'll let you eat your hangover away. Once you're full, we can start discussing our next move."

Nereyda stuffed herself full of eggs, bacon, and sweet rolls and her headache subsided. "Okay, I'm ready. What do we need to talk about?"

"Not here," said Devrim as he stood. "Follow me."

"Are we going to your study?"

"No, that is too easy to find if someone were to break into my house, as you so skillfully demonstrated not long ago." He winked at Nereyda. "You'll see."

Nereyda followed him into the kitchen and to a door at the back. He pushed the door open to reveal a staircase that descended into a basement.

"Really? The cellar? This isn't hard to find."

He gave her a small smile. "As I said, you'll see."

Devrim lit a lantern from the kitchen counter, then carried it down the stairs. At the bottom, he lit a lamp on the wall. In the dim light, Nereyda looked around the cellar. The ceiling was low, less than two feet above Nereyda's head. The walls consisted of gray stone bricks. Along one wall were several casks of wine. Other barrels and crates lay strewn around the room, which Nereyda assumed contained the mansion's food stores.

On the wall opposite from the casks, Devrim pulled on a lamp, which moved slightly as if it were a lever. Next, he ran his hand over the wall, scanning it for a moment. He stopped his hand on a specific brick and pushed in. As the brick slid into the wall, a click sounded, and a section of the wall swung open. Nereyda's host beckoned her into the darkness beyond and slid the stone door shut behind them.

In the glow of his lantern, Devrim yanked a chain on the wall, and a number of wall lamps flickered to life, revealing a spacious conference room with a large table occupying the middle. A map of the Cambisian continent was on the top, with various flags and wooden carvings of soldiers in various colors dotting the surface; a handful of blue pieces were scattered across the map, a large number of red ones, and a few green.

"What's all of this?" Nereyda asked, waving at the map.

"This is our battle map, if you will. I use this to help plan out where our support comes from. The red pieces are Imperial units and cities, the blue are known allies, and the green are cities where I think we can get some more supporters or that we have a chance of taking."

"That's a lot of red."

"It is, but as we have some success, we can turn some of that to green, then blue."

"Why did you bring me here? Just wanted to show off your toys?"

"No, I wanted to ask where you think we should go next. If you're going to help me wage this rebellion, I want to know what your thoughts are."

"I'm not a general. I've never run a campaign like this."

"I don't want a general. I want someone who thinks differently. Just take a look and see what you come up with."

Nereyda scanned the map and studied the cities with green markers. She didn't know much about most of them. The only one she was familiar with was Trabizan, where she had blackmailed an Imperial captain to get a message to Brynja in the mines. Her eyes flicked toward the western coast, where she saw Antalia.

"Have you thought about trying to take Antalia?" Nereyda asked.

"Antalia?" He let out a short incredulous laugh. "Are you joking? Maybe once it would have been easy, but not anymore. It's surrounded by some of the strongest walls in the Empire and has a permanent squadron of frigates guarding the harbor. To have any chance of taking the city, we'd need to destroy those ships, and we don't have a fleet yet. And it's under martial law, so I can't just try to become friends with the noble in charge like I would with most places. That's why it has a red marker. Our support is growing, but we only have maybe a thousand fighters ready to go and close enough to help right now. Not nearly enough to take a city like that."

She tilted her head and focused on the map as a plan started to form in her mind. "What if we could take it from the inside?"

"What do you mean? How would we do that?"

"I have some friends still inside Antalia. Many people there resent the iron grip that the Empire has them in. With the right nudge, we can probably get them to rise up." She nodded with excitement. "Yes, this could work."

"Maybe, but they'd need weapons, and civilians in Antalia aren't allowed to own them."

Nereyda looked up and smiled at Devrim. "Then we give them weapons."

"You still haven't told me how you plan to get into what might be the most heavily fortified city in the Empire."

"Can you get us some fishing boats? Enough to carry all of my pirates and the Islanders."

"What are you going to do with fishing boats?"

"We're going to bring fish to Antalia. And under the fish, we'll bring enough weapons to arm the city."

"So you need fishing boats, weapons, and . . . fish? This plan seems a bit crazy."

She shrugged. "You said you wanted someone who thinks differently, right? And what better way of continuing your rebellion than taking a city that can't be captured?"

He grimaced. "True, but it's incredibly risky. What if you're caught? What if the wrong people hear what you're up to?"

"I'll deal with that if it happens. But we're just pirates and they don't know we're with you. If we're caught, we'll be tried as smugglers, but we won't rat you out. We bear all the risk."

"And you're willing to take that chance?"

Nereyda nodded. "For my friends in Antalia, yes."

Devrim glanced back down at the map for a minute, considering the plan. "Fine, let's do it your way. If this works, it could be a great start. And it would give us one of the best harbors on the continent. Is there anything else you need?"

"You have a blue marker not far from Antalia. What's there?"

"That's the estate of one of the other nobles friendly to us."

"Good. Bring as many of your troops there as you can and keep an eye on the city while we're there. I'm sure you'll be able to tell when the fighting begins. When it does, we'll try to get the gates open, and you can walk right in to help."

"I hope this works." Devrim furrowed his brow as he gazed at the map. "If it doesn't, this rebellion is going to be awfully short."

"Trust me. It'll work."

Devrim chuckled. "I can't believe I'm trusting someone who tried to rob me."

Nereyda smiled and winked at him. "That's all in the past. I'm sure we'll be the best of friends from now on."

"At least until you get a ship again?"

"Are you implying that I'm using you until I get what I want? How dare you!" Nereyda put a hand over her chest in mock insult. "I would never do such a thing. Anyway, aren't you using me until you win your little rebellion?"

"I guess that's one way to put it. So we're using each other, then?" He grinned. "As long as we're open about it, that's not a problem."

"Good. I should go tell my crew to start getting ready to leave. Come find me once you have the fishing boats." Nereyda turned and left the war room without waiting to be dismissed and found her way out of the house. As she made her way back to the tavern, she thought about how she could turn her crazy half plan into an even more ridiculous full plan that just might work.

CHAPTER NINE

The harbor of Antalia was noticeably emptier by the time Brynja reported to the docks the next morning. She found an Imperial frigate with Tavara printed on the side. A number of people moved about the deck, preparing it for departure. A man with dark hair waited for her next to the helm, a gray jacket wrapped around his lanky form.

"Hello," he said, fixing her with piercing green eyes. "You must be Brynja."

"That's right. Who are you?"

"I'm Ilker, and the good admiral has decided that I should be his representative aboard your vessel." He tapped a golden ring with the shape of an eye inscribed onto it. "That means that you'd better keep me happy and healthy," he said with a predatory grin, "whatever it takes."

"We'll try not to disappoint you."

"Good. I should hope so. We can set sail as soon as you give your crew the orders. Supplies were stocked overnight, and some additional crew members are here already, so we're fully staffed."

"Where did the other ships go? This harbor was full yesterday."

"Oh, the rest of the fleet is being redeployed to patrol the sea near the mines. You don't need to concern yourself with that now, though. Now it's time to get ready to leave. I'm eager to blow some Stalstans out of the water." He grinned at her. "So get going, please."

Brynja turned away from the man and addressed her crew members on the deck. "You all know what your jobs are. If you're new and don't recognize me, my name is Brynja. Once we're at sea, we'll have time to get to know each other better. Finish preparations, then we'll be off."

The crew muttered their obedience, which was much different than the usual exuberance they had shown on the Storm Raven before setting out on a raiding expedition. She shook her musings aside as she focused on observing the crew and issuing specific orders when necessary. Once the ship was ready, they cast off from the dock and drifted out into the harbor.

Brynja piloted them out through the narrow water passage that connected the harbor to the ocean. "Now that we're at sea," she said to Ilker, "do we have a particular place where we're supposed to go?"

"You know where Stalsta is, right?"

"Of course."

"Then head west. As we get closer, we'll watch for any ships and attack them as the opportunity arises."

"No specific target?"

He shook his head. "Not right now. Perhaps eventually we'll get a narrower focus. For now, if we see an easy target, we take it out."

"Okay, then we just sail for now, I suppose." She angled the ship to head west. "Full sail," she shouted. Once the sails were unfurled, and everything had been secured, they settled in to cruise toward Stalsta.

As they sailed, Brynja almost forgot that she was still a prisoner. The fresh sea air and wide-open sky felt like total freedom after the cramped confines of the mines. Energy returned to her and the weight of her sentence diminished. After several days of sailing west at full speed, the first islands of the Stalsta Federation appeared on the horizon.

"Ah, good," said Ilker. "We should start to find some prey soon."

An hour later, they found their first potential target as a speck of a mast moved at the edge of Brynja's vision. "I think I see a ship," she said.

"Not surprising," Ilker replied. "We're coming up on a popular trading route that runs between Akureyri and Husavik. I bet this isn't the last ship we find here today. Turn toward that one and chase it down. If we're feeling bold, we can even sail closer to one of the ports and take out some fishing boats."

"Fishing boats?" asked Brynja with surprise as she spun the helm wheel. "Why them? They aren't exactly enemies of the Empire."

"On this ship," he said with an edge to his voice, "I decide who is and who isn't an enemy of the Empire." He looked away from her, showing that he considered the matter settled.

Before long, the distant mast grew into a gigantic barge. Crates and barrels covered the deck and it lay low in the water, weighted down by its cargo. It had no cannons, not even a deck gun. When the other crew spotted the Cambisian vessel, they panicked and scurried about their deck. Their helmsman frantically spun his wheel away from the Tavara.

The barge lumbered into a turn and Brynja adjusted her course with a slight turn.

"Fire a warning shot," Brynja called to her crew as they closed within firing range.

"Cancel that," Ilker shouted.

"We're not going to give them a chance to surrender?" Brynja asked in disbelief.

"Of course not. I know you were a pirate, so you're used to capturing what you can, but we don't care about that. It doesn't matter what it's carrying or who's on board. It could be a barge with a hold full of gold or a passenger ship of orphans, and it wouldn't make a difference. If it's something that can't fight back, we're going to sink it."

Brynja swallowed her disgust and angled the Tavara so that its broadside faced the defenseless ship. "Prepare to fire," she ordered.

People on the other ship scurried around their deck and took what little cover they could find. Not that it would make a difference.

The Tavara loomed parallel to its target. "Fire," she yelled. A chill came over Brynja as she gave the command.

The trading ship stood no chance. As the cannons erupted, their shots tore straight through the hull. They had been aimed at the waterline, so their target started taking on water and slowing down with the added weight and drag.

"A good start," said Ilker, "but they're still floating. Finish them off."

"Reload," she ordered.

While her crew readied the guns for a second round, she ordered the sails trimmed. They slowed down, then turned around the front of their target as they passed it. By the time they maneuvered parallel to the other side of the vessel, the cannons had been loaded.

"Fire!"

Again, the cannons ruptured the hull. Their target became engulfed in rising water, and the crew scrambled off of the ship and grabbed whatever they could to stay afloat.

"Very well done," said Ilker. "I think that's good enough for now. We don't need to bother with the survivors." He spoke as if he gave them no more thought than he would a cockroach under his boot.

"You want to leave them here? We can at least take them and ransom them."

"As far as I can tell, we don't have the space to house any prisoners, so capturing them isn't an option. And, while I have no problems just finishing them off right here and now, it would take a lot of time better spent finding another target. Besides, it can be useful to have some survivors to go home and talk about what happened here. We want Stalsta to find out about these attacks."

Brynja hated the idea of leaving people to drown, especially people who had done nothing to deserve their fate. An ember of resistance started to glow within her, but it wasn't enough to catch flame. "So where to now?"

Ilker shrugged. "That's up to you. You saw where this ship was going and where it was coming from. Pick a direction, and we'll encounter another ship sooner or later."

A few hours later, they came upon a ship lazily sailing through the water. The hull featured intricate carvings, and each post that supported the railing was a unique wooden sculpture.

A boy bounced an orange ball as he ran up and down the length of the ship. "There's a child on board that ship," Brynja noted. "It looks like a pleasure cruise vessel."

"A child, you say?" Ilker asked. "As far as I can tell, it still has a Stalstan flag flying on the mast, so it doesn't matter who you see on deck."

She glared at him and said with a growl, "I can't give the order to fire on a ship that's carrying children. We never went that far when we were pirates."

His gaze toward her contained the same natural hatred with which he observed the Stalstan ship. "You aren't pirates now. Either you give the order, or I will. If I have to do it, be prepared to be punished. I packed a whip, so I can administer a flogging right here on deck. Or perhaps you can pick a crew member and do it yourself. The third choice is to sail straight back and report to the admiral that you have decided you'd rather serve your sentence somewhere else. Is that what you want for you and your friends?" He smiled as if inviting her to test him.

Ilker's words brought back memories of when Brynja had been forced to whip members of her own crew in the mines. The echoes of their cries ringing in her mind, she hung her head. "No, I don't want that."

He loomed next to her and brought his lips right next to her ear. "Then give the order, pirate."

She took a deep breath, then nodded and gave the command.

Their target exploded from the impact of the volley. Bodies flew into the water and floated lifelessly. Screams echoed from the wreckage as it slipped beneath the waves. As Brynja turned the wheel to leave, an orange ball bobbed up and down in the waves.

Ilker observed the scene with a pleased gleam in his eyes. "Very good, pirate. You're learning. Now, if you're feeling bold, let's get a bit closer to shore and find some fishing boats."

They sailed farther up the trading route and, a few hours later, saw land on the horizon. Soon afterward, the Tavara encountered a cluster of fishing boats trawling the water, drifting with the current and waiting for their nets to snag some fish.

"Don't hesitate this time," said Ilker, his voice razor sharp.

His threats still fresh in her mind, Brynja ordered her crew to attack. Their shoulders drooped as they aimed the guns and worked the sails.

The Tavara made quick work of the fishing fleet. The small vessels weren't made to withstand cannon fire, so it only took one shot per boat to sink it or break it apart entirely.

In the chaos, one boat slipped out of their range, its tiny sail wide open. Frantic sailors paddled with wooden planks in pursuit of an extra touch of speed.

"Should we pursue that one?" Brynja asked.

"No, let it escape. They'll go back and tell everyone about what happened."

Brynja let out a sigh of relief. "In that case, I recommend that we pull away from the shore. A Stalstan patrol will be out soon to catch whoever did this, and we should be as far away as we can."

"I agree. We've had a good first day, so I think we can end it here. I'll leave it up to your judgment where to go and drift for the night."

Brynja tightened her grip on the wheel as a floating orange ball haunted her thoughts.

CHAPTER TEN

Nereyda stood at the helm of her fishing boat as it glided through the water toward Antalia, her eyes on the Imperial frigates that floated just outside the harbor. Devrim had gotten her five fishing vessels. Nereyda piloted the one in the center, with two others on either side. Each fishing boat had a hold full of crates of weapons, with fish covering the contents of each crate in case they were inspected. They also had some casks of wine to use as bribes if necessary.

Six frigates drifted on the water, with several more docked in the harbor. One of the patrol ships cut off the fishing vessels and ran up its colors. A yellow flag indicated that the fishing boats should stop and prepare for boarding. Nereyda and her crew brought their vessel to a halt, then waved to the other ships to do the same. A rowboat pushed off from the nearby frigate with a squad of armed Imperial marines.

They rowed up next to Nereyda's boat, and a young man in an officer's uniform gave her a crisp wave. "Hello, there. I'm Lieutenant Metine, and we request permission to board and inspect your vessel."

"Request permission? Somehow, I don't think this is something I can say no to," Nereyda called over the water.

"You're correct. I am merely being polite. If you refuse, there will be consequences."

"I'd hate to break the rules and have to suffer any of those consequences. Come on aboard. Elvar," she waved him over, "help secure their boat to ours and throw a ladder down so they can climb up."

"Aye, Captain," said Elvar.

Once the ships had been secured together, Nereyda waited at the ladder for the lieutenant and his men.

"I must say, I don't think I've ever seen a woman captain a fishing boat before," he said as he climbed onto the deck and straightened his uniform.

"It runs in my family. My father taught me everything he knew, and I took over once he died. Allow me to show you around." She kept her stride a humble saunter rather than her usual swagger as the officer followed her.

Metine's eyes scanned the deck and he gave an impressed nod. "Well, you seem to be doing well for yourself. Are these other boats with you, as well?"

"Yes, I own the fleet." She gave a casual wave toward the other boats. "It's not much, but we do well enough. Will you need to inspect the other vessels, too?"

"I will, but it won't take long if you're cooperative. What brings you to Antalia?" He kicked a pile of rope aside, looking underneath it.

"We had a good haul not far up the coast and wanted to bring it to market as soon as we could. It'd be a shame if it spoiled in our holds."

"Ah, yes. I've heard they've been biting lately. I hope you find a buyer."

"Thank you. Can I ask why you need to inspect us, though? I haven't been to other cities that do this."

"You don't know?" The officer arched an incredulous eyebrow at her.

"Should I?" She feigned simple ignorance. "I'm just a fisherman's daughter and am too busy to pay attention to much else."

"I thought everyone knew. Antalia is under martial law. It was a hive of criminals and other undesirable elements. We've since cleared all of them out, and we aim to keep it that way."

"Oh, I had no idea." Nereyda held her hand up to her mouth. "I'm very glad that you have helped calm things down here, then. And these inspections are to prevent those sorts of people from coming back?"

"Yes, that's exactly right."

"Very commendable, sir. It would be a shame if someone came in to stir up any trouble."

"You speak very well for a fisherman's daughter," Metine remarked.

"My father insisted that I be able to read, so he'd buy me books at every port we visited. Anyway, I think I've taken enough of your time with chatter. Please follow me to the hold. Then, we can all be on our way. I'm sure you have more important things to do." Nereyda led the way to the short staircase down to the hold.

"More important than protecting the city, you mean?"

"Oh, certainly not, sir." Nereyda acted embarrassed. "I didn't mean that."

"Don't worry, I'm kidding. You've been friendlier and more cooperative than most of the people I deal with."

"Oh good. Just step down here, and you'll see all the fish we've hauled in."

Nereyda led him into the small hold and forced herself to ignore the smell of fish that permeated the air. She stopped at the bottom of the stairs. "Feel free to open any crates that you want." She gestured at the stacks of crates that filled the tight space.

"Definitely smells like a fishing boat." Metine wrinkled his nose and pulled the top off of one of the crates, revealing the fish underneath. He pushed a few around, which only showed more fish underneath. After replacing the top of the crate, he moved to the next one and rummaged through it.

Nerves prevented Nereyda from waiting quietly. "Has anyone actually tried smuggling anything into the city?" she asked.

He glanced over his shoulder. "It would surprise you what people think they can bring in. Mostly it's unlicensed alcohol or goods, just so they can avoid paying the taxes on them. What they get is much more expensive, though."

"Nothing more dangerous than that, though?"

"Like what? Weapons?" He shook his head, moving to the next crate of fish. "Nobody would be that stupid. Unlicensed alcohol just costs you a fine, a few days of working on the docks, and the loss of the vessel. Steep, but you get to live. If someone is caught with weapons, it's straight to the gallows. Too much risk and not enough profit to make it worthwhile for anybody."

Nereyda's pulse quickened at the reminder of the punishment that waited one wrong move away. "Sounds like you've figured out how to prevent trouble from even getting close."

"That's the idea." He closed up the crate he was inspecting. "I think we're good here. I just see fish, and you don't seem like the dangerous sort. I'll just take a quick glance at your other boats, but that won't take long."

"Good." Nereyda led him back up to the deck and watched him step back onto his rowboat with his men. "Thank you for your service!"

"You're welcome. Enjoy your stay in Antalia." He bowed his head quickly, then ordered his men to row to the next boat.

As they rowed away, Nereyda let out a deep breath.

"That wasn't so bad," said Elvar next to her.

"Could have been worse. Still, I'm not really one for the obedient citizen act."

"You pulled it off well, I thought. He didn't know you well enough to realize you were mocking him." He chuckled.

"They never do."

For the next while, Nereyda stood at the helm and gripped the wheel tight as she watched the rowboat go from one fishing boat to the next. The first two went quickly. On the third, they spent longer below deck than the others. Several minutes longer. Just as Nereyda was working through a backup plan, the officer emerged, and he moved on to the next boat. Soon, they finished the final inspection and rowed back near Nereyda's boat.

"You're all clear to dock," called the lieutenant.

Nereyda waved in response, color returning to the fingers that had clenched the wheel. Her boat led the others past the line of frigates and into the harbor. She found five open docks near each other and had her small fleet pull into them.

"Elvar, can you see about getting all of the fish loaded up onto carts? I'm going to go find Fariha and see if she'll help us out. Once the boats are unloaded, have the crew and our cargo come to the Bawdy Bard."

"Are you sure she'll let us stay there? Antalia has been through a lot, and she might not want to take the risk."

"Then we'll have to figure something out. But judging from the last time I talked to her, I think she'll be itching to take in some troublemakers like us."

Nereyda patted Elvar on the shoulder as she sauntered past him and up from the docks into the city, which sloped up and away from the harbor. The people that Nereyda passed all made their way through town with their shoulders hunched and voices low. Patrols of Imperial soldiers eyed anybody wandering the streets. Nereyda didn't know how people could stand living in a place like Antalia, where the air felt heavy with oppression.

She picked up her pace. A few blocks from the harbor, she found the faded sign for the Bawdy Bard.

Nereyda pushed into the tavern and let her eyes adjust. The warm lantern light welcomed her, but the silence echoed and the empty tables were too clean. After a second, she heard the sound of water splashing from the kitchen in the back. At the bar, she called, "Hey Fariha, is that you back there?"

The sound of water stopped, and a young woman appeared in the doorway to the kitchen, then smiled as she saw the captain. Her braided copper hair lay draped over one shoulder. Fariha's green eyes carried the hint of a sparkle that seemed to defy the oppressive atmosphere that weighed on Antalia. "Reyda. You're back. I thought I'd seen the last of you."

"Same here, but I'm back." Nereyda tossed Fariha a smile and a shrug. "I see business hasn't really changed."

"No, it never changes. How'd things go with Brynja? Did you get your crew out?"

Nereyda rubbed the back of her neck. "We got them out, but it wasn't easy. Brynja . . . she's not with me right now, but a lot of the crew is."

"What brings you to Antalia again?"

Nereyda leaned forward against the bar. "I think that conversation is going to need a drink."

Fariha smirked. "What kind of trouble did you bring into my tavern this time? What do you want?"

"You pick. You might need one more than I do."

"Take a seat, and I'll get us a couple of mugs of ale."

Nereyda perched herself on a stool at the bar.

Fariha came back with a pint in each hand and eased around the bar to sit next to Nereyda. "Okay, so what is it that I need a drink to hear?"

Nereyda sipped her ale and took her time setting it back down. She wished she had planned this conversation better. "Last time I was here, you told me about what happened to this city. How they rounded up all of the pirates, smugglers, and other criminals that they could get their hands on."

"That's right. They strung them all up in the square. It was a forest of gallows . . ." Her voice trailed off, a distant look in her eyes.

"Some of those people had to have escaped that fate though, right?"

"Some of the clever ones are still alive, yes. But most didn't make it. Where's this going, Reyda?"

"Just bear with me for now. The ones who were killed—they must still have friends and family around here."

"They do . . ."

"Do you have a way of getting them all to meet here?"

"Maybe. But you need to tell me why."

Nereyda took a deep breath, then held her friend's eyes with a steady gaze. "We're going to take the city back."

Fariha's eyes widened. "You're even crazier than I thought. You want to take Antalia back? How? This place is full of soldiers. We don't even have weapons."

"That's where you're wrong. We have weapons. Several boats full."

"This is nuts, Reyda. Do you have a plan for all of this?"

"I have part of a plan. Enough of a plan."

Fariha rolled her eyes. "That's reassuring."

"Listen, do you want to keep living like this? Running an empty tavern in a city full of people who walk around like dogs with their tails between their legs?"

"It's not the life I would choose, but I also want to keep living."

"Is this living, though? Or are you just surviving?"

"Maybe you're right."

"Get as many people in this bar as you can. Say whatever you have to in order to get them here. Once they're here, then I'll worry about what we'll do next."

"Fine. I'll get them here and hear you out with the rest of them."

"Great, thank you. We'll also need rooms if you can spare them and some space in your cellar for some crates."

"Do those crates contain what I think they do?"

"That depends on what you think is in them."

"I'm probably going to regret this, but sure, if I'm going to hang for helping organize a rebellion, I might as well add weapons smuggling to the list of charges. They can't kill me twice."

"They'll probably try, though."

"That's true enough."

"How soon can you get your people here?"

"Nobody in this town has anything to do, so I'll get them here tonight."

"Couldn't we end up with some random people who might rat us out?"

"I know whom I can trust to spread the word to the right people. And if a stranger wanders in, I'll just tell them we're full already."

"Sounds great. Set it up." Nereyda heard a creak from outside. "Sounds like our cargo just rolled up. Which way to the cellar?"

"In the back." Fariha pointed through the door to the kitchen.

Nereyda took a big gulp to swallow the rest of her ale, then stood up and strode across the room. Outside, six carts full of crates sat at the side of the road. Elvar leaned against one of the wheels of the front cart.

"Have any trouble?" Nereyda asked him.

He shook his head. "Went as smooth as possible."

"Nobody thought it was strange that six carts rode through town together?"

"If they did, I think the smell of fish convinced them otherwise."

"Good. Let's get everything moved into the tavern. Fariha's got a crowd coming tonight."

"What are you going to say?"

"No idea. I'll make it up as I go."

"Didn't you tell Devrim that you had a plan?"

"I had a plan to get in. Now we work with what we find. Let's get to work."

Nereyda and her crew spent most of the afternoon and early evening hauling the crates into the basement, then removing the fish from the crates to let the weapons air out. Nereyda dug out her own cutlass, dagger, and pistol. She had felt naked without them, and their weight on her hips restored her sense of security and balance.

After they had stored all of the weapons, the crew relaxed around the tavern, and Fariha kept them supplied with drinks and food cooked from the fish they had hauled into port. As she brought orders out, she'd stop and chat with old friends from the original crew. A couple of hours after sunset, other people trickled into the Bawdy Bard. A few minutes later and the trickle became a stream. Nereyda scanned the faces to see if she recognized anybody, but didn't see any of her old friends. A couple of times she thought she saw someone familiar, then realized it was just family resemblance. A room full of strangers surrounded her. Before long, the whole tavern was packed with people whom Fariha had invited.

The crowd gave her the same warm, giddy feeling as when she recruited people for her crew, but her excitement was weighed down with the fear that she was sending them all to their deaths.

A hand landed on her shoulder. "Looks like it's time, Captain," said Elvar.

Nereyda nodded at him, then stepped up onto the nearest table so that she could see over the crowd.

"Hey, everyone!" The chatter in the crowd died down to a murmur. "Quiet! That means all of you!"

"Who the hell are you?" called a voice.

"I'm Captain Nereyda, and I'm the evening's entertainment," she said with a smile to the watching faces. Once everyone had focused their attention on her, she turned serious. "I'm here to help you win back what you've lost."

"What do you know of what we've lost? You're not from here."

"You're right," said Nereyda. "I'm not from here. But I used to call Antalia a second home. And I do know what you've lost. I know that I'm a stranger to you, as you are strangers to me. And that saddens me. It saddens me because it means that the many friends I once had who lived in this city are gone." Emotion cracked into her voice and Nereyda let it hang in the air. She paced along the length of the table, scanning the crowd.

"Even though I don't recognize your faces, I still recognize what your faces tell me. I see people who have lost friends and family members. I see people who have had their ways of life torn from them. I see people who have been stuck living in the cage that this city has become. I see all of these things because I have been exactly where you are. Maybe not in this city. Maybe not in the exact same way. But I've been where you are in spirit."

She raised her voice, recalling the moments when she rallied her crew. "I've spent my life on the sea, as has my crew. That all ended when we were captured by the Empire. My crew was tossed into the mines to work themselves to death, while I at least had the freedom of being pressed into service on an Imperial ship. Eventually, I thought I could free my crew, but my first mate betrayed me in the hopes of getting our crew out herself. The Empire that captured us and made us slaves made my own sister betray me because it was the only way she saw to help our people. We just managed to escape during the attack on the mines, but not everyone in my crew made it. I've lost people whom I consider to be my family.

"I'm here to help you take your life back. We're going to hit these Imperial bastards where they never saw it coming, right in the middle of the most heavily guarded city in the Empire. They don't think little people like you and me can stand up to them. We're going to prove them wrong. Together, we're going to take back Antalia."

A cheer erupted from the crowd as it whooped and clapped its approval.

"Wait, wait," called the same doubtful voice from earlier. A man with a stubbly face stumbled to the front of the crowd. "That's all great, but if we're going to fight, what are we supposed to fight with? Just beat Imperials to death with our hands and beer mugs?"

"You'll be using these. Crew, bring out our gifts."

Some crew members hauled out some of the crates and dumped them onto the other tables. Swords, daggers, and pistols poured out, overflowing the surfaces of the tables.

"We have many more where those came from. Now, who among you has fought before?"

Some hands started to rise, but the same man interrupted again with a scoff. "Is that all we have? Just us against the whole garrison?"

"We're not going to fight them all at once. We're going to be smart about it," said Nereyda. "Plus, I have yet another surprise." She reached up toward the ceiling while summoning the power inside her. Sparks of lightning shot upward from her hand, crackling in the air. "How many Imperials do you know who can do that?"

As she lowered her arm and shook out the tingling sensation, she fixed her eyes on the man who had questioned her. "Is that enough of a demonstration?"

The man had no response aside from an impressed nod.

"As I was saying, does anyone here have experience fighting?"

A handful of people around the tavern raised their hands, including a pair of burly twins, a tall man with a graying beard, and a woman with straw-blonde hair around her shoulders.

"Good. Meet me here tomorrow morning so we can start planning. The rest of you, come back tomorrow night and we'll have our plan ready for you. Aside from that, don't change your schedule tomorrow. We don't want to tip off the Imperials that anything is about to happen. Also, if anybody decides to tell the Imperials about what we're doing and I find out about it, you'll learn what it feels like to be struck by lightning."

Some nervous laughs sounded through the crowd.

"I'm serious. Now, enjoy yourselves and get some rest tonight. You'll need it very soon."

Nereyda hopped off the table and found Elvar waiting with a drink in hand for her.

"That was a good speech," he said.

"Thanks. Now we have to make it count for something," she responded as she slumped down on a bench.

"We will," said Elvar. "You remind me of Captain Nogre. You definitely picked up his knack for getting people ready for a fight."

"And you helped teach me how to win those fights."

"I don't know about that. You've always been a natural fighter. But Nogre would be proud of you, and so am I."

"Proud of the captain without a ship?"

"A ship is just a piece of wood. The Storm Raven is here, with the crew."

"Half of the crew, at least."

"We'll find the others. I have faith in us." The wrinkles on his face creased into a smile. "In you. We'll do it together."

"I hope so. Let's just make all of this worth it."

CHAPTER ELEVEN

Towering peaks loomed on Erhan's left and right as his horse trotted toward Goremia. The city occupied the Turhan Pass, the only large gap in the mountains that separated the western portion of the Empire from the rest of the continent. Placed in such a key location, Goremia had become a hub for commerce, full of shops and inns looking to capitalize on the travelers and merchants making their way across the continent. The city took up most of the valley, with a wall stretching from slope to slope. Up the slope to the south of the main part of Goremia, the gold and ivory domes and spires of the Temple of Ameretat overlooked the city. As the seat of the church, it was the largest temple in the Empire, even surpassing the one in Manisa, the capital city. The large religious presence had driven brothels and other unsavory businesses further into the shadows than they normally were, especially when compared to the more liberal western cities such as Trabizan where prostitution was practiced openly.

Erhan rode his horse into the town and through the winding streets to the bottom of the slope that led up to the temple. A short wall separated the temple grounds from the rest of the city, and no horses were permitted beyond it. He stopped at a stable just outside the gate and left his horse with the stablehand, along with enough coin to cover a day of boarding. He left his belongings in the saddlebags to retrieve after visiting the priests.

He passed through the gates to the temple grounds and started up the stairs to the temple proper. Blossoming flowers lined the path, almost glowing with blue, pink, and yellow in the late-morning sunlight. As he hiked away from the city up the winding stairway, the noise of the town quieted, and a gentle peace hung in the air of the gardens. Erhan had never been to the Temple of Ameretat, but he now understood why the church had resisted any push to move to the capital. It would be very difficult to achieve the same sort of serenity that they found in the mountains.

The hike up the stairs tired his legs, but at least he wasn't straddling a horse anymore. As he reached the top of the stairs, he stopped to catch his breath. The golden doors of the main temple building rose in front of him. Smaller buildings surrounded it and several paths led through the grounds and farther up the mountain. So far, Erhan had not seen any priests wandering about the grounds.

His muscles ached as he lumbered up to the large temple doors and pulled the right side open. Inside, he saw the familiar configuration of any temple: benches surrounding a central platform. The dome above featured a glass center, allowing light to shine down into the cavernous sanctuary. It differed from other temples in size and opulence. The room was bigger than the deck of any ship Erhan had ever served on. Vast murals covered the walls, each depicting a different scene from the church's history. On the left, they started with a scene of the gods handing humanity a gift of tremendous power. Turning to the right, he saw the next scene, which showed people glowing and performing miracles, including healing the injured, summoning rain, and raising colossal buildings. In the next panel, a woman portrayed as a demon with dark hair and hands glowing with fire, known as Corinna, tempted people to her side. The fourth scene depicted a terrible battle between Corinna's army and the rest of the world, with both sides using their powers to kill and destroy. Following the battle, the gods smashed the world, creating the Shattered Sea, and took back the powers that they had gifted to humanity. The final scene showed people kneeling before the gods, pleading for their forgiveness, but the gods had turned their backs on humanity. For hundreds of years since then, the church had been seeking that forgiveness, but so far, it seemed as if the gods had ignored all pleas for help. Erhan thought it was fitting that the depiction of the demon woman resembled Nereyda, with dark hair and purple eyes.

An old priest in blue robes emerged from a door on the other side of the sanctuary. "Hello, there," he called. "I thought I heard the door open. I am Sabah. Please, make yourself at home. All are welcome here." He strode across the room with a younger man's energy and appraised Erhan with icy blue eyes. "What is your name? What brings you to the temple today? You're rather early for our noon service."

"My name does not matter. However, I've made a long journey to come here for answers. I hope you'll be able to help me."

Sabah held his hands open and bowed his head. "Of course, I'll provide whatever guidance I can." While he spoke in a kind tone, his face remained stern.

Erhan furrowed his brow. "May we sit down?"

"Of course." The man let Erhan sit down on the nearest bench, then joined him. "I can tell that something is bothering you. What is it?"

"I've heard some troubling rumors after what happened at the mines. Something about unnatural forces attacking." Erhan didn't want to admit that he had been at the battle and risk being labeled a deserter.

Sabah nodded. "Ah, yes, I've heard those same reports. Stories of fire demons from Stalsta. So far, all of these tales are just rumors. I have yet to see any convincing evidence that these are anything more than exaggerated war stories. I don't blame people for being scared, though. Battle is terrifying, and that fear can cloud how we see the world."

"Have you heard any other stories? Anything about a woman, a pirate actually, who shoots lightning or throws water?"

The priest shook his head. "No, I haven't heard anything about that."

"What would be the church's stance if such a person existed?"

Sabah narrowed his eyes. "What do you know? Who are you?"

"I'm just a concerned citizen, and I only know what I've heard."

"Well, as a single priest, I don't think I can speak for the whole church on such a serious matter. But if there was such a person free in the Empire, the church would take that very seriously. I could only imagine that this woman has stolen power from the gods. If this woman is a pirate, as you say, then I doubt they would gift their powers to such a person."

"Would it be enough to start an Inquisition?"

The priest drew himself up. "That is a strange thing for you to know about. I would need to review the texts about how an Inquisition works, but I am quite sure that it takes more than rumors from a concerned citizen. It would require witnesses to come before the church and tell us what they saw. If you meet any such people, tell them to come here, and we will listen to their testimony and decide how to proceed. While you're searching, I will review what the texts say about . . . extracting information from the sort of person you describe." The eagerness in his voice unsettled Erhan. "Until then, there isn't much more I can tell you. Now, if there isn't anything else, I need to get ready for the noon service."

Erhan shook his head. "No, I'll leave you to prepare." He rose from the bench, his legs stiff as he staggered out of the temple. He had spent days on the road, yet his journey had produced few answers and more to do. Now he needed witnesses, but the battle at the mines hadn't left many that he knew of. He needed to find a place to gather more rumors from the western part of the Empire. A large city at a crossroads would do. That meant Trabizan.

CHAPTER TWELVE

Nereyda quickly regretted picking random people to help strategize. Despite having combat experience, the handful of people that had come to the tavern in the morning could not agree on a plan.

"We should ambush their patrols in the streets," said one of the stout twins. He fidgeted with his moustache. "Make them fear to even walk through our neighborhoods."

"That won't work. They'll just do another sweep and purge of the city," said the older man. "All that will do is get us and other people in the city killed. We need to take the walls. Then we control the way in and out."

"Except for the sea," said the woman with straw-colored hair. "They'll still have their ships out in the harbor, and all of their soldiers will be inside the city. Who cares if we have the wall if they control the city and can easily reinforce it from the sea? We need to take out their ships first."

"How?" asked the second twin. This one had a shaved face. "They have ten frigates, and five of them are always out on patrol. Even if we could hit all of the docked ships at the same time, there would be five of them left, and they'd expect trouble."

A pain grew in Nereyda's temples, fed by the constant bickering as her makeshift war council made the same arguments for what felt like the eighty-fourth time. She slammed her mug down on the table. "Enough. This conversation is going in circles."

"What do you suggest, Captain?" asked the woman. "Are you going to say you have a better idea to take back our city than we do, even after living here for years?"

"Even though none of you agree about what to do, what you've said has helped me understand what we face in trying to take Antalia. Between the garrison, the walls, and the fleet, it's clear that we don't have the numbers to deal with all of this at once. But as I told you before you started arguing, we will have allies coming to help. Tell me, if it looked like we had a real chance of winning, do you think more people in the city would rally to us?"

The group glanced around at each other for a moment, then back to her. The older man spoke, stroking a beard that was more gray than black, "It's possible. It's hard to know exactly what their fighting spirit is like because nobody talks openly about this kind of thing, but many resent the Empire's strong hand in Antalia. If we somehow demonstrated that we were serious about pushing them out of the city, I think we could gain some more people to our cause."

"Good. And if we did, we'd need more weapons. Tell me, where does the Empire keep its stock of weapons? Is there an armory of some kind?"

The older man furrowed his brow and rubbed his throat before answering. "They do have a central armory. It's attached to the main barracks, a couple of blocks from the main city gate."

Nereyda nodded. "Perfect. Sounds like that needs to be our target."

"Are you crazy? That place is heavily guarded. It's also the headquarters for the entire city garrison."

"An even better reason to hit it, then. If it's the headquarters, that's where they would normally coordinate their defenses against us. If we cut them off from the rest of the city, they'll be confused. And we'll be close enough to the gate to let in our allies outside the walls."

"How do we attack it, though? It has its own wall. We don't have enough people to assault it, and I doubt the rest of the soldiers in the city would just let us lay siege to it."

"Then we just need to get inside those walls before they attack."

"And just how do you propose we do that?"

"How many of the people from the crowd last night can sing, dance, or play an instrument?"

They exchanged perplexed expressions. "How should we know? Why does that matter?"

"Just find out. I have an idea," she said with a wink. "Also, you'll need to talk to any tailors you know. We're going to need some costumes."

Nereyda felt ridiculous in the sleek purple dress that she had found. She hated wearing the dress. It wasn't the revealing neckline or the hip-hugging cut of the dress—she wasn't modest or shy. She hated how it confined her and made her feel trapped by her own clothing. The corset cinched around her torso only made it worse. At least she wouldn't have to wear it very long. It only needed to stay on long enough to get them into the Imperial garrison that sat just up the hill.

They had arranged as many instruments and costumes as they could for their makeshift entertainment troupe. Anyone who had a costume marched next to the carts that carried their props and instruments, which concealed their weapons as well as another surprise that Nereyda had arranged. There had been more volunteers to fight than there were costumes, so the spares lurked in the alleys near the Imperial fortification. Nereyda hoped that they could stay hidden from any patrols, but she pushed that worry out of her mind. She couldn't do anything about it at the moment.

Their caravan rumbled up to the gate into the barracks compound, where two guards kept watch.

Nereyda waved to the cart drivers to stop, then sauntered up to the guards. "Hello! We're the Marvelous Ravens, and we're here to brighten your camp."

One of the guards arched an eyebrow at her. "I don't remember seeing anything on the schedule about this. And we've never had something like this happen before."

She beamed at him. "Exactly. You haven't received the warmest welcome from the people of Antalia, but we're here to change all of that. All of us in this troupe appreciate the protection of the Empire and what you've done to make this city safe. We would love the opportunity to come in and show you just how much we appreciate it."

"This is not the normal procedure for these things. You can't just show up and expect us to let a strange group of musicians into our fort."

"Strange? What do you mean strange? We're renowned in the west. Surely you've heard of the Marvelous Ravens!"

"I can't say that I have. But, if you want, I can go see if our commander will make an exception for you. If he's in a good mood, maybe he'll let us enjoy some music."

"Perfect! Want me to come talk to your commander with you? Perhaps I can convince him of how entertaining we can be?"

"I'm sure you are all very entertaining, ma'am, but I don't think he would approve of me letting some random lady into our base."

"Very well. I'll wait here, then. I hope you return soon and with good news. You and your friends always look so glum, and I think some of our music might be the perfect cure."

The guard didn't give her another response before he turned away and knocked on a small door in the gate. She heard something moving behind the door, then it opened, and the guard disappeared into the fort.

She spent the next few minutes pacing next to the front cart. Her corset squeezed her ribs, forcing her to take shallow breaths. Nereyda acted like she was dancing as she practiced a couple of sword moves and winced as the rigid garment confined her movement. She fidgeted with it to loosen it as much as she could without ruining her disguise.

Soon, the guard emerged from the door. "I'm sorry, miss, but the commander will not permit you to enter the fort. However, if you wish, he has granted leave to perform outside the walls so that the soldiers inside might hear you."

Nereyda forced a smile despite her frustration. "If that's the commander's wish, we will set up out here. Where would you like us? Here on the road?"

The guard shook his head. "You'd better pull off the road, in case anybody needs to get in or out of the walls. We have space near the walls on either side of the road. Move your carts there, and you can give your performance. If it's good enough, maybe the commander will change his mind and invite you inside."

"I don't think he'll be able to keep us out after what we perform for you today."

"I hope your music matches your confidence."

"You won't be disappointed."

Nereyda turned to the drivers of the six carts and directed them where to go. She didn't much care where the first five went, but she made sure that the sixth was parked as close to the gate as possible without being on the road. She kept it a bit farther from the rest of the other carts.

As the other members of the fake troupe got their carts and

instruments ready, Nereyda lit a fuse in the back of the sixth cart. The long fuse led to a pile of barrels of explosives. They were actually fireworks, since that was the closest thing to gunpowder that they could get on short notice in the city.

Nereyda introduced the musicians and dancers to the soldiers who watched over the wall, then the entertainment started. She kept a countdown in her head based on the length of the fuse. As it drew closer to detonating, she positioned herself near the cart where her own weapons were held.

With a loud boom, a blast of color erupted from the cart of fireworks.

At the explosion, all of the rebels with Nereyda grabbed their weapons from their carts. Those who had guns opened fire on the soldiers along the top of the wall, sending several of them falling off the other side.

Nereyda hurried to strap her weapons to herself. Through the fire and smoke, she saw that the explosion had opened a small hole in the wooden wall. She dashed toward it but fell down as her dress caught midstride. She rolled as she tumbled on the ground, then tore the front of the skirt from ankles to thighs, leaving her long legs free to move. She had never tried to fight in a dress and, based on her experience so far, never wanted to do so again.

She shoved herself back to her feet and sprinted toward the opening in the wall. The guards who had stood outside the gate and near the cart lay unmoving on the ground. She drew her sword as she leaped over the pile of debris that remained in the gap.

The garrison was running around, trying to figure out how to respond to the unexpected threat. To her right, two guards stood next to the gate with their weapons at the ready, though their eyes were wide and their hands shook.

"Open the gate!" Nereyda shouted at them.

"What?" said one of the guards in a loud voice. "Drop your weapons!"

"I don't think so. Open the gate!" she repeated in a louder voice, gesturing at the gate with her cutlass.

"Drop your weapons. Stay there," said the other guard. He rubbed his ear with his free hand.

The blast had clearly damaged their hearing, so she dashed toward the gate to open it herself. The closest guard blocked her path with his sword, but with a twirl of her cutlass, she knocked his weapon from his shaking hands, then shoved him to the ground. She glided around him, and the other guard blocked her path.

Nereyda couldn't tell if his eyes held courage, recklessness, or just shock. She easily danced around his attempted sword strikes. When he left an opening, she lunged and struck him in the gut with the pommel of her sword, knocking the wind out of his lungs. With her left hand, she wrenched his sword out of his grasp. She swept his feet from under him and let him fall to the ground. Finally, she got to the door and pulled the lever to unlock it, then turned the wheel to raise the gate.

When it was open, she yelled to her crew and the rebels, "Get in here! The gate's open." They ran from behind the carts to the open gate, and the others who had been waiting in the nearby alleys poured into the streets to attack the fort. Another group should be taking up positions near the other gate on the other side of the compound to prevent anyone from getting out that way, but Nereyda could only hope that they were doing their job.

Imperial soldiers emerged from their barracks. Her army of rebels should be able to handle the soldiers, so she wanted to find the garrison commander and deal with him. If she could take him out, and anyone else on his staff, that would cut off the head of the entire Antalian garrison.

She found the largest building, which sat in the middle of the fort against the tall outer wall of Antalia. Nereyda dashed across the courtyard toward the structure, skirting squads of soldiers. Unnecessary fights would only slow her down.

She reached the main central building. Nereyda ran up the staircase that wrapped around the outside, taking the steps two at a time. Her heart was pounding by the time she burst into the room at the top. A tall man in a general's uniform yelled orders to other officers who rushed around the room. Tables and desks with maps and other papers lined the walls.

He stopped when he saw Nereyda standing in the doorway, then glanced at a man in the back of the room.

"Temel," said the general, "get the word to the other garrisons and the fleet. Use the other roads."

"Yes, sir," responded Temel, before he disappeared through a door in the back wall of the room. The wall that was pressed against the dark, solid walls surrounding Antalia.

"Who are you?" asked the general, as he examined Nereyda. "You're a strange sight. I don't see a lot of people wearing dresses and fighting with swords."

"Get used to it. It's very comfortable, and I'm sure I look great. I expect it'll catch on soon."

"Maybe. But that still doesn't answer my question."

"It doesn't matter who I am," said Nereyda. "We're taking back the city. Surrender your garrison to us, and we'll spare your men."

The man laughed. "You're going to take back the city? You caught us by surprise, yes, but that won't help you with the rest of the city."

"Maybe. We'll see. Draw your sword and face me, or surrender."

The man sighed, then pulled his shield from his broad back and drew a sword from his belt. "Very well." He almost sounded bored.

With her cutlass in her right hand and the guard's sword in her left, she circled the general, watching how he moved and carried himself.

His eyes maintained an intense focus on her. He kept the face of his shield pointed directly at her, in front of his torso, and his sword was ready to engage.

She danced toward him and swung her cutlass toward his exposed left shoulder.

He shifted his shield, and her blade kissed off of the face.

As he moved his shield, she thrust her other sword toward his belly, but he swept it out of the way with his sword.

She took a step back to regroup, but he advanced on her.

Nereyda feinted from her left, but he didn't fall for it.

She tried striking at the same time with both blades, attacking both of his shoulders.

As her blades swung toward him, he shoved his shield directly into her, slamming into her chest.

The staggering blow sent her to her knees, and she dropped the sword in her left hand.

As the general raised his sword above her, she swiped her blade toward his ankles, below his shield. Her sword carved into a gap in his armor and he lost his balance, his sword striking the floor next to her.

The large man fell to his knees as Nereyda sprang back onto her feet. The general tried to stand, but his ankles wouldn't bear the weight.

He tried to bash Nereyda with his shield, but Nereyda dodged out of the way. She circled around him and placed the tip of her blade at the back of his neck.

"Stop fighting. It's not worth your life."

"I swore to defend the Empire. I'll never surrender."

Nereyda kicked him in the back, and he fell forward, his shield falling from his grip as he caught himself. She stood on his back to keep him from rising and used her other foot to kick his weapons away.

"Don't try to run anywhere. I'll be back."

She dashed to the door in the wall and pulled it open. On the other side, she found a stairway carved into solid dark stone, descending to the right. It was a stairway hidden inside the wall of Antalia itself. Torches provided dim light. Iron reinforcements were built into the wall, making the walls of Antalia the strongest in the Empire. Supposedly, they could endure days of barrage from cannons and stay standing. Nobody had yet put the walls to the test.

Nereyda hurried down the steps. They descended considerably lower than the height of the building. When she reached the bottom, a corridor with more torches went to the right, underneath the fort.

She sprinted down the hallway until she reached a four-way intersection. None of the connecting hallways provided any clue about where the officer had gone. Nereyda held her breath and listened for footsteps, but didn't hear any. The only sound came from a rat scurrying down the hallway to her left. Without any clue to where he had gone, it would be pointless to pursue him. Her best bet was to go back and try to get ready for a tougher fight.

She dashed back to the stairs and up to the command center. Inside, the general remained on the floor but had grabbed his sword and shield. He was still making a futile effort to haul himself up, along with pulling himself toward the exit. Nereyda ran up behind him and kicked him down again and wrenched his equipment from his hands. "I told you to stay here. You're just going to make it worse by trying to put weight on it."

As her legs recovered from her run, Nereyda staggered to one of the windows and looked over the compound as she caught her breath. The rebels had almost finished securing it while she had been inside. The bodies of Imperial soldiers were strewn around the compound, and survivors were sitting on the ground in the corner of the fort, guarded by a woman in a purple leotard and a man in a billowing orange shirt. She caught Jax's eye and waved at him. He nodded back, then he ran out of the walls with a group of rebels.

Turning back to the general, Nereyda grabbed him under the

shoulders and helped him into a chair at a table on the side of the room. She dragged another chair over and faced him as she sat backward on her chair.

"I have some questions. Then I'll decide whether or not to put you out of your misery."

CHAPTER THIRTEEN

Gunfire erupted from within the city walls, and Limbani could do nothing about it. From her position standing on a hill outside the high black walls of Antalia, she could only listen to the sounds of violence and watch as wisps of smoke rose from the site of the battle that had started. She hoped that the pirate captain knew what she was doing and could get the city gates open to let Devrim's forces in to join the fight.

She looked back over her shoulder to scan the small army that they had assembled. It numbered perhaps five hundred soldiers gathered from the household guards of nobles friendly to Devrim's cause, along with a detachment of army reserves under a captain who had decided to join their side. While a good start, it was not nearly enough to take Antalia, at least not from the outside. Trying to do so would be suicide. She hoped Devrim had judged well in placing his trust in Nereyda. From Limbani's interactions with the pirate captain, she seemed to mean well and certainly appeared to be capable, but it was a big gamble to take on such an ambitious target as their first choice. If it didn't go right, their rebellion would die against the black walls ahead of them and be swiftly forgotten.

A rattle of chains and a groan sounded from the direction of the wall. Limbani turned her focus forward as the giant main gate of Antalia rumbled open. Nereyda had done it. Now they had to do their part before the pirates inside were crushed.

"After me!" she cried as she charged down the hill.

The rest of the soldiers followed after her, pouring around and over the hill, then down toward the gate. As they dashed over the open field to the opening, very little fire came toward them from the walls. The battle within had drawn the attention of the guards on the wall, distracting them from the additional threat outside.

When she reached the gate, she spotted a group of Islanders, including Jax, fending off some Imperial soldiers attempting to retake the mechanism that opened and closed the city gates. Jax growled as he whirled his battle-ax over his head, blood dripping from the blade. A soldier blocked it with his shield but was staggered from the blow. Without slowing down, Limbani drew her saber and stabbed it into the side of the soldier fighting Jax. The rebel troops behind her engaged the other Imperials, driving them away from the Islanders and securing the gate for the time being.

Limbani paused to catch her breath next to Jax. "Good work with the gate," she said between breaths. "How are things going everywhere else?"

Jax shrugged. "Fine, as far as I know. We took the main Imperial fort. Nereyda and the others are there finishing securing it now."

"Others? Is it more than just the pirates?"

"Way more than just us. Plenty of folks in the city seem to want to fight. Nereyda managed to raise quite the uprising."

"Sounds like it. If you took the main fort already, what's a good target for us?" she asked in a clipped tone.

"The other two gates have fortifications too, but not as well defended as this one," he said quickly. "If we want to finish taking out the city garrison, we need to take those bases."

"Okay, we'll start working on that. Are you going to join us?"

Jax shook his head. "We need to get back to the fort. I told Nereyda we'd return once we opened the gate."

"All right. We've both got work to do."

"We do, but I think we're almost there. The Imperials didn't plan on the city rising up beneath them. See you when we're done."

Limbani watched as Jax ran off, leading the Islanders back to the main fortification, then called her company leaders over. "We need to secure the other two enemy forts and the walls. Lieutenant Adnan, you and I will take First Company toward the southern fort and take that. Captain Kadri, you will take Second Company to the northern fort. And Captain Erol, Third Company will climb the wall and clear any enemies up there. Any questions?"

Nobody said anything.

"Good. Let's move out."

Limbani led her company as they double-timed their way south through the city. She ordered each platoon to scatter to different alleys and side streets so they couldn't all be ambushed at once.

The disorganized Imperial soldiers that they encountered panicked as they saw enemies inside the city walls. They waited for orders that weren't coming and scurried about in attempts to take cover. Limbani's company easily cut through any resistance they encountered.

As they twisted around a bend in a side street, Limbani's platoon faced an overturned cart.

"You," Limbani said as she gestured to half of the troops in the platoon around her, "take cover. The rest of you, approach that cart with caution." The rebels slowed their approach to navigate their way around it. When they had almost reached it, Imperial troops popped up from behind it.

Limbani's men dove behind cover and opened fire on the enemy position. Each side held the other pinned down. All of her troops had found good cover in doorways and alleys, so they weren't taking hits, but neither was the enemy.

Yells sounded from an alley that connected to the street behind the cart. A horde of civilians with axes, hammers, and other improvised weapons dashed out. The confused Imperials turned toward the new threat, but not in time before the mad rush of people reached them.

When the last of the Imperials fell, Limbani emerged from cover. "Who are you?" she asked.

"We're the people of Antalia. We're taking back our city. And who are you?"

"We're rebels like you and we're here to help. I'm General Limbani. We're going to take the south camp."

"We'll come with you. It's time to kick these bastards out of our city."

Limbani pursed her lips as she looked over the group of Antalians. The lack of discipline in their attack worried her. Would they listen and follow orders? However, several of them had cuts and scrapes that they ignored or even laughed at. The fire in their eyes and their disregard for danger would be valuable.

"Excellent," she said. "Stick with us, though. We'll have better luck if we work together as a group."

"Hope you soldiers can keep up, then." Their leader turned and dashed up the street toward the fort. Limbani sighed and signaled to her troops to follow the civilian rebels.

A few blocks later, they reached an intersection and took heavy fire, with bullets chipping the buildings and street around them. Limbani kicked open a door and ordered her men and the civilians into the building to take cover. Once everyone was safe inside, she crouched near a window next to Adnan. "Have the men send some covering fire across the street while I take a look at what we're facing."

"Yes, ma'am."

After a moment, their platoon began their barrage, taking turns firing and reloading. Limbani peeked up over the windowsill. Some Imperial soldiers had set up a firing position to ambush rebels at the intersection. They had set up cover on the ground using barrels, crates, and wagons. Some others had taken position at windows and balconies and watched for anyone who stepped into their view. Limbani started forming a plan.

She slid along the wall toward the person who had led the charge of the Antalian rebels. "If we can cover you, how do you feel about charging the Imperials?"

"As long as you take the pressure off, we can do that. We're eager to fight, but we don't want to run into a hail of bullets."

Limbani nodded. "First Squad," she said in a loud voice, "I want you to head upstairs and take up positions to provide cover. Second Squad, once they're settled up there, follow them up. Third, you do the same when Second is ready. I want everyone with a gun on the second and third floors." She turned back to the rebel leader. "Once they're all in position, they'll give you the cover you need, and you can go."

The three squads in the platoon took turns hurrying upstairs.

"Lieutenant, go upstairs and give the order to begin a cover volley when everyone is ready."

A few moments after Adnan had gone upstairs, a rolling series of shots erupted from above Limbani. "Now's our chance," she said to the rebels. "Follow me."

Limbani dashed out the door and drew her saber as she sprinted across the street. Their Imperial enemies kept their heads down and blind fired at them. Two civilian rebels fell during the charge.

The first to reach the line of cover, Limbani vaulted over a waist-high crate and thrust her sword into the belly of the Imperial using it as cover. Around her, the Antalians savaged the Imperials with their scrounged makeshift weapons.

As they finished clearing the enemies on the ground, they dashed into the buildings to force out the Imperials on the upper floors. Limbani ran toward one of the ground-level doors. When she was halfway across the street, the second story exploded in a shower of wooden splinters. She dove out of the way of the debris as more buildings nearby had holes blown in their walls and roofs. Imperials, Antalians, and rebel soldiers all spilled out on the street in the chaos. A man screamed as a wall collapsed on top of him.

She returned her focus to the current battle with the Imperials. She caught two fleeing soldiers and dispatched them with slices of her saber.

When the last of the Imperials had fallen, Limbani paused to watch where the artillery fire was coming from. The sounds came from the harbor. Were the Imperials bombarding their own town? What were they trying to accomplish? Limbani and her group couldn't stop it at the moment. Their only option was to continue on to the enemy fort and take it. They would deal with the Imperial Navy later.

As they ran through the streets, they encountered a few more groups of Imperials, but defeated them quickly. The Antalians would rush the soldiers while Limbani's men provided covering fire. The Empire's forces froze as they stared at the Antalian charge in disbelief. A couple of times Limbani and her lieutenant had to pull civilians away as they continued to strike an enemy who had already fallen and died. Meanwhile, cannonballs from the frigates continued to rain debris and death.

CHAPTER FOURTEEN

Nereyda stared at the general across the table from her, his face contorted with pain and defiance.

"What can you tell me about the rest of the garrison? What are they going to do now that we've taken your main camp?"

The general laughed at her.

"What's funny?"

"You're never going to take Antalia."

"Why not? We already defeated you here, and more of the city is going to join us."

"It doesn't matter, because there won't be a city to take."

"What do you mean?"

"I don't need to tell you anything."

Nereyda rose, marched around the table, and swept the chair from under the general. As he sprawled onto the ground, she pointed her sword at his throat.

He groaned in pain. "Fine, I'll tell you. I'm sure you noticed the fleet in the harbor."

"Of course. What about them?"

"Did you notice the oversized guns?"

"I did. What's special about them?"

"They're shore bombardment guns. Sure, they'll tear through another ship easily enough. But they're made for attacking a city or fixed fortifications. And, as far as I can tell, there is only one city here."

"The Empire is going to attack its own city? Why?"

The general shrugged, with a menacing grin on his face. "One of two things will happen. Either you'll give up, and the barrage will stop. Of course, everyone who has rebelled will be executed. If you don't give up, the city will be destroyed, and no other city will ever think of doing something similar. Even if they want to, they'll remember what happened to Antalia."

The door opened, and Jax burst into the room, his chest rising and falling as he caught his breath, the strand of beads swaying in his hair.

"What is it?" Nereyda asked.

"We did it." His broad smile radiated energy. "The gates are open."

"Good. But we have another problem. Let's go get Elvar."

"What about him?" Jax pointed at the general.

She glanced down and plunged her sword into the general's chest. "Can't afford to leave him alive."

Nereyda and Jax ran down to find Elvar directing people in colorful costumes into a large warehouse full of crates of ammunition, barrels of gunpowder, and racks of rifles, pistols, and swords. In the corner, a man in a red and blue jester's outfit checked the balance of a rapier.

"Elvar," said Nereyda, "we need to do something about the fleet in the harbor. They're going to start bombarding the city."

His eyes widened. "Why would they do that?"

"It doesn't matter why. We just need to stop it. Elvar, help me gather the crew. We're going to go take one of the frigates that are still docked and see what we can do about the ships that are already out. Jax, can you take your people to stop the rest of the frigates from leaving? One versus five is going to be hard enough, and I don't want to worry about the odds getting worse."

Jax nodded, then ran off to organize the other Islanders.

Nereyda and Elvar found the Storm Raven crew members and led them off into the city. Nereyda ran as fast as she could without tumbling down the hill that sloped to the docks. In the gaps between the buildings, she saw the five frigates lining up in the harbor. When they were halfway down the hill, cannon shots sounded. A second later, a cannonball hit a tower to Nereyda's left. She dodged the stone debris that rained down.

Some buildings had gaping holes in their walls. Others teetered on the verge of collapse. Civilians in the streets screamed and ran for whatever cover they could find. When Nereyda arrived at the bottom of the hill, she surveyed the docks. A couple of docks down, one of the frigates sat mostly unmanned, except for a few guards standing on the dock next to it.

Nereyda led the charge toward the guards. When she reached them, she quickly defeated one while her crew members took care of the others.

"Elvar, make sure there is plenty of ammunition and powder. Everyone else, start getting her ready to sail. You don't need to be fancy, just get it done as quickly as you can."

Her crew began preparations for sailing. The frigate was a little larger than the Storm Raven, but it shouldn't be too difficult for them to pilot.

Nereyda stepped up to the helm and untied the line that held the wheel in place. As she finished, Elvar joined her.

"The ammunition stores are about half full. I've got the gunners getting the cannons ready now."

"Half full is fine. We can make that work. And make sure the guns are all manned, even if it means taking people from other parts of the ship. We need every cannon ready."

"Aye." Elvar shouted orders to some of the crew to report to the guns, taking them away from less essential stations.

Within a few minutes, the ship was ready to sail. At least, it was ready enough for what they needed to do.

"Okay, cast off and full sail," Nereyda commanded.

One crew member chopped the line connecting the frigate to the dock, then the sails fell from the yardarms, snapping in the wind. The ship pulled away from the dock and into the harbor. The other frigates in the water seemed to pay them no attention as they kept blasting the city with barrage after barrage of fire.

Nereyda piloted the frigate toward the space between two of the ships. "Prepare to fire!" she called, and the order was relayed to the gun crews below. "Aim at the waterline."

She waited until they were in the middle of the ships and angled the ship to deliver two broadsides at once.

"Fire!" she ordered.

The cannons on each side roared as they blasted the ships nearby. The frigate shuddered from the simultaneous broadsides. Ships weren't normally designed for that kind of stress.

The barrages tore through the aft of one target and the bow of the other. The cannonballs struck just where Nereyda had ordered her crew to aim, creating gaping holes in each hull along the surface of the water. Both frigates angled down into the waves as their holds filled with water. The crews abandoned their bombardment of the city and hurried to deal with their sinking vessels.

That still left three other enemy ships. As their captured frigate pulled out beyond the line of ships, toward the open sea, one of the other ships stopped firing and dropped its sails, then turned out toward Nereyda's frigate.

"Full speed," she ordered. At least she could lead one of them away from the city.

From the harbor, a narrow strait led out to the ocean. Nereyda piloted her frigate toward the gap, as the other ship stayed on their tail.

When they were a short distance from the opening, a chain sprung from under the water, spanning the whole gap.

"Full stop! Hard port!" she ordered.

As the sails were furled, Nereyda spun the wheel hard to the port. The frigate tilted hard to the starboard as it strained against the change in direction. When it stabilized in the water, the Imperial ship was heading straight for them. The ram on the prow of the ship would smash right through the middle of their exposed side.

"Fire!" she ordered.

The guns on the port side blasted a volley at their target. Some struck their mark on the bow of the ship, and it started to tilt forward and slowed down. It didn't slow enough though. Before Nereyda could give the order to bring the vessel back up to speed, the Imperial ship struck them low on the port side. The slow speed minimized the damage, but Nereyda's ship became sluggish as it took on water. They needed to defeat the other ships quickly.

"Drop the sails!" she yelled.

Once again, the sails filled with wind and they started moving. They pulled away from the ship that had rammed them, which continued to take on water. Three ships had been disabled, but the remaining two had turned away from the docks and sailed for them. Nereyda wasn't quite sure where to go in the confined harbor. She felt the frigate begin to lean to port, and it was becoming more difficult to maneuver.

Despite her best efforts, the two ships closed in from behind, one pointing toward their port side and the other heading starboard.

"Prepare to fire," she ordered. Their best shot might be another double-sided broadside.

Before Nereyda's crew was ready, however, the two enemy frigates pulled up alongside the captured frigate, aiming their own broadsides at it.

Nereyda ducked just as a combined volley erupted from the two ships and blasted into the side of her frigate. Crew members screamed as splinters tore into them. The mainmast cracked and collapsed over the side. Their entire ship tipped forward as water poured into the hull.

A cry sounded from her left. When the dust cleared, she saw that Elvar lay on the deck with a spike of wood sticking out of his belly, blood pooling next to him. His face had turned pale.

Nereyda rushed to his side and knelt down, wrapped her arms around him, and rested his head on her lap. "Elvar, hold on. We've almost won, and we'll get you out of this."

He shook his head. "No, I don't think so," he said as he gasped for air, blood trickling from the corners of his mouth. "Don't fuss over me. I've had a good life. And I've had the privilege of watching you become the best captain I've ever known. Now, go finish this and get back to the sea where you belong."

Elvar's eyes glazed over and he went limp in Nereyda's arms.

As the life of her friend and mentor faded, a dam broke inside of Nereyda. The storm inside of her demanded an escape. And she didn't want to contain it.

By this point, the two Imperial ships had pulled past the front of their ship. She had neglected to give the order to fire as she had tended to Elvar.

Nereyda ran the length of the ship and stood at the bow, now just feet from slipping beneath the waves, where she could see both of the remaining enemy frigates. As the storm swelled inside of her, she held out her hands and let everything out.

A torrent of energy surged from within and her nerves sizzled as electricity blasted through her arms. From each hand, a lightning bolt shot through the air with a crack of thunder. The scent of a storm permeated the air as the energy bolted toward the enemy ships.

Lightning struck the frigates. They erupted in plumes of fire and splinters. An odor of charred wood and flesh invaded the harbor. Once the energy inside of her was expended, Nereyda collapsed on the deck and passed out.

CHAPTER FIFTEEN

A bolt of lightning flashed in the corner of Limbani's eye, followed by a huge boom of thunder, which was strange because there were no clouds in the sky at all. She turned toward the harbor and saw two broken and burning frigates, with bits of debris still flying through the air and splashing down in the water. She hadn't been paying attention to the sea battle, but the only ship left floating seemed to be the one that Nereyda and her pirates had commandeered.

The squad of Imperial troops that Limbani and her own soldiers had been facing threw down their weapons, their eyes wide with terror. "We surrender!" said their sergeant as they came forward, their hands raised. "I don't know who you are, but I want no part of fighting you."

Limbani and her troops held their weapons on the Imperials as the sounds of gunfire and violence subsided in the rest of the city.

"Lieutenant, take these prisoners and secure them in one of these houses. Hold them there until I send for you. And you, Private," she addressed another soldier in her platoon. "Leave the city and go find Lord Devrim. Tell him that the city is ours."

"Yes, ma'am," he said before running off toward the gate.

Adnan directed the other soldiers to bring the prisoners into one of the houses.

Limbani kept her pistol drawn as she made her way through the city in the direction of the harbor. As she wound through alleys and side streets, she saw that other groups of rebels had captured Imperial soldiers. She instructed them to take shelter and hold position. No more pockets of resistance remained. It seemed that whatever had destroyed the ships had frightened the Imperials into giving up the fight.

In the harbor, the pirates' frigate limped its way toward the dock. Some of the Islanders milled about near the city administration building. Jax waved at Limbani before approaching.

"Quite a fight," he said. "How did you do?"

"It was dicey when they started bombarding the city, but once they stopped to deal with Nereyda, it went pretty well. They're all surrendering now."

Jax laughed with a booming voice. "I think they got nervous when their ships blew up."

"Get anyone important when you took the headquarters?"

"I don't think so. Mostly just officers and bureaucrats who keep the city running. The admiral who was in charge left with the main fleet and the replacement hasn't arrived yet."

"Lucky for him."

"I suppose so. Looks like our pirate friends finally made it to the dock."

Limbani and Jax hurried toward the heavily damaged frigate as it pulled up next to the dock. As soon as the gangway had been extended from the ship, two of the pirates rushed across carrying a limp body.

Nereyda.

###

A few hours later, Limbani stood at the front of the assembled crowd as Devrim approached the central platform with the three gallows that rose above the square. Next to her stood Jax, who shifted back and forth uneasily.

"Stand still. I'm sure Nereyda will be fine soon." That was a lie, though. Limbani was far from certain of anything.

Jax frowned at her, but settled a bit.

As Devrim neared the short staircase up to the stage, he stopped in front of one of the Islanders. "May I borrow your ax, friend?" he asked with a hand on the man's shoulder.

The Islander nodded and handed over his weapon.

"Thank you," said Devrim as he accepted the ax and ascended the platform. He stepped next to the gallows on the left and hefted the ax behind him and swung it at the wood. The post shook as Devrim's powerful stroke bit into it. Wordlessly, he struck it with swing after swing. His strong arms wielded the ax with practiced precision. Soon, the post fell onto the ground behind the platform. He wiped beads of sweat from his forehead as he paused to catch his breath. He hoisted the ax up to rest on his shoulder and turned to face the crowd of assembled rebel soldiers, pirates, Islanders, and captured Imperials.

"I'll finish chopping down the other two later, but that is exactly what I came here to do. The time of the Empire's reign of terror in Antalia has come to an end."

The crowd erupted in cheers.

He nodded for a moment, then waved to them to quiet down. "Yes, it is a day to celebrate. But I'm not the one who deserves your cheers. I might have helped organize this, but it's the people who actually led the charge, the people who fought, and the people who gave their lives who deserve the most praise. I cheer for all of you standing in this square here today. You all chose to rise up and throw off the heavy boot that the Empire had stomped down on you." He strode the length of the platform, his head held high.

"I especially want to recognize someone who isn't even here right now. You might remember the thunder and lightning in the harbor. That was our own Captain Nereyda, who managed to destroy two frigates with power from her own hands. She also led the triumphant rebels from within the city."

They cheered at the mention of Nereyda, especially the citizens of Antalia.

"Yes, she was heroic. However, her act of courage has left her unconscious." His head drooped.

The crowd fell into silence.

He spoke in a low tone, yet it still carried over the crowd. "The very act that ended this battle took her to the threshold of death itself. I dearly hope that she will recover soon and will be ready to lead us to future victories." His voice rose in a crescendo as he lifted his gaze to the crowd once again. "If we have someone with her abilities on our side, nobody can stand in our way. When the Emperor and his allies hear about Nereyda and about the rest of you and what you're capable of, they will tremble even in their comfortable mansions because they'll know that we can't be stopped."

Cheers roared again.

"Now, I want to talk to our Imperial friends who have surrendered to us."

Boos murmured through the crowd.

Devrim waved for them to settle down. "No, no. Do not boo these people. They are not our enemies anymore. At least not right now. Many have been raised in a darkness that hides the true nature of the Empire. They've been indoctrinated to believe that the Emperor is right in all things. Some of them have been forced into service, or perhaps they found that it was the only job available and they had a family to provide for. No, soldiers may fight for our enemies, but they are not our enemies themselves. Our true enemies cower behind high walls and refuse to put themselves at risk, letting others do so for them as if their lives somehow matter more."

He stared at the portion of the square where the captured Imperials stood. "So, Imperial soldiers who have surrendered to us, I want to give you a choice. If you are tired of following orders from people who don't care about you and only use you to further their own positions without sharing the benefits with you, stay with us. We will find a place for you within our movement, and you can enjoy newfound freedom. And any soldiers who don't join us will be free to go. We will not keep you as prisoners, nor will we murder you for our own convenience. We will give you enough supplies to journey to the nearest town and escort you out of the walls. I give you this option because we can't truly say that we're fighting for freedom if we won't let you have yours, even if we disagree with what you do with it.

"Those of you who wish to join our cause, step up into this open area here." Devrim indicated a space directly in front of the stage to his left. "If you wish to leave and return to your life as an Imperial soldier, remain where you are."

After a moment, about half of the captured soldiers moved toward the open space, while the other half stayed where they were. Devrim waited for them to finish moving.

"Excellent. To those who have chosen to join us, welcome. You are now a part of our ever-growing family, and we will take care of you. Those of you who want to leave, I have some final instructions for you. Please make a full report of what you saw here today to your superior officers and any nobility that you encounter. I do not want this battle or how we won to be a secret. Tell them that the people are rising up and that we are bringing a storm with us. They need to know what they are about to face so that they can choose where they want to stand.

"Everyone else, we'll have at least a few days before we think about where we're going next. So enjoy yourselves in this new free city for a while so that you're well rested when we go to liberate the next city from the Emperor. Because now that we're started, we won't stop until we take this straight to the gates of the Imperial Palace itself."

As the crowd roared its approval of his conclusion, Devrim waved Limbani to the edge of the stage and knelt down to speak to her. "Have four days of rations and a bedroll prepared for each of the soldiers who are leaving. Let's get them out of Antalia as soon as possible."

"Yes, sir." Limbani left to carry out her orders with new vigor after their victory.

CHAPTER SIXTEEN

"And then, she shot lightning out of her hands and the ships were completely destroyed," said a man with eyes as wild as his short hair as he animated his story with his hands.

Erhan listened from a booth in the corner of a tavern in Trabizan. He had come to the crossroads city in search of anyone who had seen or heard news of Nereyda. After a week, he had almost moved on after not discovering anything. Then, this man had started telling a story of a woman with raven hair performing miracles.

The man's friend on the other side of their table shook his head. "I don't believe it. Nobody can do that. Not since the gods took that from us."

"Now you become religious. I don't care about what the church says. Maybe this woman got her powers from the gods, maybe from someplace else. I know what I saw."

Erhan slid out of his seat and rushed over to their table, helping himself to a seat.

"Excuse us, do we know you?" asked the storyteller's friend.

"No, but I heard your story." He focused on the storyteller, whose well-kept clothes clashed with the rest of his appearance. "You said you saw this in Antalia?"

"Yes, that's right." The man's dark eyes sparkled.

"What's your name? What can you tell me about this woman?"

"My name is Hayri. And I don't know much. I was up in the city, and she was on a ship in the harbor. I could only see that she had dark hair. But I also heard she organized the whole rebellion that kicked the

Empire out. Her name is Reyda, or something like that." Hayri's expression carried a steady honesty as he spoke.

Erhan's heart hammered at the discovery of a new lead. "How did you get out of the city?" he asked with excitement. "Wasn't it sealed off?"

Hayri shook his head. "No, after they kicked the Imperials out, they made it much easier to come and go. Merchants like me no longer need to get a pass for every trip. Now, they just make sure we're not Imperial soldiers in disguise."

"Would you be willing to come with me to tell your story to some other people?"

Hayri shrugged and eyed Erhan with suspicion. "Maybe. Where would we need to go? And who wants to know?"

"We'd go to Goremia and tell the priests there what you saw."

The man shook his head. "That's several days out of my way. I have no need to go that far, not this time of year. My carts sit empty and I need to restock. Goremia has nothing I need. And what would the priests do with this story? I don't want to get this woman in any sort of trouble."

"This woman could be a sign that the gods have turned their favor back to humanity and given her the chance to prove that we're worthy. And I can pay you to come with me. One hundred gold. Half now and half after you tell the priests what you saw."

"I'd easily make that or more in the time it would take to make that trip."

"Two hundred?"

The man's eyes widened. "If you're sure this won't be bad for her, I suppose I could make time for that kind of money. When would we leave?"

"As soon as we can."

"I can probably be ready tomorrow morning."

"Meet me here at sunrise, and we'll leave."

Hayri proved to be a fine travel companion. He did not complain about long days on the road and helped set up camp each night. Conversation had been sparse, but that didn't bother Erhan. When they strode into the Temple of Ameretat in Goremia, a high priest with a familiar face emerged from a door at the back of the sanctuary. "Ah," Sabah said, "you're back. With a friend, I see. What can I help you with this time?"

"This is Hayri, a witness who saw the woman I talked to you about last time."

Sabah raised his eyebrows. "Interesting." He turned to Hayri. "Tell me what you saw, Hayri."

Hayri told the story of Nereyda destroying the two frigates with lightning, admiration ringing in his voice.

The priest frowned as he finished his tale. "This is concerning. I should go get the rest of the priests. They need to hear this. Both of you, please wait here while I summon them." He hurried into the back.

"You're sure this isn't going to cause problems for that woman?" Hayri asked. "The priest didn't seem happy with what I told him."

"He's probably just worried about what it means for the church. It's existed for centuries without anyone doing anything like this. Someone suddenly showing up with powers from the gods will change everything. Besides, you came all this way. You can't turn back now. And you don't want to leave before telling the priests your story. They have the authority to force you to come before them. It's much better to be cooperative."

"If you say so. When do I get the other half of my payment?"

"After you talk to the priests."

A few minutes later, Sabah came out with four others in blue robes. The five of them gathered on the central platform.

"Both of you," said Sabah, "come forward and sit on the front bench."

They moved up and sat before the priests.

"Now, Hayri, tell them what you told me."

The man repeated his story to the priests. After he had finished, they turned to each other and spoke in whispers that Erhan couldn't overhear.

When they stopped, Sabah spoke. "This testimony is most troubling, indeed, and is much more concrete than the rumors you brought to me before. However, we need more than one account from an average citizen before we can act. Unless you have another account to offer us, we cannot do anything yet. Perhaps, concerned citizen," he said with a pointed gaze at Erhan, "if you were more forthcoming about who you are and where you heard your stories, we could proceed. If you're reluctant to reveal yourself, I want to remind you that the church does not have to disclose anything to other Imperial authorities."

Erhan scowled down at the floor. Either he'd need to go out and find a second witness, or he'd have to serve as a witness himself. He couldn't waste time. He needed to trust that the priests wouldn't report him as a deserter or worse, a traitor.

Erhan rose, his head held high, and announced, "I am Commander Erhan of the Imperial Navy. I was present at the battle at the mines, though I have been hesitant to return to duty due to the questions that might be asked about my absence. A while ago, I apprehended the pirate captain Nereyda. At that time, she did not exhibit any talents with these strange abilities. After she and I were shipwrecked on an island near the Shattered Sea, I observed her throw some sort of fire demon through the air with a blast of wind. As we were about to board a raft we had made, she struck me with lightning and tied me up so I couldn't follow her, though I did manage to hail a civilian vessel as it passed through the area. I knew that she would want to go to the mines to attempt to free the rest of her crew, so I went there to intercept her. After being captured there, she made an escape attempt with her crew and was caught. She decided to bear the full punishment for her crew, and while she was being whipped, she froze her restraints until they shattered and killed the guards with lightning. Shortly after that, Stalsta attacked, and I made use of Nereyda and her pirates to help fight them. During that fight, she destroyed most of the fire demons with a wall of water and tossed me against a wall with her wind. That is my full account of what I know about this Nereyda and the abilities she has come to possess."

Sabah rubbed his chin, pulling on his beard. "That is an extensive testimony about this alleged gift thief. Do you have proof of your identity?"

"Gift thief?" asked Hayri. "I thought you said this wouldn't get her in trouble?"

Erhan ignored him. From a pocket in his jacket, he pulled out his commander's patch, which had his identification number, along with his service papers. He also handed over the original order from High Judge Aydin instructing him to arrest Captain Nereyda.

Sabah took the papers and studied them. "This order seems to have authentic signatures from both the High Judge and the Emperor himself, along with their seals. These papers are all either real or very convincing forgeries. We will, of course, need to do our own verification of what you've given to us. You understand that committing perjury before the church is a serious offense and that it could cost you your tongue, or even your life, depending on the severity of the lie. If you are false, this is your last chance to admit your lie without consequence. However, if you make us go through the work of verifying who you are and we find that you are dishonest, you will not leave this temple without punishment."

Erhan nodded. "I understand and swear that my testimony is true."

Sabah turned to Hayri. "Do you say the same about your own account?"

"Yes, I told you everything that I saw. I didn't make it up."

"Very well. Both of you will remain on the temple grounds as our guests while we check some of our sources. If we can confirm that you are who you say, this may be enough for the Inquisition that you asked about when you last came here."

"Wait," said Hayri, "we're prisoners now?"

"No, while you are confined to the temple grounds, you will be free to use any of our trails, and you will not want for comforts. If you need anything from the city below, we will send a courier to retrieve it. Also, as we don't have any current guests, you can stay in our best guest suites. These are the rooms used by the Emperor himself, along with high-ranking nobles and military officers."

"It still sounds like a fancy prison. What about my life?" he yelled. "I'm a merchant and have a business to run."

"The church is not blind to the economic needs of others. I assure you, you will be compensated for your time away from your daily affairs."

"So you'll pay me to stay here? Fine, that doesn't sound so bad." He nodded, then stopped with a frown. "Wait, what was that about an Inquisition? That doesn't sound good for this woman."

Sabah smiled at the man. "'Inquisition' is simply a church term for an investigation. Before we decide what action is appropriate, we need to learn more about this woman, how she obtained these gifts, and what her intentions are. I assure you, we will do what's best for her, the church, and the Empire."

"If you say so." He leaned back against the back of the bench and crossed his arms.

Sabah tilted his head toward Erhan. "Do you have any concerns about the church's hospitality?"

He shook his head. "No, of course not. I'll stay here as long as it takes."

"Good. We'll get started on checking these right away." He waved the papers in his hand. "We won't keep you waiting any longer than necessary. An acolyte will show you to your temporary quarters."

After four days, Erhan and Hayri were summoned back to the sanctuary, where all of the priests were assembled. Once they reached the front bench, Sabah spoke with them. "Commander Erhan, it seems that you are who you say you are. I verified the authenticity of your order with the High Judge himself. Also, Hayri, we heard some other rumors coming out of Antalia that support your own account. Some of them featured exaggerations, as these stories often do, but there was enough there for us to believe that you were honest in your testimony."

"What's next?" asked Erhan.

"Based on what you've told us, we have enough information to pursue an Inquisition. And we believe that you should lead it yourself. You have the military qualifications to lead such an effort. And, given your history with this individual, I believe that you are the best suited to bringing her in. Here, we have the tools for a proper examination once you bring this Nereyda to us."

Erhan cracked a rare smile at the thought of properly and finally pursuing his revenge.

CHAPTER SEVENTEEN

Every inch of Nereyda's body hurt with a sharp pain as she woke up, as if a thousand wasps had stung her all over. Her muscles were leaden and sluggish as she rolled onto her side. The sheets stuck to her clammy skin. Sunlight streamed in through the window next to the bed she lay in. She recognized the room as one in the Bawdy Bard but didn't remember arriving. The last thing she remembered was the battle against the frigates out in the harbor.

And Elvar. Her breaths felt heavy as she remembered how he had died in a volley of cannon fire. After that, she didn't remember much. Her inner storm had surged, but nothing after that came to her. Not that it mattered anyway when she had lost someone close to her.

Her muscles felt like fire as she forced herself out of bed. A clean robe lay on the dresser nearby. She wrapped it tight around herself as she stared out the window at the harbor, where ship wreckage still floated in the water. Tears flowed down her face as she thought about losing her friend. The crew of the Storm Raven would not be the same without him. It broke her heart that Elvar would never get to live free on the sea again.

The door behind her clicked, and Nereyda turned around to see Fariha with a wet cloth in her hand. "Oh, Reyda, you should have waited for me to help you up," she said with concern in her emerald eyes. She closed the door as she entered, her copper hair swaying in a braid.

"I can stand on my own," Nereyda said. She tilted toward the wall and caught herself. "What happened? How did I get here?"

"Let's sit you back down." Fariha grabbed Nereyda's arm and guided her back to the bed. "Some of your crew carried you in. You've been out for a few days. I was coming to put this cloth on your forehead for a while. You've been running hot."

"How did they bring me here? We were losing to those frigates."

"Apparently, you didn't lose." Fariha dabbed the cloth on Nereyda's face and wiped away the sweat. "From what I heard from your crew, you shot lightning out of your hands and destroyed their ships. I don't know about that, but I did hear an awfully loud bit of thunder from the harbor right before the Imperials surrendered."

"Wait, the Imperials surrendered? You mean we won?"

Fariha set the cloth down. "Oh, forgive me. I probably should have started with that. Yes, Antalia now belongs to its people again. Some soldiers in green uniforms came in through the gate and helped take the rest of the Imperial camps. Between their help and what happened in the harbor, the rest of the Imperials threw down their weapons quickly. You should hear what the people are saying about you. They're calling you the Savior of Antalia."

Nereyda grabbed her pillow and clutched it to her chest. "I'm no savior. If I was, I'd have saved Elvar."

Fariha's mouth hung open and she put a hand on Nereyda's shoulder. "Oh, I'm sorry, I didn't know he was gone. I just figured he was somewhere else when the crew brought you in."

"He was right next to me on the ship." She clenched her fingers into the pillow. "Maybe I could have done something. I could have used wind to protect him, maybe." Her voice cracked. "I don't know exactly what, but I should have tried."

"You did your best, Nereyda. I know you. You always do whatever you can. He died doing what he loved."

"What do you mean?" Nereyda gave Fariha a sideways glance. "He never got to be a pirate again."

"That's not how I see it. Isn't stealing a ship being a pirate? And he helped you take out four ships with a single frigate. But I'm not talking about being a pirate. He died standing side by side with the people he cared most about. And remember, you got him out of those damn mines. A death fighting on the sea has to be better than a life slaving away in that place. You've given him the best life and the best end you could. He would be incredibly proud of you. And he'd want you to cheer up and go out and celebrate your victory."

A tear slid down Nereyda's cheek. "Thank you, Fariha. I'm sure they've been celebrating the last few days, though."

"They have, but they've been holding back. I think they've been waiting for you. Your crew definitely has. Also, a Lord Devrim has been asking about you. He came in with the green-uniformed soldiers. He's been by a few times a day."

"Ah, yes, he's the one behind all of this. He'll want to know I'm not dead. Do you know where he is?"

"He stayed here the first night, but I think he's moved into the administration building."

"Where is this place?"

"It's on the south side of the harbor. You won't be able to miss it, especially with our green friends running in and out of it."

"Okay, I'll head out in a bit. Do you have any food downstairs? I'm starving."

"Sure. I'll find something for you and have it ready by the time you come down. Your clothes are in the wardrobe next to the window. You might want to grab a bath first, though. I did what I could but, well, you did fight in a battle and have been in bed for three days."

Nereyda smelled herself and wrinkled her nose. "Yeah, you're right."

"You can use the washroom through that door." Fariha pointed at a door on the other side of the room from the bed.

"Do each of your rooms have a washroom?"

"No, but you lucked out and got our suite. I give it out as a free bonus to anyone who successfully leads a rebellion in Antalia."

Nereyda let out a short laugh before wincing in pain. "I'll have to do it again someday. Thank you, Fariha, for all of your help."

"Not the first time I've taken care of you while you've been passed out."

"You're not wrong. Are there many people downstairs right now?"

"It's the busiest it's been in years, aside from the night after you showed up."

"Can you bring food up here, then? I don't feel like celebrating at the moment, and I don't want to bring the mood down for everyone else."

"Sure, I can do that. It'll be waiting when you're clean and dressed."

Fariha left the room, and Nereyda went into the washroom. The bathtub even had running water, a benefit of a well-developed city like

Antalia. She turned the faucet and undressed as the tub filled with hot water. She let out a sigh as she slid into the bath. If she hadn't already slept for three days, she would have been tempted to take a nap. As it was, she enjoyed how the water relaxed her muscles and loosened them up. After washing, she dressed and stepped back into the bedroom. A tray of eggs, bacon, and toast sat on the dresser. She barely tasted any of it as she shoveled it into her mouth.

When finished, she set the tray back on the dresser and slipped out the door. She snuck down the stairs and toward the kitchen to use the back door, avoiding the noisy crowd gathering in the main dining area of the tavern. She'd meet her crew and the other rebels soon. She wanted to go talk to Devrim first, though. It was less daunting to face someone one on one than to wade into a crowd, at least as she wrestled with her conflicted feelings about losing Elvar while still winning the battle.

She left the tavern for the administration building.

"Nereyda," called a voice from behind her.

She turned around to see Jax slip out from the same back door.

"Hey Jax," Nereyda said.

"Why are you sneaking out?" His dark eyes narrowed with concern as he studied her face. "You've been out for days, and your crew misses you."

"Devrim wanted to see me when I woke up, so I'm heading down to the admin building. I'm not quite ready for my crew and everyone else yet."

"Elvar?"

Nereyda shrugged and shook her head.

"I'll be fine," she said. "Don't worry about me."

"You don't have to keep everything buried, you know."

She ignored him and glanced out over the harbor. "You know, we can have any ship we want. There's a frigate right there in the harbor. If we wanted, we could take it and sail your people back to the Shattered Sea right now."

"We could do that, but we won't. I don't think you really want to do that."

"Why not? Stealing a ship isn't really beneath me." She flashed him a smirk.

He gave her a concerned frown. "I know that, but I don't think you're in this for a ship."

"Then what am I doing it for?"

"What you said to the people in that tavern to convince them to join us—that didn't come from someone who only cares about a ship. That was a woman who cared about the people of this city and wanted to help them. You're fighting for them, even if you don't want to admit it."

She shrugged off his words. "I know how to rile up a crowd." Nereyda started to turn away.

"Reyda, Elvar died knowing what he was fighting for. Elvar thought you were worth it, so don't throw that away."

Nereyda turned back to him.

"I know what it's like to lose someone important to you," Jax continued. "I didn't mention this before, but I used to have a wife." His eyes held an aged soul. "We had been friends since we were children, and it grew into something more than friendship.

"A month after our wedding, we left for the new settlement to begin our life together. We built our marriage and the village on the same foundation. We'd flirt and sneak kisses even as we worked with the others. She set up a school and taught the young ones. Then, the Imperials came. I've never seen such fierce courage from anyone as she showed when she protected her students. She got them to the ship and helped them escape. She had intended to go with them to keep them safe on the journey. We both had. I tried to provide cover for them as they got ready to cast off, but there were too many enemies. When Avra saw that I was being overwhelmed, she told the kids to cast off without us and rushed to my side with just a spare oar as a weapon. She fought fiercely, even more than I did. A soldier circled around behind her, and he ran her through with his sword. I don't remember if the scream I heard was hers or mine. As soon as she collapsed, I fell to my knees and dropped my weapon. My wife was dead, and I was captured. For a long time, I wondered if saving those children was worth our sacrifice—if it was worth her life and my freedom. But it was. I don't know what became of those kids. I hope I get to find out. But we gave them the best shot that we could. That's what you've done here. You've given this city a chance to be great. What will the children of this city get to do, what opportunities will they have because you and Elvar fought for them, even if it did cost him his life? I didn't know him long, but from what I've seen of him, I think he would be comfortable and happy with what his death bought for the city."

Nereyda stared up at the puffy clouds floating through the sky as she digested Jax's story, then turned her eyes back to him. "Maybe you're right. Thank you, Jax. And I'm sorry about your wife. You've lost even more than I have."

He nodded. "Now it's up to us to honor the memories we have of Elvar and Avra. Want company on the way to see Devrim?"

"No, I think I'm fine by myself. I'll see you later, though."

On the streets, her muscles ached as she made her way downhill to the harbor, then followed the edge. A large marble building, several stories tall, occupied a space of at least two blocks. Armed men in green uniforms hurried in and out of the building. She had no idea where to look for Devrim in such a vast building. She asked one of the guards at the door, "Do you know where I can find Devrim?"

"Lord Devrim has taken the city administrator's office, on the top floor in the middle of the western side, looking over the harbor. It's a big room. You won't be able to miss it."

"Thanks." Inside, a staircase ascended straight ahead of her. After hiking up several flights of stairs, she found the western side. It was easy to figure out which room was the administrator's office. Two guards stood outside an ornately decorated door. Battle scenes from the Empire's history were carved into the door and lined with gold.

"Hello," she said to the guards. "I'm here to see Devrim. He asked for me."

"Oh, the pirate," said the guard on the right. "He said you'd be coming. He's in a meeting right now, but you can come back in a bit."

"I'll go in now. Thanks, though." Nereyda strode past the guard and ignored his protests as she shoved through the door and into a spacious office. Devrim sat behind a desk, with two other people in chairs in front of him. One of them Nereyda recognized from the night she had broken into Devrim's mansion. The other she didn't recognize.

"Does she know about the Inquisition yet?" Nereyda heard one of them ask.

"Inquisition?" she said. "What's that?"

Devrim's eyes flicked up at her. A glimmer of surprise flashed across his face before it disappeared. "Nothing I would worry about. It seems that news of what you did to the ships in the harbor has got around and the Empire is scared that they don't have anything that can stand up to you. They're trying to make you out to be some sort of demon. I'm not sure they're wrong, but at least you seem to be the right kind of demon. You're among friends, and you don't need to be concerned."

She gave a weak shrug. "If you say so."

"Sorry, sir," said the guard. "I tried to tell her you were busy, but she just walked in."

"That's fine," Devrim said. "I'd expect no less. Excuse me, gentlemen, but we'll have to continue this discussion another time. The Savior of Antalia has finally woken up, and I've been looking forward to talking with her."

The two men got up and nodded to Nereyda as Devrim showed them out of the room. Devrim clapped her on the shoulder. "Glad to see that you're up and about now. I was worried that my best general would be gone after the first major battle. Please sit." He pointed to an empty chair as he returned to his seat.

Nereyda crossed her arms and leaned back against the wall. She bit her lip as the solid surface pressed against her back. "General? Really?" Titles didn't mean much to her.

"You did win Antalia for us." He gestured out the window behind him. "From what I hear, you pulled off a bit of a miracle in the harbor."

A weight sank in Nereyda's gut at the mention of the battle. "Who were you meeting with? What was that meeting about?" Nereyda asked.

"You recognize Rahmi, I believe."

"I do, but I didn't think he wanted me to know his name."

He waved her concern away. "It's fine, now that we're all outlaws together. Those two are our strongest supporters in the nobility. They've been working on building alliances with others in the Empire, especially the western portion."

"Hope they've made some progress. Maybe turned more of those green markers to blue? You know it's confusing that you use blue markers for your allies, but you have green uniforms."

"Yes, I know. It's just a strange mismatch we'll have to live with."

"What did you want to talk to me about?"

"Please, sit down." He once again pointed at the seat across from him.

"I'd rather stand, but thanks."

"Very well. First, Nereyda, I want to thank you. I could never have imagined taking Antalia, let alone as quickly as you did."

Nereyda looked away and out the window. "It didn't come without a cost."

He rubbed his chin and gazed down at the desk. "Yes, your friend. I heard."

"Elvar," she said with an edge. "Not just a friend. He's been part of the Storm Raven crew ever since I was hauled out of a barrel. If Captain Nogre was my father, Elvar was my uncle."

Devrim clasped his hands and perched his chin on top of them, his eyes sympathetic. "I'm sorry that this battle cost the life of Elvar. I didn't know him, but if he helped turn you into the person who could accomplish this, he was clearly a good man."

Nereyda scoffed. "Not just good. The best. Even if we return to the sea, it won't be the same without him. I'm starting to wonder if it's even worth the cost."

Devrim rose, crossed the room, and put his hand on her shoulder.

She fought back a wince as he touched a spot that was still healing. Then again, what part of her body didn't hurt?

"I understand how you'd think that," said Devrim. "It's not easy to bear the loss of someone you care about. But Elvar probably knew what he was doing. He knew that he might die fighting this fight. And he did it anyway. He faced his death because he believed in something bigger than himself. He believed in you and your crew. He didn't waste his life. He invested it in your future."

"I'd rather have my friend than an investment."

"I know, but now you have the opportunity to make the most of that investment. After what happened at the mines, and what you did here, I believe in you too. Together, we'll win this and get your crew back home on the sea."

Nereyda pulled away from Devrim's hand and drifted around the room, her fingertips grazing the bookcases that lined the perimeter. She was ready to talk about something, anything, else.

"What's next for us?" she asked. "The best way forward is to start moving."

"We're still figuring that out. After we get established here, we need to figure out what city to take next. I'm also interested in how the Empire will react to the fall of Antalia."

"I doubt they'll stand by and let us rest here for long. I'm not sure how they'll take it back, though."

"No, I don't think they'll try anytime soon. They might try besieging the city, but only if we wait around and let them do it. I want to take at least one more city before they can mount a significant counterattack. The closest major city is Trabizan, so that might be our next target. So far, Lord Feridun, the appointed mayor of the city, has been resistant to our efforts to bring him to our side. I even sent a messenger after taking Antalia, and he still refused."

"Will you need my crew again?"

"Yes, but first get your rest. While I do want to take Trabizan soon, it will be at least a week before we're ready to move out. Spend some time with your crew and enjoy your time as a celebrity here."

"Since we have time, mind if I borrow one of the fishing boats for a few days? I need to see a friend and see if I can figure out what happened in the harbor. I don't want to burn myself up again if I can help it."

"Of course. Anything that can help you better use your power. We could use that again."

"That move nearly killed me. You can't ask me to do that again."

"I hope your friend can help you get it under control, at least. I think we'll need some of that lightning and whatever else you can do in our next fight."

"I'll see what we can do. Is that everything?"

"I think so, for now. When you return, feel free to stop by anytime for a drink."

She raised an eyebrow at him. "Are you sure you should be asking your general on a date?"

"It's not a date. I just want to get to know you."

"Whatever you want to call it. Sure, I'll stop by sometime when we're taking a break from taking over the Empire."

Nereyda gave him a slim smile, then slipped out of the room.

CHAPTER EIGHTEEN

Gentle beams of sunlight roused Nereyda from her slumber. She climbed out of the bedroll on the deck of the fishing boat, then weighed anchor and sailed from the spot she had spent the night. In just a couple of hours, she would arrive at Manu's. Hopefully, he would have some answers or at least be able to help her learn more about her powers.

As the boat bobbed through the sea, propelled by the morning breeze, the solitude of the last few days weighed on Nereyda. She tried not to think about Elvar or how she had nearly killed herself with her powers, but she couldn't turn off those thoughts. Despite her conversations with Jax and Devrim, which had provided some comfort, her mind was still stuck in a loop.

The roar of dozens of cannons. The screams of her crew members. The feeling of Elvar's blood on her hands. The scent of lightning in the air. Nereyda's brain forced her to relive all of those sensations again and again. She gripped the wheel of the boat as she tried to drive the thoughts away, but the more she fought, the worse they seemed to get.

Why can't I get it together? It's not like I haven't been in battle before.

Thankfully, the dock near Manu's shack came into view. She wrestled her focus from her memories and concentrated on bringing the boat to the dock, then tying it up. Nereyda strode quickly along the beach, as if she could outpace her brain.

The weathered wood of Manu's place came into view, with its slight lean away from the shore. Nereyda marched up to the door and knocked three times. A moment later, it opened, and Manu poked his head out.

He beamed as he recognized her and swung the door wide open. "Ah, Nereyda! I thought you were away. I wasn't expecting to see you."

"Yes, I hadn't planned on it either, but recent events made me seek you out."

Manu tilted his head. "Recent events? What can I do to help?"

"I've just come from Antalia. I helped Devrim's rebellion take it. In the fighting, well . . ." Nereyda gazed down as she shifted her feet in the sand. "Something happened, and I destroyed two frigates with huge blasts of lightning."

Manu took a short step back in surprise. "What prompted that response from you, I wonder?"

"That doesn't matter right now," Nereyda snapped. "What does matter is that it knocked me unconscious for days, and I can't let that happen again."

Manu stroked his chin with a thoughtful expression. "Hmm, I've read about such things happening, and worse."

"Can you help me learn more and control this?" Nereyda asked, hope in her eyes.

"I can certainly try." He leaned into his house and emerged with a fishing rod and a satchel in one hand and a pail in the other. "Can you carry this please?" He passed the bucket to Nereyda.

She took it and he shifted his satchel to his shoulder. Inside, the pail held a lump of butter, wrapped in paper, and a bag of flour. These rested in one half of the container, divided from the other half by a piece of wood.

"Follow me," said Manu as he closed the door behind him and hiked along the beach. "I was just about to go fishing when you arrived. It will be a good time for us to talk."

"You said you know about what happened?" The wind off the ocean blew a strand of hair across her face and she tucked it back.

"Perhaps. I've read about people who pushed themselves too hard, channeled too much of their power at once, and were consumed by it. Some fell unconscious, like you. Others went mad or even died. You may have gotten lucky."

"It didn't feel lucky. When I woke up, everything hurt."

Manu turned toward the water and waded in until he was ankle deep. "That is not surprising," he said, "considering how much energy coursed through you. If you want to prevent this from happening again, you need to learn to control yourself."

Nereyda stayed on the dry sand. "I wish I could, but I didn't exactly get an instruction book to go along with this. Do you know anything that could help me?"

"I don't have much practical knowledge of this, so I'm not sure how much help I'll be," he said as he strung a line onto his rod.

"You know more than I do. Unless you can recommend someone else, you're all I have."

He stopped fidgeting with the fishing rod and turned toward her. "What if I teach you something wrong? There's no guarantee that I'll guess the right things to do."

Nereyda trudged down through the wet sand and into the water. "It still gives me a better chance than doing it on my own. Please, help me."

"Of course. I only want you to be aware of the risks. But I do know a bit, I suppose. And I'm eager to learn more about your abilities." He took a piece of bait from his satchel and hooked it onto his line. "Why don't you practice while I fish?"

"Where should I start?"

Manu lifted the rod, then cast the line into the sea. "Begin by repeating what you did with the water the first time I saw you use your power."

"That trick?" Nereyda rolled her eyes. "That's easy. Let's work on something hard."

"No, when learning, you always start with the basics. Begin with what you can do consistently, then we'll build out from there. Also, go take your boots off. It will help you get better in touch with the elements. And one more thing, roll your eyes at me again and you'll be on your own," he said in a stern voice.

Nereyda pivoted and scowled to herself as she marched out of the water. At the edge of the grass that lined the beach, she sat and tugged her boots off. As she hiked back down, the dry sand scratched and tickled her feet. She waded into the cool water and the muddy sand squished between her toes.

She paused and took in the aura around her. With her eyes closed, she focused on the warm sun on her neck, the refreshing breeze across her face, and the scent of salt in the air, with a hint of rain. As she continued, she sensed energy in the air, but thought it was subsiding.

"Did it storm yesterday?" she asked as she opened her eyes.

"It did. It was quite a strong one in fact." He slowly reeled his line in. "That's why it should be a good day to catch some fish. Do you feel it?"

"Yes, I do."

"Good. Let's see what you can do."

Nereyda held her hand out and focused on the power within and the atmosphere without. She thought of the sea wrapping around her and passing through her. An arm of water stretched out and caressed her hand.

"There, I did it."

"Very good. Now see if you can do more with it." He finished reeling in his line and recast it.

Nereyda reached out with her other hand and, while she kept the first column of water, she summoned a second. Her face scrunched as the simultaneous concentrations stretched her mind.

Manu glanced over at her and smirked at her expression.

"Not so easy anymore, is it? Have you ever used your hands to do two different tasks at the same time? How did you learn to fight with two swords? Imagine you're doing that. At least, that's what I've gathered from the hints in my reading."

She listened to him and moved her hands as if she were tying a knot, with each hand guiding one end of a rope. The tendrils of water followed her gestures. Nereyda swirled her hands around each other and the two ropes of water twisted together. A grin escaped her lips at such a simple yet beautiful display.

"Ooh, looks like we caught one," said Manu as he tugged on the line.

Nereyda broke her concentration and retrieved the bucket. Once Manu reeled in the fish, he dumped it into the empty half of the bucket.

"What was it like studying these kinds of powers?" Nereyda asked, shaking out her arms as she took a break.

"Rigorous and intense," Manu answered as he cast the line out again. "It often took months of searching to find new material for our research. Then, it took months of comparing it to our other materials to see if it supported or disproved current theories. Still, despite the arduous process, it was rewarding. It felt like we were peeking through a tiny hole and seeing a small image of what the real history of our world is."

"And what is that real history?"

"Someday, when you have hours or days to spare, we can start that conversation. Now, however, you should continue."

"Okay, but I'm going to try something else."

"Very well. I suggest trying lightning, since that's what you used at the harbor. But please, stand out of the water," he said with a wry smile.

Back up on the dry sand, which had warmed under the late-morning sun, Nereyda held her hand out and focused on the storm inside. After a couple of seconds, she found it and tried to latch on to the electricity there, but it retreated further within her.

She closed her eyes and tried again. Once more, the storm pulled back from her, but this time she pursued it. Deeper and deeper she went, always a fingertip away from touching it. Soon, the nerves in her arms started to sting. She ignored it and pressed on.

As the pain grew, memories flooded her mind. The battle in the harbor. A ship ramming them. A cannon barrage. Elvar, dead in her arms.

She shoved the images aside, but they always returned. Elvar's still, dead face haunted her as she chased her storm. With her arms on fire and Elvar seared into her mind, Nereyda opened her eyes and dropped her hand.

The pain in her arms dissipated and sweat dripped down her forehead as she panted.

Manu set his rod down and rushed across the sand to her. "Are you all right?"

Nereyda wrapped her arms around herself. "I kept seeing my friend Elvar. I tried to ignore it, but it just got worse. And my arms were burning up."

"What's special about Elvar?"

"He was killed in Antalia." Her voice caught for a moment. "He died in my arms, then I let out that blast of lightning."

"You don't have to keep trying, if you don't want to."

Nereyda shook her head. "I need to do this."

"Very well. I caught a second fish while you were trying that. Let's take a break while I cook them. You can use the time to talk through what you experienced." He retrieved his bucket with the fish, butter, and flour, then led her up a short path through the grass and away from the beach to a firepit. "Please sit." Manu pointed to a long log that lay near the pit.

"What should I talk about?" asked Nereyda as she perched on the log. "I don't see how that will help me."

"Trust me. What are you feeling at the moment? What is going through your head? Don't hold back. I'm not someone you need to impress, so you don't need a mask with me." He shuffled through the grass beneath the nearby trees and grabbed various bits of wood.

"I guess I'm feeling a bit lost at the moment," said Nereyda with a distant look. "Elvar taught me a lot of what I know and I could always turn to him for advice. My friend is dead, and I want to move on so that I can give his death meaning." She rubbed her hands up and down her upper arms as she hugged herself. "But I still have nightmares about how he died. When I wake up, his face lingers in my vision as my arms sting. It goes away after a few seconds, but I can't escape it. And what's the point of being able to control lightning if I can't save my friends?"

Manu piled the wood he had collected in the firepit and flicked a flint and steel from his satchel. "When I was at the academy, I too suffered a loss that took me a long time to get over."

"Your friends who went to the island?"

"No. Their disappearance saddened me, but they had embarked on a dangerous journey to the other side of the world. I knew they might not come back." A spark caught and fire grew among the wood. As it burned, Manu filleted the fish. "The loss I speak of happened much earlier, just after my own graduation. I had a longtime advisor, Karthik. He guided me through many difficult times in my life. My studies, of course, but also the deaths of my parents. He was as much a friend as a mentor."

Once the fire had grown, Manu extracted a small pan and a spatula from his satchel. He cut off a chunk of butter and dropped it into the pan, then heated it over the fire. "Karthik set out on a journey to another city across the continent to retrieve a newly discovered text. I stayed behind to help around the academy. Once he returned, we planned on studying what he found. But he never came back."

Once the butter had melted, he coated the fish with it, then dredged the fish with flour before he cooked it over the fire. "Karthik fell ill with a plague while on his journey, and died quickly. For weeks after learning the news, I could not motivate myself to work. I refused to travel at all out of fear of the same plague. Then, another messenger brought the text he had set out to retrieve. As I gazed upon that tome, I realized that I needed to work on it. I needed to do it for Karthik."

Nereyda digested the story that Manu had told her as the scent of frying fish wafted through the air. "So what you're saying is that perhaps I need to embrace and accept the loss of Elvar instead of running from it."

"Yes. And I think that will help with controlling your abilities, as well. You can't be ashamed of who you are or what has happened, otherwise you'll always hold yourself back. In extreme cases, such shame has even made people tear themselves apart with their pent-up power. Too much inner conflict can stir the elements inside of you in dangerous ways. Why don't you give it a try before the meal is ready?"

Nereyda stood up and found space a bit away from the fire. She closed her eyes and searched for the storm inside. At the same time, she pictured Elvar's smile in her head. She remembered the pride he displayed after she had rallied the people of Antalia. Rather than pain, a warm tingle spread upward and through her arm. She opened her eyes just as sparks shot out and danced between her fingers and the sand.

She practiced the same thing a few times until she summoned lightning at will without closing her eyes. Manu and Nereyda shared a grin. "I knew you'd get it," he said.

"Thank you for listening, Manu. And for all of your help."

He shrugged. "I only helped point the way. You did all of the real work. Join me for fish?"

Nereyda sat next to him on the log and enjoyed the freshly cooked fish.

"What's next for you? Once this rebellion business is done, I mean," said Manu.

Nereyda chewed on her lip. "I'm not sure right now. I want to get a ship and return to the sea, but aside from that, I don't know. Especially with my new talents. I feel like they mean something, but what that is remains a mystery."

"I know that you'll figure it out when the time comes. And if you need someone to talk to, you know where to find me. Care to spend the night? I can make space."

"Sounds good. Then, in the morning, I'll head back to the war."

CHAPTER NINETEEN

The night after Nereyda returned to Antalia, she looked up from her mug of ale and spotted Limbani on the other side of the Bawdy Bard. The general leaned against the wall near the doorway, apart from everyone else, with her arms crossed tight across her chest. She was the only person still in full uniform. Excusing herself from her crew, Nereyda took one last swig to polish off her drink, then sauntered up to the general.

"You still on duty, Limbani?"

"No, not right now. Why?"

"Why don't you come sit down and have a drink?"

Limbani shook her head. "I'm not really comfortable drinking with my men around."

"That's never stopped me. If it bugs you though, come with me, and we'll grab one of the booths in the back. I see one that's open. I'll even buy the drinks, and we can chat, captain to captain. Or general to general now, I suppose."

Limbani thought for a second. "I suppose one drink would be fine."

"That's the idea. Come on." Nereyda led her back to the booth that sat in a shady corner of the tavern and waved to get Fariha's attention, holding up two fingers.

The two women sat on either side of the table.

"Isn't it against regulations to drink in full uniform?"

Limbani arched an eyebrow. "Since when does a pirate care about regulations?"

"I don't, but I think you do."

"So now you're trying to talk me out of drinking with you?"

"No, I'm just teasing you. But you can take your jacket off if it makes you feel better."

Limbani took off her green jacket, folding it and setting it on the inside of the booth's bench, leaving her with a white undershirt that contrasted with her dark skin.

Fariha brought two ales to their table and set them down.

"Thanks, Fari," said Nereyda.

"Of course."

Nereyda took a sip of her drink, keeping her gaze on Limbani. After she had swallowed, she asked, "So, what's your story?"

Limbani kept her posture straight as she lifted her mug and set it back down in measured movements. "I have a few stories. Which one do you want to hear?"

"How about how a Takondwan woman ended up a guard captain for the Empire. It's not exactly common."

"I'm good at my job, and I follow orders. Devrim saw that, and it's worked out," Limbani said efficiently.

"There has to be more to it than that, though. How did you become a guard in the first place?"

Limbani took a big swig of her drink, gazing off into a corner of the tavern, then looked back. "Fine, I suppose it won't hurt to talk about it." Her perfect posture relaxed a bit. "I was very young when we moved to the Cambisian Empire, so I don't remember the reason. When I was a girl, my family worked in the textile factory that Lord Devrim ran in Manisa. During a break, I was playing with a broom like it was a sword. After I had been playing for ten minutes or so, I saw Lord Devrim watching me. He said he was impressed with me and asked me if I'd like to be trained as a guard. I said yes, of course, and he arranged everything else. He paid for all of my training and equipment. When I asked him how I could repay him, he simply asked me to swear loyalty to him. That's all there is to tell, really."

"I'm glad I never came up against you in a fight."

"Why's that?"

"You seem tougher than any other soldier I've faced. And I know the determination that it can take to succeed when you're different than your peers."

"I could say the same about you." Limbani leaned forward, resting her elbows on the table as she pointed at Nereyda. "You've obviously done well for yourself. It's strange what turns life can take. It makes you wonder how much you really choose and how much just happens and you have to deal -with."

"What do you mean by that?"

"Did you ever consider not being a pirate?"

"No, not really. I've been doing it for as long as I can remember."

"Exactly. You didn't choose it."

"But you chose to be a guard."

Limbani shrugged and leaned back in her seat. "It wasn't much of a choice. Slave away in a factory, even one run by someone like Lord Devrim, or have some amount of freedom as a guard?"

"I suppose that part of what happens in life is determined by where in the ocean you're born and what direction the wind is blowing, but it's still up to you to chart a course to get you where you want to go. I chose to work hard and become a captain. I chose to work to get my crew back after they were captured. And now I have to make new choices about how I use these crazy new abilities I've discovered. You're much the same. You chose to take the opportunity to get out of the factory. And it seems that you've chosen to work hard enough to prove yourself worthy of being a captain, and now a general. From what I hear about how you fought in the battle, you're more than worthy. You might think you're lucky that Devrim discovered you, but I think he's the lucky one. He needs you. Needs both of us, really."

"Someone has to do all of the fighting. Might as well be us."

Nereyda exchanged a smile with Limbani. "At least we get to have all of the fun. By the way, where is Devrim tonight?"

"Still in his office. I tried telling him to take it easy, but he doesn't listen."

"I might go and see if I can change his mind. Let's grab a drink again sometime."

Limbani cracked her own sliver of a smile. "Anytime."

Nereyda finished her ale and headed out into the street.

The hall leading to the administrator's office glowed with a mix of the golden flames of the wall torches and the silver moonlight that shone down through the skylights in the roof. "I'm here to see Devrim," Nereyda said to the guards standing on either side of the door.

They just nodded at her.

This time, neither guard moved to stop her as she reached for the door and let herself into Devrim's office. The room was dark except for the light that came in through the windows. To her left, the red glow of a fireplace in a small, attached room caught her attention. Devrim rose from a high-backed chair near the flame with a warm, welcoming smile. The top two buttons of his white shirt were undone and his sleeves were rolled up.

"I'm glad you decided to join me," he said. "I was hoping you might stop by tonight. Please, come sit." He pointed to an identical chair that sat empty next to his. A small table between the two chairs had two glasses and a bottle of wine.

"Seems like you've trained the guards since I last came," Nereyda said as she joined him in the sitting room.

Devrim let out a short laugh. "They know that you're a part of my high command now. They also know that you won't let them stop you even if they try, so they don't."

They sat in their chairs and Nereyda welcomed the comfortable warmth emanating from the fire.

"Want a drink?" Devrim offered, holding the bottle.

"In the future, assume the answer will always be yes. So what did you want to talk about? Got some grand plan for where we should go next?" she asked as he poured two glasses of wine.

"No, not right now, at least. I don't want to talk to a general or a pirate captain. Tonight, I want to talk to Nereyda." He held a glass out to her.

She arched an eyebrow at him as she took the glass. "Me? Why? There's plenty of entertainment around here if you're bored."

He shook his head and gave her an amused look. "I'm not interested in entertainment. I want to get to know you."

Nereyda took a drink and smiled. "Okay, then, what do you want to know?"

"How does someone like you become a pirate?"

"Someone like me?"

"I mean, you're not exactly what I would imagine when thinking of a pirate."

"What do you imagine? Someone with a hook for a hand, part of a tree for a leg, and a parrot on their shoulder?" She smirked at him.

Devrim laughed. "No, not that. You're just younger and different than most captains I know."

"You mean because I have breasts and don't have an extra appendage between my legs?"

"I wouldn't be so crass about it, but yes. I don't have a lot of experience with women of authority, aside from Limbani."

"That's too bad. We're pretty good at it."

"Clearly. But anyway, how did you get into this life?"

Nereyda shrugged. "It's what I've always done. My parents set me adrift in a barrel—I don't know why—and I was picked up by the Storm Raven. I've been there ever since, and it's all I know."

"And you've never thought about leaving and finding a more, well, legitimate life?"

"Is this about trying to straighten me out?"

"No, only curious."

"Leaving's never really occurred to me. Leaving the Storm Raven would be like abandoning my family. Unless I took them along and helped them find their own happiness, I don't think I could do anything else."

"How did you become captain so young?"

"When Captain Nogre died, I got us out of a bad spot. I was the best choice, and the crew voted to make me captain after that."

"You don't exactly have any problems with confidence, do you?"

"That's not a problem if I know what I'm doing, which I generally do."

"What about when things go wrong, though? Like when your crew was captured or when Elvar died?"

Nereyda frowned as she set her drink down and shuffled over to stare out the window, crossing her arms. "I try not to think about that."

She heard Devrim put his own drink on the table, then his footsteps as he came up beside her and put his hand on her shoulder. She didn't turn to look at him but didn't pull away, either. His pine scent comforted her. "I'm sorry. I don't know why I said that. I didn't mean to pick at that wound."

"It's not your fault. And you're not wrong to ask. I think I just don't like to think about it because I don't really have anyone in the crew that I can share my fears with. I love them, but they need me to be a captain. And for that, I need to be sure of myself."

"I don't know if it helps, but I don't know what I'm doing with this rebellion. I'm making it up as I go along. I'm used to running a factory where I can plan everything out. This is new territory for me."

Nereyda turned to him, leaving his hand on her shoulder. "Don't worry. This is where I live my life." She gave him a slim smile.

"Good, then it looks like I picked the right general."

"Why lead this rebellion if you don't know what you're doing?"

The embers reflected in his dark eyes as he fixed her with a determined gaze. "Because I might be the only one who can. Some of the people I grew up with are still stuck working in the factories, barely earning enough to feed their families. I was lucky, and I hate to leave them behind."

"They're your crew." She reached up and touched the side of his face. "I get it."

"You get me, I think."

Nereyda's heart quickened as she pulled him toward her and placed her lips on his, nibbling slightly on his lower lip before he pulled back.

"I'm not sure I should be getting involved with someone working under me," said Devrim. He turned his face away and lightly held Nereyda back with the hand he still had on her shoulder.

However, he didn't resist as she sidestepped and pulled his chin toward her again. "Are you saying it's against the rules? You know that will just encourage me."

He flashed a tempting grin. "I'm counting on that."

Nereyda kissed him again, then brushed her lips alongside his neck up to his ear. "And who said I'd need to be under you?" she asked with a purr in her voice.

"Tempting. Maybe I can persuade you to stay the night?"

She gasped as he nibbled at the base of her neck. It was almost enough to make Nereyda give in. "You are very persuasive, but I think I'll make you wait a bit," she said as she slipped away from him, running her fingers down his arm.

Devrim caught her wrist in his hand, then his light caresses and rough callouses performed a duet across the top of her hand. "You shy?"

"Absolutely not. I'm not afraid of having a night of fun. But I don't usually see those guys again. You, though, I think I'll be seeing a lot. Don't want to complicate things too quickly." She gently tugged her hand from his grasp.

"If that's what you want, I can be patient."

"Good. Trust me, I'll make it worth the wait when it does happen."

"So you're saying it will?"

"As long as you don't screw anything up." She winked at him. "But I suppose I should head back and call it a night. We still have our meeting about Trabizan in the morning?"

"Yes." He picked up the wine bottle and waved it at her. "Want another drink before you go?"

"So you can keep seducing me?" She winked again. "After we take Trabizan, we'll make time for another evening together. We'll see what happens then. Have a good night, my lord." She swayed her hips as she glided out of the room, feeling his gaze follow her.

CHAPTER TWENTY

"Are you ready?" asked Devrim.

"After Antalia, this should be easy," said Nereyda.

They stood on top of a hill, overlooking Trabizan and the stone bridge that led to it. The rebel army stood behind them at the bottom of the hill, a patchwork of the green uniforms of soldiers, the mixed black and gray of the pirates and Islanders, and the smattering of colors worn by the volunteers from Antalia.

"Looks like you were right," Nereyda continued. "Only a single regiment is stationed in the city right now. They haven't reinforced at all."

"Hopefully, we won't need to fight. They can see our army here. You shouldn't have a problem convincing them to surrender the town to us."

"I hope you're right. Might as well head down." Nereyda took a step forward, then halted as Devrim gently gripped her shoulder.

"Be careful," he said as he gave her a squeeze.

Nereyda smiled to herself as she slipped from his touch and hiked down the hill toward the edge of the city. Imperial soldiers were taking positions, despite being outnumbered by the rebels. The Empire still hadn't figured out how to react to the rebellion that had erupted.

The gravel crunched under her feet as she followed the road toward the large crossroads town ahead of her. From behind a low wall that wrapped around the edge of the city, a squad of soldiers trained their rifles on her as she approached and crossed the bridge. Before they got too antsy, she raised her hands above her head and kept them visible.

Nereyda stopped about twenty feet away, still on the bridge, and raised her voice. "I've come to parley with the commander of your garrison. I represent the Free Cambisian People."

"That is not a recognized nation," shouted one of the guards. "Our commander is only required to give an audience to officials representing recognized governments."

Nereyda had expected this. "Would you prefer that I signal my friends to attack? Are you ready to die today? You know you won't win."

He frowned and glanced at the army at her back. "Fine. Stay here while we convey your message. Perhaps he'll spare a minute." He nodded to the soldier next to him, who strapped his rifle over his shoulder, then jogged into town.

"Can I lower my hands? Or do you expect me to keep them raised for the whole time I wait?"

"You can lower your hands, but if I even think you're going for your weapons, I'll shoot you where you stand."

"Fine by me." Nereyda sat down on the bridge wall and crossed her legs. "Nice day for a fight, don't you think?" she asked.

The soldier scowled at her but didn't respond.

"Of course, it'd be an even better day for a nice walk. I hear the road east from here is quite lovely this time of year. I think you and your comrades would enjoy a stroll in that direction."

"We're not going to just leave town and let you have it."

"We'll see."

The guard who had left returned with a man in an officer's uniform. A scar cut down the side of his square jaw. "This is Captain Nurullah. He's in charge of the garrison in Trabizan."

"Oh, so you're a captain, too? It's nice to be speaking with someone of equal rank. I didn't think you'd actually come out. Did you see our army and get scared?"

He avoided eye contact and instead peered over her shoulder at the army gathered beyond. "We'll hold our ground as long as we can. And I'm not here to negotiate with you. I needed to see you for myself." His attention turned to her as he looked down his arrow-like nose and sized her up.

"And now that you've seen me in all my glory, what do you think?"

"I think that I don't owe you any more of my time." He turned to one of the other soldiers. "Get the civilians out of their homes and line them up between us and the enemy. We'll see how far these rebels are willing to go." He gave Nereyda a sneer, then turned back toward town.

"In that case," she said with a raised voice, "I demand to face a chosen champion so that I can earn recognition in the Empire's eyes for the purposes of these negotiations."

"Are you really serious about facing our champion?"

"Of course. You think I came all this way with my friends to just turn around and leave?"

He had a dark laugh. "Very well. Our champion has been preparing for battle anyway, so he should be ready." He waved over a nearby soldier. "Run and let him know."

The soldier nodded and ran off.

"Where should we fight?" asked Nereyda. "Here?"

"No, it'll be in the center of the town, so that people can see what happens to someone like you."

"Are you sure you want everyone to see this? It could be pretty embarrassing when he loses."

"Even if you win, that merely grants you an audience and free passage to leave without being arrested as a rebel. It doesn't mean that we will surrender or even listen to you."

Nereyda shrugged. "Let's get this over with, then."

"Follow me," said Nurullah. He pivoted and marched off without waiting to see if Nereyda came along.

The captain led her from the bridge and into the main square of the town. As she swaggered through the streets and projected an attitude of confidence, Nereyda recognized the inn where she had faked the death of a prostitute and framed an Imperial guard captain for it. It would be an amusing memory if it didn't also remind her of Brynja's betrayal.

A raised platform stood in the middle of the square.

A man in shining blue armor sat near the edge of the stage, sharpening the blade of a greatsword. His helmet sat next to him. He looked up as Nereyda approached. "You're the one who challenged me?"

"That's right."

The man chuckled to himself. "And here I thought today was going to be boring." He slowly rose to his feet. He fitted his helmet over his head, then hefted his sword up to rest against his shoulder. He gestured to the stairs that led up onto the stage. "After you."

Nereyda accepted his invitation and hopped onto the platform, but didn't take her eyes off of the knight as he stomped up the stairs behind her. When she reached the center of the stage, she turned to face him, drawing her cutlass.

Around them, soldiers filtered into the square to watch the fight.

With her opponent towering above her, Nereyda circled around him on the platform.

He spat to the side without taking his eyes off of her. "You can start whenever you work up the guts."

Nereyda studied his armor. Aside from the narrow gaps at the joints, there weren't many vulnerable spots for her to stick her sword. Still, she might be able to wear him out.

She lunged and thrust her blade toward a gap near his hip.

He merely turned his torso so that the blow kissed off of his armor, then swung his sword across.

Nereyda ducked and rolled back out of reach. She struck at his left shoulder, and he batted her blade out of the way.

With surprising speed for wielding such a large sword, he brought it back around with a swipe that nearly sliced across Nereyda's chest.

As she sidestepped around him, he lunged and caught her sword with his own. Before Nereyda could yank it free, he backhanded her across the face.

She reeled back, dropping her cutlass.

As he swung his sword down toward Nereyda for a killing blow, she threw her hand out, and a wall of wind rushed out from her hand. The surge of air tossed the knight off of the platform, his armor rattling with the blast. A few loose boards and a handful of nails sprayed through the air as the wind rushed across the stage. The crowd of soldiers kept silent as the knight lay still for a moment. He groaned as he sat up, leaving his sword laying on the ground.

Nereyda wiped the sweat off her forehead and turned to look at the captain, whose eyes were wide. "I knocked him off, so I'm the winner, right? Can we talk about how you're going to leave the city, now?"

"You," said Nurullah. "I should have recognized you from the poster." He rushed over to a building and pulled a piece of paper from the wall, then shoved it toward her. "You're her, aren't you? I should have seen it at first, but now that you cheated with that foul sorcery, I know who you are."

Around the platform, the soldiers shifted uneasily. Some reached toward their rifle straps or rested their hands on the swords on their hips.

Nereyda took the poster from him. A sketch of her own face stared back at her, complete with her purple eyes. She didn't know how the sketch could be so accurate. Underneath her picture, she read,

An Inquisition has been called to find and apprehend the gift thief known as Nereyda. She has been known to manipulate the elements to stir up trouble in the Cambisian Empire and has been declared an enemy of the church and of the Empire. If seen, inform the nearest Imperial garrison or temple as to her whereabouts.

"What's this about?" she asked. "What's a gift thief?"

"You've stolen the power of the gods and are using it for evil. Nereyda, you are under arrest. Champion, grab her for me."

The large man shoved himself up off the ground and picked up his sword, climbed back onto the platform, then stomped toward her. With each step, the wooden platform vibrated under Nereyda's feet.

"You don't want to do this," she said as she tossed the poster to the ground. "I can do more than blow wind at you."

He continued, stepping across the platform.

Nereyda held up her left hand and created sparks between her fingertips. "You really don't want to do this."

Still, he didn't stop.

Before he could reach her, Nereyda held out her hand and sent a bolt of lightning into the armored man. Thunder boomed around the square. He screamed as the electricity coursed through his metal suit. He collapsed onto the ground, and his screams stopped. Looking back at the captain, Nereyda said, "I warned him. If anyone else wants to try, they're welcome to see what they can do. But even if you do take me or kill me, my friends are moving on the city now. You won't last the rest of the day, especially after I take out everyone standing in this square. So, Captain, are you going to surrender Trabizan and live to fight another day, or are you going to see your command wiped out?"

The Imperial captain scowled at Nereyda for a long moment. "Fine. The city is yours. You can tell your rebel friends that we will leave it to you. But your tour of terror won't last forever."

Nereyda watched as he started ordering his troops to prepare to leave the city, then turned to return to the rebel forces. As she left the platform, she snatched up and studied the poster again on the way through the town. In the windows and doors on either side of the road, people peeked out, their faces etched with fear, rather than relief at being liberated.

She picked up the pace to leave behind the accusing stares.

CHAPTER TWENTY-ONE

Back in Antalia, Nereyda huffed as she stormed into Devrim's office. "I don't get it. Antalia was happy to see me sink those ships with lightning. But Trabizan is scared of me? Why do they believe the lies that the Inquisition is spreading?"

Devrim strode from his desk and put a comforting hand on her shoulder. "Most of the Empire's citizens are raised in a rather small bubble. They don't understand anything that's different or anything that challenges their worldview. It's easier to condemn something that you don't understand than it is to learn to understand it."

"What are we going to do about it, though? My powers aren't going away, and I doubt that this Inquisition will suddenly shut up and leave us alone."

"No, I don't expect that it will. However, as more people see you and get to know you, they will realize that you're not here to kill everybody and that you're not some sort of demon. They'll hopefully start to question what the church and Empire are spreading about you. In some ways, I think these people are also scared of the change that our revolution represents. They're so used to living in a cage that the thought of being let out of it scares them. And when that freedom comes from someone who shoots lightning from her fingers, it becomes even scarier. Once they see that life under our leadership is better than life under the Emperor, that fear will go away."

"So what do I do until then?"

"Just keep being you and don't let this Inquisition get to you. Plus, I have something that might help you take your mind off of things for a short time. There is a gathering of nobles coming up, arranged by one of our allies, and I would like you to come with me. The host has invited supporters and potential supporters, and I want them to meet my favorite general."

Nereyda arched an eyebrow. "Favorite general, huh? Is this a professional outing or are you asking me on a date?"

Devrim shrugged. "Can it be both?"

She flashed a smile. "I suppose. What kind of gathering is this?"

"It's a ball at Lord Volkan of Mardin's estate. He's one of our most dedicated supporters, as well as one of the wealthiest."

"Just so I understand you, you want me to go hang out with a bunch of stuffy nobles? I'm not sure if you've paid attention, but I'm not exactly the refined-lady type of person."

"And that's fine. I don't expect you to be. If I wanted a polite lady who would stay quiet, I would bring one."

"When is this ball happening?"

"Five days from now. It isn't far, so we can leave that afternoon and arrive in time for the event in the evening. I have arranged to stay at Volkan's place that night, since I don't know how late it will go. Limbani will also be with us as security."

"Sounds good. Who knows, it can always be fun to mess with nobles."

"Remember, though," he said in a chastising tone, "these nobles are our allies."

"I'll try not to make you regret bringing me, but no promises."

"Great. Now we need to set you up with something to wear."

"Isn't this good enough?" She waved at the clothes she had on.

He raised his eyebrows and laughed. "I'm afraid that walking in dressed like a pirate might put them off a bit. I'll have the tailor bring in something more traditional for you to wear. This is their first time meeting you. Don't want to scare them off just yet."

Nereyda sighed. "Fine, I'll see what you can get for me."

"Great, I'll have my friend Zeki find something for you."

In a spare office that had been turned into a dressing room, Devrim stood next to a small mousy man. A rack of clothes lined the wall, near a three-paneled full-length mirror. "Nereyda, this is Zeki. He's been my tailor and armorer for years. He'll help you pick out something fashionable to wear to the ball."

"Oh good, an afternoon of trying on frilly dresses."

"I'm sure he'll help you find something that you'll like. I'll leave you to it." Devrim closed the door behind him, leaving her with Zeki.

"So, where do we start?" asked Nereyda.

"First," said the tailor, "I need to take your measurements. If you could undress, please."

"Excuse me? I'm not shy, but at least get me a drink first."

The man turned red. "Just down to your undergarments is fine. I don't need to see everything."

"Okay, then." Nereyda pulled off her clothes down to her underwear, and tossed them onto a chair in the corner.

Zeki pulled out a tape measure and spent the next several minutes holding it up to her limbs and wrapping it around her hips, waist, bust, and shoulders, taking notes on a piece of paper as he went. "Very good," he said as he finished and put away the tape. "I think I have something that you might like." He scratched his chin with one hand as he rummaged through the rack with the other. His hand paused on something and he pulled it out, then handed what seemed like a pile of purple fabric to Nereyda. "This should fit you. Step behind the screen and try it on."

She took the dress and stepped behind a divider in one corner of the room and spent several minutes pulling the dress on. When she finished, she felt like she was wearing a mountain of silk. The large billowing skirt reached all the way to the floor, and loose ruffles covered her torso. She shuffled out from behind the screen, trying not to trip on her skirt. "What the hell am I wearing?" Nereyda asked.

"This is what all of the noble ladies wear to formal events. Keep in mind, you'll be wearing a corset underneath it, so it might fit a bit differently when you wear it for real."

"What's the point of a corset? Not like you'll be able to tell under all these ruffles."

The tailor shrugged. "That is the style lately. While you may see some more risqué outfits among the lower classes, the nobility is still quite conservative."

Nereyda tried to practice some fencing footwork, but the skirt proved cumbersome. "How is someone supposed to fight in this?"

Zeki chuckled. "And why would you need to fight in your dress?"

"In case you haven't noticed, we're in the middle of a little rebellion. Who knows what could happen at this ball? If anyone finds out about it, it could be an easy target."

"I think you are perhaps a bit paranoid, miss."

"Maybe, but I'd rather be ready."

"As a lady, you will not be expected to fight in the event of such an attack."

"But I will fight nonetheless." She held her skirt up and shuffled her way toward him. "Tell me, Zeki, don't you ever get tired of making the same style of dresses, without being able to do something truly creative?"

He shrugged. "It's what the lords and ladies order. I don't get a lot of room for creativity."

"Devrim said you're an armorer, too, right?"

"That's right, though only for leather armor."

"Perfect. I want to place an order for something a bit different than what you're used to making. Something that I can fight in. We're fighting a rebellion, so why not start a bit of a fashion revolution at the same time?"

Zeki smiled. "I think I'd welcome the chance for something new. What do you have in mind?"

Nereyda spent the next several minutes describing what she wanted as the tailor took notes and sketched out a rough drawing to visualize the design. As they went, his eyes lit up, and his writing became faster and more animated.

"How long will it take to make this? Can you get it done in time for the ball?"

"Don't worry, I'll make it happen. This is the most excited I've been to make a dress in a long time. I'll get started as soon as I get back to my shop. I'll deliver it myself the day of the ball."

CHAPTER TWENTY-TWO

Erhan stewed in the back corner of a shady tavern in Trabizan. He took a large swig of his ale, finishing his second mug of the evening. He had received a message from an unknown sender to meet at the tavern. Erhan knew that it could only be one person. After nearly getting stabbed at the previous meeting, he had considered skipping this one. However, if his contact could find him so easily, he doubted he could run far.

A familiar figure in a cloak swept into the tavern and glided across the floor toward Erhan's booth, helping himself to a seat.

"Hello, Commander." An unsettling smile crept across the man's face, though the shadow from his hood obscured his eyes. "I see you got my message."

"Why do you want to meet? To chastise me for missing Nereyda? I got here just after she left following the rebel attack. I'm lucky that nobody recognized me. Otherwise, I doubt they'd have let me wander into town."

"No, I am not here to express any sort of disappointment." Somehow, the friendly tone came across as creepier than any chastisement might have. "Quite the contrary, in fact. Since we last spoke, you've managed to start an Inquisition, and you've made this town scared of our pirate friend."

"The only thing I did was hang up some posters with her face on it."

"Yes," he said with a hiss. "And then she walked into town and fried a man with lightning, confirming the horror your posters warned them about. I'd say that's quite a good start."

"But a start is all it is. This Inquisition is a joke so far. The church priests have been encouraging with their words, but they've barely given me any resources aside from some paper and ink to print posters."

The man pointed at Erhan with a long, spindly finger. "Don't talk yourself into being frustrated. My employer has a lead that might help you in your search. That's why I wanted to meet you as soon as possible. This may be the best opportunity yet to catch our target unaware."

"I'm listening."

"There are reports that Lord Volkan is holding a ball for potential rebel supporters, and the rebel leader is going to be in attendance to try to secure allies. We believe that Nereyda will be there with him. Following this ball, the next logical target of the rebels is Goremia. You are to apprehend our person of interest while she is on the road."

"Why is Volkan willing to help the rebels? Hasn't he been one of the Emperor's strongest servants in the west?"

"We can only guess as to what the good lord's motivations are."

"He's not your employer, is he?"

The man's lips stretched like two worms across his face as he smiled. "He might be. Or he might not be. Even if you did guess correctly, I couldn't possibly tell you. You're welcome to keep guessing, though. It's endlessly entertaining."

Erhan furrowed his brow. "Why can't I go to this party and capture Nereyda there?"

"Because my employer does not want you to interfere with this event. The Inquisition cannot be an organization that invades the homes of the nobility on a whim. And if you do so and are caught, that will drive the nobles toward the rebellion and away from us. You will take her on the road as instructed."

Erhan did not care about that. It would be far easier to catch Nereyda at a party than on the road when she would be surrounded by the rebel army. Still, the man seemed adamant, so Erhan would play along for the moment. "Very well, I'll set a trap to catch her on the road."

The man clasped his dexterous hands and rubbed them together. "Good. My employer will be pleased."

He rose and started toward the door. Erhan slid out of his seat, rushed behind the cloaked man, and pressed his dagger to his back. With his other hand, Erhan caught the man's hand before he could grab his dagger.

The man went rigid. "What are you doing?" he said with a snarl.

"I'm tired of being played like a pawn. How can I get into that party?"

"You've made a terrible mistake. My employer will not stand for this."

"And you won't stand at all if you don't help me." Erhan pressed the point into the man's back.

He tried to pull away, but couldn't. "Fine. You need an invitation."

"Who would have one?"

"A lot of people."

Erhan shoved him down into the booth and pointed the dagger at his throat. "Make a list and I'll find one of them."

CHAPTER TWENTY-THREE

Nereyda paced back and forth as she waited for the tailor to arrive with her outfit. Devrim had no idea that she had arranged a special order with Zeki. She couldn't wait to see his face when she revealed the rather unorthodox dress she had helped design.

A knock came at the door to her room at the rebel headquarters in Antalia, and she hurried to open it. When she pulled the door inward, Zeki stood outside, holding a large garment bag with a hanger sticking out the top. "Here it is. This has been the most fun I've ever had making a custom dress." He handed the bag to Nereyda.

"Thank you, Zeki. I can't believe I'm actually excited to wear a dress."

He drew himself up with pride. "My dresses do have that effect on people."

"I don't doubt it. Let me put this on, then you can see your work in action."

"You should be able to put it on yourself, but if you need any assistance, I'll be standing just out here."

First, she put on the black leather corset, with laces on the front so she could dress without help. The steel ribbing proved stiff as she laced it up, but she yanked it tight enough to provide the support she needed while leaving it loose enough for her to breathe. She pulled sheer black stockings over her legs. Next, she pulled on the long purple dress and laced up the front. The skirt extended down to just above her ankles so she wouldn't trip over it. A slit on each side of the dress ran from hip to hem, revealing the sides of her legs. The upper portion of the dress had long sleeves with laced forearms. The neckline was open and low-cut. Finally, she pulled on the bodice, which featured an interior of black leather and an exterior of dark violet silk. It hugged her waist and came to a point at the top of her skirt. An open diamond from the bottom of her bust to a clasp on her neck revealed a hint of cleavage above the dress fabric. Sitting on the edge of her bed, she pulled on black, low-heeled boots that reached the middle of her calves.

Standing up, she took a look at herself in the mirror, turning to catch every angle that she could. She smiled to herself. It was exactly what she had imagined. The form flattered her figure, the color matched her eyes, and she felt as if she could actually fight in it. She practiced a lunging thrust and was thrilled when her legs didn't get caught. "Zeki," she called through the door, "come on in and see how you did."

The tailor entered and looked her up and down, making her spin around as he examined every inch of his outfit. He beamed. "It fits perfectly."

"It feels great."

"You'll be the biggest scandal at the ball," he said with a devilish smile.

"Oh, I hope so," she replied, winking at him.

"Do you want to do anything with your hair? If so, I can go grab a hairdresser."

"No, I'm all right. I'll leave it loose. I like it this way."

"You do look lovely. You'll turn some heads tonight, I think."

"You didn't tell Devrim about this special project, did you?"

"Of course not. It'll be a surprise to him."

"Then let's go see how far his jaw drops."

She instinctively grabbed her sword belt and had begun to fit it around her waist when Zeki cleared his throat, and she realized what she was doing. "This isn't going to work, is it? I'm making enough of a statement without carrying a sword."

"It would likely get in the way of dancing, miss."

Nereyda pulled the belt off and wrapped it around the sheath. "I guess I'll give this to Limbani to hold on to."

She left her room with the tailor behind her, and glided down the stairs with a sway in her hips to the foyer of the building. Near the main double doors, Devrim leaned against the wall, reading a note in the light from a sconce next to him. "I was beginning to think you might be standing me up, pirate. Our carriage is waiting just outside."

"Oh, I'm ready. It's been a while, so I wanted to make sure my dress was on just right."

He lowered the note and turned to look at her, his eyes widening. "What are you wearing? Zeki, that's nothing like the dresses I had you bring for her to try on. Nereyda, what was wrong with those choices?" Despite the exasperation in his voice, his eyes traveled the length of the slits in her dress and stopped at the opening in her bodice before his gaze returned to her face.

"I wanted something that I could move in." She put her hand on her hip and flashed him a smile. "Besides, it seems that you enjoy the view. I'm sure you won't be the only one to look at me like that tonight."

"This isn't a night to attract unnecessary attention." His eyes kept returning to the more revealing parts of her dress. He caught himself and cleared his throat. "This is not the sort of dress the noble ladies wear. Zeki, do you have anything else that she could use?"

"I don't need another dress, but I think we do need to get going. Aren't we running late?"

"We can wait for you to change into something . . . more suitable."

"It's not like I'm walking into the ball naked. Besides, you're the one who wanted to bring me even though I'm not your average lady." She waved her weapon toward him. "If you want to bring me, that includes what I choose to wear."

"And why, exactly, are you bringing your sword?" he asked with a snarl. "Do you plan on killing our host? Challenging the other guests to duels?" He extended his hand and attempted to grab the cutlass from her.

She yanked it out of reach. "I'm bringing this sword because, in case you had forgotten, we're in the middle of a rebellion. Do you trust our host to keep us safe? I can fight, so I should be ready to do so. Now, let's not keep our host waiting any longer than we have to." Nereyda whirled away from him and strode to the double doors and shoved through them.

Outside, a dark blue carriage with silver trim along the edges and around the windows and doorframe stood hitched to a pair of horses. Limbani stood at attention next to the carriage. Devrim stomped to the front to talk to the driver who sat above and behind the horses.

Nereyda shoved her sword belt toward Limbani. "Hey Limbani, can you keep track of this for me tonight?"

Limbani arched an eyebrow at her, and she tentatively reached out and grabbed the belt. "You're bringing a sword to the ball?"

"You're bringing it, and if I need it, you can toss it to me."

The rebel general wrapped the belt around her waist and situated it so that Nereyda's cutlass hung off the opposite hip as her own saber. "If you say so, though I don't expect trouble at this thing."

"I learned firsthand that wandering into something without being ready can get you into trouble. That's how I got captured. Twice. I don't want to take any chances. Besides, you wouldn't turn down instant backup, would you?"

"No, at least not after seeing you fight. I like your dress, by the way."

"Thanks. I've never been into dresses since they're not practical on a ship, but I could see myself enjoying wearing something like this more often. But Devrim's not too keen on it. He thinks I'll stand out too much." Nereyda leaned toward Limbani and whispered, "I think he likes it, though. He's definitely been checking me out."

Limbani chuckled. "I don't blame him."

Devrim marched over to them and pulled the carriage door open.

"That's usually my job, sir," remarked Limbani.

"I know. After you, Nereyda." His words were terse. He tried to keep his glances at her furtive, but he had trouble keeping his eyes away. She couldn't tell if he was glaring at her or checking her out. Perhaps a bit of both.

Nereyda smiled as she ducked her head down to climb into the carriage and sat on the rear bench, facing the front of the carriage. Devrim sat across from her, while Limbani closed the door behind them and took a spot next to Devrim.

"Maybe you missed out on all of the etiquette training since you didn't grow up as a noble, but aren't you supposed to compliment your date on how she looks?" asked Nereyda.

Devrim smiled at her and let out an amused huff. "You do look gorgeous. I'm sorry that I've forgotten my manners. You took me by surprise, and I reacted poorly."

"What's so wrong with standing out, anyway?"

"These people we're about to see—most nobles, really—are surprisingly sheltered from the world, despite the education that they can afford. They wall themselves off, often literally, and pay servants to take care of any dirty work. Any sort of change can seem intimidating to them."

"If someone feels threatened by a woman in a dress, they're not going to be a very worthwhile ally, are they?"

"Unfortunately, this is the game we have to play. I can't imagine being successful without at least some support from the nobility. And you know we're broke. We need the money."

"But if they're so afraid of change, why would they help us? Isn't overthrowing the Emperor rather a big change? Do they actually care enough about the average person to invest in our rebellion?"

"Most of them are blind to how the average citizen lives. While some of them are sympathetic, as I am, many of them are interested in our cause for less than altruistic reasons. They may see it as a chance to gain influence or wealth. Some of them are from families who have fallen into disfavor with the Imperial court and are looking to change their fortunes."

"Seems like that would make them unreliable allies. How can you count on them to stick with you when it gets tough?"

"The pirate's complaining about potentially unreliable allies?" he asked with raised eyebrows. "Aren't you just in this for a ship?"

Nereyda smiled slightly. "You know I could have taken a ship anytime I wanted to, right?"

"But you didn't. Why not?"

She shrugged. "Maybe I care about my friends in Antalia."

"I saw that. They saw it, too, when you led them. You've also been on the receiving end of what the Empire considers justice. You, perhaps, deserved it for being a pirate, but not everyone did."

She nodded at him and turned to look out the window as the countryside rolled by. They passed verdant hills and towering forests. Peasants worked the land and chopped trees, seemingly oblivious to the civil war around them. On top of one of the hills, a small château looked out over the area, the sun glinting off its blue roof.

A couple of hours later, as the sun sank toward the horizon, they crested a hill, and one of the largest estates Nereyda had ever seen came into view. The center of the grounds was dominated by a sprawling mansion that rose four stories, made with white marble walls and golden trim. Lush and colorful gardens stretched out from the building. Outbuildings such as a stable, gardening shed, and guardhouse were scattered around the edge of the area. A wall of marble pillars and iron grating surrounded the complex.

"I haven't seen a place as big as this since I was at the Imperial Palace," said Nereyda.

"Well, that's fitting since our host is sometimes called the 'Emperor of the West,' though not within earshot of the actual Emperor."

"Where did he get the money for all of this?"

"Lord Volkan consulted in the expansion and further development of the whole mining complex. It was a very lucrative contract."

Nereyda's eyes narrowed. "We're allied with someone who profited off of creating that terrible place?"

"I didn't say I like it. But someone with his wealth is an incredible ally, or could be a very problematic enemy."

"That place was hell for my crew. Enough so that it broke my first mate to the point that she betrayed me. I'm not sure I can set that aside and play nice with one of the people most responsible for creating that place."

"If you can't play nice, then fake a smile and stay quiet. I know you're not really one to bite your tongue, but do it as a favor to me. I'll handle talking to our host, and you can go make friends with everyone else."

"I'll do my best not to piss people off."

"With that diplomatic mouth of yours, I don't think you'll have any problems," Devrim said with a smirk.

They pulled up to the gate of the estate, and a guard reached up to the side window of the carriage.

"Invitation, please," the man said.

Devrim pulled his invitation out of his jacket pocket and handed it to the guard, who gave it a quick scan before passing it back.

"Welcome, Lord Devrim. We'll open the gate for you, and you can pull in. Passengers may exit directly in front of the house, then your driver can park in an area that we've set aside near the stable. Our staff will attend to your horses."

"Very good, thank you and your lord for your hospitality."

"My lord aims to be a gracious host, and he appreciates your attendance tonight," the guard said with a bow before he returned to his post where he awaited the next guest.

The iron gate rattled open in front of them, and the carriage trundled through and up the driveway toward the house. When they stopped, Limbani stood and opened the door ahead of them. Devrim stepped out next and held up a hand toward Nereyda. She gave a soft laugh as she took his hand and accepted his support as she climbed out of the carriage.

"Such a gentleman," she said.

"I'm good at pretending. And you're good at faking being a lady."

"Let's see how our disguises hold up. Lead the way," she said with a wave toward the house.

Devrim held out his arm and Nereyda linked hers through it. Giant doors stretched up two stories of the front of the structure and appeared to be made of solid gold. As they approached, one of the guards standing on the side of the doors reached up to one of the heavy knockers and swung it against the door three short times. With each knock, the door boomed with a deep tone. A moment later, the doors pulled open. Limbani trailed behind them as they entered.

Nereyda's eyes threatened to pop out of her head as she took in the opulent entrance hall. The hall rose three stories, with staircases both to the left and the right of the doors. They spiraled up to walkways that lined the second and third floors, then disappeared up into the fourth floor above. The hall stretched at least the length of a frigate toward another set of golden doors at the other end. A shimmering reflecting pool occupied the center of the hall.

"I've never seen anything like this," she said to Devrim, her eyes devouring the statues and paintings that lined the grand hall. Hallways led into other wings on each side.

"Me neither. I've never been here. I've only heard descriptions from other people, but I always thought they were exaggerations. He's not afraid to show off his wealth."

"Maybe he's just compensating for something."

Devrim chuckled. "Don't say that to his face."

As they reached the other end, servants pulled the doors open, and they stepped into the ballroom. The wooden dance floor stretched out in front of them, while staircases on each side led up to a second floor that surrounded the dance floor. Another pair of stairways led to a third tier. A small orchestra was setting up in the corner of the dance floor. Scattered groups of people were on the two levels above, wandering around or leaning on the railings. Heaps of billowing fabric roamed the floors, with women's heads poking out the tops of their dresses.

"Looks like we're just a bit early, which is good," said Devrim. "It'll give us a chance to greet our host without feeling rushed."

Devrim and Nereyda climbed the stairs to the third tier, while Limbani drifted toward a group of servants and bodyguards. Nereyda felt the eyes of the other guests on her as they walked up to a man and a woman standing at the far end of the cavernous chamber, where they could gaze down on anyone who entered. The man appeared to be about middle aged, with a trace of silver in his black hair and faint wrinkles on his otherwise strong face. He stood tall and broad-shouldered in his light-gray suit. The woman wore a green dress with a wide skirt and had her golden hair twisted into a coil on her head. She wrinkled her nose when her eyes fell on Nereyda.

"Ah, Lord Devrim of Ascaya," said the man in a booming voice as he held out his hand. "I'm glad to see that you've arrived safely. How was the trip here?"

Nereyda gave Devrim a sideways glance at the formal title, but held her tongue.

"Very smooth," said Devrim. "Thank you, Lord Volkan, for hosting this ball for us."

"You don't have to thank me. You're the one doing all the hard work out there."

"Well, it isn't just me. I want to introduce you to General Nereyda. She's been instrumental in our campaign so far. Without her, we wouldn't have captured a prize like Antalia."

"Oh, yes, the pirate," he said with a touch of condescension. Their host's eyes grazed down and back up, looking Nereyda over, before he extended his hand. "Pleased to meet you, General. I must say, your dress is quite unique. Very lovely, as well, if a bit unexpected." His smile contained half of a sneer.

Nereyda took his hand but didn't quite turn her body fully toward him, looking at him at an angle. "Thank you. Devrim's tailor is quite creative. And you can just call me Nereyda. I'm not really one for fancy titles."

"Still, we took Antalia for the price of just a few pirates and rebels. Quite a bargain for us. It is a title you've earned, I'd say."

Volkan's words stabbed into the memory of Elvar's death and of the civilians who died in the bombardment. "True, I did earn it, which is more than can be said of some people."

The lord's eyes narrowed at the remark. "What do you mean by that?"

Devrim tugged on her elbow and cleared his throat. "I'm sure you have more guests that would like to speak with you, my lord host. Perhaps we can speak later about some of our more formal business."

"Very well, I would like that. Please enjoy yourselves."

"Come, Reyda, let's sample some of the food that looks so delicious."

"I'm not hungry right now," Nereyda said as she pushed Devrim's hand away. "And our host asked me a question." She ignored Devrim's warning look as she turned back to Volkan. "I meant exactly what I said. Not everybody earns or deserves the titles they've been given. Some are born into them. Some buy them. And some very special people get there by profiting off of the suffering of others."

Volkan leaned back and took in a deep breath through his nose, puffing up his chest. "It seems Lord Devrim has told you of my success with the mines."

"Success? That's what you call it?"

"Nereyda, please, now isn't the time," said Devrim.

She pulled away from Devrim and crossed her arms in front of her chest. "And when exactly is the time? It's easy for you to tell me to be quiet when none of you have been to the mines to see what it does firsthand. I have been there. I know what it does to people. I may have only been there for a few days, but my crew was there for months. I still see the scars on their backs and how they wince in pain sometimes as they move. I've listened to them cry out in the night and held them as they calmed down. Have you done the same? Have you witnessed what your 'success' does to people?"

"The Empire would have made that facility with or without my help. Someone else would have done the work to expand and develop it. If it had to happen, why shouldn't I be the one to do it?"

"Is that what you tell yourself to keep your own demons away?"

He placed a dramatic hand on his chest and spoke with a practiced sadness. "My heart breaks for the people, like your crew, who have been made to suffer there. It truly does."

"Perhaps, but I bet it's more comfortable to cry in a beautiful house like this than it is to weep in a dark hole in the earth. Is your broken heart why you've decided to back this rebellion? All of a sudden, you want to make up for the damage you've done and become a friend to the poor? Or are you just hoping to take your mines back and fill them with the prisoners of this war?"

He stood rigid and peered down his nose. "You're questioning my dedication to our cause?"

"You're damn right I am. If you're so dedicated, why hide in your fancy mansion, away from the fighting? You smell like a coward and an opportunist."

Volkan's face turned bright red. "Why, I've never been so insulted."

"Good. Maybe you should be insulted more often. It might teach you something."

"Okay, that's more than enough, Nereyda," Devrim said with a hint of a growl. He yanked her away and tugged her outside onto one of the balconies that lined the third floor. "What was that all about? I thought you agreed to play it cool."

"I did before I heard him talking like that. You heard what he said. He brushed off the people who gave their lives to take Antalia. They and the people in the mines are nothing more than objects to him. He doesn't care about people. He just wants whatever's best for himself."

"I know all of that. But we need to be pragmatic. This war isn't free, and with his support, we can buy a lot of supplies."

"Is it worth it though? Do you really want an ally like that? If he's an opportunist and is backing you, that means he thinks you're going to win. And if he ever senses that you could lose, he won't hesitate to turn on you."

"If that wasn't true before, it definitely is now after you called him a coward to his face." He relaxed his grip on her arm. "Look, I'm going to go try to fix this mess and smooth things over with him. Maybe it's best if you get some food and mingle with the other guests."

"You trust me to talk to more nobles? I don't need a babysitter?"

"None of the others have helped with anything like the mines, so I think you should be fine. Maybe stick with small talk this time. We don't need another incident." He slowly moved his hand away from her.

"Oh, nobles always love me." She winked at him. "Don't worry about me."

Devrim hesitated before turning away and heading back to their host.

Nereyda scanned the people nearby and spotted a group of four nobles clustered together near a tall table, with glasses of dark crimson wine and small plates of grilled calamari. They appeared to be two couples. A tall, thin man in a crisp black suit stood next to a woman in a flowing red dress who had her golden hair pulled up. The other couple consisted of a woman in a billowing blue dress with brown braided hair and a broad-shouldered man in a dark brown jacket.

They faced Nereyda as she approached. "Mind if I join you?" She slid into the space between the couples without waiting for a response.

"Oh, please do," said the blonde woman. "I'm Aliya, and this is my husband, Kerem of Sanliurfa. And our friends are Idris and Nebila of Kas."

"I'm Nereyda." She shook all of their hands.

"So you're the pirate, then," said Aliya.

"I suppose I am. My name keeps reaching places before I do."

"From what I've heard, I can understand why. You're not here to rob us, are you?" the woman asked with a twinkle in her eye.

"Not tonight, at least. Figured I should take the day off. Unless you're carrying something valuable; then I might make an exception." She smirked at the nobles.

Aliya laughed, but the others stiffened up.

"I'm not sure this is the company we should be keeping, Aliya," said Kerem.

"Lighten up. This is supposed to be a fun evening. Nereyda, do you have any good stories for us?"

Nereyda shrugged. "Several, but I'm not sure many of them are good for polite company."

"Maybe you can start with how you met Lord Devrim?"

"Well, I was trying to rob him, actually."

The nobles stared at her with wide eyes.

Since she had their attention, she jumped into the whole story about how she had broken into Devrim's mansion and found him conspiring to start the rebellion.

"So you blackmailed him into helping you?" asked Nebila.

Nereyda swiped a piece of calamari from Aliya's plate, though she didn't seem to mind. "That's right. I told him I would spill his secret if he didn't."

"And yet he trusts you now?" asked Idris.

"I think so. Nothing like a little rebellion to bring people closer together."

"I want to hear more," said Aliya.

Nereyda acquiesced and shared a few more stories from her time as a pirate. Her new noble friends seemed both horrified and amused, though maybe a touch more amused.

As the group of nobles laughed, something brushed her arm. She turned and found Devrim standing at her shoulder. "Ah, you're back," she said. "Devrim, do you know these fine people?"

"I don't think I've had the pleasure." He shook hands and exchanged introductions with the group.

"Oh, we know who you are," said Aliya. "You're part of the reason for all of these festivities. After talking with Nereyda, my husband and I will certainly make a donation to the cause."

"Us, as well," said Idris.

"Wonderful!" Devrim clapped his hands together and bowed slightly. "I can't tell you how grateful I am. We'll put it to good use."

"As long as you can change things so we can wear dresses like hers," Nebila said as she pointed to Nereyda, "that's good enough for me."

"Thank you, again. Nereyda, would you perhaps like to go dance for a bit?"

She shrugged a shoulder. "Sure, that could be fun."

Nereyda accompanied Devrim down to the dance floor, where other couples were swirling around each other in time to the music. They found space in between the other people.

Devrim took her hand and placed his other hand on her waist. As Nereyda put her hand on his shoulder, she couldn't help but appreciate the solid muscle she felt through his dress jacket.

Nereyda allowed Devrim to take the lead since she didn't have much experience with ballroom dancing. However, she picked it up quickly. The steps weren't too different than sword fighting and lacked the distraction of someone trying to kill her. And while her dress had been designed to make fighting easier, it also let her move freely as she twirled around the ballroom.

Devrim guided her effortlessly around the dance floor. As she settled into the rhythm, Nereyda asked, "So did I mess everything up for us?"

"No, I had him laughing about it after a couple of drinks. He admires your spirit and just isn't used to someone doing that to him. Don't beat yourself up over it. He needed to hear what you had to say, even if it ruffled him a little. And I'm sorry I got angry with you. You shouldn't feel bad about speaking your mind, especially when you're right."

Nereyda smirked at him. "When I'm right? Generally, assume that

I am."

Devrim laughed. "So far, I think that's true." He surprised her by spinning her around, and she giggled. It had been a long time since she had had this kind of fun with anybody.

After a couple of songs, Nereyda felt warm, either from the dancing or how her heart raced when she was with Devrim. "I'm going to step out onto the balcony to cool off for a minute."

"Sounds good. I'm going to take a look at the food table."

Nereyda climbed the stairs and drifted out onto the balcony, finding a spot with nobody else around. The fresh air on her face refreshed her as she caught her breath. She closed her eyes and inhaled the cool air.

"Hello, pirate."

Nereyda spun around to find a sword pointed at her chest. Her gaze followed the blade to its owner. She gasped as she recognized him. "Erhan. How the hell did you get in here?"

"I have an invitation." He gave her a smug smile as he reached into his jacket with his free hand and pulled out an envelope, then held it out at arm's length.

Nereyda kept her eyes on him as she took it and flipped the envelope open. Just as Erhan had said, it contained what looked like a legitimate invitation. "How did you get this?"

"I have friends. You don't need to know the details. What you do need is to start moving."

"Somehow, I don't think people are going to let you shove me out of here at the point of a sword."

"Let me worry about that. You turn and walk that way." He pointed toward a door that led into the main house, rather than the ballroom.

"Fine." Nereyda dragged her feet as she moved toward the door.

"I know you can move faster than this."

"I'm in a dress. It slows me down."

"I don't care. Pick it up."

She lengthened her stride and picked up the pace. After a few steps, she feigned tripping on her dress and rolled onto the ground.

"Get up." Erhan grabbed her left arm to haul her to her feet.

With her right hand, she punched Erhan in the face, then wrenched his sword from his grasp.

"My turn to tell you what to do," she said with a snarl. Nereyda paused to snatch Erhan's invitation from where it had fallen on the ground and tucked it into her bodice. Then, she grabbed Erhan by the collar and shoved him into the ballroom with her sword digging into his back.

Spotting their host, she marched toward him.

Nereyda threw Erhan down at the feet of Volkan, then grabbed Erhan's invitation from her bodice and shoved it into Volkan's hands, all while holding Erhan's sword at the ready.

Erhan tried to scramble away, but Nereyda stomped down on his ankle before she returned her gaze to Volkan.

"Want to tell me how he ended up getting invited to your party? Seems like quite a coincidence that someone who wants to kill me managed to get in."

"I swear, I'd never let a guest be harmed under my roof. I have no idea how he got an invitation."

"Why should anyone believe you? You clearly do anything for a profit, no matter who gets hurt along the way. You're trying to play both sides by selling me out to the Empire." She sprang closer and pressed the tip of Erhan's sword against his chest.

The crowd let out a collective gasp.

Devrim and Limbani pushed through the crowd. "What's going on here?" Devrim asked.

Nereyda ignored him. "Limbani, make sure this one doesn't go anywhere," she said, pointing at Erhan.

Limbani nodded.

Nereyda glanced around at the crowd, who stared at her with wide eyes and open mouths. "What? Is it rude to threaten the host even after he probably tried to kill me? I'm sure the rest of you are tired of living in his shadow. If you actually care about the rebellion, join us. Don't do it for money or position, because if you do, I think you'll be sorely disappointed and quite likely find yourself on the wrong side of the next revolution. Either stand with us and be prepared to make some sacrifices or get the hell out of our way because we're coming for you one way or another."

"What do you want from me?" Volkan asked in a shaky voice.

Nereyda turned back to him. "I want you to open your treasury to us. You're going to fund this rebellion with every last bit of gold you have. You accumulated it on the backs of the lowest people in the Empire, and now it's time to give it all back to help make it right."

"You want everything? I refuse."

"Really?" She pressed the sword harder against his sternum. He winced at the pain. "I could kill you in front of your guests, take what I want, then let your other guests pick over the scraps. Cooperate, though, and you'll at least get to keep the house."

Sweat dripped down his face as he stared at Nereyda with gritted teeth. "Fine," he spat. "Take whatever you need, then get the hell out of my house."

"Perfect. We'll probably have to wait until the morning to get started on hauling away what we need, though. In the meantime, I want to use your quarters." She gave Volkan a nasty smile, then winked at Devrim. "Let's go."

After making sure that Volkan and Erhan had been properly secured for the night, Nereyda retired with Devrim to the lord's quarters.

As she pulled open the gold-inlaid double doors, she gawked at the interior. Everything seemed over the top. Between the extra-large mattress, the painted tile floors, and the intricately carved furniture, their host hadn't spared any expense.

"Well, he definitely knows how to waste money."

Devrim laughed. "His tastes are definitely . . ."

"Gaudy?"

"I was going to say opulent, but yes."

As Devrim pulled the doors shut, Nereyda paced around the quarters, looking into the spacious washroom and the lady's bedroom that attached to the main bedchamber.

"Hmm, I guess if I was married to that bastard, I wouldn't want to sleep in the same bed as him, either," Nereyda remarked.

"Reyda, I have to say, you were remarkable down there. I never expected tonight to go the way it did."

"What can I say? I know how to get what I want."

"You certainly do. I don't think I could imagine tonight going any better."

"Really?" Nereyda asked with a wry grin. "There's nothing else that would make it better?" She let her hips swing as she glided up to him.

His eyes glanced down then back up to her face, and he smiled. "I suppose there might be something. Are you sure you want this?"

She leaned into him and teased his earlobe with her teeth before she whispered, "Oh, I've been sure since before we left the ballroom.

And, as we both know, I know how to get what I want." She started undoing Devrim's shirt, deftly moving from one button to the next.

"This is going to be quite the scandal, the two of us."

"I don't care." As Devrim's shirt fell from his shoulders, Nereyda ran her hands over his bare chest and bit her lip as she felt his firm muscles, her heart hammering in her chest. She took a deep breath of his pine scent. "This, though—this I do care about. Your turn." She pointed to the laces on the front of her bodice.

He pulled the laces loose and, after tossing her bodice to the ground, pushed her dress off of her shoulders. "You know this is completely improper."

"And you know that makes me want it even more." Nereyda let the dress fall to the ground and kicked it to the side, then let Devrim undo her corset.

He started working on the laces, but his hands shook, and his fingers fumbled. "Sorry, I should be better at this."

"As long as you're better at using your fingers for other things, we'll be just fine." Nereyda took over and undid her own laces, then let the corset fall to the ground, stepping back to let Devrim gaze at her bare body.

His eyes devoured every inch of her. "You're even better than I imagined."

Nereyda put her hands on her hips. "So you've been imagining me, huh?"

"Of course, though I didn't quite know what to expect."

"Then shut up and let me outdo your imagination again."

Nereyda dropped to her knees and undid Devrim's breeches. Finally, she got Devrim to stop talking.

CHAPTER TWENTY-FOUR

Erhan sat in a cell below the mansion, with Volkan on the ground next to him. The dungeon around them was small and gloomy. A lone guard sat dozing in a chair at the base of the stairway that led to the house above.

"I can't believe I'm being held captive in my own home. That pirate's ruined everything."

"Oh, I'm familiar with that feeling. That's why I chased her down to your party."

"Don't try to be friendly with me. You're part of the reason I'm here. I don't know you, and I certainly don't know how you got an invitation."

Erhan had no shortage of disdain for Volkan. He had been one of the Emperor's strongest servants and had grown absurdly wealthy as a result. Yet, he had tossed aside his loyalty to support the rebels who would burn it all down. However, he resisted the temptation to argue and instead focused on escaping. "I have my ways. But now we're both in the same predicament. Do you know a way out of here?"

"Out of the cell? No. But if we could get out of the cell, there is a secret way out of the dungeon. Though, as I said, we'd need a way out of our cell."

"Don't you have a wife? Shouldn't we bring her with us?"

"Ah, yes. They put her up in one of the servants' rooms. She should be comfortable enough for the time being," he said in a bored voice. "I'll get out and return once they leave my house."

"Is that guard one of yours?" Erhan nodded toward the sleeping man.

"He used to be. Who knows right now?"

"Try asking him."

Volkan stood up and peeked through the bars on the side of the cell closest to the guard. "Hey, Haluk, wake up."

The guard's head jerked up, and he squinted as he overcame his disorientation. "What is it, sir?"

"Can you let me out of here?"

"I'm sorry, but I can't do that."

"And how long have you been a member of my household guard? How long has your family served me?"

"I've served for five years, and my family has served yours for generations. But I'm afraid the other nobles are quite insistent that I watch you. I'm trapped as much as you are. I'd let you out if I could, but they've made it quite clear that they know where my family is."

"If you let us out, I'll make sure they're unharmed."

"I'm sorry, sir, but I can't take that risk." Haluk gave a regretful smile, then pulled a small figurine out of his pocket, drew his dagger, and started whittling.

Volkan whispered into Erhan's ear, "Any other ideas?"

"One, but you're not going to like it."

"If it gets us out of here, do whatever you need to."

Erhan inhaled deeply, then raised his voice. "If a traitor like you didn't host a party like this in the first place, I wouldn't be stuck in a cell with a damn rebel." He hauled his fist back, channeling his disdain for the traitorous noble, and struck Volkan across the jaw with an unnecessarily hard hit.

Volkan staggered back and gazed at Erhan with wide, disbelieving eyes.

"Whoa, whoa, whoa," called Haluk. "Break it up." The guard jogged to their cell and fumbled with his keys.

Realization dawned in Volkan's eyes. "How is this my fault? If your Imperial ass hadn't crashed my party, I'd be up in my own bed right now." He charged Erhan and shoved him into the wall.

The cell lock clicked open, and Haluk hurried into the cell. As soon as he was inside, Volkan and Erhan tackled him to the ground, taking his sword and key ring.

They rushed out of the cell and Volkan locked it behind them. "I'm sorry, my friend," said Volkan to the stammering guard who was still processing what had happened. "I hope they don't punish your family for this."

"Come on," said Erhan. "Where is that secret passage?"

Nereyda smiled to herself as she lay curled up in bed later that night, with Devrim's arms wrapped around her. It had been a long time since she had had that much fun in bed. She had especially enjoyed surprising Devrim with her willingness to do things he'd never tried before.

A knock sounded at the door.

Devrim snorted but kept sleeping. Nereyda ignored the sound.

It came again, more insistently.

"Go away," Nereyda yelled.

"It's me, Limbani," came a voice through the door. "It's about Volkan and Erhan."

"Fine, just a second," said Nereyda.

She shook Devrim awake. "Get dressed. Limbani needs to talk to us."

He grumbled as he rolled out of bed and tossed on a shirt and pair of pants. Nereyda sprang out of bed and found a robe that must have belonged to Volkan's wife. As she tied it around her waist, she rushed to the doors. She pushed one open. "Come in."

Limbani slipped into the room and averted her gaze as she took in Devrim and Nereyda in the bedchamber. A professional, she composed herself quickly. "Erhan and Volkan have escaped. I don't know how. Their guard was locked in their cell and said they didn't use the stairs, but he didn't see exactly where they went."

"Bastard must have another way out," said Devrim.

"And you've searched the estate?" asked Nereyda.

"Entirely. No sign of either of them."

"Where do you think they'd go?" asked Devrim.

"Did Volkan know about our plan to attack Goremia?" asked Nereyda. "If so, he's probably told Erhan by now. We need to make our move now."

"Yes, Volkan knew." Devrim shook his head. "But we're not ready to attack them there yet. We need at least another week."

"We don't have that long. We need to get ready and hit it as soon as possible. Erhan's already going to beat us there and rally a defense, and we can't afford to give them any more time. Especially if Volkan still has some other noble friends who might join them."

"Very well. Limbani, send a message to have the army assemble as soon as possible."

"Yes, sir," Limbani answered before running out of the room and down the hall.

"We might still be able to capture Goremia if we move quickly. I hope the two of you can come up with a way of taking the city."

"We haven't let you down yet," said Nereyda with a cocky smile.

CHAPTER TWENTY-FIVE

Brynja slumped in her seat next to Ilker in a spacious audience hall, where they had gathered with a large number of Imperial officers and others, including some who sat with the same lack of enthusiasm she did and had people next to them in gray jackets who wore rings inscribed with eyes.

"What do you think this is all about?" she asked.

"You'll have to wait and see," said Ilker, looking sideways at her. "The admiral himself called this meeting."

"Why did he pull us off of the sea?"

"I'm sorry, did you want to keep attacking helpless boats? I thought you hated it."

"I did, but it was easy."

Ilker scoffed. "Do you think Admiral Mansur really cares about fishing boats and cruise ships? This is part of a larger game."

"Do you know what that game is?"

"I do, but it's not my place to tell you. Wait a few minutes, and you'll find out for yourself. But remember what happened the last couple of times we attacked ships."

"You mean the frigates that almost caught us?"

"Exactly. That didn't happen at first. Stalsta has changed its strategy. That's the most I'll say though. Besides, it looks like our admiral is about ready to reveal what's next for us."

Admiral Mansur marched onto the short stage so he stood where the seated assembly could see him. "Hello everyone. I'm excited to see the western fleet assembled all in one place. It doesn't happen very often, but we have good cause to gather here today. I know many of you crave revenge for the vicious attack that the Stalsta Federation launched on us not long ago. It has left our mining operations crippled and our people hungry for justice."

Brynja frowned as she remembered a drifting orange ball. Is it justice to leave children to drown?

Mansur continued with a voice of measured and practiced confidence. "Some of you have confided in me your frustration that our only response has been to send privateers after tiny fishing boats and ships hauling goods from city to city. I'd like to remind you that any dead Stalstan is worth the effort." He let out a dark laugh. "Still, you'll be happy to know that this was only the first stage in our plan. I couldn't share it with you before, because if it leaked to the wrong person, it never would have worked. While the work of our privateers has inflicted some damage on the Stalstan economy, the true achievement has been to draw out the full Stalstan Navy. It's kept itself hidden ever since the attack on the mines. While we do not have any desire to invade the Stalstan lands, we do want to destroy their ability to attack the Cambisian Empire for the foreseeable future. To that end, our entire western fleet, including both our official mainline ships and our privateers, will sail out to engage their main fleet. We believe that we can catch them off guard and cripple their navy.

"I know some of you might be hesitant to face the Stalstans while we face a rebellion within our own empire. There are even rumors of a purple-eyed pirate who can destroy ships with lightning."

Brynja perked up. She only knew of one purple-eyed pirate. Of course, Nereyda would get herself tied up in a rebellion.

"Believe me, I hear what you're saying. The loss of Antalia hurts. However, imagine what might happen if the Stalstans decide to back these rebels. We've all heard the stories about the sort of monstrosities that the Stalstans brought to attack the mines. I wasn't there, so I can't vouch for the accuracy of these legends. I hope they are merely the exaggerated stories of soldiers in a hard battle for their very lives. However, even in myths and tall tales there is a kernel of truth. Whether the Stalstans have developed some sort of new weapon or have become proficient in witchcraft that turns them into fire beasts, or even if they just fight fiercely, we can't afford to have them aiding the enemies on our own shores. I trust our friends in the army to contain this rebellion. It's one thing for rebels to mount an unexpected uprising in a single city. It's quite another to sustain a long campaign to take the entire nation and force out the Emperor. I do not believe they even have a navy, so our own usefulness against them will be limited. However, if they are intent on taking the whole Empire, they will need a fleet eventually, and our job will be to either deny them that resource entirely or destroy whatever ships they do acquire."

Brynja did not relish the idea of facing Nereyda in battle. The idea of fighting her former friend saddened her. And she knew how deadly Nereyda was in a fight, even without the ability to summon lightning.

The admiral paused to consult his notes before droning on. The officers and representatives still paid perfect attention, but the others glanced about the room and out the windows. If it weren't for the reference to Nereyda, Brynja would likely do the same. Mansur continued, "I'm getting ahead of myself. Talk of dealing with these rebels is premature, so I will return to the task at hand of destroying the Stalstan fleet. As you all know, we have been sending privateers to harass Stalstan civilian vessels in the waters just on the east side of their main island. In the wake of our attacks, their main battle fleet has been sent to destroy the marauders. A few of our more expendable privateer ships are still out there to keep up an illusion that the attacks are continuing. Meanwhile, every ship represented in this room will sail out in formation with the goal of destroying that fleet. Officers of the Imperial Navy, you already know your command structure and whom you will report to for this operation. Privateers, you will consult with your designated representatives. They will know where you fit in the hierarchy and where you will sail in our grand formation. This is the largest assembly of Cambisian ships in history. It will be a proud moment to cripple our rivals and prevent them from ever again invading our beloved Empire. You're all dismissed so that you can begin your preparations. The fleet will set sail at dawn two days from now."

The assembled officers and privateers stood and began filtering out of the room.

"Did the reps on the expendable ships know what they were getting into?" asked Brynja.

"Yes, they all volunteered," said Ilker. "They were well aware that they were likely going to be sacrificed to help complete the ruse. Their families are being well compensated for their lives and they will be remembered for years to come."

"What's our role in all of this?"

"We get a very special assignment. Due to your record as a rather skilled pirate, your exemplary performance in our coastal raids, and my superb negotiating skills, we will be in the headquarters formation. This means that we will sail near the admiral's flagship. If the fleet breaks into smaller formations, we will stay with him and prevent enemy ships from getting too close."

"Seems like a pretty good assignment. And we finally get to shoot at something that can fight back."

"It is a great assignment. We'll be at the center of all the action, but won't be in too much danger unless the rest of the fleet doesn't do its job well."

CHAPTER TWENTY-SIX

As the sun sank below the horizon behind them, golden light shone off of the snowcapped mountain peaks on either side of Goremia and highlighted the top of the wall that stretched in front of where Nereyda stood next to Limbani. Even from a distance, they could see the glint of helmets as a host of Imperial soldiers prepared to hold off the rebel army that had approached. So far, the rebels had remained out of range as they formed a plan, but they'd have to move forward with the attack at some point.

"We should have come up with a plan to take the city earlier," said Limbani.

"We didn't have the time. The Empire is reinforcing the city and more troops are only days away. We need to take it before they get here."

"We need to think of something, and I'd rather not just throw our army at their walls. The only other way in is a hard climb into the mountains, followed by dropping a hundred feet off of a cliff, all at night. It would exhaust the men to do it all in one night, and we don't have enough climbing equipment to make it worthwhile—even if the Imperials didn't see us, which they would."

"Do we have enough for one person?"

"Yes, but don't do that."

"I haven't even told you my idea yet," said Nereyda.

"I've fought next to you long enough to make a pretty good guess, and it's crazy."

"Why? It's the best option. If I go alone, I can move faster, and there's less of a chance that I'll be caught. And let's be honest. If we waste time arguing about it, you'll forbid me to go, then I'll go anyway. Or you can just let me go in the first place."

Limbani sighed. "Fine. How will we know that you've succeeded?"

"When you have a way into the city that doesn't involve vaulting a thirty-foot wall."

"So you'll slip in and open the gate?"

"Something like that, or whatever I can manage."

"Then what do you need?"

"A horse, some warm clothes, and a hundred feet of rope."

"Fine, you can use my horse. Check with our supply wagons to see about the other things. Just remember that I hate everything about this."

"I'll keep that in mind. You'll hate it less when we take the city."

"I hope you're right. Take care of my horse."

After Nereyda acquired the equipment she needed, she waited for the sun to set, then mounted Limbani's horse and rode hard for the mountain that stood at the northern side of the pass. In the diminished light and with her rather unpracticed riding skills, Nereyda trusted the horse to handle any obstacles that might be on the ground. When she crossed the plain and reached the edge of the thick forest that stretched up the slope, she slowed down. Her pulse quickened as she imagined what might lurk within. The moon rose above the city to the east, providing faint but much-needed light.

As she looked for a trail that led up through the dense woods and heavy underbrush, she shivered. Not used to the dry cold of the mountains, she pulled a wool coat out of her pack and wrapped it over her shoulders as a shield against the chill that encroached in the night, and that would only get worse as she ascended the mountain. She spotted a gap in the trees and urged her horse toward it at a trot.

The rough ride left her butt feeling bruised, but after two hours of winding through the woods and up the slope, she arrived at the edge of a clearing at the top of the cliff overlooking the city.

Within the shadow of the forest, she dismounted and directed the horse to return to Limbani with a slap on its hindquarters. Outside the forest, a guard tower rose above the cliff, with a wooden staircase spiraling around the perimeter up to the guardhouse on top. An alarm bell dangled from the side. The Imperials hadn't been stupid enough to leave this spot entirely unprotected, at least. Torches glowed along the edge of the cliff, so she couldn't walk up to it without the risk of being spotted.

The top of the guard tower wasn't lit, so Nereyda couldn't immediately tell how many guards had been stationed there. She watched for a few minutes and made out the occasional flicker of moonlight reflecting off of a helmet. Based on the glimmers of metal she caught, it appeared that two guards wandered around on the top of the structure. When it seemed like they were both moving toward the other side of the tower, Nereyda dashed out from the trees toward the closest torch. A cap dangled from the torch, so she used it to snuff out the flame before running back to the trees, where she waited for the guards to respond.

After a moment, one of the guards said, "One of the torches is out."

"Don't just gawk at it. Go down and check it, and relight it if nothing's there."

A flame flared at the top of the tower as the guard lit a torch of his own. He descended the stairs, the wooden steps creaking beneath his footsteps. A few moments later, he emerged into the light at the bottom of the tower. As he meandered past the remaining lit torches toward the extinguished one, Nereyda moved toward the other side of the tower as quickly as possible, remaining in the trees.

"Anything down there?" asked the man from the tower.

Nereyda wrapped her rope around a tree and tied it off.

The guard on the ground waved his torch over the ground near the extinguished torch. "Nothing I can see. Not sure what put the torch out."

With the guards' attention fixed on the other side of the tower, Nereyda grabbed her coil of rope and ran toward the edge, then tossed the rope off the edge before grabbing it and sliding over the side. Totally exposed on the cliff, she rappelled down as quickly as she could. Despite the darkness, anybody could look up or down and see something moving. She was glad she had remembered to bring a pair of gloves to spare her hands from the friction of sliding down a rough piece of rope.

Nereyda landed at the base of the cliff and glanced around. She had landed in what appeared to be the slums of the city, pressed up against the natural wall. Flimsy shacks sat densely packed on the ground. She slipped along the cliff toward the city wall so she could figure out a way to open it for Limbani and the other rebel troops.

As she moved west, she emerged from the ramshackle slums and into a section of two- and three-story buildings. Many of them appeared to be shops with apartments above them. Strangely, she didn't see any taverns or brothels. The church's influence must have kept out the more unsavory places of business.

The streets were all deserted. She only encountered a couple of patrols and easily evaded them by ducking into alleys. When Nereyda was a block from the wall that kept out the rebel army, torch sconces lit a bustle of activity. Soldiers marched along the wall, their footsteps clapping on the stone. Others, even some not in uniform, scurried at the base of the wall and moved supplies with squeaky carts. Officers strode behind their soldiers, giving them orders and empty pep talks about how they were doing their duty to the Empire and the gods.

Nereyda kept to the alleys and side streets, looking at the wall for a way to open it. Under a less guarded section between two guard towers, a drainage ditch led to a grate that let water flow under the wall and out of the city. Brown stinky water splashed her legs as she hopped down into the ditch and snuck toward the grate. The bars were solid iron, too thick to cut through. She made a note of the location, then returned to where she had seen people shuffling supplies around.

From a hiding spot in a darkened doorway, she observed the Imperial soldiers and their servants for several minutes. The servants moved with lowered shoulders and worked just quickly enough to avoid being yelled at. They were clearly civilians who had been drafted into helping defend the city.

An old woman pulling a cart stumbled onto the street below the wall. A guard strode over and laughed at her. "Come on. Keep moving that gunpowder. We need to be ready in case those rebels decide to do something stupid."

The woman scowled at him from beneath a head of wispy white hair but didn't say anything as she dusted herself off and resumed pulling the cart, her shoulders hunched and a limp in her step.

Nereyda slipped out of the shadows and made her way toward the woman without being seen. "Mind if I help you with that?" she asked.

The woman whirled around and eyed Nereyda with suspicion, then relaxed with relief as she looked over the helpful young woman. "Fine, I suppose it wouldn't hurt to let a younger person handle the heavy lifting."

"Perfect. Can you give me directions?"

"Sure. I was taking this barrel to that guard tower down there." The woman pointed toward a guard tower a couple of blocks north of where they were.

"And where do you go for barrels of powder?"

"Ah, that's back the way I came. There's a storehouse near the center of the wall. You won't be able to miss it. It's a hive of activity tonight."

"Excellent. I'll take this from here."

Nereyda grabbed the handles of the cart and, after making sure nobody kept watch in her direction, veered into one of the alleys. She hauled the gunpowder between the buildings until she reached the drainage ditch. Parking the cart near the grate, she dropped down into the ditch, then pulled the barrel down before setting it into the gap.

After climbing out of the ditch, she hauled the cart back toward where the woman had said the storehouse was located. As she approached, she worried that the Imperial soldiers would recognize that she didn't belong there. However, she strode with purpose right up to the storehouse without raising any suspicion.

"What are you hauling for us?" asked a guard outside the large door that opened into the warehouse.

"Gunpowder."

"Good. It's in the back there."

Nereyda nodded at him, then went in to retrieve another barrel of powder. She made several trips over the next hour, going back and forth between the storehouse and the drain. As she shoved the last barrel into place, she knew she needed a way to ignite it since a fuse wouldn't work in the wet drainage ditch. She climbed out of the ditch to get out of the water as she brainstormed. Her teeth clicked as a cold wind hit her wet clothes.

"Hey, what are you doing down there?"

Nereyda glanced up to see an Imperial soldier on the wall with his gun aimed at her.

"I'm just out to enjoy some fresh air. Is something wrong with that?"

"You should know it's after curfew. You don't look like a child. You should know better."

"I'm sorry, my mistake. I'll head home now." Nereyda backed away from the wall with her hands in the air, careful not to step into the drainage ditch next to her.

"No, you stay right there."

Nereyda backed away faster. "There's an army of rebels outside, and you're wasting your time with someone out for a walk?"

"I said stop!" he shouted.

Nereyda turned and sprinted away.

A shot rang out and struck the ground behind her.

She glanced over her shoulder. As she did so, she ran right into another person, sending them both tumbling to the ground.

A strong pair of hands hauled her to her feet. "What are you doing running away from an Imperial soldier?" said the man who had lifted her up.

"I was scared. I'm so sorry I ran into you," she said as she reached down to the man she had run into. He slapped her hand away and jumped to his feet on his own.

Both men wore dark uniforms with a silver flame insignia on their shoulders. "Who are you?" Nereyda asked. "I don't think I've seen that symbol anywhere else."

"We are Sentinels of the Temple," said the man who had helped her up. He looked down his nose at her. "We help keep order in this holiest of cities. And to that end, not only are you guilty of being out past curfew, you are guilty of failing to obey the command of someone in authority."

"As well as assaulting an officer of the church," added the other.

"Indeed. I'm afraid you'll have to come with us to answer these charges."

"Again, I'm so sorry." Nereyda held her hand to her collarbone. "I was stupid to be out past dark. I needed some fresh air and got scared by the guard. I didn't mean to run into you."

"Even so, you will come with us. Besides, how many people go for an evening stroll with a sword at their side?" He pointed at the cutlass on her hip. At once, both men drew a sword and pointed it at her, moving to stand on either side of her.

Nereyda considered fighting them off, but she still needed to detonate the gunpowder in the drain hole in the wall. Could she summon lightning and draw her weapon fast enough to do both? Or could she shock both of them and the barrels at the same time? She had never tried striking three separate targets at once.

Dammit.

She slumped her shoulders as she made her choice.

"Fine, I'll come with you," she said as she raised her arms. "I need to do one thing first." Nereyda thrust an arm out and sent a jolt of lightning toward the barrels of gunpowder. The air sizzled with the smell of a storm.

The wall erupted. Chunks of stone flew through the air. The gap would be enough for at least twenty rebels to pass through at once.

Limbani had her opening.

As the lightning left her fingertips, one of the Sentinels grabbed Nereyda's arms and yanked them behind her back. "You're not some random person. You're the gift thief that this Inquisition is all about. Do you have any idea what you just did?"

Nereyda laughed. "Yeah, I did exactly what I wanted to do. Blew a hole in your wall so my friends can come in."

"Hey Celik, tie her wrists together."

The other Sentinel grabbed a short length of rope from his belt and wrapped it around her wrists before tying it tight. He pulled hard on her arms to test the restraint. She winced at the pain of the rope digging into her skin.

"How did you get into the city?"

"Does it matter?"

"Not really, I guess."

With one Sentinel in front of her and the other shoving her from behind, Nereyda was forced to move along as they made their way through the streets toward the temple grounds that sat above the city on the slope of the southern peak. The faint sounds of swords clanging and guns firing rang from the direction of the wall. Eager to join Limbani and the others in the fight, she struggled against the rope, but only managed to scrape up her wrists.

She concentrated on freezing the ropes enough to break them. While she projected cold into the fibers, they held fast as she tugged on them. Nereyda gave up fighting, not wanting to exhaust herself. She'd watch and wait for an opportunity to escape or fight back. The men brought her through the winding city streets to the wall that stood at the base of the slope leading to the Temple of Ameretat.

"What do you have there?" asked a Sentinel standing at the gate.

"The gift thief herself walked right into our city."

The man leaned forward in surprise. "Really? The priests will be thrilled to finally have her in their possession."

"I know. Mind opening the gate so we can show them?"

"Oh, of course. My excitement got the better of me. Forgive me."

"Nothing to forgive, brother. This is a great day for the church."

The escort behind Nereyda prodded her ahead through the gate and they began the ascent to the large temple building that loomed above. She supposed that the spires and domes were intended to inspire awe. In the moonlight, though, they took on a sinister look. Nereyda dragged her feet as they climbed the stairs, but the Sentinel shoved her so she tripped. He yanked her back to her feet, and they resumed the climb.

When they reached the temple at the top of the stairs, Nereyda glanced toward the battle at the city wall below. From what she could see, the rebels had poured into the city through the hole that she had blown open, though the Imperials had organized into their usual three ranks, and rotated through them as they fought. This slowed the rebels down, but did not stop them.

"Hey, pirate, come on." The lead Sentinel had opened the large golden doors, and they hauled her inside the sanctuary.

The murals covering the walls were filled with images of legends and myths that formed the basis of the church's teachings. All superstitious nonsense to Nereyda.

A man in blue robes emerged from the back of the sanctuary. "Ah, Firat and Celik, what brings you here? Who is your friend?"

"Sabah, this woman destroyed the city wall with lightning. And she matches the description of the gift thief."

The old man's eyebrows rose and he sprang up to the platform in the center of the room to get a better view of her. His icy eyes matched his robes. "Exceptional. Our inquisitor said she might be coming our way, and now she walks right to us. Bring her closer." He beckoned with his hand.

Nereyda was brought to him. "What's your problem with me?" she asked. "I've never met any of you before. Why do you want to capture me?"

"Our problem isn't with you. It's with what you've stolen, whether intentionally or not. We want to help you."

"If you want to help me, then this whole Inquisition might be a bit much, don't you think? Why not just send a nice card or a messenger to sing me a song to invite me here? And I don't think I need your help."

He flashed a wolflike smile. "Ah, but you do. This lightning, and whatever other power you have, is a gift stolen from the gods."

"I didn't steal it from anybody. I just touched some glowy light stuff in a fountain, and I woke up like this. Nobody was there, unless the crazy fire demon counts, but he wasn't really in a talkative sort of mood."

The high priest jumped down next to her and used one hand to turn her face toward the murals while pointing at them with the other. "Do you know the story these paintings tell?"

Nereyda shrugged. "Some bullshit to trick people into following you, probably."

"This is the story of Corinna, and how she destroyed the world as it was. Long ago, the gods gifted us with tremendous power, which we used to perform wonderful feats for the benefit of all. But this Corinna only craved more and more power. She rose up to take the world for herself, using powers much like yours. For her hubris and greed, the gods punished us all. They smashed the part of the world that she had claimed, creating what we know as the Shattered Sea, and took all of our powers away from us. Now, here you are, with abilities of your own, helping enemies of the Empire tear down everything we have worked to build these last centuries." His face contained pure zealous rage. "It is as if you are Corinna reborn, determined to lead us astray and attract the wrath of the gods once again."

"Look, I might be a pirate, but this is one of those rare times when I'm not trying to take things for myself. Sure, I might get a ship out of the deal, but aside from that, I just want to help my friends so they can give people a better world than you've given them. Besides, how do you know your men are telling the truth? You haven't seen me use any of these abilities. As far as you know, your minions grabbed someone off the street who happens to look a bit like the woman in your murals."

"You're right," said Sabah. "We need to make sure you are who they claim you are. Men, take her to the back room. You know which one."

The Sentinels hauled her toward the rear door of the sanctuary, with the priest behind them. They passed doors that led into offices, bedchambers, and small private chapels. They reached a closed wooden door with a lit torch on the wall next to it.

The lead Sentinel grabbed the torch off of the wall and shoved the door open, then led the rest of them into the room. As he lit torches around the small room, the purpose of the chamber became clear. Near the middle of the room, but slightly off-center, stood a rigid wooden chair with ankle and arm restraints. Next to it, chains dangled from the ceiling and connected to a winch in the corner of the room. Light from a glowing fireplace in the corner glinted off of a wall of sharp and otherwise uncomfortable-looking implements.

Ice crawled down Nereyda's spine and her mind raced in search of an escape, but she concealed her fear with a snarky mask. "What, are you going to torture me until these powers go away?"

"Perhaps, but that's not our purpose here today. We're going to torture you until you show us everything you can do."

"You could just ask. I'd be happy to put on a show for you."

"I'm sure you would, but our chief inquisitor has told me about how pain and distress bring your powers to the surface. So that's how we're going to start."

"How does he know that?"

"Because he knows you." The nasty grin reappeared. "Men, chain her up."

There was only one person who could be the chief inquisitor. Erhan.

The Sentinels removed the rope that restrained her, moved her arms in front of her, and locked her in a set of iron handcuffs. One of the Sentinels went to the winch and used it to lower one of the chains. They hooked the handcuffs to the chain, then winched it back up. The chain lifted her arms above her head, then kept going. Her shoulder muscles stretched and ached as she was hauled up inch by inch until her toes barely touched the ground. She gritted her teeth as her shoulders took all of her weight.

"Where is Erhan now?" she asked. "Why not wait for him?"

"Oh, he was here. He warned us that the rebellion was coming. But I made him leave the city. If Goremia falls, someone needs to carry on our work."

"What's the point of doing this right now? Wouldn't you rather run from the city? What are you going to do when Goremia falls? Keep me in here forever and hope the rebels decide to ignore the temple?"

"You know what? You're exactly right," said Sabah. "Celik, go spread the message that the church is ordering all civilians within the temple's walls. The power of faith will protect them from the invaders."

Celik bowed his head briefly, then slipped out of the room.

"You're hoping that the rebels will hesitate to attack the temple if civilians are in the way," said Nereyda.

The priest shrugged. "We are their shield as they are ours. However, we have no time to waste on continuing this discussion. Firat, cut open the back of her shirt."

The Sentinel took out his dagger and ran it up the length of the back of her shirt. The blade nicked her skin, leaving a gash that dripped blood down her back. The pain from the cut and the chill from the air raised goosebumps on Nereyda's skin.

Sabah paced along the wall of torture instruments. "No need to get too creative yet. We'll start with the basics."

He grabbed an iron poker and looked it over before setting it in the flames within the fireplace in the corner. "We'll save this for later, in case we need it." His voice contained an unsettling amount of joy. Going back to the wall, he took down a cat-o'-nine-tails. "We'll start with the one without the hooks. If this doesn't work, we'll upgrade to the other." He held the handle to Firat. "You may start. Not too hard at first. Let's work our way up."

Nereyda took short, quick breaths to prepare herself as the Sentinel stepped behind her. A whisper sounded a fraction of a second before the nine knotted cords struck Nereyda's back. She bit her lip to stop herself from crying out.

Firat fell into a rhythm as he struck her back again and again. Each stroke hit harder and carved deeper into her flesh. As the whip snapped, warm blood crawled down the skin of her back. An iron scent permeated the air. The storm rose inside her of its own initiative. A blizzard charged forward from within.

Icy cold grew inside her. A chill spread through her arms and to her wrists. The shackles strained as they froze.

When they felt cold enough, Nereyda yanked her wrists apart and shattered the handcuffs before falling to the ground. As she tried to push herself up, her arms wouldn't give her their strength. Her shoulder muscles ached with a deep pain from supporting her weight, and her arms had fallen numb. Before she could summon the strength to stand, Firat grabbed her and yanked her arms back behind her.

"Did you use the iron shackles?" asked Sabah. "The inquisitor told us she's done this before. Weren't you paying attention?"

"I'm sorry, sir."

"Never mind, use the gold shackles and string her up again. With her arms behind her this time."

"Didn't you get what you wanted? You saw me freeze those handcuffs," Nereyda asked as Firat shackled her wrists again.

Sabah ran his fingers through the blood on her back, and she recoiled. "And you did very well with that. But let's see what else you can do. And if, at the same time, we can set an example for the world and show it what happens to people like you, all the better." He laughed to himself.

As the Sentinel turned the winch and the chain pulled her arms up behind her back, Nereyda's shoulders strained with agony. She pressed herself up as high as she could on the tips of her toes as the chain tightened, but that only got her so far. Her shoulders strained with ever increasing pain as the chain lifted her off the ground. With two pops, her shoulders dislocated, allowing the chain to lift her arms the rest of the way above her head. Nereyda's head spun as she felt herself going into shock.

She groaned in pain. "Haven't you done enough?" she said through gritted teeth as she tried to push the pain behind her.

"Hardly. Firat, continue."

Firat took up the cat-o'-nine-tails again and resumed his flogging of Nereyda. The welts on her back broke, and more blood dripped down her back. One stroke, in particular, felt like it ripped a piece of flesh from her.

"Sir, one of these cuts is bleeding pretty badly."

"Well, we can't have that."

Sabah strode to the fireplace and grabbed the handle of the iron poker. The tip glowed with heat as he pulled it out and paced behind her again.

"Where is it? Hard to see among the rest of your work."

"Right there, sir."

"Ah, yes."

Nereyda's back lit on fire as the priest pressed the hot iron against her. She finally let out an agonized scream. She had suppressed it throughout the whipping, but the scorching metal crossed the line.

"Perhaps we should try something else. We don't want to accidentally make her bleed out on us. What would you like to use next, Firat?"

The door crashed open, and Celik burst into the room, panting.

"Sir, all the civilians we could find are within the temple walls."

"Excellent. Care to join us for the next part?"

"That's not all. The rebels are nearly at the temple gates. The people are scared and don't know what to do."

"Ah, then we might have to cut this little session short. Firat, lower her down and bring her outside with us. Let's show them our prize."

As the chains lowered her down, Nereyda still had to use them to support her weight, despite the agony that it caused in her shoulders. Her legs wouldn't support her, and she didn't want to fall down. Firat unhooked her handcuffs from the chain but left them on her wrists. He caught her as she collapsed. Her arms hung uselessly from her shoulders. She tried to concentrate on breaking out of her handcuffs with what little strength she could summon. While the gold became frigid, it wouldn't shatter no matter how much she strained against it.

"Ah, yes, those golden handcuffs are quite a good investment for something like this," said Sabah. "Iron becomes brittle in the cold, but not gold, as you're discovering."

Nereyda wished she could come up with something to say but saved her energy.

The priest and the Sentinels brought her through the sanctuary, out of the temple, and to the top of the stairs. Hundreds of people had gathered inside the temple walls and covered the mountain slope that led up to the temple. They huddled tightly together and cowered. Outside the walls, silver moonlight reflected off the rebel army's armor. They had closed in and maintained a siege of the temple grounds, but had stopped short of a direct attack on the temple itself. The wall only stood one story tall and would not stop an invasion for long if they decided to make an assault.

"Friends," called Sabah. "Friends, I have some wonderful news to share."

The crowd of civilians quieted and looked up at the priest and his curious guest.

"I know that our city has fallen on dire times, but not all is lost. For it is this very day that the gift thief we have been pursuing so relentlessly has walked right into our city. Here she is." He nodded to the Sentinels, who threw her on the ground in front of the priest.

Nereyda yelled in pain as she landed on her dislocated right shoulder.

The crowd took an instinctive step back, pressing itself against the wall.

"I understand your fear. She is indeed dangerous and has killed many of your fellow citizens. However, rest assured that she is properly restrained and has been broken." He projected a calm confidence. "You will not face any threat from her today. Now, you are probably wondering what good this does us when we're surrounded by our enemies. While these walls keep them out for now, they will not last long if those rebels decide that your lives are worth sacrificing. Even if they don't attack, our walls will not keep out those deadly enemies of starvation, exposure, and thirst. Fear not, for the gods provide a means for our escape, as they have always provided for us."

The high priest raised his voice louder. "To those rebels outside the walls, we have someone that seems quite important to your cause. We will not offer her to you, but if you don't want to see her die right here on these steps, you will let us out of these walls so that we can head east. We will take this gift thief with us, and if we catch any sense that you are following us or attempting to reclaim her, we will execute her. Consider this offer and send a messenger to the gates within an hour. This offer will expire then."

CHAPTER TWENTY-SEVEN

Limbani's eyes were wide as she took in the scene at the top of the stairs where the slope rose above the temple wall. "My lord, what are we going to do?" she asked Devrim, who had come in to the city once it had been mostly secured.

Devrim's face was white and he spoke with a distant voice as he gazed up at the priest and Nereyda. "It wasn't supposed to happen like this. I'm not ready."

"We won't let her die. Focus. We need a plan," said Limbani.

He shook his head. "For once, I don't know what to do. How could you let her run into the city like that?" He turned and grabbed Limbani's shoulders. "You didn't even consult me."

She shrugged his hands off. "What should I have done? She wanted to go, and she did. Nothing I could have said would have stopped her. We needed a way into the city, and she volunteered, then delivered. But we don't have time for this debate. We need to get into the church grounds."

He paced back and forth, his hands clenched. "What would you have us do? Storm the temple? We'd kill hundreds of civilians, and they'd kill Nereyda before we even get close."

Limbani stared up the mountain. Even from this distance, moonlight reflected off of the wet blood that darkened the spot where Nereyda had been dropped. The pirate couldn't even stand. Limbani's new friend, someone who had fought at her side, lay in visible agony. "Let me come up with something."

A sharp shake of his head. "No, it's too much of a risk."

The thought of abandoning an ally to die was too much for Limbani. "I can't just leave her there without trying to help. I'm going to do something," Limbani said with resolve, then stormed through the ranks of soldiers to find her lieutenant.

"Come back here, General," he yelled after her. "I order you to stand down."

Limbani kept going, for the first time ignoring an order from Devrim. When duty conflicts with friendship, one needs to win out. Today, it was going to be friendship. She'd deal with the consequences later.

She found Adnan and got his attention. "Lieutenant, we need to get Nereyda out of there."

"Agreed, but how?"

"Select your best nine soldiers and send them to meet me at the east end of the temple walls. I'll be there soon."

"Yes, ma'am." He turned to go but Limbani caught his arm for a moment.

"Do you know where the pirates and Islanders are?" she asked.

"They're toward the back of the formation. If we're lucky, they might be far enough back that they're not aware of what's happening."

"Maybe, but they're going to know what's going on after I talk to them."

"Whatever you think is best."

"Go find the men. We don't have any time to waste."

Limbani rushed away from the wall and found Jax huddled with the rest of Nereyda's pirate and Islander crew in a small plaza. Some of them refreshed themselves in a fountain, others slumped on the ground after the fight.

"What's going on up there?" Jax asked.

"The church has Nereyda. They want to use her to get them out without a fight. They're taking her with them and they'll kill her if we try something."

"But we're going to try something, right?"

"Of course. I need ten of you to come to the east end of the temple wall. Along the way, stop at a supply cart and grab some rope and climbing hooks. At least ten. Twenty if possible."

Jax nodded. "I think I get what you're thinking of doing. I'll find our best people and meet you there as soon as we're ready."

Limbani jogged back through the formation of rebels and found the squad her lieutenant had assembled waiting under some trees that hung over the east end of the temple wall. The plant life obstructed the view of anyone within the temple grounds, which would prevent them from being detected for the time being. Even with the moon, they were lucky that it was still dark.

Once Jax arrived with some crew members, Limbani waved all twenty people to gather around her.

"Now that we're all here," she said in a low voice, "we're going to free Nereyda and get the church to surrender. Our friends picked up some climbing equipment on their way here. How many did you get, Jax?"

"They only had ten. Sorry we couldn't get more, but I didn't figure we had time to check the other supply carts."

"You're right. We'll make ten work. First, I will take my soldiers over the wall. We'll stay hidden and keep watch as Jax and the others climb over to join us. This is the only spot along the wall where this could work because of the trees. Once all of us are assembled in the small grove on the other side, Jax, I need you to take your people toward the gate so you're ready to open it when the time comes. You're not in uniform, so you will hopefully blend in with the crowd. Once you're in position, let me know, and we'll do our jobs. I don't see any guards other than the two who are by the priest and Nereyda. You two," she pointed to two soldiers and beckoned them forward.

They stepped ahead of the others.

"Can you take out those guards when I give the order?"

"Absolutely," said one.

"Of course," said the other.

"Good. I'll face the priest and get Nereyda away from him. The rest of you," she said, looking at the remaining soldiers, "cover us and keep an eye on that crowd. You also need to protect this spot on the wall so we can climb out of here if this goes wrong. Everyone understand their job?" Limbani looked around at all twenty and got nods in return. "Good. Let's get over this wall."

The pirates slung the lines and hooks up and over the wall, then passed the ropes to the soldiers. Limbani took hers from Jax and put her weight on it to test it. When it held, she walked her way up the wall, which was only about twice as tall as she was. Once they reached the top, the soldiers hopped down to the ground on the other side. Limbani stayed crouched, behind the tree branches that overhung the wall. When the pirates finished their climb, they hung the ropes off of the other side of the wall, in case they needed them to get out.

Once everyone had landed on the ground on the inside of the wall, Limbani crept in a crouch toward the edge of the grove of trees. Peeking out from behind a wide trunk, she had an unobstructed view of where the guards and priest stood over Nereyda's crumpled form at the top of the stairs.

She remained conscious, but barely. The pirate's eyes contained none of her characteristic purple spark. Sweat matted her black hair. If Nereyda wasn't trying to fight back, that meant they had broken her, either physically or mentally.

Limbani's jaw clenched. I made the right decision.

As soon as her sharpshooters took out the guards, Limbani would have a clear path to run around the crowd to reach the priest and Nereyda.

"You all know your jobs," she said. "Jax, head to the gate."

He nodded and gestured for the small group of pirates and Islanders to follow him along the wall. They slipped into the crowd and disappeared. Limbani held her breath as she waited for Jax to give the signal. The crowd was becoming increasingly rowdy.

Someone started a chant. "Kill her! Kill her!" The rest of the crowd soon joined and pumped their fists in the air.

So far, the priest had convinced them to stand back, but it wasn't clear how long that would work. With only those two temple guards, there wasn't much he could do to stop the mob if they decided to rush them.

At the gate, Jax's head appeared in a gap in the crowd as he raised his hand and waved at her.

"Okay, it's time." She looked at the two shooters she had chosen. "When I give the signal, take out those guards. Everyone else, make sure we don't get swarmed by that crowd."

"We can't stop all of them, ma'am."

"I know, but I doubt many of them are willing to be among the ones who die."

The two shooters took positions, leaning against trees to steady their aim. They each gave her a slight nod to show that they were ready. As she flicked her hand toward the guards, they took their shots and Limbani sprinted out of the grove.

The guards yelled and fell to the ground. The priest jerked his head around as he searched for the source of the shots. The crowd screamed and cowered. Some ran for any available cover, but most stayed where they were, not knowing where to go or who to run from.

The high priest spotted Limbani as she ran up the slope. He bent and grabbed the sword of one of the fallen guards. Kicking Nereyda onto her stomach, he stretched her left arm out to the side so that its hand hung off of the top step, then stood on her arm with his left foot and raised the sword over her.

"Stop right there if you want your friend intact," he said.

Limbani almost tripped as she brought herself to a halt twenty feet downhill from the priest. Nereyda struggled, but she couldn't get enough strength to push herself from under the priest's weight. Her shoulders looked malformed, bulging out in a strange way. Limbani's heart hurt to see her friend suffer.

"You know what," said the priest. "Maybe it will be better if I do it anyway."

He swung the sword down and through Nereyda's wrist. She screamed in agony as her hand fell onto the step below her, blood pouring from the wound.

Anger poured an extra surge of adrenaline into Limbani's blood. Her heart pounded in her ears with every stride as she powered up the slope. Her vision narrowed until her sole focus was on the man who had hurt Nereyda. All sound became white noise to her ears.

The priest raised the sword to strike again, but Limbani leaped the final distance and thrust her sword into his chest, then shoved him off of her blade and to the ground.

Trusting her soldiers to cover her, Limbani knelt next to Nereyda, who lay on her side and clutched her stump of a wrist and writhed in pain as blood dripped between her fingers. The back of her shirt had been cut open, and her back was a mess of blood and torn flesh. Tearing the sleeves off of the priest's robe, Limbani used one to fashion a tourniquet around Nereyda's upper arm to slow the bleeding. The other she used as a bandage around the severed wrist. Guilt seeped into Limbani's mind. *I took too long. I shouldn't have even let her go on that stupid mission.*

She shook her mind clear and reminded herself that it wouldn't help Nereyda to sulk in the past.

"Can you stand?"

"I think so, but I need help," said Nereyda, her words labored.

Limbani started to pull Nereyda up by her right arm, but she let out a scream.

"My shoulder!"

Following what she had seen medics do, Limbani held the top of Nereyda's shoulder at the base of the neck with one hand while grabbing her arm with the other. In one motion, she pulled the shoulder out, moved it up, and popped it back into the socket. Tears welled in Nereyda's eyes, though the pirate didn't make any noise.

"Better?" Limbani asked.

"We'll see. Still hurts."

Limbani wrapped her arm under Nereyda's arms and helped her stagger to her feet. She glanced down the hill and found Jax. "Open the gate so Devrim can come in," she called.

Jax and his group shoved the guards out of the way and unlocked the gate.

"Grab my sword belt," said Nereyda. "One of the guards had it."

"Can you use a sword right now?"

"Probably not, but I want it."

Limbani found the familiar sword belt and wrapped it around Nereyda's waist, helping her fasten it.

"You're freeing the gift thief!"

Down the stairs, a man shoved his way out from the crowd of civilians.

"I won't let you take her." His eyes gleamed with a wild rage.

He sprinted up the stairs.

A shot rang from the grove, and he dropped to the ground, rolling back down the steps.

Instead of settling the crowd, this just made them angrier. Stones flew up toward them, mostly aimed at Nereyda.

The crowd hurled stones and insults at Nereyda as she stood next to Limbani at the top of the temple slope. As they kept falling, a breeze rustled past Limbani as Nereyda tossed out a wave of wind that pushed the crowd back. They became silent and froze, staring at the pirate.

"What do you want from me?" Nereyda called out to the crowd. "This was good enough for Antalia." She held out her remaining hand and sparks sizzled between her fingertips, then cascaded to the ground. Blood dripped from her stump and spattered on the ground below. The irises of her eyes glowed purple.

Those nearest to her took a step back.

Even Limbani edged away. She knew what had happened at Antalia, but it was entirely different to witness Nereyda's abilities in person.

"Are you afraid I'm going to use it on you? Why? Are you an Imperial soldier trying to kill me? No? Then what do you care?"

"You're a gift thief! You took your powers from the gods!" called a voice from the mass of people.

Nereyda scanned the crowd. "I don't know who said that, but there were no gods where I got this. And I certainly didn't choose this. Do you want to take this from me?" she asked, her voice pleading. "Do you know how? If so, please, let me know."

Limbani hated to see Nereyda so broken and desperate. "Reyda, let me get you out of here." She put a guiding arm around Nereyda, but the pirate shrugged her off.

There was a shuffle in the crowd, and Devrim stepped out from the masses.

"Nereyda, you're scaring them. We've won the battle, so step away and let me handle this," he said, his voice and face filled with concern.

"They're only scared of me because they've been fed a steady diet of bullshit about how I'm some sort of demon."

"I know you're not a demon." He climbed the stairs as he spoke. "And that's all I need to know. But these people put a lot of stock in their church. This Inquisition has gotten much bigger than I could have predicted and it's gotten people fired up about what you can do. They don't know what to make of it. But just settle down. They'll see that you're only here to help."

"So this Inquisition is the problem? Where did it start? That church on the hill, right?"

"The Temple of Ameretat? Yes, but the priests aren't there right now. They evacuated before we got here."

"You mean the same people who have been spreading rumors about me being some sort of witch ran away at the first sign of trouble?" Nereyda spat on the ground. "While they're out, maybe I should let them know what I think of their Inquisition."

Nereyda turned around to face the mountain and raised her hand upward. Dark clouds formed above. Limbani's hair stood on the back of her neck. Reyda closed her fist, then pulled down. As she did, a lightning bolt surged down into the top of the temple. The building, which had stood for hundreds of years, exploded. Bits of stone rained down on the mountainside, and the remaining structure of the sanctuary collapsed.

Nereyda turned back around to face the crowd, barely staying on her feet as a wave of exhaustion came over her. She forced herself to stand up straight and pointed her cutlass up the mountain. "See? Your church couldn't even protect itself. What makes you think it can protect you?"

"Nereyda," said Devrim from a couple of steps down, shaking his head, "you've gone too far. Limbani, arrest her."

"What?!" asked Nereyda.

Limbani nearly said the same thing, but Devrim would just get someone else to do it if she refused.

She wrestled Nereyda's arms behind her back. Nereyda struggled against Limbani, though her attempts lacked any real strength. It seemed that the combination of her dislocated shoulder, hand loss, and calling down that lightning had exhausted her. After a moment, she passed out and went limp in Limbani's grasp.

With the remains of the temple smoldering up the mountain and Nereyda collapsed in Limbani's arms, the crowd had, at last, become quiet with fear.

"All of you," said Limbani from the stairs, "are you ready to stop fighting? You're not soldiers. You don't need to fight. It's time to be at peace and let us show you that we're on your side. I don't want to fight you. None of us do. But, if you do choose to fight, you will lose."

"So are we your prisoners now?" asked one of the citizens, a scowl across his face.

"No, you're not prisoners. Drop the rocks and walk out that gate. This city is still yours. You don't have to leave. We're not here to take anything from you."

"Tell that to your friend who destroyed our temple. And you killed the high priest. We're people of faith in this city. You can't attack our church and be our friends."

"You're right," said Devrim as he stood next to Limbani. "We have not shown ourselves to be good friends so far, but we are going to work to make it up to you and prove that we are indeed on the same side. General," he said in a terse tone, "why don't you take Nereyda and lock her up in my tent, then get a medic to tend to her wounds? I think you've done quite enough. Leave the crowd to me."

"Why do I need to lock her up?"

"She has committed a crime against our new friends here. I need to contemplate what the consequences will be. Please don't argue with me on this." His eyes delivered a warning.

Limbani glanced down at Nereyda's still form and nodded. "Very well, sir." Limbani hated to haul off a wounded ally like this, but she chose to be glad that at least she didn't have to calm the crowd down. Devrim was much better at dealing with people.

She leaned the unconscious pirate against her as she staggered down the slope. Jax hurried out of the crowd and took hold of Nereyda from the other side, taking some of the weight off of Limbani. "Thanks," she said.

"Of course."

Once they made their way down the stairs and out the gate, she found a stretcher on a cart. Jax and Limbani laid Nereyda down and wheeled her through the city to Devrim's tent.

An hour later, Nereyda remained unconscious on the cot as Limbani and Jax tended to her to the best of their abilities, along with the medic that they had grabbed on their walk through the city. The bleeding from her wrist had mostly stopped, and her other shoulder had been set. Now, they were cleaning and dressing the wounds on her back.

"This is ugly," said the medic. "Even by my standards. There are a couple of places where there are more than cuts. Chunks of flesh have been ripped off. This burn stopped some of the bleeding, but it wasn't a proper cauterizing. It's going to get infected if we don't care for it. Even then, it still might. It's a burn on top of a deep cut."

"Will she recover?" asked Limbani.

The medic shrugged. "Maybe. If she gets through the next couple of days without an infection, she'll probably live, though there is permanent damage, even beyond the severed hand. And if her back or wrist do get infected, she'll get a slow, feverish death as it overtakes her."

The tent flap opened, and Devrim stepped inside. "How is she, Doctor?"

He chewed on his lip as the medic gave him the same information he had just told to Limbani and Jax.

"Do you think she'll go off again?" Devrim asked with a whisper, fear creeping into his voice.

"Go off? What do you mean?"

Jax spoke. "I think he means her powers. But I've never seen her accidentally use them while sleeping."

The medic scrunched his face with confusion. "I don't know anything about that."

"So what can we do for her?" asked Devrim.

"I don't know," said the medic. "We just have to wait and see for now."

"Well, do everything you can."

"Yes, sir."

"This tent is starting to feel a little crowded," said Jax. "I'm going to go update the others." Jax slipped out through the tent flap.

"How is the crowd now, sir?" asked Limbani.

"They've settled down for the most part," said Devrim, "though they still clearly want Nereyda dead. This city is going to be a problem. We can't afford to have a city that hates us in this key location. And we can't spare the troops to leave a large garrison. That leaves one other option. Have someone find a criminal who looks like Nereyda, preferably one who is sentenced to death."

Limbani narrowed her eyes. "Sir? Are you sure you want to go down this path?"

"Absolutely. We can give the people what they want and keep Nereyda alive."

"So you're going to kill someone in Nereyda's place and hide her away forever? I'm not sure I like this plan."

"It's the best we have right now. And you've done your share of disobeying me today, I think," Devrim snapped. "I'm going to ignore your earlier transgression because you did get Nereyda back to us. But if you want to protect the friend you saved, go do what I told you to do."

"Yes, sir." Limbani resigned herself to obeying Devrim as she slipped out of the tent to start her search for a Nereyda look-alike.

Nereyda woke to the sound of voices above her. A million sharp pains crisscrossed her back. Her shoulders throbbed with a deep ache. And her wrist hurt inside and out with the most intense pain she had ever experienced. Her eyes still half-closed against the bright morning light, she tried to push herself up and off of the cot she was lying on.

Except something wasn't right.

She couldn't feel her left hand.

Her eyes popped fully open. The sun shone through the tent walls. She took in the blood-soaked bandages that covered the stump of her wrist, where her hand should be. Nereyda cried out as she remembered everything that had happened to her.

On the other side of the tent, Devrim, Limbani, and a medic jumped at the sound of her voice.

Nereyda tried to roll out of her cot, the muscles in her back protesting in pain. Her right wrist caught on something, and she glanced at it. A chain locked her to a post next to the cot. Her eyes shot to Devrim.

Nereyda erupted. "What the hell is this? After everything I did, you chain me up?"

Devrim looked her straight in the eyes and spoke in a calm voice, "I'm glad you're finally awake. If you promise not to try to kill me, I'll have Limbani let you go, and I can explain."

"I won't kill you right away, at least. We'll see how I feel after we talk."

"Good enough. I'll take it. Limbani, please undo her restraints and leave us."

"Of course," Limbani said as she stepped forward.

"Thank you. Then return to the task I gave you."

The general gave Devrim a silent glare, but unclasped Nereyda's handcuff and left the tent.

Nereyda's building anger gave her the strength to shove herself to her feet.

The medic rushed forward, his hands out. "No, no, no. You can't get up yet."

She ignored him and the pain that screamed throughout her back. She could barely stand up straight. "Okay, she's gone, so now tell me why you had your general arrested in front of a town full of people?" she asked, staggering up to Devrim's face. "You wanted me to use my abilities. We wouldn't have Antalia or Trabizan without them, yet the more I keep using them, the more people seem to hate me. Then you go and humiliate me by hauling me away like the criminal they claim I am. I took that city for you, and this is how you treat me?"

"I had to get you out of there." He placed a hand on her shoulder, but pulled it back after she winced. "That crowd would have torn you apart for destroying their temple—which was rather a small overreaction, don't you think?"

Her eyes flared. "An overreaction? You see what happened to me, right? Priests are calling for me to be killed for something I didn't choose. They tortured me! Didn't you tell me that the Inquisition would be no problem? Clearly, you were wrong. Why am I paying the price for it?"

"Yes, Reyda, I was wrong about the Inquisition." He held his hands up in apology. "But I have a plan to give us some extra time."

Nereyda narrowed her eyes with skepticism. "How?"

"We start by having you go away for some time. While you're gone, this whole Inquisition business should blow over."

"You want me to leave? Don't you need me here? And what about the other night? I thought you cared about me, as more than just your general."

"I do care about you." His voice emanated warmth. "That's why I don't want you to get any more hurt by this religious nonsense. And I don't want you to go away, but unless you step back for a bit, this won't clear up."

Nereyda wanted to keep fighting back, but her head spun, and she staggered back.

A gentle hand took her arm and supported her. "Nereyda, please, rest," said Devrim's voice.

She let Devrim help her back onto her cot. "Everything hurts," she cried.

"I know, and we're going to do everything we can for you." He kept his voice low and reassuring. "You've done more than enough, so now it's your turn to rest and recover."

"How can I recover from this?" she asked as she waved her wrist in Devrim's face, wincing at the pain in her shoulder.

He wiped a tear from his cheek. "I don't know, but we'll help you."

"I don't want to need your help. I don't want to feel useless."

"You're far from useless, Nereyda. What you did let us take the city, and saved many lives since we didn't have to try to climb the wall."

"I don't care about what I did. I care about what I can do next. Where did Limbani go? What was the task you gave her?"

"She's taking care of something for me. You don't need to worry about her right now."

"When she's back, I want to talk to her. I need to thank her for doing what she could to get me out of there. How bad is the damage? To me, I mean."

"Don't focus on the negative. It won't help."

"Screw that. I want to know how bad it is."

Devrim nodded to the medic, and he came over to Nereyda's side.

"I've been tending your wounds, General. The bleeding from your wrist has slowed, and your shoulders have been set. What I'm most worried about is what happened to your back. Some of the cuts are quite deep, and I believe they have damaged the muscle underneath. Recovering full mobility will be a difficult road, I'm afraid, if it's possible at all. I've done all I can, but there is little I can do to repair the damage. The best we can hope for now is that it doesn't become infected. That's the biggest danger for both your wrist and back. If they are infected, I fear there is little I can do to save you. You have to rest and keep them clean."

Nereyda refused to accept that her body may be permanently broken. "I know a place where I might be able to heal," she said.

"What do you mean?" asked the medic. "Someplace with healers with more skill? I don't know of anyone who can do a better job than I have."

"No, not healers. It's hard to explain, but I'll need a ship."

Devrim knelt next to her. "When I said you should go away, I meant somewhere close and comfortable on land. You're in no condition to sail far, Nereyda."

"You're right, I'm not. But I might not ever be ready to sail again if I don't go."

Devrim looked at the medic. "What do you think?"

"I think it's dangerous to consider moving her much, let alone putting her on a ship to who knows where. In my professional opinion, she should not go anywhere, except to a more permanent hospital."

"Too bad I'm too hurt to run away and do what I want," said Nereyda with a dark laugh.

"Exactly where do you plan to go?" Devrim asked.

"I want to go to an island I found south of the Shattered Sea."

"The one where you were shipwrecked?"

"That's the one. When I was there, after I touched the fountain that gave me these abilities, it also seemed to heal some scratches I'd gotten from a panther."

"And you think if you go back there, it will help heal all of this?"

Nereyda shrugged, then winced as she regretted it. "Hard to say, but it's worth a shot."

Devrim paced around the room, his hand stroking his chin. "Who will you take with you?"

"Jax and my crew, of course. I also want to bring my friends Manu and Fariha. We'll need to set out from Antalia anyway, so we can pick Fariha up there and grab Manu on the way north."

Devrim nodded. "Fine, you can go. In fact, you've done more than enough for this cause." He stared in her eyes with a kind look. "I will give you a ship and you can keep it. You do not need to come back. Go heal and rest. Your part of the bargain is fulfilled."

"Are you serious?" Nereyda asked. "What about the rest of the war? What about us?"

"After what happened here, I worry if you'll survive if you come back. They nearly killed you and may succeed next time. I'd rather know that you are safe and healthy far away than risk watching something horrible happen to you."

"Thank you, Devrim, for giving the sea back to me." She gave him a deep kiss.

CHAPTER TWENTY-EIGHT

As their ship, the Morgiana, pulled closer to the island's shore, Nereyda recalled her last arrival there. Most of the wreckage of the ship she had been pressed into service on remained in the clear water, near a rock that jutted sharply out of the water. She recalled how she had pulled Commander Erhan to shore, in an act of stupidity that Nereyda had increasingly come to regret. She should have let him drown after he had hit his head and fallen off of the ship in the storm that had wrecked them. It wass unfortunate that her instincts to protect members of her crew overcame her hatred of the man who had become her nemesis.

Today, at least, the weather was clear. A few clouds drifted above as the sun shone down on them. It might have been hot except for the breeze blowing off of the ocean. Palm trees swayed at the top of the sand that lined the coast.

Nereyda forced herself to stand up straight as she stood near the helm, though the muscles in her back strained to keep her upright. Her crew needed to see her as strong, even though her back ached with the effort. For now, at least, her fever seemed to be held at bay. It had started a few days ago and had grown steadily worse since. Yesterday, she had spent the whole day in bed.

Fariha had given her an herbal tea that supposedly helped with fever. Nereyda didn't know if it was the tea, the wind, or the hope of finding healing that helped, but she was glad that she wasn't debilitated for this part of their journey.

Manu had an eager, maybe even hungry, gleam in his eye as he gazed out over the coast. He had jumped on the ship as soon as they had swung by and offered him the chance, and he'd spent the trip helping the crew with surprisingly youthful vigor.

"I think we're as close as we can get," said Jax from the helm.

"I agree," said Nereyda. "Let's not beach ourselves. As nice as this place is, I'd rather not get stuck here again. Once was enough."

After they dropped anchor, Nereyda, Jax, Manu, and Fariha all boarded a rowboat and set out for shore. Nereyda kept trying to help row, despite the remaining ache in her shoulders and the torn muscles in her back, but the others wouldn't let her. Sweat dripped down her forehead as the sun stirred up her fever once again. She grumbled as they helped her out of the boat and through the forest toward the pond. She hated being fussed over.

"Manu," said Nereyda, "do you want to see the remains of your friend? The one whose journal I found? It's on the other side of this pond."

"Yes, I would very much like to pay my respects, though I think it can wait until we see if this fountain can heal you."

"We're here now, and it's light out. Once we get inside, I figure you might want to explore for a while."

"Very well. How do we get there?"

"There's a cave entrance on the other side of the waterfall."

Manu led the way around the pond as Nereyda's friends helped steady her. "It's flat sand. I think I can manage."

"I'm sure you can," said Fariha with amused incredulity, "but let's be safe."

Nereyda groaned but resisted the urge to shake their hands off. She hoped that the fountain would heal her, if only so that they would let her walk on her own without fussing over her through every step.

They passed into the cave where Nereyda had spent a night during her time shipwrecked on the island. In a corner, the burnt skeleton lay on the stone ground with a journal with charred edges next to it. Manu knelt to pick up the book and flipped through the pages. "This is Adil's handwriting," he said. He flipped back to the beginning and skimmed the content, nodding to himself. "Here are his notes on our preliminary research." As he kept going, he slowed down his reading. "It just stops," he said as he closed it. "You didn't take anything out of this after you found it?"

"No, that was it."

"How much did you read?"

"Not all of it. I only saw the part at the end."

"My friend wrote about what happened when Lochan touched the fountain and was drawn to touch fire. It consumed him. Burned through his whole body as he ran through the ruins, trying to stop it. Where did you defeat the fire demon you spoke of?"

"Right outside. I threw him into the pond with wind as he tried to grab me."

"Show me," Manu asked as he put the journal in his travel pouch.

Nereyda climbed out of the cave and shuffled around the pond, occasionally leaning on Fariha or Jax as her damaged back muscles started to give up on standing up straight. The pond tempted her to jump in as her fever continued to rise. Pressing on, she arrived at the spot where she had first discovered the powers the fountain had granted to her. The place was marked by blackened sand where the demon had stepped. "This is it. I stood on the edge here, and blew him out into the middle, about there," Nereyda said as she pointed.

Manu stood next to her, his hand on his chin and his eyes narrow as he gazed into the pond. Suddenly, his eyebrows shot up. "I see something," he said. He leaned close to her and pointed to a spot closer to the shore. "There's something catching the sun under there. Looks like it's made of metal."

"What is it?"

"I have a guess, but I'd need to see it to know for sure."

"I can go get it," said Jax. Without waiting for a response, he waded into the water up to his waist, then bent down to retrieve the object. As he pulled it out, it appeared to be a pendant of some kind, with a gem in the center. Jax slipped out of the water and handed the pendant to Manu.

He turned it over in his hands. "It's what I thought. This belonged to Lochan. He must have become the fire beast."

"I'm sorry, Manu. I didn't know. Maybe there is some way I could have spared him . . ." said Nereyda.

"No, don't feel guilty. He was not a violent man. If that thing you described attacked you, then none of my friend remained within his body. And even if a trace was there, you did him a favor by freeing him from that existence. It seems that you got quite lucky in your own experience with this fountain."

"I don't think I'm a fire demon yet, at least. I might have a fever right now, but I don't think I'm actually on fire."

He gave her a small smile. "No, I think you're safe. Adil's journal said that the negative effects came on quickly."

"How did the pendant survive the heat, though? He was hot enough to melt my dagger when I threw it at him."

"That is the wonder of engineering from Hariana. We can treat metal and other materials to be heat resistant. We don't usually use such technology on trinkets like pendants, but my friend did enjoy splurging on this kind of thing." He gazed at it for a moment longer before tucking it into a pocket. "I suppose we should be on our way. I think we've learned as much as we can from this place."

"Sounds good. You can see the spire up there, at the top of the waterfall. That's where we're going." She started to lead them into the forest but winced as her back tightened up in protest.

"Enough stubbornness," Fariha said. "Let us help you the rest of the way."

"Fine." She reluctantly put her weight on Jax and Fariha. They helped her through the forest and up the hill to the rocky spire that jutted upward like a dagger from the center of the island, a natural guide to their destination. Under the afternoon sun, a light breeze carried the smell of the sea inland. Manu followed a few steps behind them.

"This is much better weather than when I climbed up here before," Nereyda said as she reminisced. "Just as well; I don't think I could make it in a storm. Last time, I had to crawl on my hands and knees to avoid getting blown off of this ridge. Wouldn't work so well with one hand." She let out a mirthless laugh. She didn't want to let on that she felt like she was burning up. The infection in the wounds on her back felt like it was on fire and her fever had reached the boiling point. She ignored it, knowing that her best chance to recover was in front of her.

"We'll get you there. It's not much farther," said Jax.

"You can finally see where all of this trouble started."

"I've known you for a few years," said Fariha. "And I think the trouble started long before that."

"Ha, ha. And you still decided to come along with us."

"Only because I don't think any other healer could put up with you for an entire voyage. You need me to keep you in your place."

"If I had both of my hands, I'd like to see you try."

They reached the opening in the spire and all of them squeezed into the gap, forced to walk sideways so they could keep hold of Nereyda.

She winced as they helped her maneuver through the passage, but didn't complain. The chamber within contained the familiar low wall, surrounding a ladder that led into the main section of the ruins. A low blue light glowed from below, causing Nereyda to let out a breath of relief.

The fountain must still work.

"Okay," said Nereyda, "Fari and I can climb down and see if this works. The two of you can wait up here."

"Can't we see this fountain in action?" asked Manu.

"You can, right after I do this. I'm going to undress to get into the fountain, and I'd rather not have a crowd."

"Feeling shy?" asked Jax.

"No, I just don't feel like putting on a show." Nereyda didn't tell them that she still hated them seeing her wounds fully uncovered, even though they had plenty of times. "Now, head on down," she said to Fariha, "and I'll be right behind you."

Nereyda walked to the low wall and climbed over to the ladder.

"Are you sure you don't need help climbing down?" asked Jax.

"Should I have help? Probably. But I don't want it," she said with stubborn determination. "I'm going to do this myself."

"Okay. But if you need help, let us know."

Nereyda's instinct was to just vault over the side and land on the ground since she knew it wasn't very far. However, she had to restrain herself due to her current condition. Instead, she sat on the edge of the low wall and rotated, so her legs dangled into the hole. With her only hand on the edge of the wall, she eased herself down until her feet reached the rungs of the ladder. She clung to the top of the ladder as long as she could as she stepped down. When she arrived at the limit of her reach, she rested her left forearm on one of the rungs to support her as she brought her right hand down. Placing weight on her half-healed stump hurt, but she forced herself to bear it for a moment. Slowly, she worked her way to the bottom of the ladder.

She stopped for a minute to take in the large room. The fountain's basin sat in the middle of the chamber and looked about twenty feet across. Three tiers rose from the center. A bright blue cascade of wispy energy fell down from the top into the basin, where it swirled. The light from the fountain illuminated the entrances to several passages that led in all directions out of the chamber. Nereyda hoped that there wouldn't be another fire demon lurking in the dark this time. One chase through ancient ruins was enough for a lifetime.

"You ready, Nereyda?" asked Fariha.

"Definitely."

Her friend offered her an arm for support, but Nereyda strode past her toward the fountain. Her long, quick steps pounded pain into her back as she crossed the stone floor, but she didn't care anymore. As she reached the edge of the fountain, she started fumbling with her clothes as she tried to undress one-handed. Without a word, Fariha stepped beside her and helped her.

"Thanks," said Nereyda as her friend took her clothes.

"I'll keep track of them for you. Enjoy your bath in the weird light."

"Let's hope this works."

Near the perimeter of the fountain, she noticed details she had missed before. Carvings covered the knee-high wall that surrounded the basin. Flames. Waves. The sun. Lightning bolts. Others that were less clear.

Nereyda slid over the wall, setting her feet in the blue wisps of light that pooled at the bottom as they flowed from the central sculpture, a stone flower that blossomed at the top of the tiers. So far, she felt nothing other than the cold stone against her bare feet. She lowered herself in and lay facedown rather than put her weight on her back. The light whirled across her face as she rested her head on the ground.

She breathed in a lungful of the substance, and warmth filled her chest. As she held it in, the heat spread out from her chest to her back and through her limbs. Instead of rushing into her and overwhelming her as it had the first time she interacted with the fountain, the light filled her slowly. The nerves all over her body tingled with a pleasant sensation somewhere between a tickle and a sting. Nereyda took slow, steady breaths as the energy coursed through her. Gentle heat crisscrossed the gashes across her back, and the constant ache subsided. Her fever dissipated, and a renewed vigor filled her spirit.

She also felt something else.

Her left wrist started to itch under the bandages. Quickly, she tore them off with her right hand. She let out a cry as bones, blood vessels, sinew, and skin all extended from her wrist and stitched together. Her mouth hung open as the flesh and bone of her wrist morphed and grew, creating a brand-new hand.

She gasped, breathless with amazement. She'd only wanted to take the edge off of her infection and heal her back. Nereyda stared at the new hand as she flexed and moved her fingers. It was a perfect regeneration. Too perfect, in fact. As she felt the palm of her new hand, it felt smoother than it should, lacking the callouses that came with years of using her hands to work with rope, operate her ship's helm wheel, and fight with a sword. She relished the chance to toughen it up again and even looked forward to dealing with some blisters as her hand adapted.

The warm tingle that had spread through her body subsided, and she sat up, still fiddling with her new hand.

"Mother of the gods," shrieked Fariha. "Where did that come from?"

"I don't know. This healed some scratches last time, but this is a bit beyond that."

"Well, I'm glad to see you'll get back to being useful on a ship again, rather than just lazing about," Fariha said with a smirk.

Nereyda hopped out of the fountain. The cool air of the chamber tickled the skin across her back. She stretched her arms and reveled in being able to move without feeling like her back would rip apart. "Yeah, I'm ready to get back into trouble now that I have two hands again."

"I recommend not losing this one, though. It's quite a trip back here."

"I'll try to keep track of it. How does my back look?"

"It's completely healed." She ran a hand over Nereyda's bare skin. "The light isn't very good in here, but I don't even feel any sign of scarring. It's perfectly smooth. I'm a bit jealous, actually."

"Well, take your time and appreciate it if you want."

Fariha giggled. "While it's been a lovely view of you, I think you should probably get dressed. Our friends are waiting up top. Besides, aren't you with Devrim? What would he think?"

Nereyda's mood fell a bit as she wondered if she'd get to see Devrim ever again. She forced back the wave of sadness and shrugged a shoulder. "No clue, but everyone's allowed one of each, right? But you're right. We shouldn't keep them waiting any longer. Manu is probably jumping out of his own clothes in excitement to check out this fountain," she said as she took her bundle of clothes and started putting them on.

Fariha pressed her eyes shut and shook her head. "I don't need that image in my head. You, sure, that was fine."

"Just fine?" Nereyda raised an eyebrow.

Fariha blushed. "Err."

"I'm just teasing you, Fari. You make it too easy. But I'll try not to say anything else to make you imagine an old man naked."

"You just did."

"Anyway, I have clothes on again, so let's get our friends."

Nereyda yelled up to the opening, "We're done. You can come down and explore now."

Manu scurried down the ladder a moment later, his academic curiosity driving him with a speed beyond his years, letting himself drop the last several feet in his excitement. His eyes immediately went to the glowing fountain.

"This is incredible. I've read bits and pieces of information about something like this, but to see it for real . . ." He glanced down at Nereyda's new hand, his eyes widening. "Your hand is back! I never saw anything about that in any of my research."

"What did I just hear?" asked Jax as he stepped off of the ladder.

"I have a left hand again," Nereyda said as she waved at him, wiggling her fingers.

"That's amazing. And your back?"

"That's all healed, too."

Manu grabbed her hand and turned it over as he ran his fingers over the skin. "Incredible. Simply incredible. The fountain did all of this?"

"It did. Do you think it could heal anybody who goes into it?"

"It's hard to say. In some of the tales that I've read about these fountains, people can become overwhelmed by the power. I believe that's what happened to Lochan. I don't know if it was something about him that caused him to be overcome by fire, or if you have a particular quality that allows you to absorb the power without negative effects. Either way, I would not risk touching it myself, and I would recommend that others stay away as well, at least until we can learn more about the nature of this power. Someday, perhaps, we can arrange safe experiments to study how it works."

"Do you think it could bring someone back from the dead?"

"You're thinking of your friend, Elvar."

"If we had brought him here right away, would he have had a chance?"

Manu shook his head. "Doubtful. Healing your hand was quite a miraculous surprise, but I think I would have seen something in my research if these fountains could resurrect people. That seems like a large omission if such a thing were possible. And there is no telling if Elvar would have come back in the same state of mind as when he died. I would hate to bring back the body just to find that the mind and soul had become corrupted. Besides, it could become a dangerous game to decide who or who not to bring back. While I don't believe in the gods' wrath as far as your abilities are concerned, playing god yourself with other people's lives would invite trouble."

"You're probably right. Now that I'm healed, you want to look around for a while?"

"I don't even know where to begin."

"Just pick a doorway and see where it goes. When you run out of hallway, come back and pick another one."

"What are you going to do while I explore? Don't you want to come with me?"

"Nah, I saw enough of this place the last time I was here. Bad memories, even with the fancy new abilities I picked up. I want to head outside and fight something."

Manu raised his eyebrows. "Are you suddenly in a bloodthirsty mood? Did the fountain affect you in other ways?"

"No, I don't want to kill anything. Jax, want to come spar with me down by the pond?"

He shrugged. "Sure. It'll be good for you to give that new hand a try, and see if it's as good as the old one."

"Exactly. My last one did some pretty awesome things, but I hope to top that with this guy. Let's head out now. Fariha, are you cool with keeping an eye on Manu while he wanders around?"

"I can do that. I'd rather watch you two spar, though."

"Next time," said Nereyda. "I don't think Jax will be too thrilled with an audience while I lay him on his ass."

"We'll see," he said with a smirk.

They climbed out of the chamber and hiked back down toward the pond. As she moved through the forest with an energetic bounce in her step, Nereyda took out her cutlass and waved it around with her left hand, getting a feel for how it moved. It seemed to be the same as her old hand. Swiping at branches and leaves in their path, she struck as accurately as ever. She smiled as she looked forward to winning some more fights. It did feel as if she had lost some strength in her arm over the last two weeks, without using her hand. In fact, her right hand had even atrophied slightly since she hadn't been doing as much physical work in general.

Not a problem; she'd get herself back into shape in no time with some drills on the ship. She had always practiced fighting with both hands, in case something happened to one or the other. She had forgotten which hand was dominant, as she did some tasks with one and others with the other. Even if she didn't get disarmed or lose a hand, it was useful to be able to switch up her combat stance in the middle of battle. If her opponent thought she was right-handed, switching to using her left usually threw them off balance, giving her an opening. Plus, since most people were right-handed, nearly everyone had less experience facing someone fighting with the left.

Nereyda and Jax arrived at the pond, and they found an open patch of beach for a sparring match, a spot with plenty of room for footwork and without overhanging branches that could get in the way of their sword swings.

They faced off a couple of arm lengths apart and held out their swords, Nereyda keeping hers in her left hand. "Go ahead and start," she said.

Jax took a timid swing at her left shoulder, which Nereyda batted away with little effort. "What was that?" she asked. "I wanted a sparring match, not an insect to swipe away. Don't hold back. You don't have to be gentle with me." She winked at him.

"Fine, if you want a fight, then I hope you can keep up."

This time, a wild look gleamed in his eyes, and he lunged toward Nereyda with a full-strength swing from her right. She blocked it and felt the familiar pang of her muscles straining against the force of the hit.

She laughed as she shoved his blade away and thrust at him with an attack of her own.

Jax gritted his teeth and swatted her cutlass away.

With her right hand, Nereyda shoved his sword arm away, spinning into an elbow to his gut with her left arm.

"Oof, what the hell?" said Jax. "Isn't this supposed to be a fun match?"

"I'm having fun. I don't know what you're talking about. You can't be afraid to fight dirty. Low blows, blind hits—anything that gives you an edge is fair game. And don't complain. I barely hit you. In a real fight, I would have laid you out on the sand."

Jax set his face with determination or frustration—Nereyda couldn't quite tell which—and came at her with a series of fast strikes, which kissed off of Nereyda's blade as she whirled around him. As she moved, his foot struck out and caught her in her footwork.

Nereyda tumbled to the ground and lost her grip on her cutlass, sending it falling out of her reach. As Jax pointed his sword down at her and smiled, she instinctively threw her hand in front of her, and a blast of wind flew into him, tossing him through the air and into the pond with a splash.

Even as the move took the wind out of her, a silent laugh came to her lips as she watched Jax splash around in the water, pulling himself to shore. He waded out with a scowl on his face, having managed to keep ahold of his sword.

"That's definitely not fair. I finally trip you up, then you go and do that. Even if I fight dirty, how am I supposed to outplay that?"

"You're not supposed to, that's why I do it. Don't act so glum. That was a good trip. I didn't think you'd do it, and you caught me off guard. You read me well. And look on the bright side: there aren't a lot of other people out there who can do what I can do. None that I know of, at least. And I won't try to kill you."

Jax relaxed his shoulders and smiled. "You're right. Would you mind showing me more of how you fight as we sail?"

"Absolutely we can do that. I need to keep working out both of my arms after taking it easy for too long. I suppose I've given my hand enough of a test for now, though. How about we go check on Manu and Fariha and see if they're ready to head back to the ship?"

"Perfect. I'm ready to head out. We can finally head home and see my people." Jax's eyes lit up as he mentioned going home.

"I look forward to meeting them. I hope we can meet some of the children you saved."

"I'd like that very much, as well."

After they retrieved the others from the ruins, Manu wouldn't stop talking about everything he saw there. "I wish I had paper to transcribe all of the inscriptions. Some of them matched what I've seen in books, but others were entirely new. And we'll have to rewrite our model for power absorbance entirely after what happened with the fountain." He chattered the whole way through the forest and back to the ship. Nereyda thought the fountain was interesting but got lost in some of the details that Manu told her.

Once they emerged onto the beach, Nereyda took a fast stride toward their rowboat, sitting down at one of the oars.

"Giving me a break this time?" asked Fariha.

"I want to keep testing out my back," said Nereyda.

She set a fast rowing pace for Jax and herself as they pushed out toward their frigate, feeling the muscles in her back work without feeling like they were tearing apart. The familiar ache of muscles working hard returned in a way that made her feel rejuvenated. She perspired with the natural sweat of exertion rather than fever.

When they arrived at the side of the Morgiana, she scrambled up the ladder. As the first one to the top, she turned and offered her new hand to help the others climb aboard. Fariha paused for a moment to marvel once again at the regrown hand. As Nereyda pulled each of her friends up, she gave them a clap on the back and thanked them for helping her get herself back together in one piece. She bounced up to the helm and ran her hands over the wheel, welcoming the feeling of the wood.

She looked over the crew. They had been making preparations for their cruise farther north into the Shattered Sea. Pirates and Islanders mixed together as they secured lines, swept the deck, and stowed cargo. They joked and laughed together, their spirits renewed by their time at sea. Each group took turns teaching the other sea shanties. Raunchy pirate songs contrasted with soaring Islander pieces.

Some other shore parties had gone out to collect water and any other resources that they might be able to scrounge, but all of them had returned. She watched as a few crew members hauled the boat they had used up and over onto the deck, securing it in place. Once that was done, she raised her voice over the ship.

"As you all can see, I'm feeling much better now. You've all done a great job of keeping things together while I haven't been well. Now that my back is healed and I even have a shiny new hand, it's time to get underway to the Shattered Sea and take our Islander friends home." The crew cheered at her words.

She let the cheers die down before continuing. "We'll need to be wary, though. We've never sailed the Shattered Sea before. Even our Islander members are not familiar with all of it. The air is misty, and the islands are unpredictable and scattered. There are narrow passages where danger could lurk around any corner. Both Stalstan and Imperial ships patrol there, so we need to watch out for possible enemy ships in addition to the treacherous terrain. Still, this is what we were made to do. It's time to head out and find an adventure."

She gave the orders to pull away from the island and put her hands on the helm wheel to guide the ship out. Once they were on the open sea, she called "Full sail!" to the crew, and they accelerated north toward the depths of the Shattered Sea. The wheel in her hands filled her with life, even more so than fighting with her cutlass. She remembered many more exhilarating times piloting the Storm Raven, but this came very close: just the simple feeling of holding the wheel with both hands again.

CHAPTER TWENTY-NINE

Brynja and the other captains of the headquarters formation stood on the deck of the flagship of the Western Cambisian Fleet, listening to Admiral Mansur go over their strategy for facing the Stalstan fleet. Around them, the other squadrons of ships bobbed in the water, awaiting their orders.

"If our scouts are correct," he said as he paced the deck, "the enemy fleet is not far over the horizon. We are mere miles away from our chance to punish Stalsta and cripple them for years to come." He gazed out over the water before returning his attention to them. "What we need is someone to draw them to us." His eyes fell on Brynja. "You, pirate; you'll do."

"Wait, aren't we supposed to be part of your headquarters formation?"

"The headquarters squadron is for the most important ships. And wouldn't you agree that this is a critical role to play? You get to lure our enemy into our trap. That's quite an honor. Do you really want to refuse such a prestigious assignment?" He looked down on her with an arrogant smirk, challenging her to dissent.

Brynja knew better than to try to argue her way out of it. "No, sir. We'll do it. Gladly."

"I knew it. Now get going, and the rest of us will be behind you as soon as you've gotten them to engage you."

Brynja gave a weak salute then strode across the bridge linking her ship to the flagship, Ilker at her heels. "I thought you said we were going to be in one of the safest spots for the battle. Now we're stuck doing the most dangerous job."

"I know what I said," he snapped. "And I'm not any happier about this than you are. I'm loyal to the Empire, and I'll make sure you do your job, but that doesn't mean I have to be excited about putting my life at the tip of the spear."

"Now you see how much the Empire really cares about returning your loyalty."

Ilker didn't have a response, so Brynja set about ordering her crew to get ready to sail over the horizon in search of a fight. They made their preparations in silence, a nervous air hovering over them. She eyed the flagship and the rest of the fleet, in case an opening had been left open. She hated the idea of her crew being used as bait and would escape if she could. Unfortunately, no escape route presented itself. As soon as they were ready, they set full sail and cruised away from the rest of the fleet.

After several minutes, she spotted a forest of masts poking above the horizon, then specks of color from the Stalstan flags waving in the wind. As the enemy fleet came into view, her heart accelerated as she counted its ships. The Stalstans must have had several dozen vessels. Looking back, Brynja could barely see the Cambisian fleet and hoped that she and her crew weren't being sent to their deaths.

She returned her gaze to the Stalstans. Her hands grew clammy and she wiped them on her shirt before gripping the wheel tight. Three ships had broken formation and zoomed out from the larger fleet, which had also started cruising in Brynja's direction.

"Half sail," she commanded.

Their ship slowed down, and she waited for the Stalstan ships to approach. As they surged closer at full sail, they came into focus as frigates. Two dozen guns, divided between two rows, protruded from both sides of each ship. Marines scurried about the decks and formed up into boarding parties.

One ship aimed straight for the Tavara, while the other two maneuvered around to either side. Brynja and her crew would soon be surrounded. When they were almost within firing range, Brynja turned the ship and headed back toward the main Cambisian fleet.

Shots sounded behind them, followed by the splash of cannonballs landing in water. A couple of droplets landed on the back of Brynja's neck. Glancing over her shoulder, she saw that the other ships gained quickly.

"Full sail!" she yelled. The Tavara sprinted over the water, though the Stalstans kept pace. Ahead, the Cambisian fleet had started to close the distance.

The three pursuit ships fired their deck guns toward the Tavara again and again, still falling short of their target. Through the portholes on their lower decks, gun crews watched, waiting for the chance to deliver a broadside.

A distant barrage of cannon fire sounded. A second later, the three ships around them exploded. Two shots also struck the hull of the Tavara.

Brynja was momentarily confused about the source of the fire, but then she glanced toward the Cambisian fleet. The heavy ships of the line had formed a wall of ships, their broadsides aiming at Brynja and the Stalstan ships behind her. Plumes of smoke billowed from the guns of several of the ships. They had fired on the Stalstans, not caring that Brynja and the Tavara were in the strike zone.

Even though they couldn't see her, she scowled in the direction of the Cambisians. The Stalstan fleet loomed ever closer as it continued sailing toward Brynja and whatever had destroyed its vanguard. Stuck between the two large groups of ships, Brynja had no choice. She would sail back to the Cambisians and get ready for the larger fight.

A minute later, the Cambisian ships of the line fired again as the Stalstan fleet entered their range. As before, they showed little regard for the privateer ship that sailed in the middle. This time, three shots struck the Tavara, one damaging the foremast, another striking just above the waterline off the port bow. The last smashed across the deck, killing and wounding several members of her crew.

With the next shuddering barrage that rocked the Tavara, Brynja stumbled and her momentum carried her over the railing and into the sea below.

CHAPTER THIRTY

Nereyda's initial elation about sailing subsided as they drew nearer to the Shattered Sea. The gray peaks of islands poked above the horizon, shrouded in a thin mist that Nereyda knew would only grow thicker and darker. When they drew near, she had the crew go to half sail to maneuver through the tight spaces. Nereyda had only been to the Shattered Sea once and not long enough to learn every nook and cranny or where every passage led, so Jax stood next to her and shared what tips he could.

Now, unlike her time with the Imperial prisoner ship, she didn't even have a map to help guide her or help her plot a course. The Empire held those maps closely, not letting just anyone have access to them, not even—in fact, especially not—traders. The Emperor didn't want the average person to be able to associate with Islanders. It made it easier to demonize them and portray them as inhuman monsters set on marauding and destroying anyone who got close, Nereyda supposed.

During her time with Jax and the others, she hadn't seen any sign of the violence they supposedly were capable of. She supposed that it was similar to the church's lies about her. She was a victim of a massive misinformation effort to fool the population into hating her, as the Islanders were.

She turned to Jax and asked him, "So where do we go? I've only piloted a ship for a bit in these waters."

"I can only help you find where the capital was the last time I was there."

"Why wouldn't it still be there?"

"It can move. You'll see when we get there."

"And if it isn't there?"

"Then we hope for a clue about where it went. For now, keep wending your way north." He pointed in that direction. "I'll let you know if I think you're heading down a dead end or going the wrong way."

"That's reassuring. I don't want to end up smashing against any rocks."

"Didn't you tell me you went through here at full speed before? If so, this should be nothing." He winked at her.

"I did, and that was crazy, even by my own standards," she admitted. "I had to do it, though. That Stalstan ship had burned a village to the ground. We weren't in a good place to fight them, but at least we were able to determine who the culprits were. I don't know what the Empire planned on doing with that information, though."

As the Morgiana pierced through the fog and slid through the channels, the mountainous islands consisted of dark rocks along the water's edge, then sharp cliffs that led up to dense, tall forests.

"Whatever the Empire's purpose, it wasn't to protect the lives of some random Islanders. They only care about Stalsta being here because they don't want them moving in on their territory." His voice took on a growl as he spoke of the Empire. "If Stalsta figured out how to ally with the Islanders, or take the territory for themselves, it would give them a massive edge against the Cambisians. The only reason the Empire cared about what happened to that village is so they know whom to fight for their own sake."

In a relatively straight passage, Nereyda took a moment to stretch her arms and fingers before she gripped the wheel again. "It's strange. Erhan, the commander I was with, the one who convinced Brynja to betray me and had me whipped in the mines—he hates me. He hates us. Well, at least my crew because they're pirates. I don't know if he cares one way or another about you aside from the fact that you're with me. But he actually did seem to care about the lives of those villagers. He seemed genuinely distraught when we were there, among the charred houses and burnt corpses."

Jax shook his head with a disbelieving look. "I'm sure it was all an act to gain your sympathy. Didn't he also murder your friend in front of your eyes? I was there outside the mines when he did that."

Nereyda sighed and nodded. "That was the second time he'd done that, actually. The first time, when we were brought to Manisa right after being caught, he killed one of my best friends. Jovan hadn't even been a pirate, just my fence, but Erhan didn't know that. He only came along with us after a rival pirate burned down his warehouse. We always got along well and made sure to get a drink or two whenever I was in port. Jovan hadn't even done anything wrong. I had tried to run away, and Erhan murdered my friend in order to punish me." She squeezed the wheel for a second as she recalled her friend's death.

Jax leaned against the railing near the helm. "He doesn't seem like someone who could truly care about what happened to the Islanders, to my people. He's the sort of person who can kill in cold blood, like the person who killed my Avra was."

"You're right. I don't know why I keep trying to redeem him in my mind. And I don't know why I saved his life when we crashed on that island. I should have left him to die."

"No, I don't think you should have left him, even though he's caused a lot of pain for you. You're loyal to your crew, or anyone whom you view as your crew. And Erhan, for all of his faults and even though he was your captor, had become a part of your crew, at least for a bit. That's why you did that. Don't lose that. It's going to help keep your friends with you. It's why we stick around. We believe that you're going to help us. And it makes us want to help you. That said, don't lose sight of the fact that Erhan has convinced a lot of people who haven't even met you that you're evil, just because you can do some fancy tricks with your hands."

"Oh, I can do quite a bit with my hands," she said with a laugh.

"That's not what I meant. Get your head out of the gutter." He stifled a chuckle as his face turned red. "Where was I? Oh, those people need to see that you're there to help them. That means doing things that make their lives better without scaring them."

Nereyda arched an eyebrow. "You mean without destroying a temple with a lightning bolt in front of their eyes?"

"That would probably help," Jax said with a smirk.

Nereyda chewed on her lip for a moment. "I'll keep that in mind. At least I don't have to go back at all now that Devrim gave me a ship and told me I've held up my end of the bargain."

"Do you miss him at all?" Jax tilted his head.

"I do." Nereyda frowned. "I would like to go back someday, once things settle down. For now, though, it's too dangerous for all of us. And your lot have earned their trip home. And maybe I can stick around for a while and see what the life of an Islander is really like."

"Good, and I can show you around." He clapped her on the shoulder. "You can worry about what to do about the people of the Empire if and when you decide to go back. Try not to dwell too much on it."

"I hope they give me a chance without throwing stones at me and demanding my execution."

"At the very least, fear might keep them at bay until they see the good things you can do. I'm sure the rumors about what you did at the temple will only spread and grow. Even as amazing as what you did was, you know how rumors tend to get pretty crazy."

"You're with a bunch of pirates." She waved toward her pirates working on deck. "Every time we tell a story about a raid, the ship is bigger, there are more guards, and the size of the loot grows. At this point, I can hardly remember the truth of some of our stories."

"Ah, you're not too different from some of our own then."

"Maybe we can compete to see who can tell the most outlandish tale sometime."

"I'd like that. Besides, we'll have plenty of time while we're sailing the Shattered Sea."

"Let's get farther in first and get comfortable, then we can do it when we're stopped for the night."

After a few days of traveling through the Shattered Sea, Nereyda felt lonely in the expanse of mazelike islands. They had yet to see a single other ship or even hear any sounds of life, aside from the bird calls and random wolf howls from the islands, way up in the forested peaks. Many of the islands were quite barren—whether from the great force that had broken up the sea or from exploitation by the Cambisians or others, Nereyda didn't know, and probably never would. They only took a few wrong turns that took them to dead ends where they had to turn around. At least they always kept their bearings though, and kept their heading generally in a northern direction.

One afternoon, a shadow appeared on their tail. As Nereyda glanced back from the helm, the vague shape of a ship lingered behind them, just at the edge of their vision in the fog.

"Jax," she said, "do you recognize that ship?"

"No, I don't," he said.

"You were one of them; don't you know how they greet outsiders?"

"I didn't serve on a patrol ship. We're not all marauders, like your emperor would have everyone believe." He gave her a wry smile.

"I know most of that was bullshit. I only figured you might know something."

"I'm afraid not. And things might have changed. It's been many months since I was here. After the Imperial attack on our settlement, and the Stalstan attack you've described, the Islanders may have become more reclusive and defensive."

"Keep an eye on that ship and let me know if anything changes."

Nereyda focused on piloting her ship through the narrow passages ahead, winding between the twisted and jagged islands.

She couldn't afford to watch behind her. Too many hazards lay in wait for them, from unexpected rocks and sudden changes in the coastline to sudden strong currents that she would need to counter with her steering and orders to her crew.

"Captain," said Jax. "I think they're closing. Not fast, but their shape is gradually becoming clearer."

"They are tailing us, then?"

"It seems that way. They don't seem to be making any aggressive moves. Probably keeping an eye on us and determining if we're friendly, hostile, or otherwise."

"Okay, then we have to not make any crazy moves to provoke them into thinking we're an enemy, and we should be fine."

"Sounds good."

As the Morgiana pulled into an intersection between passages, Nereyda heard a whoosh behind them. "Nereyda," said Jax, "something's changed. They launched a flare and started accelerating."

"Shit." Nereyda turned down one of the side passages to evade the ship.

"Are they pursuing us?" she asked.

"Let me see," said Jax.

They continued down the new direction for a second.

"Yeah, they're turning down to follow us," he said. "They're still picking up speed, too. Are you sure you want to run from them?"

"We haven't determined who they are, have we?"

"No, we haven't. They could be friendly Islanders."

As Jax finished talking, a shot echoed from behind and splashed into the water immediately behind them.

"Does that settle the question of whether they're friendly?" asked Nereyda.

"I suppose so. I don't see any flags or any other attempt to communicate with us."

"Neither do I. And a cannon shot is generally a form of communication that says 'we want you dead.'"

"True. Let's keep going then."

"That's what I'm doing," said Nereyda through gritted teeth.

Against her better judgment, Nereyda ordered the ship to go to full sail.

Her stunned crew hesitated for a second, then followed her orders.

The ship picked up to a reckless speed as Nereyda focused entirely on what was in front of her.

"Let me know what they do. I need to concentrate on not getting us killed on these rocks."

"Yeah, I'll do that."

The Morgiana twisted as it flew past the rocks and islands on either side of them. She gripped the wheel with white knuckles and remembered the last time she had done this. This time, an even thicker fog clouded her vision. Another shot rang out from behind them, followed by another. They didn't come close to striking their ship, landing in the water behind them with a pair of splashes.

They came to another intersection of watery passages, and Nereyda had to choose a direction to go. She could take a sharp right to head southeast, or a gradual left to take them back toward the north.

She chose left and sped into the new direction.

"Are they with us, Jax?" she asked.

"Oh yes, they are definitely with us. They're picking up speed, too. They're still closing."

"How?"

"They've gone to full sail to match you, and they're taking the corners closer. They must know these waters. I think they're Islanders, though why they're reacting this way rather than flagging us down to talk, I don't know."

They reached another set of branches, but before Nereyda could make a decision, a second ship came out in front of them and sped past the opening to the intersection. Some sort of material stretched out behind it.

A net.

At full speed, Nereyda could do little to slow their approach toward the net that stretched behind the ship and across the passage. The Morgiana would hit it with full force.

"No sails!" she ordered, trying to bring the vessel to as much of a stop as possible.

Still, they hit the net hard. The wood creaked as the ship lurched to a sudden stop, and the crew tumbled forward. Nereyda caught herself on the helm wheel. She bit her tongue as she came to a stop.

The other ship had slowed down, knowing the trap that Nereyda was piloting toward. Now it turned its side to them and pulled right alongside their ship.

Hooks flew across the gap, and people on the pursuing ship's side pulled the two ships together. The Morgiana was about to be boarded.

Nereyda didn't know how to react.

In the interest of avoiding an unnecessary fight, she chose to wait and see how this played out. When the ships had been brought close enough together, a number of people jumped across the gap and surrounded her crew with weapons drawn and pointed toward them.

The Islanders certainly had a unique and varied look to them. One man with a bald head wore a patchwork of hides and hefted a war hammer in his hands. A leather cord on his armor held his beads, which included mostly yellow, some red, and a few black. Another figure, a woman, wore a long dark green cloak. Curls of golden hair dangled from beneath her hood, along with a braid full of black, green, and yellow beads. She had no visible weapons, but her hands were concealed beneath the cloak. The outfits of the other Islanders were equally varied, assembled from whatever they had collected.

Fariha and Manu huddled next to each other down on the main deck, while Nereyda's own crew pulled their weapons out and aimed them at the new arrivals, waiting for any order from Nereyda about whether to fight or not. "What do we do, Captain?" asked Jax.

"I don't know."

A man with broad shoulders jumped across the gap and strode up to the aftercastle, next to the helm. He looked them over, judging Jax and Nereyda. His leather armor featured an assortment of jewelry sown into rows like military medals. The strand of beads that trailed down along his face contained yellow, some black, and a couple of gold, and was capped with one purple bead.

"I am Bessarion, of the Islander nation. I am here to ask why you are among us. I need to speak with your captain." He drew a black greatsword from his back. "Disarm yourselves or be destroyed."

CHAPTER THIRTY-ONE

Screams rang down as the rebel guards dragged Nereyda to the top of the stairs. Not actually Nereyda, but someone who looked close enough. With black hair and a lithe athletic frame, plus some cuts and bruises on her face, she passed as the pirate captain to anyone who didn't know her well. The guards shoved her to the ground on the top step, the ruins of the massive Temple of Ameretat in the background. The people of Goremia had assembled on the mountain slope and were jeering at her.

"You bastards," the woman growled. "Why are you doing this?"

The guards ignored her salty mouth. She attempted to crawl away, but she had only a stump where her left hand should be. Limbani didn't remember the woman missing a hand when she had found her in the city dungeon for some petty crime. Revulsion and regret spread like a cold chill. It should never have come to this. Devrim had gone too far.

One of the guards kicked Nereyda's look-alike to the ground and planted a foot on her back while the other backed up and watched for any sign of real resistance, but the prisoner could offer none.

The guard on her back raised his sword.

The woman's scream pierced Limbani's ears and darted straight into her heart.

Limbani glanced away as the sword fell.

Then silence.

Limbani jolted awake. The screams of the woman still echoed in her mind. It had merely been a dream, but the memories that fueled it were very real.

The rough fabric of her bedding clung to her clammy skin as she tossed her blankets from her. A slice of morning sunlight cut between the flaps of her tent. Limbani stared at the tent walls for a moment as she settled her pounding heart. The image of the woman, executed for the crime of looking like Nereyda, refused to budge from her brain.

She rolled out of her cot. As she dressed herself, the familiarity of her uniform on her skin comforted her and reminded her of her duty. It was her responsibility to protect Devrim, even from himself.

After she slipped on her boots, she pushed aside the tent flaps and emerged into the cool morning. Crisp air breezed off of the mountains and carried a hint of pine. Rows of tents stretched out around her on the field outside of Goremia. Groups of rebel soldiers marched around the camp on patrol. Others huddled around campfires.

Laughter and banter rippled from the pockets of soldiers. Limbani smiled at the combination of order and comradery that her troops displayed.

She marched through the camp toward Devrim's command tent. As she passed a larger campfire, the savory aroma of roasting meat drifted past her nose. Her stomach growled at the scent of food, but she didn't think she could eat with the woman's image still fresh from her nightmare. She'd join the troops later for some breakfast.

Two rows of tents later, Limbani arrived at the large command tent Devrim had set up. No voices sounded from within, only the rustle of papers.

She peeled back a flap of the tent and poked her head in. Devrim sat at a portable folding desk as he read through a pile of documents. "May I come in, sir?" Limbani asked.

He kept his gaze on the papers as he waved her in. "Yes, of course."

Limbani ducked into the tent and approached the desk. "Any important news?"

Devrim tapped the stack of papers. "Yes. More towns and villages have sent letters of support. They are rising up against their reigning nobles. Even some of the lords have been pressured into flipping sides."

"That's good. Maybe this will be over soon."

"I hope so. It seems that the news of Nereyda's apparent death has been tremendous for our recruiting efforts," Devrim said in too casual a tone.

Limbani picked at a button on her uniform. "That's part of why I'm here. I'm not sure that was the right approach."

He planted his elbow on the desk and rested his chin in his hand as he studied her. "How could it not be? As we just discussed, our numbers have swelled. What's the life of one criminal compared to overthrowing the Empire?"

Limbani chewed on her lip before responding. "I understand that it has been good for expanding our reach. I'm just worried that perhaps we're paying too high a cost."

Devrim rose and strode around the desk, then stood in front of Limbani, gazing down his nose at her. "Too high a cost? We killed some worthless nobody so that Nereyda, your friend and the woman I care about, could live. This single death has also gained us more support than any of our hard-fought battles. It seems like a pretty low cost to me."

Limbani crossed her arms. "I did not sign up for your household guard to murder innocent people."

"Innocent? We hauled her from jail. She committed a crime."

"That woman broke into a shop for a loaf of bread and was serving the time for that. She was only executed for the crime of looking like Nereyda."

Devrim loomed closer and dropped his voice into a sinister whisper. "Listen, if we're going to win this, we have to be willing to make sacrifices. This is a war. People die in war."

Limbani held her ground and stiffened her posture. "That doesn't mean you have to throw them away. Sacrifices are only worth it if you gain more than you lose. And this rebellion is not worth losing our humanity."

Devrim spun around and kicked his desk over. Papers flew around the tent. He whirled back to her and jabbed a finger toward her chest. "I did not scrape you off of my factory floor so that you could question me. We are a sliver away from having everything come together as planned. I did not work this hard for it to all come crashing down because of your crisis of conscience."

Limbani gave him a sideways look, unshaken by his outburst. "What do you mean everything is working out as planned? You have to admit that things have gotten a bit off track."

He lurched back. He stared at her for a second before he shook his head. "Yes, you're right," he said, his voice suddenly calm. "I only mean that we are on the path to victory as people realize we can get things done that the Emperor can't." He bent down and hauled his desk upright.

Limbani let it go. It wouldn't help to press Devrim any further at the moment. However, she resolved that she would not allow him to cross the line again. "Speaking of the path to victory, what's next for us? Keep waiting for more letters to pour in?" She knelt and gathered papers from the ground.

Devrim relaxed his shoulders, apparently relieved at the change in topic. "Our progress on land is excellent with our new allies. However, we will not be able to finish the job without a fleet. The Imperial Navy will make it nearly impossible to take the capital or any other city on the coast that remains loyal to the Empire."

Limbani passed the papers she had collected to Devrim. "In that case, we need a fleet of our own. Send letters back to all of these new allies and ask them to outfit any available ships for war. Have them meet us in Antalia."

"Antalia? That's on the opposite side of the continent from Manisa."

"I know, but it's the most protected harbor and our largest. We can't afford to lose whatever fleet we assemble."

Devrim rubbed his chin and nodded. "You're right. I'll send the messages. I only hope that it will be enough. Taking on both the western and eastern fleets is a dangerous proposition."

"It can't be true," said Erhan. "I don't believe Nereyda's dead."

He stared across at the broad-shouldered cloaked figure. Together, they sat at a rickety table in an abandoned house a week's ride east of Goremia. The trees outside rustled in the wind and the door creaked back and forth on its hinges, the latch rusted to the point of not catching.

Erhan had hated being left out of what happened in Goremia. When Sabah had told him to leave, he nearly disobeyed, but had changed his mind when the Sentinels escorted him from the city. Sabah had not said as much, but the message had been clear.

He was being forced out of Goremia.

Now, it was up to him to finish the work of the Inquisition.

"Why don't you believe she's dead?" asked the man as he leaned back in his chair.

"Because it doesn't add up." He drummed his fingers on the coarse wood. "I saw Devrim and Nereyda dancing together at the ball. He clearly cares for her, or he is very good at acting. And why throw away one of his best assets?" Erhan sighed. "As much as I hate to give her any praise, it would take a lot of troops to add up to her worth."

"You think the news is fabricated?"

"To some extent. I think they killed someone, but I don't think it was Nereyda."

"And the pirate conveniently vanished around the same time?" A wormy smile slithered across the cloaked man's face. "Why would she do that?"

A chill breeze penetrated the cracks in the old house. "It's hard to say. But it might be easier to guess where she'll appear next, if she is in fact alive."

"What are you thinking, Commander?"

The sarcastic emphasis on his rank irked Erhan, but he ignored it. "Nereyda's greatest value is at sea. And you can't take the capital without a navy."

"You think the rebellion will reach Manisa? You're willing to write off your Empire already?"

Erhan pounded his fist on the table. "I'm not writing it off, but I can see where things are going. When the rebels go for Manisa, Nereyda will be with their navy if she's alive. And I'm going to be there waiting for her."

CHAPTER THIRTY-TWO

The black blade glimmered in what sunlight penetrated the fog. Nereyda glanced around at the situation, looking at the heavily armed Islanders and the rows of cannons aimed at them from the ship alongside them. The commander of the Islanders stood in front of her with his sword drawn, alternating between pointing it at her and Jax. The bald man clutched his hefty war hammer just behind him.

"I need to speak with your captain. Drop your weapons if you don't want us to kill you right now. I won't repeat myself again."

"Jax, how do I respond?"

"Do not address each other," Bessarion interrupted. "I am speaking, not this Jax."

"I am Captain Nereyda," she said as she offered her hand.

He pulled away, keeping his sword on her.

"You are the captain? Tell your crew to disarm, then we can speak."

"Very well. Okay, friends, drop your weapons, and we'll see what this is all about."

Her crew hesitated.

"Do what I said. I'm sure this will all be fine. We won't win a fight, anyway."

With that, her crew dropped their weapons to the ground and watched their guests warily.

"Excellent. Thank you for complying. Most do not. Most try to fight as soon as they see our ships. You chose to run rather than fight. Why?"

"We didn't recognize your ship, and we aren't here to fight. We're just bringing your people home."

Bessarion scanned the faces of her crew and let out a grunt. "Still, you came into our territory uninvited, in an unfamiliar ship, and did not submit immediately upon hearing our warning shots."

"I didn't know how to interpret your shots. If you had been Stalstan or Cambisian, we could not afford surrender."

"Perhaps, but do Stalstans and Cambisians navigate our waters at full speed without crashing into the islands? Only we can do that. You seem to be pretty good at it, though." His gaze held both suspicion and admiration.

"I've done it before. This isn't my first time sailing in these waters."

"Are you one of us? Have you come home?" he shuffled back and let his sword fall a bit.

"No, but I was here on an Imperial ship, and I piloted as it chased a Stalstan ship."

He paced closer again and raised his sword once more. Cool metal rested against Nereyda's throat. "You are an Imperial? Are these Islanders your prisoners?"

"No, I was a prisoner when I was on that ship. And these people were prisoners in the mines with me when I was returned to the Empire."

"So how do you come into our sea now?"

"We escaped during a Stalstan attack, and we want to come home. Well, the Islanders want to come home. I'm helping them. The rest of us may also stay a while. Can you lead us to your home?"

He remained silent for a moment, then said, "You are here to join us?"

"Possibly. We are enemies of the Cambisians, as you are. I was part of, well, we all were part of, a rebellion to overthrow the Emperor."

Bessarion removed his sword from her throat, then tilted his head as he gazed at her. "You are the one whom we saw do the impossible feat of bringing an Imperial frigate through the Tempest's Corridor at full sail. I remember now. You are a legend. No outsider has ever done that. How did you do it without being familiar with the waters?"

"I guess I'm a natural. I feel where the water is going to go and I follow my intuition. But we can talk about that all day long somewhere else. Can you lead us through the Shattered Sea?"

"I need some verification from your Islander guests first." He turned to Jax. "What is your name? Is what she says true? Are you indeed Islanders come home? You aren't prisoners or perhaps even spies sent here by the Cambisians or Stalstans to undo our people?"

Jax cleared his throat. "My name is Jax, and what she says is true. We have all been friends and allies through many battles. She and her crew have yet to let us down. In fact, we would not have been free of the mines without her. Do you know what happened in Lamia? Here is a scar I earned while fighting there." He lifted his sleeve and revealed a long scar that trailed from wrist to elbow. "My wife died to send the children to safety. I hope they arrived safely and that they told the story of how the Cambisians slaughtered us."

The bald man leaned closer to Bessarion. "Sir, my daughter came from Lamia and spoke of this woman. I think he's telling the truth."

Bessarion's eyes widened as his eyebrows rose. He took a deep, measured breath. "Ah, yes. That was a somber day. A boat full of children arrived and they told us a tale of great death. A village of people put to the sword for no reason. Did you ever learn why they did that?"

Jax shrugged. "Our captors merely told us that we were impeding on the claimed territory of the Cambisian empire—though we saw no sign of a claim or settlement on their part."

"Yes, we have heard similar reports of anyone who attempts to settle or even camp too far south in the sea. The Stalstans may be up to something similar, perhaps. In fact, they may be up to something even more sinister. I've heard stories," he said looking at Nereyda, "of villages burned to the ground, with no sign of prisoners being taken. No message left, and nobody left alive to tell the tale."

"I have a guess about what is doing the killing," said Nereyda.

"Then perhaps you may be able to help us." Bessarion's posture relaxed a bit further. "I don't need to hear the full story now. Because of your willingness to surrender and the fact that you are among other Islanders who vouch for you, I am comfortable helping you bring these people home. However, we understand that our islands remain largely uncharted to you southerners, and we wish to keep it that way."

"We understand and will not reveal your secrets to anybody."

"Be that as it may, we can't rely on your word alone. Too much depends upon your secrecy and outsiders have not treated us in a way to be viewed as trustworthy."

"So what do you propose?" asked Nereyda. "You going to wipe our memories after the trip?"

"Nothing so complicated. You will leave your ship here and board our own vessel. We will blindfold you until we reach our capital city. When you get there, I will have you speak with our leader, who'll be interested to hear any news from outside of the Shattered Sea."

"What about our own ship?"

"Your ship will be towed safely to port. It will take some time, as sailing with a towed ship through the Shattered Sea is quite dangerous. However, we know what we are doing and will do so with care. Your ship will not be damaged."

"Fine," said Nereyda with a deep breath. "We'll do it. Tell us where to go and how to behave while we're on your ship."

"Good. Have your crew cross to my ship just there." He pointed at the ship that had boarded them. "The other ship, the one that drew the net across the channel, will be the one to tow your ship into port."

Nereyda led her crew across a set of boards that had been lowered across the gap between the ships. The Islanders, both on the Morgiana and their own, still had their guns drawn and swords unsheathed, watching the strangers warily. Some of the Islander crew recognized people who traveled with Nereyda and came up to greet them.

Bessarion came across the gap. "I know that some of you may know our new guests, at least those of Shattered Sea origin, but there will be time for reacquainting ourselves later. Now, quartermaster, please escort our friends to the hold and blindfold them so they can't see how we're provisioned. Once they have been secured comfortably, please let me know, and we will be off. And I do mean comfortably, my friend. They are our guests, not prisoners."

The bald man with the war hammer stomped up to them. A string of shark teeth wrapped around his neck. "I am Photios," he said. "Follow me and tell your crew to keep their eyes forward and hands to themselves."

Nereyda waved for her crew to follow the new person along with her. "We'll behave. Lead the way."

They climbed down a hatch in the deck, then down a couple of sets of stairs. They entered the dank hold of the ship. The scents of fish, salted beef, and unwashed sailors hit her nose. "Is this your idea of housing us comfortably? It stinks."

"We are not a luxury ship. We don't have much space for guest quarters. You will be comfortable because you won't be in chains and you will get to pick whatever spot you'd like to stand or sit in while you're down here."

"Fine. Put on the blindfolds, and we'll get this over with."

One by one, Photios and his assistants bound cloth hoods over the heads of Nereyda's crew. They saved her for last, putting a hood over her head after she had picked out a spot to sit and lean against the hull of the ship. A few minutes later, after she had heard the quartermaster go back up to the deck and call to the captain that everyone had been secured, the ship started to move.

Nereyda tried to focus on how the ship turned and how long it went in each direction. First it turned left, which meant they were going west. It went that way for five minutes. Next, the ship turned right to head north. Good, the right direction to the Islander capital, or so she guessed. It went that way for twenty minutes, by her estimation. Then it took another right—east—for ten minutes. Another right.

That's not right. Now we're going back the way we came.

The ship made a series of tight turns that made it difficult for Nereyda to keep track of all the maneuvers. Frustrated, she gave up her efforts of tracking. The Islanders weren't stupid. They were intentionally making random maneuvers designed to throw off any of the pirates below trying to figure out where they were going.

Nereyda couldn't blame them. She'd probably do the same thing in their position. It just was frustrating to be on the other end of it. She leaned back against the wooden hull and closed her eyes. She listened to the sounds of the ship. The creak of the hull as it bobbed in the waves and turned down the many passages of the Shattered Sea. The voices of the Islanders above, shouting commands and singing sailing songs to keep their rhythm. It was nice to hear that some things crossed cultural lines.

She even recognized some of the songs they sang from her time with the Islanders in her crew. They set the pace for various activities, whether it was making a turn, setting the sails, or pacing how fast the ship should go. She hummed along with the more familiar tunes.

Eventually, she dozed off against the hull.

A bump as the ship stopped brought her back to alertness.

Wood creaked as a couple of people descended into the hold. "Okay," said the voice of Photios, "we're here. You'll all be led onto the deck, where you can relax while we find a place for you. Captain Nereyda and Jax, you'll come with me first so you can meet with our leader."

Hands grabbed her and helped her to her feet, then guided her up the stairs. When they reached the deck, someone pulled the hood off of her head. Nereyda shielded her eyes with her hand until her eyes adjusted to the daylight. A haze of white fog hovered in the air. Jax stood next to her, along with Photios and another member of the Islander crew. Then she took in the city around her. It was unlike anything she had ever seen.

The city consisted of a large series of docks. Hundreds of ships sat next to the docks, ranging from tiny fishing boats to sizeable frigates. Closer to the shore of the nearest island, a number of buildings floated next to the docks, tied together so they didn't drift apart.

"Your crew will be fed while they rest on our deck," said Photios. "I wish we could make their time more comfortable, but it's the best we can do until we have approval from our leader, confirming that you are indeed the friends you say you are."

"Don't worry about it," Nereyda said. "They were living in the mines not too long ago. A a little longer on a ship is pretty luxurious compared to that."

"I've heard about that place. Many Islanders disappear there, never to return."

"I returned, and the others with us," said Jax.

"Then I am happy to see you. I hope that you shut that place down on your way out."

"We did," Nereyda said with a smile.

"Glad to hear it."

As they walked through the city toward the largest of the floating structures, Nereyda noticed that the buildings weren't just floating. They were ships themselves. They all had openings in the walls for oars, too low to be windows. The larger buildings had sails and masts tied along their sides, out of the way until they needed to set sail.

"Do you have anything on land?" she asked. Hills and a spike of a mountain loomed further into the island, their details obscured by fog.

"Not really," said Photios, as he swaggered a step ahead of them. "The dock network is tied to the shore, and we have anchors down to keep the whole thing from floating away. But this is designed to be completely mobile. Our capital is wherever we want it to be. If we ever suspect the Cambisians or Stalstans of learning where we are, we can pack up and move to another island."

None of the ship buildings rose more than a single story. All were made of wood and featured a range of paintings as varied as the Islanders' outfits. A shark pursuing its prey. A kraken with its tentacles wrapped around a ship. An island with towering peaks and dark green trees.

"How do your people know where to go if it moves when they're gone?"

"They know to find a settlement or a sailing ship to find a friend who can tell them. We have ways of communicating our capital's position in a way that is safe for us. Perhaps, if you become more trusted, we will teach you the best way of getting here and through the sea in general, without having ships follow you. We've long since learned how to shake a tail from us."

As they passed a group of children playing, a woman scurried out of the nearest houseboat and shooed the young ones inside as she stared at the strangers.

"You literally have a sailing city," she said.

Photios grunted his agreement. "Yes, it can all pack up and move in less than a day. Our fighting ships will buy us time if there is a threat close enough. However, our scout ships are supposed to warn us well ahead of time if there is an approaching enemy ship or fleet. But I've never seen more than one Cambisian or Stalstan ship at once in our waters. One lone vessel is not enough to present a true threat, but if it found us, it could lead a much more substantial force to us."

"Jax, have you ever been here?" Nereyda asked.

"I've been to the floating city, but I don't think I've been to this location. Has it moved lately?"

"Perhaps—I'm not sure I'm free to share that with you yet. We also conceal the timing of our moves. We don't want our enemies to find out their information is out of date. If they think our city is in one location when it isn't, that is advantageous to us."

Their guide led them over the docks to an expansive building that had two masts strapped along its side that Nereyda could see. She even saw the rudder hanging off of what must be the back of the ship when it sailed.

Colorful flags hung off the sides of the building, and intricate carvings were etched into the walls and two pillars that bracketed the entrance. "This is it," said Photios. "Our leader is inside, and will make sense of what you've told us and any news you have."

"Is there anything we should know to do, or not do?"

"You mean like courtly etiquette? No, not especially. Don't be too much of an asshole and you'll be fine."

"This sounds like my kind of place. I've gotten tired of all the rules and manners that the Imperial nobles shove in people's faces. It makes it tough to figure out exactly what a person's like when they keep it behind a mask."

"No masks here. That said, don't be rude. If you walk in like you own the place or like you're owed something, that will not end well."

"I'll do my best."

Jax smirked. "She does seem to have a problem with acting like she owns places."

Nereyda shot Jax a look. "Only when people are jerks. These people have brought us to their home without killing us or even locking us up. That's a head start on a lot of the people I've met."

"Fair enough. Should we get this over with?" he asked.

"Sure."

"Okay, I'll lead the way," said Photios. "Then I can make an introduction and get back to the ship."

The quartermaster pushed into the longhouse and Nereyda and Jax stepped in behind him.

CHAPTER THIRTY-THREE

Lanterns around the perimeter cast a warm light around the room. As outside, paintings adorned the walls. Each told a story, such as a naval battle or a fishing expedition.

A woman sat in a simple chair on the other side of a small table in the center of the single room that occupied the structure. She wore simple clothing and clutched knitting needles and yarn in her hands. An ornately carved wooden pendant adorned her neck.

The woman, who had gray streaks in what had once been black hair, looked up at the door as they entered. "Photios, what brings you here? Weren't you and the Bythos on patrol duty? I don't think you were due back in for several days? And who are these guests you've brought?" Even as she questioned Photios, her voice carried the feeling of a mother's warm embrace.

"These people are the reason we came back early, Sibylla. We found them sailing through our waters, and they entered the zone of warning. They weren't Cambisian or Stalstan, so we boarded their ship to learn who they were. They are just pirates, and are returning some of our people that we thought lost, including some from Lamia, like this one." He pointed at Jax. "They surrendered peacefully and with no resistance to our practice of blindfolding our guests. We are towing their ship here as we speak. So far, they have shown no sign of hostility. Bessarion and I thought you might want to meet these two and learn more about what is happening outside of our waters."

"Interesting." Sibylla appraised Nereyda with black eyes. "You did well to bring them to me. You may return to your ship, Photios. If I

224

have need of any more information from you or your captain, I will send for you."

Photios nodded his head in respect as he left the room.

Sibylla gave them a small smile. Her pendant, carved in the shape of an octopus, hung just at her clavicle.

"Thank you for returning our lost to us," she said to Nereyda. "It is rare to see such a kind deed from an outsider." She set aside her knitting, leaned forward, and clasped her hands. "Did you do this out of the goodness of your heart, or do you expect some sort of reward?"

"If it's not a problem, my crew would like to stay here and see what it's like to live among the Islanders."

"Ah, you want to live with us? Why?"

Nereyda appreciated that Sibylla didn't waste time with small talk and greetings. "You may have heard of the war back on the continent. We fought in it for a time and decided we'd had enough." A story about how she blew up a temple probably wouldn't make a great first impression. "Since we love sailing, maybe this can be a good new home for us."

"How did you meet Jax and the rest of our people that have come with you?" asked Sibylla.

"We were prisoners together in a mining complex. While we were there, the Stalstans attacked. We fought through them, then escaped after the battle."

Jax let out a short laugh. "That understates your own contribution, I think. You singlehandedly destroyed most of those fire demons."

"Fire demons, you say?" asked Sibylla. "We've had a few reports of Stalstan ships here in the Shattered Sea, along with villages burned to the ground in the areas where they've been spotted." Sibylla stroked her chin. "You've already earned our favor by returning our people to us, and you have my personal gratitude for that, but I'm afraid I must ask another favor of you, if you're willing."

"I'm listening," Nereyda said.

"These Stalstan ships always outrun us by the time we can get there, leaving behind a village of fire and little else. It might have something to do with these fire demons you mentioned. With your experience facing them, perhaps you'll have more luck than we've had so far. Would you be so kind as to find one of those ships and figure out what they intend to do? If you could even go so far as to capture or destroy it, I would be most grateful."

Nereyda was equal parts scared of facing the Stalstan fire demons again and eager to learn more about them. "You just want us to deal with one of them?"

"One is a good start for now."

"Will we be able to have a map of the sea? It would be quite helpful in finding these ships and noting where they are."

The elder thought for a moment, looking away as she considered. "Very well," she said as she looked back at Nereyda. "We will lend you one of our maps. It will not, however, have the location of our capital on it. No offense meant, but as you are still strangers, we need to be cautious."

"Will this map have some locations of your villages on it? That will give me a starting point to begin looking."

"We will mark the villages that have been attacked and those that are in the same region as the attacks. Any more information should be unnecessary for your mission, and we don't want to put our people at more risk in the event that your map is leaked."

"If this will make your people safer, we'll do it. Is there anything else we need before we go?"

"Your ship should be arriving soon. I would also like you to take one of our own with you. When you talk to Bessarion, tell him that I told you to take someone. He can pick someone from his crew, and that person will be your guide and observer."

"Observer?" asked Nereyda as she arched an eyebrow.

"We need to watch you and how you act. If you aren't who you say you are, the observer will tell us."

"Fine, we'll take a babysitter."

"It doesn't have to be babysitting. The person will probably be someone capable and will be useful to you on your short journey."

"Very well. Should we see ourselves out?"

"Yes. Do you know the way back to the ship you came in on?"

"I remember the way. Jax, do you have anything you wanted to ask about?"

"Ah, yes; thanks, Reyda." He looked at Sibylla and rubbed the back of his neck. "I heard that a boatful of kids arrived from Lamia. I was there when the settlement was attacked. What became of them?"

"They have been adopted by various families in our city, though any orphaned child is truly adopted by the whole city."

Tears welled in Jax's eyes. "That is a relief to hear. My wife, Avra, and the others who died on the island would have been thrilled to hear it."

Sibylla rose and hurried around the table, then embraced Jax's shoulders in her hands. "Avra made a great sacrifice and is being remembered in our songs and stories. She lives on still, if you listen to what people have to say. You should be very proud of her. Her loss was not in vain. Through her death, she has allowed many to have the chance at life."

"Thank you, Sibylla," Jax said. "Some of their parents came here with us. I can't wait to give them the news."

"You've waited a long time to hear this, I see," she said.

"Yes. It has been a long time between the trip to Cambisia and the time in the mines. I didn't know if I'd ever see the outside world again. I could never have hoped to see our city or our islands again."

"It is wonderful to have you back." She smiled at him. "I wish I didn't have to send you back into harm's way again so soon." She stepped back and glanced from Jax to Nereyda. "I will let you go on your way now. As soon as you return, seek me out, and we can talk about what you find."

Nereyda nodded her head while Jax gave a slight bow, then walked out of the longhouse.

They meandered their way through the grid of interlocked wooden docks and floating buildings back to the Bythos. The idea of living in such a place, one that wasn't locked to a permanent spot, appealed to Nereyda. A place to call home combined with the freedom she loved.

The free expression of the Islanders, shown through their outfits and ships, created a wonderful tapestry. She smiled as they passed a ship with a lewd painting of a mermaid. When they reached the ship, Photios was waiting on top of the deck.

"Did you have a good conversation with Sibylla?" he asked.

"We did," said Nereyda. "Sibylla gave us a mission. We need to see the captain."

"All right, follow me. We can see him in his cabin."

They crossed the deck to the room below the helm. The quartermaster pulled the door open and stepped inside.

"You don't need to knock?" asked Nereyda as she followed.

"This isn't a navy. We're friends who sail together."

"Sounds familiar."

He turned away from her, and she looked around the cabin. It was fairly sparse, with a couple of flags with krakens on them fluttering down from the ceiling next to the walls. Very different from what she had seen in Erhan's cabin. No books or personal effects to clutter the space. Only a bed, a simple desk, and a cabinet of charts. Bessarion sat at his desk.

"You don't really decorate much, do you?" she asked.

Bessarion looked up from a chart he was studying. "Why should I? This isn't my home. My house is in the city. My family is there. I'd rather not get too comfortable on my ship. I prefer to miss them so that I can be motivated to finish my assignment and get home."

Nereyda raised her eyebrows. "Not a bad sentiment."

"What business do you have here?"

"Sibylla gave us our own mission. We are to go out in search of one of the Stalstan ships to attempt to learn about it, and preferably either capture or destroy it."

"A tall order, considering none of our own have been able to do so, and we live and breathe in these waters. Why does she think you can succeed where we have failed? Are you somehow better than we are?"

Nereyda shrugged. "Not better. But I think we might have an edge where you don't. And I can do things that I haven't seen anyone else do."

The captain let out a huff. "That confident in your abilities?"

"You'll see," she said with a smile. "And your leader said that we need to take somebody with us, to help and observe us, I guess. She wanted us to take someone from your crew."

"You can take one of the sailors outside. I'm sure any of them can do the job."

"I think she wanted someone with a little more experience. Could you spare Photios?" She glanced at the bald Islander next to her.

Bessarion narrowed his eyes. "You want me to give you my own quartermaster?"

"He knows his way around. Given what we're up against, I want the most capable person I can find. And wouldn't you and Sibylla trust his word more than that of some random sailor?"

"Perhaps we could do that." He rubbed his chin.

"We aren't sailing for another couple of weeks," said Photios, energy simmering in his low voice, "since we are going to provision the ship."

"And I need my quartermaster for that," said Bessarion.

"I can leave a list of things we need. My assistants can figure the rest out. It's just a standard restocking of supplies. The ship doesn't need any significant work done, just basic maintenance. I think you can spare me for a short time."

Bessarion leaned back and crossed his arms. "Why are you so eager to join this outsider?"

"I'm curious as to what she can do." Photios studied Nereyda as he said this. "If she truly has skills we don't have, perhaps we can learn from her. And I want to be there when we capture some of these Stalstan bastards, or at the very least kill them for what they did to Iliana's family." A growl colored his words.

"Ah, yes, your daughter. I remember."

"I'm going with them, whether you allow it or not," said Photios. "For my Iliana."

Bessarion sighed but smiled at the quartermaster. "Then I might as well allow it. I don't want to lose a good quartermaster by writing you up for something like this. Go ahead."

CHAPTER THIRTY-FOUR

Three things struck Brynja before she opened her eyes. The first was that all her muscles ached and the back of her throat stung. Second, smooth and fresh linens were wrapped around her body. Finally, an aroma of cinnamon floated in the air.

She opened her eyes to a sea of blue sheets around her. Brynja flipped over and discovered that she lay in a spacious bedroom, lit by a crackling fireplace in the corner and candles that flickered on a desk across from her. The bed she occupied alone, with its smooth sheets and mahogany frame, was large enough for at least two people.

Brynja had no idea where she was. Her last memory was of falling into the ocean. Had she escaped her service to the Empire? If so, how had she ended up in a comfy bedroom?

And, if she had escaped, what had happened in the battle? Where was her crew?

She rubbed her eyes and shoved herself into a sitting position. Her muscles resisted, but she ignored the pain. Someone had changed her clothes, as she now wore a dark gray robe, which wrapped around her like an embrace. She shifted and set her feet on the ground. A fluffy red rug greeted her toes.

The latch clicked and the door squeaked open. A middle-aged woman with a white apron over a silver dress swept in, her hair in a bun. She clutched a pail in her hand, a cloth draped over one side. The woman started as her gaze landed on Brynja.

"Oh, you're awake," she said. "I didn't expect you to be up so soon."

"Well, I am. Where am I?"

"I'll explain in a moment. All that matters right now is that you're safe and comfortable." She flashed a motherly grin. "The latter is my job." The lady drifted across the room and perched herself next to Brynja on the bed. With the wet cloth from the pail, she dabbed at Brynja's forehead.

Brynja closed her eyes and enjoyed the cool refreshing feeling on her face.

"How are you feeling? You had a dreadful fever when they brought you in," the woman asked.

"Sore, and my throat hurts."

"Not surprising, since they dragged you out of the ocean." She rested the cloth on the back of Brynja's neck. "You probably swallowed your share of salt water." She placed the cloth back in the pail. "Let's get you dressed. Can you stand?" She extended her hand.

Brynja took it and groaned as she stood up. "How long have I been in this bed?"

"A couple of days. We've been caring for you in shifts."

"Whoever you are, thank you." Brynja gave the woman a weak smile.

"Oh, forgive me." She placed her hand on her chest and bowed her head. "My name is Anna."

"You're very kind, Anna. I am Brynja. What should I wear?"

"I had some of my daughter's things brought here. One of her dresses should fit you." Anna strode over to a closet in the corner and withdrew a simple light-blue dress and a pair of elegant shoes. "This should work, I think."

Brynja swallowed the urge to resist wearing a dress. Anna had taken care of her and given her clothing. It was not a time to be ungrateful.

As she put it on with Anna's assistance, Brynja asked, "Can you tell me where I'm at now?"

"You're in Kleifar, my dear—the beating heart of the Stalstan Federation."

Brynja nearly lost her balance. Anna gripped her arm and helped steady her. "Stalsta?" asked Brynja. "How?"

"I guess someone picked you up out of the ocean." Anna shrugged. "I don't know all of the details. But my lord will talk to you soon and he will have all of the answers. I'll let him know that you're awake, and bring some food for you while you wait."

Anna grabbed her pail and swept out of the room.

Brynja stared at the door as she plopped down on the bed.

Stalsta. Somehow, she had ended up captured by the enemy. Yet they did not treat her as a prisoner.

A few minutes later, Anna backed through the door with a tray. She padded her way across the room and placed it on the desk. "Why don't you sit up here? Don't want to make a mess in the bed."

Brynja floated across the room, her thoughts still buzzing in her head. A steaming meat pie waited for her, along with an apple and a tin mug of water. Her stomach growled as she slid into the chair in front of the desk.

"Do you need anything else?" Anna asked.

"No," Brynja said distantly, "this looks great. Thank you."

As Anna left, Brynja dug into the meat pie. Her hunger had been slow to wake up, but the sight and smell of the meal had woken the beast. She devoured her way through it.

When she had eaten about half of the meat pie, the door creaked wide again. A man with rigid posture stood in the doorway. He wore a gray uniform with what seemed like more medals than empty fabric. His strong chin and nose projected a calm confidence. "May I come in?" he asked in a voice as steady as steel.

Brynja managed a small smile. "Of course."

The man strode up to her and extended his hand. "I am Audo of Kleifar, Foreign Minister of the Stalstan Federation."

Brynja set down her fork, then shook his hand. "First, I'm in Stalsta. Now I'm talking with the Foreign Minister. How did I get here?"

Audo smiled down at her. "One of our ships picked you up after the battle with the Cambisians, then brought you here."

"How did the battle go? When I fell into the water, it was not going well for Stalsta." She shoveled the next bite into her hungry maw.

"It did not go well for us. The Cambisians won." His tone conveyed a complete lack of concern.

"So is your fleet destroyed?"

A twinkle was in his eyes. "The part of it that the Cambisians knew about, yes."

Brynja scraped the last bits of meat pie onto her spoon and licked it clean. "Sorry," she said as she stifled a burp.

"You have nothing to apologize for. You were out for a good amount of time. Now that you're done, will you walk with me?"

"I don't have anywhere else to be."

"Perfect. You can leave the dishes. Anna will clean up shortly."

Brynja shoved herself out of her chair, but stumbled as her muscles stiffened.

Audo steadied her with a hand on her shoulder, then offered his arm. She linked her elbow with his and followed his lead out of the room.

A deep red rug ran up and down the hallway. Candles, held in golden sconces, lit the corridor at precise intervals. "Have you ever been to Stalsta?" he asked.

"I was born here, but it's been years since I've been back."

"Ah, then I'm excited for you to see how we've developed lately. It's quite something to behold."

The rug had a cushy give beneath Brynja's feet as she angled her face toward Audo. "Why did you rescue me? What's special about me that I get to meet the Foreign Minister?"

"Our sailors hauled you from the sea out of an obligation to help a person in need. They saw you fall from your ship and that you did not wear a Cambisian uniform. Once their information trickled up to me, I sensed an opportunity."

"An opportunity for what?"

"I'll get there shortly. How has your time been in the Empire's service?"

She tightened her grip on Audo's arm. "Service is too good of a word. I spent too long slaving away in the mines. They broke me and made me betray someone I care about. Destroying Stalstan civilian ships and leaving innocent people to drown hasn't been any better."

He stopped them as they entered the mansion's entrance hall. A staircase curled upward, flanked by two suits of armor. "I can tell it's affected you. Anna cried as she told me about the scars she uncovered while changing and cleaning you. Someone needs to stand up to the Empire. We might have what it takes."

He opened the front door and led her down the walkway, between meticulously trimmed hedges, to a driveway that wound its way downhill. Audo's estate sat on a hill that overlooked the rest of the city and the harbor.

Brynja's eyes widened as she took in the scene of the city of Kleifar. Rows of smokestacks puffed black smoke into the city. The clang of hammers on steel rang through the air. Saws carving through wood provided an accompaniment. Coal, wood, and oil created an industrial tapestry of smells.

Out in the harbor, strange steel ships floated, their decks barely above the surface. A squad of soldiers marched in a kind of armor Brynja had never seen. The steel cut angular lines and the joints were hinged. Glowing orange and red lines traced the metal on the soldiers' limbs and spines.

"What is all of this?" she asked.

He puffed his chest with pride. "This is how we will fight the Empire. Double-forged steel and other technologies will give us the edge we need."

"How did you make it all?"

"We have a new resource that has helped us immensely."

Her mind wandered back to the previous conversation. "Did you recover any other members of my crew?"

Audo's shoulders dropped an inch. "No, I'm afraid not. No Cambisian ships went down, and you were the only person our sailors found at the site of the battle."

"So they're still stuck working for them." She clenched her jaw.

"True, but that also means they probably survived. You can still get back to them."

"How? I'm in Stalsta and who knows where they are."

"I can get you back to the Cambisian mainland, if you wish to find your crew."

"You would do that?" She gave him an incredulous look. "You'd just give me a free ride? I've been through too much to believe that."

Audo chuckled. "No, it's not an entirely free ride. Have you heard of the rebellion that is happening in the Empire?"

"Yes. What does that have to do with me?"

"Much. When you get back, I want you to do what you can to help the rebellion succeed. How you do that is up to you."

She inhaled and wrinkled her nose at the oily scent that clung to the atmosphere. "You want me to weaken the Empire so you can invade it."

He gave a sharp nod. "Precisely."

"I'd like to help, especially if it means getting back to my crew. But it sounds like a big job with a lot of risk."

His face softened as he gazed down at her. "It would not be an easy task. I understand if you think it is too much. You're welcome to stay here as my guest. If you get bored, you can even captain a new ship with a new crew."

The thought of a new crew weighed her with guilt. "I want to help my old crew, but I'm also worried that I'd be trading one master for another."

"I can understand that fear. But you should know that I don't ask you to sign any contract with me. I have no way of holding you to your promise to aid the rebellion. Whether or not you undermine the Empire, you will owe no debt to me. I only hope that our mutual dislike of the Cambisian Empire can lead to a beneficial outcome for both of us."

Brynja mulled over Audo's offer as she gazed at the hazy industrial city below. "Okay, I'll do it."

Audo grinned. "Perfect. I'll arrange for one of our ironclads to sneak you back to the continent. In the meantime, please enjoy yourself as my guest. You may come and go as you wish. Let Anna know if you need anything. I'm eager to see what you can do to help us bring the Empire down."

CHAPTER THIRTY-FIVE

In the Shattered Sea, shadows hung at the edge of the fog. For now, all of them were islands, but Nereyda watched for anything more sinister. They closed on the most recent village that had been savaged in a Stalstan raid.

Wisps of smoke still drifted into the sky from the husks of buildings that sat near the beach. Embers smoldered among the once-sturdy structures.

"Should we get out?" asked Jax.

"Not unless you see something moving. If it's like the last one I saw, there won't be much left."

They passed by in silence as they gazed at the charred graveyard that had been the village. A section of wall that had survived the conflagration featured a painting of a bear cub. An acrid stench reached her nose, the scents of burning flesh and sulfur. Charred skeletons lay among the blackened buildings. One had almost reached the water, its arm stretched out on the sand.

"Any ideas on how to track these guys down?" asked Photios.

"Can someone fetch the chart from my quarters?"

"I'll get it," said Fariha.

When Fariha returned with the map, Nereyda spread it out in the air and examined it, orienting the map and her stance so that they matched their heading. She placed their position on the map and found where the wind was blowing, then looked at the passages that would lead them through the islands and to the marked villages. "Are there any currents around here I should know about? I don't see them marked on the map," she asked.

Photios strode next to her and glanced over the map to orient himself. "There is one current here, which swings around this island," he said as he pointed at the map and indicated the direction of the current. "And another one here that sort of swirls around before settling on a direction, where it finally heads this way." He indicated the other current.

"So where they went depends on if they were familiar with this place or not. If I were the Stalstans, I would try to keep the same captain, or perhaps captains depending on how many ships they have, doing these runs. It would make the most sense to have the people with experience doing them, and it would keep these raids secret if that's what they intend. Does that make sense to you, Photios?" asked Nereyda.

"I think so. Where do you think they would have gone to?"

Nereyda looked over the map, then back toward the village, watching the smoke as it blew gently in the wind—a strangely peaceful look that made the horrific setting all the more haunting. "I have an idea," she said. She passed the map to Photios, grabbed the wheel, and ordered the crew to bring the ship to half sail.

Nereyda followed her instincts, with the map in her mind and the feel of the wind on her skin. On their own, her hands spun the wheel toward just the right direction and they picked up speed.

After an hour of winding through the islands, watching for anything at the edge of the shadows and listening for the sound of men talking or singing on a ship, the snap of sails other than their own, or even the howls they had heard the fire demons send out, they saw an outline at the edge of the fog.

"Is that a ship?" asked Jax.

"I don't think it's an island," said Photios. "It's not on any of our charts."

"I believe you. It looks like it could be a ship as we get closer," said Nereyda.

She piloted the Morgiana and found a bit more wind so that they could catch up to the shape, though she didn't apply too much speed. It wouldn't do to barrel toward it if it was just a pile of rocks, or to alert the Stalstans to their presence. Upwind of the ship, the air didn't hold the stench of burning and rotting flesh that followed the fire demons. The wind also carried away any sounds that might provide a clue to what they were pursuing.

As they crossed the water and closed the distance with each minute, the shape in the fog became clearer. It held the vague shape of a Stalstan frigate, but the hull was larger and squatter than that of a typical ship.

They drifted closer. A shot rang out from the ship, though Nereyda didn't see where the shot hit or splashed. However, the ship ahead sped up as it dropped its sails.

Nereyda and her crew had been spotted.

"Give me more sail," she ordered.

Her crew dropped the sails a bit farther, letting Nereyda have more speed for the chase. She gripped the wheel and focused on their prey, remembering how she did this last time. At least this time she had the advantage of having seen a map before she tried a crazy ship chase through the islands. She remembered what she had seen on the map. Mostly, at least. Enough to get the job done, she assured herself.

The ship ahead twisted down a passage, making a hard port turn. Nereyda gave chase, and she took it at a slightly better angle and shaved a few yards from the distance between the two ships.

The passage narrowed as they kept going. Nereyda's ship was narrower than the squatter ship ahead, so it didn't really concern her. What do we do when we catch them? No time to worry about that now. From what she recalled of the map, another crossroads in the water lay ahead of them and the swirling current that Photios had pointed out sat in one of the passages that branched off. How do we get them to go where we want?

"Full sail," she ordered.

Her crew paused briefly, wondering if she had given the wrong order or if they had misheard her.

"Full sail, I said."

They hurried to comply. The sails snapped full of wind, and the frigate sprinted toward the Stalstan ship. Sea water sprayed into the air as the Morgiana rushed past jagged rocks and solid cliffs on either side.

"What in the name of the gods are you doing?" asked Photios.

"Catching that ship. That's our job, isn't it?"

"It is, but it's dangerous to sail full sail here."

"You watched me do it before."

"Yes, and I wasn't on your ship then."

"I don't have the advantage of another ship lurking ahead with a net to catch this guy. We have to do it ourselves. While I focus on not smashing us against these rocks and islands that we're speeding past, perhaps you could tell me a little more about the current nearby."

"Are you going to try to ride through it?"

"We'll see if I can get our friends to cooperate."

"It is a big risk to go that way. Even our ships avoid that passage if they can help it. We've lost some people trying to take it."

"I note your concern," she snapped. "Tell me about it."

"If you're not careful, it can spin your ship right around or at least toss it sideways. The eastern edge is where you need to be if you don't want to be turned and risk smashing against the islands on either side. It's a narrow safe corridor, though. If you miss it, then you'd best hope you can swim or survive being tossed against stone."

"East side, got it. Don't want to have our brains smashed out."

With the added sail, Nereyda closed the gap between the Morgiana and the ship ahead. The Stalstans had also dropped their full sail, but with their massive hull, they were still losing ground. I hope we catch them before that crossroad.

"Ready guns," she ordered, in case they needed them. "Portside only," she added as she coaxed the boat toward the southern side of the channel they were in.

She took a curve close, far too close for safety, really, and that shaved off some extra distance. They lurched up to the ship, their bow just next to the other ship's stern. They only needed to gain a bit more. From where she was, she could see men in the gray Stalstan uniforms running around the ship, responding to the threat that presented itself.

"Ready your firearms," she ordered her crew. "When you're ready, fire at will on the enemy crew."

Her people shot their rifles and pistols at the Stalstan crew. This caused the Stalstans to take cover rather than fire back, giving Nereyda time to maneuver around them. As she pulled her frigate along the starboard of the enemy ship, she noted that the ship had no gun ports. In fact, the hull appeared to be covered with iron. No, not iron. Steel.

She had never seen a steel ship before. Dull light reflected off of the surface with a silvery tint. It did make sense that they wouldn't use a ship of wood to carry the fire demons to, and possibly from, their raids. However, the steel plating could very well make the shots of Nereyda's ship worthless. She'd still try, though.

Nereyda held their position alongside the enemy ship, patiently waiting to arrive at the intersection. Once they arrived, she called, "Fire!"

Her gun crew unleashed a broadside against the Stalstan ship. The shots pinged off the side of the steel hull, leaving little more than dents in the metal. Its captain, however, was not immune to the effects of gunfire. In what Nereyda knew to be instinct, he took a hard port turn, away from the source of the cannon fire, taking him straight down the passage that contained the current.

Nereyda took the hard turn as well. She ordered the crew to reduce sails, causing the Morgiana to lurch around the bend as she turned the helm hard to port. In the turn, especially with slowing down to take it hard, she lost a slight bit of ground, but she didn't think it would matter.

She held their ship along the eastern side of the passage, waiting for the current that Photios had said was so deadly. She kept her eye on the ship ahead, seeing what course it would take. Did its captain know about the current? If so, did he know how to handle it properly? Or would he take his crew straight into it in his panic?

The other captain did not know about the current. The Stalstan ship hit it and flipped around completely, pointing straight back at the Morgiana as the force of the current pushed it past the whirlpool and up the passage. Its starboard side leaned way out and smashed into the rocks on the side. With the steel plating, the ship didn't take significant damage from the crash. However, a crack sounded from below the deck of the Stalstan ship, followed by the unearthly shrieking that she knew to belong to the fire demons. The Stalstans had indeed learned how to transport them and were apparently testing them on the people of the Shattered Sea.

Now past the danger from the whirlpool, Nereyda pulled the Morgiana alongside the enemy ship. "Prepare to board," she commanded.

Just then, the hatches of the Stalstan ship flew open, and a horde of humanoid shapes covered in fire poured out. They unleashed otherworldly shrieks that shook the soul and went into a frenzy. Rather than think to leap across to attack Nereyda and her crew, they raged against the Stalstan crew, burning them and throwing them into the treacherous current in the water below.

"Hold," she told her crew. "Don't rush in there to get yourselves killed. Let those creatures do our job for us, at least for now."

Their weapons would be no good against opponents like those demons. She reached down into herself, finding the power that lurked in her gut. She held on to it, ready for the moment she would need it.

The Stalstan crew had completely forgotten about their human enemies, focusing on trying anything they could do to subdue the fire creatures that had escaped. The man she figured was their captain stood at the helm, blowing a strange kind of whistle. He pulled it out of his mouth, looked it over with a frustrated grimace on his face, then tried blowing it again. Whatever it was supposed to do, it didn't seem to be getting the job done.

During the fire demons' rampage, Nereyda pulled her ship away from the other, leaving several yards of a gap between them. As the demons ran out of targets on the deck of their own ship, they started turning their attention toward the other, far more flammable ship nearby.

The creatures prowled the edge of the deck, examining the distance and staring and shrieking at them. An intelligence flickered in their eyes that Nereyda hadn't seen before. They knew that it was a long distance and were judging how to cross it. They backed up to the other side of the ship and charged across, leaping into the air.

There was no way they could make it. It was too far.

However, they achieved a surprising height, enough that Nereyda changed her mind. She threw out her hand and swept a column of water up from the sea, creating a wall between them and her ship. The fire demons all crashed into the wall of water and dissolved into ashen dust. She let the wall fall back into the channel, then looked back at the Stalstan ship. All but one of the fire demons had been eliminated by her water summons.

"How did you do that?" exclaimed Photios.

"Never mind that. Let's close the gap," she said to her crew.

They slung boarding lines across and pulled the ships together. They also set down an anchor, to keep them from drifting away or being pulled back into the dangerous current. When the ships were adjacent, Nereyda leaped across and her crew followed.

The lone fire demon looked at the approaching boarders and didn't seem to know what to do. It had embers for skin beneath the flame and had the same fear in its red eyes as she had seen when she had thrown water at the horde at the mines.

Nereyda held a hand over her face to ward off the rank odor as she approached. "What are you thinking?" she asked.

The creature simply shrieked back and took a lurching step toward her.

Jax, Manu, and Photios joined her while the rest of the crew kept their distance. "What should we do with it?" asked Jax.

"Do what you did to the others," said Photios. "Get rid of it. Nothing good can come from letting it stick around."

"Is there some way we can study it?" asked Manu.

"Study it?" Photios turned to Manu. "You must be mad. You can't study something like that. You've seen what they can do. Even if you could force it to calm down and keep it from attacking you, you could never touch it, or trust that it won't lose its mind again."

"It doesn't need to be for long. We need to figure out what Stalsta is up to. Did they leave anyone alive?" asked Manu.

"Search the ship," Nereyda ordered Jax.

"And leave you with it?" asked Jax.

"I've got this." She reached out and felt for the water on the side of the ship. She closed her hand and lifted a ball of water from the channel and hauled it over the deck. She spread her fingers, opening and hollowing the large drop, then closed it around the demon, leaving it encased in a bubble of water.

Photios jumped back from the pocket of water. "How did you do that?"

"Like I said, I have a few tricks." Nereyda winked at the large Islander.

Photios stared at it as he drifted close. "This is amazing."

The creature turned within the space she had left on the inside, peering through the water, which distorted its features. Its glow shimmered through the slow waves that pulsed around the exterior of the bubble. It tried poking a finger into the water, unable to contain its curiosity, but instantly pulled the hand back, part of its finger having dissolved in the water.

Manu paced around the bubble encasing the creature. "This is fascinating. Have you ever done something like this before?"

"I haven't. Not sure how long I can keep it up. It doesn't take too much energy, but I can feel it draining me slowly."

"Then I don't want to tax you too much. Let me take some notes while you hold it there."

Manu pulled his notebook and pencil from his cloak and studiously circled the creature, taking notes and making sketches of its features.

"Reyda," said Jax, as he rushed back.

Nereyda turned toward him. "Yes?"

"I found the whistle that the captain was trying to use." He handed it over to her. "Do you know what this could do?"

She turned it over as the effort of maintaining the bubble tugged on her mind. "Is it supposed to control them or calm them somehow?" Nereyda wondered aloud. "Manu, do you want to look at this?"

He took the whistle from her, then twisted it and looked over each side, running his fingers over the holes. He lifted it to his lips and played some notes. The creature in the bubble reacted to it, shifting its stance and tilting its head at the sound. It didn't seem to calm down, though.

"Maybe you need the right tune," Nereyda said.

"Perhaps," said Manu. "But who knows if we'll find that information here. And without some way of reliably taming it, I don't think there is much else we can do with the creature."

"Are you done taking notes?"

"I think so. I was able to fill some gaps in my understanding of these creatures that remained after what you told me. It's been a productive observation, I think."

"Good," Nereyda said. She clenched her fist and collapsed the bubble of water around the fire demon, destroying it into a puddle of ashen goo.

"What now?" asked Jax.

"We search the whole ship for anything that could tell us why they were here," she said. "Search the hold, the cabin, everywhere. Also look for anything to tell us how they handled these creatures."

Her crew dispersed across the ship, searching in every corner for clues. Nereyda wanted to see how the Stalstans transported such dangerous enemies. As she descended into the hold, the lingering smell of the creatures hit her like a wave. Her hand sprang to her face and her nose crinkled in an effort to stave off the stench. She kept her eyes alert, in case any remaining creatures lurked around the ship.

A large cage occupied the hold, with a single door that appeared to have been busted off of its hinges. She couldn't tell if the crash into the rocks had broken it or if the crash had simply knocked it loose enough for the fire demons to do the rest. The material that the cage was made of didn't appear to be regular steel.

She ran her hand over it. It almost felt as if the steel hummed under her hand, just out of hearing range. I've never seen double-forged steel before, but this must be it. Something strong enough and heat resistant enough to contain such dangerous things.

Within the cage, scorch marks covered the walls and floor. They even reached the ceiling in some places. Had the creatures climbed up or did they throw fireballs up there? Hard to tell. No chains lay around the cage, suggesting that the creatures had roamed free. However, while the double-forged steel was a good clue about how they could be contained, it didn't offer much about how they could be controlled.

Since it was double-forged steel, she was curious about how the door had been broken off the cage. The metal was supposed to be nearly indestructible. A mere crash, at least one like this that was pretty mild, shouldn't have been able to break it free. She knelt down to look at the door and found that the hinges had been made of regular steel and that they had been bent and even torn. The Stalstans' whole system for keeping the creatures contained was undone by a single oversight.

"Photios," she called up the stairs.

He came down. "What is it?"

"Do you think we could take this ship back to the harbor?"

She ran her hands over the hull itself and felt a similar humming feeling. The whole ship was made out of double-forged steel.

"Why would we want to take it back? You saw how unwieldy the ship was in these waters, especially in the current."

"I don't want it for the ship itself. Have you seen what it's made of?"

"Steel, yes. But we have steel."

"It's made of double-forged steel. We could melt it down and use it for weapons, or anything else we wanted."

"What is this double-forged steel?"

"It's the strongest substance we know of. The Stalstans make it and have never shared how to make it with the outside world. I once tried to seize a shipment, but that didn't go so well. The Imperials managed to get ahold of it somehow, and they protected it fiercely."

"I suppose we could get someone to tow this ship back to port. Want me to send up a flare?"

"Couldn't we do it?"

"We could, but after what happened here, I think Sibylla will want to receive news as soon as possible. Towing a ship like this will take a long time."

"Okay, send up a flare then. We'll get someone to take it back, and we can perhaps examine it further in port."

Nereyda climbed out of the hold. Jax and Manu were looking over some documents on deck.

"What did you find?"

"We found these in the captain's quarters," said Jax.

"They seem to be notes about their mission, including the villages they attacked . . . and the results of those attacks. It is rather grim reading. Notes about deaths, how long it took to destroy a village, that sort of thing."

"Any useful knowledge from them?"

"We're still sorting through it, but at the very least, it paints quite a picture of how efficient these things are at killing people. We are lucky to have someone like you. Otherwise, I'm not sure how we would fight them."

"Well, this whole ship is made of double-forged steel. It seems to have kept them contained. Photios is getting a ship to tow it back to the capital. We might be able to strip it down and turn it into weapons to fight these things."

"That is a good idea," said Jax.

"If you've found all you could in the captain's cabin, I think we've done all the good we can here," Nereyda said. "It's time to head back to the capital and tell Sibylla about what we found. Maybe this will be enough for her to trust us."

"We'll see," said Jax. "It should be a start, at least."

Nereyda and the crew climbed back aboard the Morgiana with whatever they had taken and waited for the tow ship to arrive.

Once it was there and they had made sure it had properly attached to the Stalstan ship, Nereyda set her ship on a course for the capital city. Photios instructed her on the best way to maneuver through the islands so as to evade anyone who might be following them.

"Even if you don't see anybody behind you, make sure to act like someone is. We don't want any surprises at home."

Nereyda nodded and followed his suggestions for the circuitous route that took them back toward the city. After a bit, she stretched her hands. "Photios, would you mind taking the wheel for a few minutes? I need a short break."

"Of course."

Nereyda relinquished the wheel, then strode down the deck where she found Jax chatting with a few Islanders. "Jax, can I talk to you for a minute?"

He clapped one of his friends on the shoulder, then followed Nereyda to a quiet spot at the bow. "What is it? Is something wrong?"

She rested her arms on the railing and leaned out over the water. "Did we make the right choice?"

He sat on the railing next to her and crossed his arms. "What do you mean?"

She filled her lungs with the air that breezed from the forested islands. "We have everything we wanted. I have a ship. You're back home. And I love what I've seen so far. A whole nation of people who love to sail and express themselves. But something's bothering me."

"Thinking about Devrim?"

Below, the waves splashed against the hull as the ship cut through the water. "Well, yes. That's part of it. He always smelled of pine, and these forests remind me of him. But that's not all of it."

"What's going on, Reyda?"

"The Stalstans aren't just going to leave you . . . us alone, are they?"

"I doubt it."

She shoved herself up and paced the deck. "If they decide to invade us, we don't have the strength to beat them, especially if the Cambisians keep raiding villages as well."

"Aren't the Cambisians a bit distracted?"

"Yes, for the moment. But the rebels don't have a navy. And there's no guarantee that they're going to win. What if we could help, though?"

Jax tilted his head and tightened his arms around his chest. "Are you saying we should go back?"

Nereyda started to nod, then shook her head. "I don't know what I want to do. We have what we wanted when we started this war, yet it doesn't feel like enough." She paced faster. "Why can't I just be satisfied with what I have? A ship, my crew, you—it should all be enough, but it isn't."

Jax strode toward her, gently held her shoulders, and prevented her from pacing more. "It's because your crew isn't all here. Devrim, Limbani, the people of Antalia. They're a part of your crew now, and you don't like leaving them behind."

Nereyda relaxed in his grip as she pondered what he said. "I think you might be right. So do we go back and help them?"

"I'm in if you want to go."

"Are you sure? You just got home."

He gave a resolute nod. "Absolutely."

Her eyes traced the grain on the wooden deck. "If you're coming with me, I have another favor to ask," she said in a deadly serious voice.

"Anything."

Nereyda held her hand up. "Listen before you make that kind of promise."

He let go of her shoulders and studied her with concern. "What do you need?"

"In Goremia, I came awfully close to hitting my limit. The way those people looked at me, how the priest treated me . . . I can't take that again. Promise me, if you see I'm going to be captured again, that you'll put me down."

Jax pulled back with a stony expression. "You want me to kill you?"

Nereyda gave a sharp nod. "Please."

He turned away and stared at the passing cliffs.

"Jax," she said as she placed a hand on his back. His muscles tensed at her touch. "That priest tortured me and cut off my hand. It nearly killed me." Her voice shook. "I can't imagine what awful treatment or experiments they might use the next time they catch me. Please kill me before letting me go through that."

His muscles slackened as his shoulders fell. Jax glanced back over his shoulder. "Fine. If it looks like you're being captured again, I'll do it. I'll hate it, but I'll do it."

"Thank you, Jax."

CHAPTER THIRTY-SIX

After a few hours, they pulled back into the docks of the capital.

"Let's go talk to Sibylla," said Photios. "She'll be excited to hear about what we've done . . . what you've done. I've never seen anyone do what you did with the water. She won't believe it, but I can't wait to tell her about what we accomplished." He bounced on his feet as he strode away without waiting for Nereyda.

"Come on," he said over his shoulder.

Nereyda hurried after him, with Jax following her. "Look after the crew and make sure they get things all set," she told Fariha.

"Got it. We'll get everything done here. Don't worry about us."

"I always do," said Nereyda with a wink.

They hurried as they followed after Photios through the winding docks of the city.

Once they reached the longhouse, he burst right in with them on his heels.

"We did it," he proclaimed to Sibylla, who lounged in a chair woven from wood and reeds.

She glanced up in surprise and bewilderment and took in the three people who had barged into the room. Her hands held a pair of knitting needles and half of a sock.

"I didn't expect you to be back so soon," said Sibylla, a sliver of a smile on her face. "So you found a Stalstan ship?"

"We did," said Nereyda. "It won't be a problem anymore. The ship is being towed back right now so we can strip it down and use it for anything we need."

Sibylla gave an impressed nod. "We will also be able to look at it for more evidence of what their goals were," she said.

"That's true. We did find some notes in our own search. We will share them with you."

"That would be most excellent." Sibylla returned her focus to her knitting as she listened. "What did you find on the ship? Any of these fire demons?"

"Yes, there were some fiery creatures," said Photios. "They had the shape of men, but their skin smoldered. They shrieked and attacked anybody in sight. They killed most of the Stalstan crew themselves and would have destroyed us, too, if not for Nereyda."

Sibylla peered over the sock, but did not stop knitting. "How did she stop them? Just one person?"

"Yes, she somehow created a wall of water as they tried to jump over to our ship, and they crashed into it, destroying themselves. I've never seen anything like it."

With that Sibylla stopped and set down her knitting. She rose and appraised Nereyda with squinted eyes. "And how, pirate, do you do this with the water?" she asked in a cautious tone.

Nereyda shifted her feet and flicked her eyes away from Sibylla as she remembered the reaction in Goremia. "It's hard to explain."

"Come now. I don't mean to scare you," said Sibylla. "We don't have the superstitions of those on the continent. Once, our people used similar abilities. Please, share what you can."

Nereyda nodded. "I found something on an island once, and ever since I can do things like that. It's taken some time to learn to control it, and it can tire me out, but in situations like this, it comes in pretty handy."

"Seems more than handy. Is controlling water all you can do?"

Jax spoke up. "She destroyed some ships with lightning and can throw people with wind. She, err, she did it to me once when we were sparring."

Nereyda smirked. "To be fair, I held back. That was only a fun little gust."

"But I've seen you throw enemies into stone walls with it."

"Seems like you've found yourself some useful abilities," said Sibylla. "But this is getting us off track, as interesting as it is. You've done us a significant service in dealing with that Stalstan ship. No longer will it attack and terrorize our people in the outlying islands. It's hard to say if it's the only ship that's been in our waters or if it will be the last, but this should at least make them think twice about trying to make incursions against us. I may see if I can get you to make some more trips like that to see if you can find more of their ships, but you've more than earned a rest. And you are certainly welcome to live among us." Sibylla gave Nereyda a tight embrace.

"Sibylla," said Nereyda as she pulled back, "I have another favor to ask."

"What kind of favor?"

"It's more of a deal, actually. What would it be worth to you to rid the Shattered Sea of both the Stalstans and the Cambisians?"

Sibylla leaned back and crossed her arms. "Quite a bit, if it could be done, but I don't see how."

"I can do it, if you lend me the ships. The Cambisians are divided in a brutal civil war. We can help win that war for the side that will be friendly to you, and then they can help defeat the Stalstans."

"Jax and Photios, can I speak with you for a moment?" Sibylla's eyes did not leave Nereyda as she led the two Islanders into a corner.

They spoke in hushed voices for several minutes. Nereyda fidgeted and shifted her legs as she waited.

Sibylla returned with a grin across her face. "Is half of our entire fleet enough?"

CHAPTER THIRTY-SEVEN

Brynja trudged through the sand as she traced her way along the coast. Just around the bend, she would find the town where the Empire's western fleet had established its temporary headquarters after the fall of Antalia. Heat radiated from both the noon sun above and the sand below.

At dawn, the Stalstan ironclad had dropped her off half a day's hike north of the town. Brynja still couldn't believe what the Stalstans had created. An entire ship assembled from double-forged steel. Rather than float above the surface, it lurked with only a hint of the hull above the waves. Most of the ship remained beneath the water. This low profile was nearly undetectable, especially at night. As she learned from the crew, the Stalstans had not yet revealed these weapons in combat. Instead, they served as scouts and spies.

When she had asked if they were concerned about her telling anybody, they had merely smiled and asked, "You really think they would believe you? So far, we're just ghosts."

Brynja reached the bend in the beach and shoved through a thicket of trees. As she emerged from the branches, she could see a large harbor town spread out a couple of miles ahead of her. Imperial ships bobbed up and down at the docks, their flags flapping in the wind. Warehouses dominated the coast near the docks. Houses and shops stretched inland.

Before she continued, Brynja waded out into the water and dunked her head below the waves. Seawater thoroughly soaked her hair. She plodded back up the sand and wrung out her hair. The warm sun would cook in the salt as her head dried.

She hiked the rest of the way into town. People bustled around the streets near the docks. Soldiers marched the length of the harbor as they patrolled. Sailors hauled supplies to and from the ships. Hammers and saws sang their tunes from the decks of the docked ships.

Brynja's eyes hunted for anything familiar. The shape of her ship, a member of her crew, even Ilker. After minutes of wandering the docks, she found it. "Tavara," scrawled across the stern of one of the numerous frigates.

An anxious flutter in her heart quickened her pace as she strode toward the ship. She shifted her walk to a stagger as she remembered that she had to play the part of someone who had floated in the sea for a while. Brynja ran her hand through her hair. Good, it had crusted nicely in the warm afternoon sun. A fishy smell even clung to her locks.

As she clomped up the gangway to the Tavara, a familiar voice shouted commands at the crew. Ilker stood at the helm, gesturing as he gave his orders. Brynja limped her way up the stairs and caught his eye.

He stopped midsentence and studied her as he scrunched his face. "You. Where did you come from?"

"Some fishermen found me drifting and took me in. They didn't have much, as you can see." She waved at her tangled and salty hair. "But it was better than dying in the water."

He squinted at her. "You came back voluntarily? We had written you off as dead. Why return?"

"I'm here for my crew, not for you."

"Did your new friends drop you in the harbor? If so, I would like to thank them."

"No, it was too crowded for their liking, but they gave me this." She withdrew a piece of cloth from her satchel. It displayed a simple seal with a fish on a hook, circled by a wreath of flowers.

Ilker took it and pursed his lips as he studied it. "A symbol of some peasant family? You could have gotten this anywhere."

"What's the problem?" She planted her hands on her hips. "You have your humble servant back. Would you find it more believable if I claimed I swam to Stalsta, ate a meat pie in Kleifar, then swam back?"

Ilker huffed out a laugh. "It seems your time away has rekindled your pirate spirit. That may be all for the better. You'll need your energy."

"Why? What's next for us?"

"Our northern scouts have reported a large fleet approaching from the Shattered Sea. It is making its way at full speed toward Antalia. We believe that it intends to link up with the rebels there."

"Are we going to try to intercept the fleet?"

"No. We're going to let it arrive, then trap it in Antalia. Once we have it pinned down, we are going to bombard it into oblivion. Antalia kindled this rebellion, and it is there we will snuff it out. We're bringing everyone with us and we'll hit them with everything we have."

Brynja kept her face placid, but her mind whirred over what this meant. This might be her best opportunity to start her quest for revenge against the Empire.

CHAPTER THIRTY-EIGHT

Nereyda balanced herself on the bow of the Morgiana, holding the line for the foresail as she stood above the rolling waves. The Antalian harbor reached out to embrace them. One of her crew took the helm while they pulled toward the harbor so Nereyda could see the looks on the people's faces as the pirates brought the massive Islander fleet behind them. She glanced over her shoulder at the ships spread out behind her. Vessels of every size cruised over the waters, their sleek maneuverable forms etched elegantly against the clear blue sky, cutting smooth lines through the waves.

The Islanders knew how to make ships. They may not be made for open combat against large formations of heavy ships, but their design, optimized for navigating the treacherous waters of the Shattered Sea, made them incredibly maneuverable. It would not matter that they had fewer guns and thinner hulls if their enemies couldn't hit them.

Turning her attention back to the harbor in front of them, she watched as they passed between the small peninsulas that created the opening into the harbor. The other ships slipped in behind them one or two at a time. They would fill all of the docks that Antalia had to offer. They might possibly need to dock in shifts, or use their longboats to bring their crews to shore. The Antalian docks were made to house the entire western Cambisian fleet, yet the Islanders might have lent Nereyda even more ships than that.

The Morgiana slipped up to a dock. Nereyda could now make out the faces of the Antalian people. They stopped walking, turning to see the vast array of ships filling their harbor. Nereyda smiled to herself.

She had delivered Devrim a grand fleet. They could finally finish this war for good.

Nereyda climbed off of the bow and helped her crew secure the ship to the dock and prepare for shore operations. When everything had been prepared, she relieved her people of duty, aside from those who would take shifts keeping watch on the ship, then hopped off the deck. Striding down the dock, she spotted Devrim and Limbani walking toward her, both beaming with surprise.

Nereyda's heart took off at full speed upon seeing Devrim. She waved at them with her new left hand as she wiggled her fingers.

Devrim and Limbani stopped and gawked at her.

"What are you staring at? Haven't you ever seen someone regrow a hand?"

"How did you do that?" gasped Devrim.

"I'll tell you later. But first . . ." She lunged at Devrim and planted a kiss on his lips. Nereyda savored the moment and filled her lungs with his pine scent.

She dragged herself away, then embraced Limbani. "Thank you for everything you did. Without you, I wouldn't have had a chance."

"You would have done the same for me."

"Who gave you so many ships?" asked Devrim.

"The Islanders. I helped them with a small task," said Nereyda, "which isn't important right now. But I also made them some promises on our behalf. I told them they could take ownership of the southern part of the Shattered Sea and that we would stop running raids against them once we were in control of the Cambisian government. I also suggested that we might be allies against any Stalstan raids they experience."

"Done," said Devrim with a definite nod. "Those all seem perfectly reasonable. More than reasonable, really, considering that they're already proving themselves to be good allies."

"We haven't seen them fight yet," said Limbani. "Their numbers won't mean much if they scatter at the sight of a Cambisian ship of the line."

"I don't know how they are in open combat, but they weren't shy about chasing us down. And the Islanders who have been on my crew since the mines have performed more than admirably."

"If you vouch for them, that's good enough for me," said Limbani.

"How should we celebrate?" asked Devrim.

"I'll talk to the assembled captains of the ships, and we'll find some way of welcoming them to our cause," said Nereyda. "They aren't the sort of party animals my crew generally are, but I'm sure we can find something they'd enjoy."

"If the weather is clear, we can do something in the square," suggested Devrim. "There are new pubs opening there since we took the city, and I'm sure they'd love to have the business."

"Did you take down the rest of the gallows?" asked Nereyda. "They would cast a bit of a shadow over any party."

Devrim gave a short chuckle. "Yes, those have been taken down. It's become a much more pleasant public space. The people have started painting murals on the walls and ground. You should see some of them when you get a chance."

"If we have our celebration there, I'll check it out."

"Not to end the discussion of our fun," said Limbani, "but we should start discussing next steps. With Nereyda's fleet and the ships our allies sent, we can now move against the eastern fleet at the main Imperial shipyard. That is the last big piece before we can take the capital. If we destroy the fleet there, it will be easy to finish the war, but we haven't dared take it without a fleet to support us."

"You're right, Limbani," said Devrim. "How about the three of us talk about what we need to do? Let's go to the administration building, and we can think things through in my office."

Nereyda gave some final instructions to Photios to relay to the Islanders, then followed Devrim and Limbani, her excitement reaching her feet. Soon, the Empire would be defeated and good people like Devrim and Limbani would take over.

Nereyda was nursing a mug of ale after discussing battle plans with Devrim and Limbani when a guard rushed into the tavern and whispered in Limbani's ear. Nereyda narrowed her eyes and leaned forward, but couldn't make out what the guard said. When Limbani dismissed the guard, she leaned toward Nereyda and said, "Our guards captured someone on shore. She is asking for you. Do you know a woman named Brynja?"

Nereyda nearly choked when she heard the name. Her face hardened as she remembered her old friend. "Yes, I know Brynja."

"That's the name of your first mate, isn't it?" asked Limbani.

"Who lured me into a trap at the mines. Yes, that's her." Nereyda kept her voice icy as she sparred with the thought of seeing Brynja again.

"Why would she be here? Didn't you say she was pressed into the service of the Empire?"

"Yes, as a privateer, I think. But I might as well go see what she has to say."

"Are you sure? If she's working for the Empire now, what if it's part of a trap?"

"It might be. I'm not sure about her anymore. But I still need to see her."

"I'm coming with you."

Nereyda shrugged. "Fine with me. You can show me where they're keeping her."

"Do you know what she wants?"

"No idea."

Following Limbani through the streets, Nereyda trudged a bit outside of town along the beach, toward a spot where the lamps from the city barely cast any light on the sand. The silhouettes of six people stood outlined against the night sky. One person had their hands raised above their head, while the other five had guns aimed at them. A rowboat had its prow in the sand, while the rear bobbed in the water as waves crashed against the shore.

Limbani carried her torch toward the people. As the light was cast over their faces, Nereyda spotted the angular face and straw-colored hair of Brynja.

"Nereyda," said Brynja, a tremor in her voice.

"Quiet, until spoken to," said one of the guards.

"No, it's okay," said Nereyda. "You all can stand down. Limbani and I will talk to her. Head back to your original posts."

The guards hesitated, looking to Limbani, who waved them away. They lowered their weapons and marched back up the beach. When they were a distance away, Nereyda turned to Brynja.

"Why are you here?" she asked as she crossed her arms.

Brynja's face and shoulders fell. "I know you don't want much to do with me. But I want to make up for what I did to you at the mines."

"How do you want to do that?" Nereyda snapped. "Are you here to ask for a place on my crew again? Because my ship is full. I have a new first mate, and he's doing pretty well so far. Hasn't sailed much, but he's learning."

"I don't want to fight with you, Reyda."

"Don't call me Reyda. That's for my friends."

Tears filled Brynja's eyes. Nereyda tried to ignore them, but couldn't help but notice her eyes had become a bit sunken.

"I'm here to offer help, not join your crew," said Brynja. "The western Imperial fleet is here. They're just off the coast, and they plan on launching a full assault on Antalia tomorrow at dawn. They want to take out your fleet."

"This seems like quite a coincidence. How did they even know we got a fleet?" Nereyda asked.

"I'm not sure. Someone saw you and reported it. It might have been a fishing boat or a merchant. Something like that. But based on how many ships it seems you have, is it really that hard to believe you didn't go unnoticed?"

"Fine, let's say I believe you. What would you have us do? Is this some sort of ruse to get us to come out and face you in open battle?"

"No, I just thought you should know."

"What made you come tell us this?" Nereyda tilted her head, looking at Brynja sideways.

"I never wanted to be a slave to the Empire. They made us attack civilian ships to lure out the Stalstan navy. Now they're turning us against you. I'm sick of it." Her face contorted with disgust. "Maybe my ship could slip away and join your fleet?" She lurched toward Nereyda, her hands held out in a plea.

Nereyda scoffed. "So you can sell us out again? No, thank you. Head back to your Imperial masters, and let us win this war without you. Limbani, have your guards watch her to see that she really goes back out to sea."

As Nereyda whirled around to leave, Brynja called out, "One thousand lashes."

Nereyda pivoted and marched up to Brynja's face. "What did you say?"

"One thousand lashes. That's how serious I am."

"You don't get to say that. Not anymore." Nereyda turned her back and stormed away from Brynja, not bothering to leave a farewell.

"Whether you believe me or not, I'll do what I can to stop them. Whatever it takes."

Brynja's words blew past Nereyda's ears.

Limbani addressed the guards at their station, then caught up with

Nereyda.

"That seemed a bit harsh," remarked Limbani.

"How would you feel about seeing the person responsible for getting you tossed into a pit of hell like the mines?"

"Fair point. But what about what she told us? What are we going to do about it?"

"I'm not sure. Does the gate tower have anything to drink?" She needed something to calm the swirling storm of thoughts that raged in her head. What's more dangerous? Trusting Brynja or not?

"It might," said Limbani.

They trailed along the beach toward the closest harbor guard tower, which stood on one of the peninsulas that hugged the harbor.

As she shoved through the door, Nereyda was relieved that nobody was on the lower level. She rummaged through a cabinet on the wall and found half a bottle of rum. A large swig later, she held it out toward Limbani. "Want any?"

"No." She stayed in the doorway. "What was that about one thousand lashes?"

Nereyda let out a dark chuckle as she leaned against the cabinet. "It's sort of a promise. It started before I was even captain. When one of us said it, it meant we were so confident in something that we would take one thousand lashes if we were wrong."

"That seems rather extreme. I thought you didn't use lashes."

Nereyda gave a dismissive wave. "It wasn't meant to be literal. It means 'trust me, I know what I'm talking about.'"

"So do you trust Brynja?"

"No, I don't." Nereyda stared at the bottle in her hand. "But if she is telling the truth, and the Empire traps us in here, we're screwed." She shoved the bottle back into the cabinet. "We might as well check if we can see anything from the top of this tower."

Nereyda took the steps two at a time to reach the top.

The guard at the top turned with a start, his hand on the hilt of his sword. As he saw Nereyda and Limbani mount the top of the stairs, his shoulders relaxed. "You two gave me a fright," he said.

"Sorry about that. Do you have your spyglass?" Nereyda asked.

"Sure." He fished it out of his pocket and passed it to Nereyda. She took it and scanned it across the horizon.

At first, she didn't see anything other than rising and falling waves. Then, at the edge of the horizon, near the coast to the south, the moonlight caught a few lines that stuck up from the water, appearing and disappearing as the water rolled. She fixed the spyglass on the water around the area. The wind died down for a minute, allowing the waves to settle, and more masts and sails appeared.

"Brynja was right," Nereyda said. "Here, take a look." Nereyda handed the glass to Limbani and guided her to the location where she had spotted the threatening fleet.

"How many ships do you think are there?" asked Limbani.

"Hard to say from this distance, not to mention how many might be lurking farther away."

"What do we do? If they're going to attack at dawn, they're going to start moving toward us soon, aren't they?"

The carnage of the Imperial bombardment of Antalia replayed in Nereyda's mind. And that was just five ships, she thought. A full fleet would level the city within a day. We need to escape and lead them away. "We head for the shipyard tonight."

"Guard," said Limbani, "light the warning fire."

"No," said Nereyda. "Don't do that. They'll see it from where they are, and then they'll know that we've been alerted."

"Are our ships ready?"

Nereyda shrugged. "No idea. But they'll have to be. Let's go. Soldier, don't light the fire now, but keep your attention in that direction." She pointed at where the Imperial fleet was anchored. "If you see movement, especially if they start moving toward us, light that signal fire and get the hell out of this tower."

"Yes, ma'am."

Nereyda clapped him on the shoulder, then ran down the staircase, nearly falling as she let gravity accelerate her as fast as she could go. She and Limbani dashed back into town and panted as they crashed through the door of the tavern where Devrim was. Nereyda slid up next to him.

"Why are you two out of breath?" he asked.

Nereyda took a couple of deep breaths until she could talk. "The Imperial fleet is here."

Devrim froze as his eyes sprang wide.

Nereyda didn't wait for instructions before she and Limbani dashed from tavern to tavern, rallying all of the crews and captains. The sailors poured into the square, staggering under the effects of their drinks. Soon, adrenaline took over and they sprinted through the streets toward the docks.

Limbani left to gather the army as Nereyda ran for the ships, hoping they could get away soon enough. As she reached the docks to help oversee the rushed loading procedure, the light from the watchtower near the harbor entrance flickered to life.

The Imperial fleet was on its way.

Nereyda swore to herself. She sprinted to her own ship and found Jax there with the crew, getting it ready. The sailors all moved cargo and secured lines with a hurried focus.

"Glad you beat me here," Nereyda said to Jax.

"We heard the news and came straight here."

"Good. We sail as soon as we're ready."

Nereyda lit a flare as a signal that the ships should move out as soon as they were ready. All the captains would know to meet at the rendezvous point near the eastern Imperial naval base. Each crew scurried about the deck of their ship as they finished their preparations. A few times, sailors ran onto the docks to retrieve last-minute supplies.

The Morgiana was mostly loaded, and the crew was waiting for their chance to get out of the harbor. As one of the ships on the docks, theirs would be one of the last out of the bay.

The Islander ships in the open water of the harbor streamed out of the opening. She didn't know how well supplied they were. They hadn't fought anything on their way to Antalia, so they would at least have a full armament of ammunition and powder. Hopefully, they had enough food for the rest of the journey to their attack on the naval base.

Rebel Antalians and soldiers dashed out of the city, heading onto the ships. A squad came down Nereyda's dock, with Limbani and Devrim leading them.

"I think we have most of the troops rallied," said Limbani. "I told some to stay behind, in case the Imperials land troops on shore."

"Hopefully, they'll be too busy chasing us."

"Are we ready to face their fleet?" asked Devrim. He kept glancing toward the harbor entrance, as if expecting the Imperials to suddenly appear and close it off.

"No, but we stand a better chance than this city does," said Nereyda.

Most of the ships that had been anchored away from the docks had already escaped the harbor. The docked ships had untied their lines and now waited for their turns to leave.

"I want us to be the last ship out," said Devrim. "Make sure everyone has a chance to get out ahead of us."

"What if we get trapped here?" asked Nereyda.

"Then I have the best captain to help us get away," he added with a shaky smile.

"Once we're out, we push as hard as we can," said Nereyda, "no matter how close they are."

"Agreed," said Limbani.

Fariha and Manu dashed down the dock and climbed onto the ship.

"What are you doing?" asked Nereyda. "You should stay safe here."

"No, we're going with you," insisted Fariha. "We don't want to cower without being useful."

Nereyda didn't have time to argue. "Fine, find something to do."

As the last of the ships pulled away from the docks, Nereyda took the helm and they shoved off. They drifted away from the dock, then Nereyda turned them toward the opening.

"Full sail," she ordered.

She kept her eyes alert for any debris or obstacles that might block their path. At this pace, any obstruction in the narrow and rocky harbor entrance would prove deadly. Fortunately, the opening remained clear.

A cannon blast ripped through the air, and the harbor guard tower erupted in a shower of stone and wood. A stray stone from the tower plunked into the water just off of their bow. The Imperials were a strong breeze away from being in range to strike the rebel ships.

Nereyda gripped the helm wheel as her ship surged through the opening between the peninsulas that embraced the harbor.

Off to their left, the first part of the Imperial fleet had closed within firing range. More ships plowed toward the harbor in formation. The darkness obscured their full numbers.

She dropped her right hand and took a hard turn away from the enemy fleet.

"Can we coax any more wind from these sails?" she asked.

Her crew moved the sails, but they couldn't catch any more wind.

Cannons boomed behind them and cannonballs struck the water just aft of their stern. A couple of droplets splashed Nereyda's neck.

Adrenaline pulsed through her body. They needed to go faster and get out of range.

Reaching up with her hand, she summoned her power within and cast a gust of wind at their sails, propelling them forward with a renewed speed.

"How are we doing with our friends behind us?" she asked, gasping between words as her power drained her breath.

Jax looked behind them. "We're losing them."

"Keep an eye on them."

Nereyda concentrated on keeping her breath as she held her hand up and propelled wind at the sail. Her lungs ached and a moment of dizziness struck her, as if she had held her breath for too long.

After several minutes, Jax said, "I think that's enough for now. They aren't following us."

"What are they doing then? Why wouldn't they follow us?"

"I don't know why, but they're forming up around the entrance to the harbor. I think their objective was to take us by surprise, perhaps."

"It was. That's what Brynja told me."

Jax narrowed his eyes. "You saw Brynja?"

"Yes. I can tell you more about it later, but she's the reason we knew to get out of here."

"So she's with their fleet?"

"Must be. She came in her rowboat to warn us."

"Why would she do that?"

Nereyda shrugged. "I don't know. For now, let's get away from those bastards behind us. Let me know if anything changes."

She relaxed and let herself settle in for a long morning of piloting along the coast.

CHAPTER THIRTY-NINE

After eight days of hard sailing, Nereyda and the others reached the rendezvous point down the coast from where the eastern Imperial naval base sat on the northeastern edge of the continent, far enough that they were out of sight of any guard towers from which they might be spotted as they approached their objective.

Devrim, Limbani, Nereyda, and Jax all gathered in the captain's quarters on the Morgiana. "Limbani," said Devrim, "why don't you go over the plan?"

"So, this is what we're going to do," said Limbani. "We can't have their ships launching to face us, not with the possibility of the western fleet coming after us. With that threat looming, the pirates are going to land first and make their way toward the base. Once they get close enough, they will sneak in and cripple as many enemy ships as they can and take out any guards in the towers if possible. The rest of the troops will march behind them and attack at first light." She turned to Nereyda and Jax. "Get as much damage done as possible before then. If they get enough warning to mount a serious fight, we're going to be in real trouble."

"We'll get it done," said Nereyda. "It's not too different from Antalia. Sneak in and cause as much trouble as possible. We're all good at that."

"Glad to hear everyone's on board. Devrim and I will share the plan with the rest of the crews and troops."

"When do we go ashore?" asked Nereyda.

"Tonight, at midnight. We'll drop you on the coast, and you'll make your way to the base. Since it will be a long and late night, I suggest that you and your crew get some rest before the attack."

"Perfect. We'll do that."

"Remember," said Devrim. "We win this fight, and this war is ours. Lose, and everything we've worked toward goes away."

The hard night hike left Nereyda's legs tired. The distance from their drop zone to the base felt like it stretched on forever. They trudged through a dense forest of towering trees. Scattered logging camps fueled the shipbuilding and maintenance of the nearby shipyard. Finally, a flicker of light from a watchtower came through the trees.

"Okay," whispered Nereyda, "our primary goal is to take out any ships that we can and clear out any guard towers. Jax, I'll take my pirates to disable the ships, if you want to take your people to go for the guard towers."

"We can do that," Jax said with a nod.

"Good, let's go." Nereyda waved to her pirates to follow her as she approached the edge of the woods. She glanced up at the guard tower.

The on-duty soldier sauntered around the tower. He proceeded in a counterclockwise patrol pattern, wandering around the perimeter of the tower, pausing at the corners. Based on his relaxed body language, he had done this way too many nights. He seemed quite inattentive as he gazed up at the night sky and went through the motions to get through his shift. This was about to be the most exciting shift of his life. He probably didn't figure anyone would be crazy enough to attack the main Imperial naval base.

Too bad for him that the Empire's enemies were as ambitious as they were determined. Nereyda waited until he headed toward the other side of the tower, then dashed across the open field to the cover of a nearby building. When she reached it, she glanced back around the corner. Two Islanders had reached the base of the tower. She held up her hand and signaled to her pirates that they should wait a moment.

The Islanders snuck up the tower. A few seconds later, a pair of arms wrapped around the guard, and a knife slit across his throat. Guilt weighed her heart for half a breath as she watched the life snuffed out of someone who was obliviously doing his job. Still, they had their own job to do.

With the guard out of the way, Nereyda waved to her half of the crew. While they ran toward her, she peeked around the building she was using for cover. No other guards. Where were the other soldiers? Shouldn't they have more guarding the shipyard?

When her pirates had gathered around her, she spoke in a loud whisper so that they could hear her. "Okay, crew, we're going to split up to cover as much ground as possible. Remember, we only need to prevent these ships from being able to sail at a moment's notice. We don't need to completely destroy them, especially since we want to use them once this war is over. If you run into trouble, shout or whistle for help, and we'll come to you. But whatever happens, we can't let them get their ships out to sea and catch our fleet."

Everyone nodded as they listened to her orders.

"Good, let's go."

She waved to a handful of pirates and had them follow her as she separated from the larger group to find a side street to make her way toward the docks. They clung to the shadows and padded in crouched stances through the alleyways.

A couple of times, groups of soldiers passed them. From the way they chatted and laughed though, it didn't seem like they were on official patrol. Still, they could alert the base if they detected the intruders.

The pirates made their way around the buildings and found the huge expanse of docks that made up the majority of the shipyard and base. Several large dry docks and a number of smaller ones sat at the southern edge of the base. Along the coast, there were warehouses and wooden cranes for keeping the eastern navy properly supplied in a timely manner. As large as the western fleet was, the eastern fleet was the pride of the Empire.

A sign creaked in the wind. Waves splashed against the docks. No voices. No footsteps.

They crossed the remaining distance to the docks and picked a row of ships to disable.

Nereyda snuck across the deck of the nearest ship and cut the rope between the helm and the rudder. It would be an easy enough fix, but it would slow the Imperials down so that they couldn't sail out and fight. Her team did much the same on other nearby ships.

As she went from ship to ship, she reached a part of the harbor full of mismatched ships of varying sizes and configurations. Bobbing at the edge of one dock, Nereyda spotted a familiar silhouette of two masts standing over a sleek seventy-pace-long brig.

The Storm Raven.

She should have known it was a possibility, but she had forgotten that the eastern naval base was where they held seized ships.

Her heart swelled, and she struggled to resist the urge to sprint toward it. They needed to finish their job of disabling the Imperial ships. She ordered her team to stay focused, then hurried through the last few ships.

At last, time to retake the Raven.

As quietly as they could, her team hurried toward the Storm Raven. The urge to sprint tugged on Nereyda, but that would produce too much noise. Instead, she padded her way over the dock, a bounce in her step.

When they finally reached the gangway that stretched to their old ship, Nereyda paused and smiled. Stepping across, she laid her hands on the railing as she walked to the aftercastle. The grain of the wood against her hands and the creak of the deck in just the right places told her she was home. She climbed the stairs and stood before the helm, feeling the handles as she gripped the wheel. It was worn in all of the spots she remembered. They weren't ready to sail yet, but they would be soon.

Once the rest of the crew arrived, Nereyda gathered them on the deck and spoke from the aftercastle above. "Okay, we've disabled all the ships we could find in our part of the harbor. Head out and steal supplies from the ships around us. We don't need anything other than ammunition and powder. Food can wait. We need to sail out and join our fleet."

While they were carrying supplies down the dock, a gunshot rang through the air. The doors of the warehouses around them exploded open, and Imperial troops poured out.

The garrison had been alerted.

"Quick, finish loading everything," she ordered.

Her crew rushed as they hauled everything on board. Meanwhile, the Islanders dashed up the dock onto the ship. The rebels under Limbani's command poured into the base, responding to the sounds of gunfire.

"Leave it all on the deck," she said. "Get to your stations, and we're going to pull out."

She had hoped for a bit more time to enjoy piloting the Raven for the first time in ages, but she'd save the proper reunion for later. She ran up to the helm and had the crew shove off from the dock. As she turned them out to sea, she heard cannons echoing from outside the harbor, in the sea.

"Full sail," she said.

A cloud drifted over the moon above. After the arduous hike from the landing zone, they probably had a couple of hours left before dawn.

The Raven sped across the water of the harbor, toward the opening. The mouth of this harbor gaped much wider than the one at Antalia, though it also was much more heavily fortified. Two large stone towers, with the same dark look as the walls of Antalia, stood as sentinels on the north and south sides of the opening. Each tower had a hint of a slit on the side that was closest to the water. Something with a metallic glimmer dangled out of each hole.

A chain.

Mechanical clicks sounded from each tower as they reeled in the chain and raised it as a barrier. The Storm Raven wouldn't have time to get through the gap before it finished raising, and they would crash into it, tearing their hull.

"Hard to port!" she ordered. "Raise the sails."

She dropped the helm wheel hard to the left, spinning the ship hard as they slowed down.

"Drop the sails a bit."

Once they were turned, she set the ship to cruise at a slow pace around the harbor. On the shore, the soldiers prepared artillery to bombard them with.

"Load the starboard cannons," she ordered.

She kept them at a slow cruise as she waited for the crew to get the guns ready. Over on the docks, the Imperial soldiers continued to rally and prepare to both resist the incoming rebel troops and launch a cannon strike at the Raven.

"Ready," she heard from the gun deck below.

She turned the Raven so its starboard broadside was pointed right at the north tower.

"Fire," she said.

The Storm Raven's cannons blasted a full broadside at the tower. Each shot roared toward the solid stone wall . . . and struck it with a sad clunk, then rolled off and landed with a poof of sand on the beach below. A few scattered chunks of rock broke away, and some cannonball-shaped dents dimpled the solid structure, but other than that the tower had sustained no visible structural damage.

"Our guns don't seem to be getting the job done," said Jax.

"I've noticed," Nereyda said. "Nik, take the helm."

"Aye, Captain."

"What are you doing?" asked Jax.

"Watch and find out." Nereyda yanked her boots off and stuck them under her belt, then sprinted across the ship and leaped off the side toward the north tower.

Shouts rang through the air at her from her crew, but she ignored them. She needed to get that chain lowered so the Raven could get out of the harbor. They were useless as long as they were stuck in this watery prison, and it would only be a matter of time before the cannons on the shore got their position right and pounded them with a barrage.

She pulled herself through the water, popping her head up to keep her eye on the tower she was swimming toward. She didn't see anybody on the coast near it, or even waiting outside. Still, she knew that it would be occupied.

She got close enough to the shore that she could wade the rest of the way. Nereyda trudged through the water and onto the shore. The wet sand squished between her toes. She paused and held her breath as she listened for any signs that she had been seen. Nothing nearby; only the distant shouts of the Imperials across the harbor and her own crew working on the Raven.

Nereyda wrung the water out of her hair, letting it drip onto the beach, then sat down and slipped her boots onto her feet. She wrinkled her nose at the gross feeling of her wet sandy feet going into the boots. No time to clean them now. She'd have to ignore and deal with it.

Standing up, she strode across the beach toward the tower.

A door stood open at the bottom of the stone building, with a soft torch glow pouring out of it. Nereyda drew her cutlass. She paused at the entrance. The hum of a couple of voices came from above her.

Cannons erupted on shore. The Imperials had gotten their cannons ready. She only hoped that the crew on the Raven could keep evading them long enough for her to open the way out of the harbor.

Nereyda pushed herself into the tower, glancing around the room.

Torch sconces along the walls provided an orange light. The bottom of the tower was the living quarters for the guards, with a couple of cots along one wall and a table in the middle, with plates of half-eaten meals on it. A couple of dressers stood near the beds.

Around the perimeter of the tower, a staircase spiraled its way up along the walls, in a square-shaped arrangement. The voices she had heard had come from the top of the tower.

She ran up the stairs, taking them two at a time.

Left panting as she summited the staircase, she was face-to-face with two guards who stood near the opening in the wall with the chain running out of it. A large wheel with the harbor chain wrapped around it sat next to the opening, hooked up to some sort of mechanism. Torches flickered in the corners.

One of the guards nodded to her. "We have a visitor."

"So we do," said the other guard.

"How did you find your way up here?" the first one asked.

"I'm looking for a new place to live, and this seemed like a good place to try. Nice and remote and has a great oceanside view."

The cannons in the harbor sounded again.

"I don't have time for this. Just drop the chain, and I can be on my way. My ship would like to leave the harbor."

"Yes, we saw that. And we won't let you leave since you clearly aren't authorized to take that ship."

"It's my ship. I am the one who says I'm authorized to take it."

"We'll see about that."

Each guard brandished a large two-handed sword. As opposed to the normal uniforms of Imperial soldiers, theirs featured gleams of metal from armored chest pieces.

"Have you ever faced the Imperial elite before?"

"Yeah, I killed one of you in Trabizan."

"One? We fight in pairs. The two of us have been fighting together since we were children."

"Good. Then you should leave so you can continue fighting with your childhood buddy. I'd hate to break up a beautiful friendship by killing one or both of you."

"We're ready to die together, as well. That's what we do."

"Then let's get you on your way to your destiny."

She pointed her cutlass at her two enemies, walking herself around them toward the middle of the room. It would be an interesting place to fight. On three sides of the room, the floor dropped off to the staircase below. A wrong step and she could fall off. Only the side with the hole for the chain didn't have a gap. Aside from the gap for the stairs, the other features were a couple of chairs and a small table.

Another short staircase led up to the very top of the tower.

As she paced around them, her two opponents split and made their way toward either side of her. She didn't want to let them surround her. Instead, she wanted to use them to get in each other's way.

She rolled to her left, bringing her cutlass up in a quick jab at the nearest guard.

He swept away the strike, and Nereyda stepped again to her left, leaving the guard she faced standing between her and the other guard.

Her back was to one of the sides with the gap.

Her opponent swung his sword up and brought it down in a heavy chop. Rather than try to block such a blow, she sidestepped it and let it pass just to her right. She felt the air rush by her cheek as the sword pushed through the air.

She aimed a glancing blow at his right arm, but he blocked it again.

She couldn't stay rooted to the spot she was in, with her back to a precipitous drop. While putting one guard between herself and the other prevented them from engaging her at the same time, her position also limited her ability to maneuver.

Opting to gain some mobility, she spun around the guard with a flurry of blows aimed at his torso. They all glanced off of his armor, but they had the necessary effect of distracting him as she brought herself to the middle of the room.

She kept each guard in her vision.

They each went for a strike, one high and the other low.

She used her cutlass to block the low strike as she ducked down.

As the high striker on her left brought his sword over her, she swung out her leg and swept his feet from under him. As he tumbled to the ground, she charged her shoulder into the other guard, pushing him back.

Her shoulder ached from where she had hit his armor, but at least she had bought herself some time. She spun around him and backed herself toward part of the edge.

She kept her distance from the guard as he swung angry chops at her. She let the strikes kiss off her cutlass, just touching them enough to deflect them without taking the full force in her arm.

Cannons sounded again outside.

The guard smiled as he pressed her toward the gap.

He raised his sword for a strong strike down.

As it fell, she rolled forward and to the right. As his momentum carried him down, she gave him a shove in his back. Dropping his sword in surprise, he tumbled down the gap in the floor, smashing into the staircase and tumbling farther down, stopping on one of the landings, his neck at an unnatural angle.

She turned around to look at the remaining guard, who had risen from his fall.

She dashed toward him and exchanged sword blows with him.

When she sensed an opening, she slashed her sword along his left elbow.

He let out a cry of pain and tried to keep hold of his sword as blood poured down his arm and stained the fabric of his uniform. But without the strength of both arms, he couldn't lift his blade.

He let it fall to the ground as he drew a smaller rapier from his belt.

Nereyda smiled. This would be more her speed.

He held his left arm close to his body, protecting it from further harm.

That threw him off balance.

When the guard made a misstep, she brought her cutlass down and cut a slash along his leg. He fell to the ground, his leg not able to bear weight.

"Just kill me," he said.

"Why? I have better things to do." She walked over to the mechanism that operated the harbor chain and studied it.

"I'm supposed to die with my brother that you kicked down the stairs."

Nereyda rolled her eyes. "No, you're not. Live your life. There's more to the world than being a brainwashed puppet. Find something to do. You can take up a hobby."

He crawled toward her.

"How does this thing work?" she asked.

"I'm not going to tell you."

She sighed. "Fine. I can figure it out on my own."

She glanced back at the wheel and spotted a lever next to it. With a swift kick, she knocked it loose, and the wheel started spinning, letting more chain go out into the harbor. Outside, the chain splashed into the water below. To prevent the catch from being engaged again, she gripped the lever and yanked it sideways, breaking it loose, then tossed it out of the chain slot.

"Have a good life," Nereyda said in a biting tone as she ran past the crawling guard and down the stairs, being careful to avoid the body of the other man. She sprinted out onto the beach.

Nereyda glanced around for the Storm Raven, not seeing it in the dark water of the harbor. Had she been too slow? The cannons on the beach had fallen silent.

A series of distant booms made Nereyda's brow furrow. They weren't coming from within the harbor. They came from the open ocean.

She ran to the harbor opening and glanced around, then let her shoulders fall in relief.

The Raven had pulled out of the harbor and was lingering just outside the opening. She jumped into the water and swam toward her ship. Someone tossed down a rope ladder, and she climbed onto the deck. She dripped water over the deck as she strode back up to the helm.

"I see you kept us out of too much trouble," she said to Nik as she took the wheel back.

"It was close a couple of times."

"What's with the guns out on the ocean?"

"I don't know. It sounds like there are quite a few, though," said Jax.

"Let's go find out."

She ordered the ship to go to full sail, making for the sounds of conflict with as much speed as they could coax out of the sails. They made their way around the bend of the coast to the north.

The Islander fleet was a bit ahead of the Storm Raven, just down the coast, while a host of silhouettes broke up the shimmer of the waves in the distance.

The western Imperial fleet had caught up to them. They launched barrages across the water as the Islander ships sailed in closer to engage the Imperials.

The Storm Raven closed too slowly.

Remembering the trick she had used leaving Antalia, Nereyda summoned her power and threw wind at the sails, filling them to the brim with air. The hull shuddered as it pressed through the water at faster speeds than it was used to. The water frothed around the ship as it plowed through the waves.

Ahead of them, plumes of fire flashed from the tiny silhouettes as the Imperials launched another volley from their ships of the line in a high arc over their frontline ships. Five seconds later, a deep boom roared. Another five seconds passed as the shots continued their journey over the gulf of water.

Two Islander ships exploded. Their men flew into the moonlit water in a shower of wood and other debris. The ships smoldered as they tilted beneath the waves.

The Storm Raven caught up to the Islander fleet as it sliced through the water and closed the distance between itself and the Imperials, its guns silent this far away. None of their ships had guns with the power of the Cambisian ships of the line. The Islanders' best chance was to get in close. While the guns of the larger ships had long range and could tear through any ship with a single shot, they'd be much less effective in close combat.

Nereyda thought she'd try to push herself further than she ever had. Rather than just throw air in her own sails, she focused on reaching as much of her power as she could and threw wind behind the entire fleet.

Immediately, her vision wobbled with dizziness, but she shoved aside her discomfort and focused on getting the job done. The rebel ships sprinted over the water, surging toward the enemy fleet with renewed vigor. Looking across at the Islanders on the other ships, Nereyda saw their faces register momentary surprise at the sudden gust of wind, but their shock turned to excitement as the water sprayed over their bows.

Another blast sounded from the Imperial fleet. However, its shots overshot the rebels, landing with a host of splashes behind them. The Imperials had their cannons prepared for a fleet sailing at a normal speed. The sudden acceleration of their targets threw their aim off.

Trying something else, Nereyda put a little bit of an angle into her wind gust, which moved the Islander fleet to the side just before another blast of the enemy cannons. She kept using the wind speed and angle to help her fleet dodge the incoming heavy cannon fire.

An ache grew in Nereyda's temple. She didn't know how much longer she could keep going.

After a couple of minutes, the Islander ships had closed to a distance where they could engage the Imperials. The long sleek shadows of the Islander ships scattered and slipped between the broader Imperial ships and peppered their hulls with cannon bursts.

Water poured into the holes carved by the rebel ships.

The sulfurous aroma of gunpowder permeated the air.

The front-line frigates struggled to maneuver around to face the rebels. Two Imperial ships cracked together as they turned the wrong way. Sailors tumbled screaming overboard.

After the rebel fleet's initial charge, several of the Imperial ships were left as broken and sinking wrecks. Men drifted in the water. Some struggled in search of help. Others lay motionless among darker patches of water.

But another full line with two dozen frigates awaited, and the behemoth ships of the line and flagships loomed behind that.

It was one thing to shred some of the frigates, with their thinner hulls. But taking on the giant ships of the line, or even the flagships at the back, would be another task entirely. Would the cannons on the Islander ships even penetrate their thick hulls with a single shot? Meanwhile, a single shot from the heavy Imperial ships would sink any rebel ship.

The Storm Raven and the Islander ships surged toward the next line of Imperial ships. With more time to prepare, this group of frigates had spread out. This deprived the Islanders of their advantage in tight quarters.

The Islanders weaved between the Imperial line at full speed and unleashed a single broadside burst. They then turned away to dodge the Imperial return fire. A few frigates tipped into the waves, but some Islander ships had gone down, as well.

Nereyda started to feel light-headed. Every time she cast a gust of air, her head would spin worse than the last time. Once her energy drained, she didn't know how long their fleet could last against the Cambisians'.

The Imperial ships of the line circled their formation around their main flagship, with their broadsides facing out. This created a floating fortress and further denied the Islanders the advantage of maneuverability. As the Islander ships swirled around the formation of ships, unable to penetrate its defenses, their numbers dwindled with each burst of fire from the Imperial fleet. They needed a way into its formation, or a way to board the ships.

The lines of Imperial frigates had now turned around and were plowing toward the Islanders. Soon, they would cut off their escape route. Nereyda had a choice to make. Fight to win? Or fight to escape?

From the helm of the Tavara, it was obvious to Brynja that the battle was turning against the rebels. The small and sleek Islander ships could not penetrate the ring of tough Imperial vessels.

As the Tavara circled with the other Imperial ships, her crew worked with solemn faces and subdued voices rather than their usual boisterous behavior and sea shanties. Only Ilker carried a good mood as he stood next to Brynja.

Flashes of cannon fire illuminated the familiar shape of the Storm Raven as it circled the perimeter of the defensive formation around the Imperial flagship. In the low light and noise, details were unclear and words indistinct, but the raven-black hair and commanding tone of the person at the helm could only belong to Nereyda.

Brynja's heart panged as she recalled their last meeting. She had hoped she might earn Nereyda's forgiveness, but understood why it had been too much to ask. Nereyda had treated her with exactly the kindness she deserved after the betrayal at the mines. Never again would they sail and laugh together as they had as children.

But Brynja could at least give Nereyda a chance at victory.

She spun the wheel hard to port and called, "Ramming speed!"

"What? What are you doing?" Ilker yelled as he reached for the wheel.

Brynja punched his face and sent him reeling.

Below, her crew set their faces with determination. They knew what she was doing and were as prepared as she was.

Nereyda watched as one of the frigates in the Imperial formation broke from its station and surged toward the main flagship. At full speed, it smashed into the flagship's hull and burst a hole in the side. The bow of the frigate snapped with the impact.

The sudden action caused the Imperial ships to pause in their firing and gave the Islanders a slight opening. Nereyda called to the crew of the Storm Raven to sail into the gap in the ships, preparing a double broadside. As they pressed between the line of ships, she gave the order to fire, shredding two of the vessels. The other rebel ships followed her lead and broke into the formation among the remaining ships of the line.

A flash of cannon fire lit a human shape that leaped across from the rogue frigate to the flagship, with a gleam of straw-blonde hair.

Brynja?

A gleam of fire glowed from within the hole in the flagship's hull.

Nereyda guessed where it was in the hold of the ship and her eyes widened. "Hard to starboard!" she called as she spun the wheel hard. "Full sail," she ordered, as she gave them an extra gust of wind and pushed them away from the flagship.

A moment later, it erupted. Fire burst into the sky, and wood and crew members were tossed into the air and out into the sea. The crews on the other Imperial ships froze. The tide had turned, and they sensed it.

As the Islanders swarmed around and picked some Imperial ships off in their stupor, several others raised white flags and turned their tails, moving away from the action. Nereyda had her crew give the signal to let them go.

The guns fell silent as the light of dawn extended from the horizon. Nereyda let go of the wheel and let the Storm Raven drift for a moment while she stood at the stern railing. The surrounding water had become the graveyard of dozens, both Islander and Imperial.

Broken hulls poked above the waves as they slipped into oblivion. Wisps of smoke drifted upward from a few of the wrecks. A forest of debris lay scattered across the surface of the water.

She thought of Brynja, who had leaped onto the flagship. If she had been captaining that frigate, then she had rammed the enemy flagship. And she had probably been the one to set the powder magazine ablaze.

Nereyda's eyes watered as she remembered her first mate along with the crew members that went down with her. She felt guilty for throwing Brynja aside so callously when she had come to Antalia to offer them help. Because of her, they had been able to get to the naval base and take back the Storm Raven ahead of the western Imperial fleet. Brynja had made all of that possible. And now, she had sacrificed herself so that Nereyda and the rebels could win their battle. Nereyda hoped to see some sign of life climb out of the wreckage, but there was none. The only movement came from waves that lapped against the lifeless hull. Otherwise, a shadowy stillness hung over the remains of the ship.

However, that was not true of the surrounding sea. Rebels and Imperials alike floated among the debris. Some swam and clung to whatever floating objects they could find. Others drifted, either unconscious or dead.

Wiping her eyes of her tears for Brynja, Nereyda went back to the helm. "Let's fish our people out of the water, along with any Imperials we can capture."

The Islander ships had already begun rescue and salvage operations. The rebel fleet spent the next hour harvesting survivors from the water.

But the sound of gunfire rang from the naval base still. The rebel army needed their help.

Nereyda returned the Storm Raven to the harbor, and the rest of the fleet followed. They pulled through the harbor opening and turned their broadsides toward the coast.

Broadside after broadside, they unleashed an unending barrage into the Imperials who had become fortified in the city. Rather than copying the indiscriminate barrages that the Imperials had unleashed upon Antalia, the rebels and Islanders took their time and picked off squads of soldiers as the dawn highlighted them. It didn't take much time of sustained attack before their support helped the rebel army advance through the city.

A short time later, the naval base was theirs.

Nereyda pulled the Storm Raven up to a dock and leaped off onto it, even before the gangway had been extended or the ship tied off. She strode off the dock and glanced around for Devrim or Limbani. She spotted the general ordering about a platoon of soldiers on the street.

Exhausted, Nereyda lumbered up to her and said, "Well, it wasn't easy, but we did it."

"It's hard to believe we're so close to winning this whole thing."

"We'll do it. Maybe after a short breather, first. Is Devrim around?"

"He should be here soon. He came in with me, and I know he wants to see you. Ah, here he is."

Devrim strode up the road, holding his arms open in a triumphant gesture and beaming. "I knew you'd do it. We're almost done. Unfortunately, I don't think we have time to rest much. We need to speed down to the capital and finish this."

Nereyda pushed a strand of hair out of her face. "Surely we have time for a little relaxation. I'd love to give you a tour of the Raven."

"Can it wait? We really need to get moving."

"Trust me, you won't be disappointed." Nereyda touched his arm and guided him onto the Raven, then whispered into his ear, "I really want to show you just one room." She led him to her quarters and shut the door behind them.

CHAPTER FORTY

Taking the capital had been easy. Without a significant Imperial fleet to oppose them, the rebels had landed right in the harbor of Manisa, the capital of the Empire. Nereyda had kept the Storm Raven offshore and watched for any lingering ships that might foolishly try to help the Empire while Limbani had led the army into the city. The lower classes rose up, swelling the ranks of the rebels and helping them take the city swiftly.

Devrim spent the final quick battle on the Storm Raven. When Limbani sent the signal that the city had fallen, he bounced with nearly unrestrained energy. As the Raven pulled into the harbor, Jax nearly had to hold him back from jumping onto the dock before the ship had stopped.

Once the ship was tied to the dock, Nereyda jogged to catch up with Devrim.

"What now? Do you want me to come with you?" she asked.

"Hmm?" His eyes darted to her, then flicked around as he scanned the city ahead. "Oh, no. You and the others can stay here."

Gravel crunched as they left the wooden dock. "What do I tell the Islanders? How long do we keep them here?"

Devrim waved his hand in the air. "We'll have plenty of time to worry about that soon enough. But we will uphold our promise to them. You can all enjoy some time off while I settle things with Limbani." He marched off into the city without slowing down.

After a celebratory drink with her crew at the nearest tavern, Nereyda went back to the Storm Raven. Even a few days after the battle for the naval base, she still nursed a headache from pushing herself during the battle.

Alone, she took a moment to appreciate that they had finally gotten their ship back. Standing on the dock, she gazed up and down the length of the ship. It had been a little battered in the battle near the naval base, with dents and bits of wood chipped off of the hull. A couple of gashes had been torn in the sails, either from gunfire or perhaps from Nereyda pushing the ship a little past its abilities with her wind. Still, it was home. They'd get her fixed up and looking good, then they could set sail and at least take the Islanders home.

But beyond that, she still wasn't sure what she wanted to do. Devrim was here, and she could hang around with him. But what should she do with him? She wasn't one to sit around as the nice lady, entertaining guests. She needed to be in a fight. Without some sort of trouble, she would feel lost. She needed to cause some chaos, at least. Maybe he'd let her have a little bit of fun every now and then.

Shaking her head away from her musings, she sauntered across the deck of the Storm Raven. This time, she appreciated every creak of the hull as she meandered her way around the ship, starting toward the bow. She ran her hand along the railing, letting the grains caress her palm and the nicks kiss her fingers. In the light breeze, the raised sails swayed gently against the yardarms. Rounding the bow, she came back toward the aftercastle. She hadn't even spent much time in her quarters since retrieving the Storm Raven. She looked forward to spending a night in her own bed for the first time in what felt like ages.

She drifted up to her door and pulled it open, smiling to herself as she took in her space. Her books were still there, along with the hanging bed along the wall. A couple of ports looked out at the harbor of the capital.

Nereyda took three contented steps into the room. Then something hit her on the back of the head, and she fell unconscious.

Nereyda came to with the sensation of floating along the ground. Her weight rested on something wrapped around her chest. When she opened her eyes, she saw that gray stones drifted beneath her. The rough surface scraped against her knees. A rope embraced her around her arms and torso. She lifted her arms, but manacles jangled around her wrists.

"Oh, are you awake?" came a familiar voice from a few steps ahead of her. Erhan's.

"You?" she asked. She tucked her feet under her and took the weight off of the rope.

Erhan turned around, his lips curled in a rare smile.

"Yes, me." A satisfied chuckle. "I figured you'd come back to your ship."

"What now? Your emperor is dead. What's the point of capturing me? You can't take me to anyone. You'll never be in the military again."

As Erhan whirled around and sped up his pace, he yanked on the rope and nearly pulled Nereyda back down. "The Emperor may be dead, but I can still work to achieve what he stood for. There's someone else who is interested in you and who is not dead. As long as someone is willing to help deal with you, I'll be there to stand in your way."

"Where are we going?"

"You'll find out very soon."

Erhan shoved her into a side passage, lined with the grime that the factories put out from their smokestacks. They must be near the forge district, or downwind of it at least.

They came to a small, dark metal door. Erhan pulled out a key and opened the door. He shoved her in and down a set of stairs.

Nereyda's temples pounded as she pushed through her headache and latched onto a mote of frost within. She drew it up to her wrists, but nothing happened.

"Don't try using your powers," Erhan said. "You'd only be wasting your time. Your handcuffs are made of gold."

"What's next? Torture?"

"Nothing quite so trivial, I'm afraid. You'll have to wait to find out your exact fate, but I hear it will be quite the hot affair. After hearing that you're back, the public is again clamoring for your death."

"So what? They can deal with it."

"And they will deal with it. They are dealing with it, in fact, through me, and my employer."

"And who is your employer?"

"Even I don't really know, to be honest. But that doesn't matter. They want me to capture you, and that is good enough for me."

They came down to a long bank of dungeon cells. "Another jail?" Nereyda asked.

"Your last, probably."

He pushed her down the length of the cell block, then shoved her to the ground within one of the cells before yanking the door shut and locking it.

"Mind taking off these handcuffs?" Nereyda asked.

"I'm not an idiot. You'll wait here until someone comes for you. You do have a bed and a bucket, at least. Clean and empty, even."

"Nice of you to upgrade me to the luxury suite," Nereyda said from the ground.

She glared at him as he spun and swaggered away. With her hands bound behind her back, she struggled to roll up onto her backside for a seated position. She kicked her legs and scooted her way to the bedroll so she'd at least have a comfortable spot as she sat and waited for whatever it was that would come for her.

Not even a single guard kept watch down here, and she had no idea where she was. It wasn't the palace dungeons. The air smelled too much of the sea for that. Besides, she had been in the palace cells. Perhaps it was the harbor brig. While most of the cells had rusted bars and doors, hers had been freshly refurbished. This must have been planned for a time.

It wouldn't take long for Limbani or Devrim to realize she was missing and comb the town for her. And Erhan couldn't do anything too public with the city under rebel control. If he gave her a mere chance to escape her shackles, then she could easily turn the tide against him. Rather than waste her energy now, especially with the golden handcuffs getting in the way of her abilities, she leaned against the wall of the cell and shut her eyes. She would use the time to refill her well of energy.

Her eyes fluttered open at the sound of someone shuffling down the hallway. She squinted into the dim light to see who was approaching. A hooded figure with broad shoulders was silhouetted, along with another person who wore a green rebel guard uniform.

Nereyda blinked and looked again.

A rebel? Why? What's going on?

"Why are there so many lights in here? Why does she have one?"

"Sorry, sir, I'll put out her light."

"Very good."

The hooded man waited while the guard marched up to her cell and snuffed the lit torch that hung just outside the door. Now she was left in almost total darkness, except for some indirect torchlight from the other sconces in the cell block hallway.

"Good, that's better."

A wet odor hit her nose as the man came up to her cell. A hint of torchlight glimmered across a strong jaw as he towered above her. "We have you now." His voice was nearly a hiss. "That commander actually did it. I had my doubts after his several failures, but finally, he has come through."

"Who are you? What's the point of all of this? You've already lost the war. Give up this hopeless cause."

"Oh, we haven't lost the war. Far from it. You've been instrumental in helping us win it. And when you have a very public death, it will be the final victory that we need."

"I have friends. They'll look for me. They won't let you go through with this."

"I'm not sure how much use your friends will be. I doubt they'll be able to do much."

"Have you done something to them, too?"

"I don't want to reveal too much. You'll find out on the big day. Which will be very soon. Tomorrow, the next day, this week—I don't know for sure, but you can count your remaining days on your two hands."

The hooded man whirled and moved away with the guard. "Oh, turn out the rest of the lights before we leave."

The guard hurried around the cell block, snuffing all of the lights. "Fantastic," said the hooded man.

The two left her, alone and in darkness.

Nereyda didn't know what to do. She started to panic inside. Her heart beat like rolling thunder. The storm inside her stirred without anywhere to go. What had the man meant about her friends not being able to help her? Had Erhan captured them, too? Had they all fallen into some sort of trap?

Taking Manisa had seemed quite easy compared to the rest of their battles. Maybe it had all been a ruse, part of a trap. But the Empire had never used this kind of subterfuge in her experience. Deception was not part of its repertoire. It charged any opposition straight on, with the might of its military. Changing its strategy now, at the last minute, was out of character.

And who was the hooded man?

For the next several days, or what felt like days—Nereyda couldn't be sure without seeing the sun or having any sort of regular schedule—she went in and out of sleep, since she had nothing better to do. They brought her neither food nor water. She struggled to sit up without leaning against the wall and she drifted in and out of consciousness. Even when awake, her mind wandered without aim or focus.

A clang at the end of the cell block signaled that someone had arrived.

"Are you awake, pirate?" asked Erhan.

Nereyda grunted, her throat too parched to respond.

He came to her cell and unlocked it. Erhan yanked a hood over her head before hauling her to her feet and shoving her out. It seemed he escorted her out of jail and onto the streets, from the light that filtered through the hood and the breeze that blew past her. They hiked a while, meandering in different directions as they hit intersections. They started going uphill.

They stopped briefly.

"Is this her?" she heard a voice ask.

"Yes," said Erhan.

"Very well, everyone is waiting."

After walking a bit farther, the sound of a crowd of people reached her ear. Many voices yelled and cheered.

Erhan pressed her closer to the assembled mob. The cheers and yells got louder as she approached.

Wet spray and objects struck her. People were spitting and throwing things at her. She didn't know why. Her throat wouldn't let her toss a retort at them. This assault lasted for several minutes, and included a few solid hits of what felt like stones hitting her body.

"Okay, up some stairs, then we're about there."

She feebly tried to yank her arms away from him, but it was no use. She didn't have the strength to fight back. Another pair of hands grabbed her on the other side, and together Erhan and the second person moved her across what sounded and felt like a wooden platform. They put her back to a post and wrapped ropes around her arms and torso, binding her to the pole.

"Today, we have found the final enemy that we need to destroy to bring peace to our nation," said a triumphant voice. The crowd cheered.

Someone yanked her hood off. Devrim stood in front of her. The hood dangled from his hand.

Her jaw dropped open.

Devrim scowled at her. "You just had to come back," he whispered.

Nereyda's heart pounded as her eyes swiveled and scanned her surroundings. Beneath the platform, a crowd filled a large plaza. At the base of the stairs, Erhan crossed his arms with a contented smirk. Next to him, the hooded man loomed in his cloak.

The clouds above seemed to mock her as they drifted through the blue sky highlighted by sunlight.

Limbani stood at one corner of the platform, and her wide eyes proclaimed that she had never seen this coming. She strode across the stage, one hand on her sword hilt. "What is this?" Limbani asked. Her eyes darted between Devrim and Nereyda as she tried to piece things together.

"We need to do this," said Devrim. "You want to make our nation safe and secure for anybody, right?"

"Of course, but she's been our ally, my friend, and your lover," said Limbani, her voice urgent.

Devrim pivoted toward the crowd and elevated his voice for their benefit. "Yes, she has been very helpful. And she will be helpful again. Her death will make us safer. We can't have someone like her running around and playing god against us." He glanced back toward Limbani, and a wicked gleam shone in his eyes. "Now, stand silent and hold your post, or at least make sure she doesn't go anywhere."

Limbani tightened her jaw, but nodded in silence, and Devrim turned back to the crowd.

Rage and confusion stirred within Nereyda as the pieces fell together. She should have figured something was up. Devrim had protested when she had worn her modified dress and brought her cutlass to the ball. He hadn't been upset at her impropriety. He had wanted her vulnerable.

Devrim had known about the impending attack at the ball. That meant that Erhan had been working with Devrim all along, which meant that Devrim wanted the Inquisition to happen. Later, he'd been very quick to send Nereyda away after Goremia. After she returned, he had been distant, especially after the battle for the capital. She had thought he was just excited and anxious.

But betrayal?

"I know it has been a long, hard war," Devrim called to the crowd as he paced the stage. "I made some mistakes in who I allied with. This pirate has proven herself to be quite a danger to society. You know that from what happened in Goremia, where she destroyed the temple you treasure so much. Even after her hand was severed from her body and you witnessed her death in front of you, she has somehow managed to return to us. Thus, the only way we can be sure to be truly rid of her dangerous presence is to burn her at this stake."

Limbani padded over to Nereyda and leaned next to her. "Do you have any way out of this?"

Nereyda croaked out a response and shook her head.

"Here's some water." Limbani lifted her canteen to Nereyda's mouth and let her drink the whole thing.

"Thanks," said Nereyda. "Won't you get in trouble for this?"

"He's busy with the crowd. They'll just think I'm getting you ready. Now, here's something that might help."

Limbani reached around Nereyda and slipped something metallic into her hand. Nereyda closed her hand around the object and nodded.

"Thank you."

Limbani gave her a small smile, then went back to her corner of the platform.

Devrim continued his tirade. "With this demon secured, we can finally move forward with building the sort of nation we want. A nation that doesn't rely upon the strength of a fallible Emperor or the wicked abilities of someone like this pirate, but a nation that seeks to give everyone a better life and that seeks to be a godly nation. If we seek to make amends with the gods and truly live in harmony with them, they may truly gift us the old abilities. But not if we abide an unholy gift thief as she."

"Unholy?" Nereyda called out. "I can think of a few unholy things we did in a bedroom not too long ago."

At the quip, Devrim halted his pacing and stomped up to Nereyda. He leaned over her. "You think this is easy for me?" he asked with a low growl. "I'm doing what I have to do."

"What you have to do? You don't have to do anything." She injected venom into her voice. "Did you plan this all along?"

He hung his head. "Yes . . . and no."

"Why?"

"I needed something to stoke the anger of the people. If not their anger, then their fear. What better opportunity than a pirate who can shoot lightning? The Inquisition did far more to stir up fear than I could have ever hoped. I could kill you and become a hero. But something unexpected happened. I fell for you."

"Don't you dare say that," she spat. "Not now."

"That's why I let you go after Goremia. I didn't know they'd torture you. Seeing it go so far tore me up inside, so I had to send you away. When everyone thought we had killed you, towns across the Empire flocked to us. Then you had to come back and ruin it all. You don't know how to lie low, and if anyone figures out you're with me, all of this will collapse."

Tears trickled down Nereyda's cheeks. "So you use me for one last fight, then toss me to the wolves?"

"I can't let this slip away from me. Not when I'm an inch away."

"You wouldn't even be here without me."

Devrim pulled away from her and glanced toward a couple of people in rebel uniforms with lit torches, then waved to them. The two of them descended the five steps to the ground, though Limbani kept glancing back at Nereyda.

The rebel soldiers stuck their torches under the platform, and a glow spread out underneath Nereyda as flames spread over the straw that had been laid beneath the platform. It wouldn't be long before the platform itself caught, and she started to cook. Heat emanated from below and sweat trickled down her brow.

Her eyes watered at the sting of hazy smoke. Below, Devrim planted his hands on his hips and watched with a stony face.

With little time to spare, she manipulated the metal object Limbani had given to her. Her fingers traced the shape of a key. She pressed it into the keyhole in the handcuffs and turned. With a click, one of her shackles opened. She slipped her hand out of it and traded the key to the other hand. After she freed the other wrist, the handcuffs clunked down onto the platform.

Devrim appeared unbothered by her efforts to escape.

Flame flickered up through the platform and threatened to engulf her within minutes. The scents of ash and ember drifted among the smoke. Her feet would start cooking at any moment. Her toes involuntarily curled and fidgeted in a futile effort to escape the heat. An odor similar to burnt hair came from her boots as they roasted.

She needed time to escape her ropes.

Nereyda focused on building energy and hunted within for the calm water aspect of her abilities. The heat made it difficult to access that part of her power. The urge to unleash a barrage of lightning sizzled. She shoved that aside in her mind.

Finally, she calmed herself and summoned a pool of water that splashed around her feet. It instantly hissed and turned to vapor, but the heat at her feet subsided for the time being.

Still, after reaching for her abilities, a burst of lightning strained against her mental restraints. She didn't know why. Maybe the energy of the flames beneath her fueled her own violent nature. It gave her an idea.

"Devrim," she called over the sizzling flames. Outside of where her pool of water had formed and calmed the flames, the fire rose almost to her knees.

"What is it?"

"I want to make a deal."

Devrim scoffed. "A deal? What kind of deal? You're not in what I'd call a strong bargaining position."

"Maybe not. But if you don't cut me loose, I'll call a lightning storm down on the city."

"Now I know you're desperate. I've never seen you go so far before."

"Want to see if I can? You saw me destroy a temple. Can you really believe I won't do that to this city?"

"Still, that was just one building. One lightning strike. You can't make a full storm."

"I haven't yet, true. But are you sure you want to find out if I can or not? I suppose then we can both know exactly how powerful I am. I still haven't found my upper limit. Is this the time you want to learn?" Lightning flowed into her hands, and sparks crackled between her fingers.

"It's a risk I'll take. Besides, if you do it, it'll prove me right. Everyone will see the threat you are."

Storm clouds gathered above the city. Nereyda felt the static that charged the air. Devrim glanced down at the hairs standing up on his arm. "Do it," he said. "I want to see it."

Nereyda debated whether she actually wanted to unleash the fury that seemed to sizzle below her surface. She had no idea what would happen if she let it go. She scanned the faces of the crowd. Faces contorted with rage at someone they never knew and had only been told they should hate.

She never had to make a final decision. Limbani leaped onto the platform, dashed over, and sliced through her restraints with one swipe of her saber, then pulled Nereyda from above the flames.

"Limbani," shouted Devrim, "what are you doing?"

"What I should have done as soon as I saw her up here."

"After all of this, you turn against me?"

"I'm not the one who betrayed his friends. Come on, Nereyda, let's go."

"The ships. They're the only way out."

Limbani tugged Nereyda off of the platform, then led the way as they dashed past Devrim and toward a narrow gap in the crowd.

"Somebody stop them!" Devrim yelled from the base of the platform.

The sea of people closed the way forward. As they pressed in, Nereyda let out a gust of wind. Bodies flew into the air. One man struck a building with a crunch, then crumpled onto the ground.

A man charged forward and brandished a sword as he blocked their path. Nereyda flicked her hand and jolted him with a surge of lightning. After that, she maintained a spark of energy in her hand and waved it at anyone who looked like they might think about stopping them.

Once they made their way through the crowd, they sprinted through the streets toward the docks. They could hear the mob pursuing them, with the shouts of Devrim and the rebel soldiers encouraging them.

Upon reaching the docks, relief swelled at the sight of the crew on the Storm Raven. Nereyda spotted Jax and yelled at him, "Are we ready to sail?"

"I suppose. Why?"

She and Limbani dashed over the wooden dock. "We need to go. Right now. All the Islander ships, too."

"What happened? Why are we in such a hurry?" Jax asked.

They leaped onto the ship. "We'll explain later," said Limbani. "Right now, we have an angry mob after us."

"Making friends already?" Jax smirked at Nereyda.

When she scowled back, he dropped his amused expression. "Fine, not in the mood for jokes, I see. We'll run up the signal to the rest of the fleet. Almost everyone has kept to their ships, so they should be ready soon."

As Nereyda rushed to help make the final preparations for the Raven to leave the harbor, Photios ran up onto the Raven.

"I just saw the signal to leave. What's going on?" he asked.

"Devrim tried to kill me, so we're running," said Nereyda as she cinched a knot tight. "You can do what you want."

"No, we're with you. We'll be ready soon." Photios ran off and returned to his own ship.

After they shoved off, the Raven led the Islander fleet at full sail for an hour. When they were sure nobody had tailed them from Manisa, she had the crew go to half sail and they settled into a good cruising speed. Nereyda, Limbani, Jax, and Manu gathered at the stern of the aftercastle.

"Okay, are you going to finally tell us what the hell that was all about?" asked Jax. His eyes locked onto Nereyda's in an unblinking stare. "First, you disappear for two days, then you turn up with Limbani being chased by an angry crowd."

Nereyda broke eye contact and leaned over the railing. She stared down into the ship's wake for a moment. "I disappeared because I got captured by Erhan. He was working for Devrim this whole time. Devrim—" Her voice caught. "Devrim tried to burn me alive in front of the city."

"Why in the hells would he do that?" Jax asked.

"He was playing me the whole time. He stoked the Inquisition so he could channel the people's anger. I'm . . . I'm still putting it all together. We should have just stayed up in the Shattered Sea."

"How did you escape?"

"Limbani freed me." Nereyda turned to Limbani with a sideways glance. "By the way, why did you do that? What happened to your loyalty to Devrim?"

Limbani grimaced as she stiffened. "I was loyal to the version of Devrim that uplifted a lowly factory worker. I don't know what happened to the Devrim I swore my allegiance to, but he is apparently gone. You've been nothing but loyal to us, even after you got your ship back. You deserve better. It was an easy choice."

"I'm very glad you made that choice, Limbani. I don't think I would take well to being roasted." Nereyda paused and looked Limbani in the eye. "Thank you. I don't think I would have gotten out without you."

"You'd have found a way. Would you really have sent a lightning storm down on the city?"

Nereyda shrugged. "I don't really know. I was considering it. Not something I would normally want to do, but the feeling of my feet cooking changed my perspective a bit."

"So now where do we go?" asked Jax.

"I don't know." Nereyda shook her head. "Wherever we can regroup to burn Devrim and his new empire to the ground. Maybe to the Islander capital, but I don't want them seeing us going in that direction."

Manu stepped up. "If I might interrupt, I have an idea."

"Don't let me stop you. Go ahead."

"After everything that's happened with your abilities, I think it might be prudent to learn more about them. If you insist on calling down storms, you can at least learn to do it without burning yourself out. And we can do so in a place that Devrim won't be able to reach you."

"Where did you have in mind?"

"My home. Hariana. My old colleagues at the university will be quite intrigued to see you, and we have an extensive library that might help you learn something. We also have . . . other means of helping you discover who you are, but I'd rather not go into that right now."

"I guess that's as good a suggestion as any. And definitely out of reach of Devrim. Let's do it. Jax, signal the ships to follow us. Today, we sail east."

After getting the fleet on course, Nereyda stood at the stern railing and gazed at the continent as it disappeared over the horizon. Her heart ached as if it had been yanked out of her chest and tossed to a shark. She wondered when she'd get the chance to come back and unleash her scorn upon Devrim.

The End

Nereyda will be back in Raven Revelation, coming late 2019

www.ingramcontent.com/pod-product-compliance
Lightning Source LLC
Chambersburg PA
CBHW052023240626
47153CB00006B/1932